The

This is a work of fiction. Names and characters are the product of the author's imagination and any resemblance to actual persons, either living or dead, is purely coincidental

Copyright (C) 2013 Lorna Cooke

This book may not be reproduced in whole or in part, by any means, without permission. Making or distributing electronic copies of this book constitutes copyright infringement and could subject the infringer to criminal and civil liability.

This work is dedicated to Alan Cooke for his infinite patience with me whilst writing it and also as a thank you for the cover illustration

Acknowledgements: To Crispin Brocks for all you have done and for always being there. My thanks also go to Irene Gamble, Melanie Grey, Anna Prokhovnik, Elizabeth Martin and especially to Michelle Macé for your help and encouragement

For more information about the author please visit www.lornacooke.com

Preface

The world of a family coping with the aftermath of a civilised divorce is rocked by the arrest of one of its members for an alleged sexual offence. The story unfolds as parents Michael and Pamela rediscover their own individual identities. Carla, their daughter, experiences her dawning pubescence while at the same time her grandparents' repressed sexuality is revealed. Each generation reacts very differently as they endeavour to continue with their lives whilst adjusting to the changing developments around them.

Secrets, deception, addiction, bullying and family dynamics all play their part in this story, but there is also loyalty, friendship, warmth and humour. The characters are fictional, and drawn from all walks of life, but their strengths and vulnerabilities will strike a familiar chord with many readers.

Chapter 1

Pamela heard the front door close softly; it was Carla coming in from school. Apart from the pain of the split from Michael, the change in Carla was one of the things Pamela was finding hardest to bear. "Would you like a glass of coke?" she called up the stairs to her daughter.

"No thanks" was the quiet reply

Before her parents had split up, Carla used to bounce in from school, telling Pamela all about her day and leaving a trail of school clothes as she changed out of her uniform before going out in search of her friends. Pamela, in her more lucid and less angst-ridden moments, assured herself that this was all a part of growing up from a twelve year old into a thirteen year old. However in the early hours of the morning, the sleepless soul-searching moments, Pamela fiercely blamed Michael for ruining their marriage and their daughter's life, as it had been.

Intending to coax Carla from her room, Pamela started wearily up the stairs, still totally fazed by the phone conversation she had just had with her mother before Carla came in. As she was half way up, she heard the phone ringing again. "Mum, it's Gran for you" called Carla from upstairs "she sounds really weird, are you going to take it downstairs?" Having said that she would, Pamela turned back, walking slowly, reluctantly, towards the phone. What on earth else could her mother have to say? That it was all a mistake, perhaps; that it was a joke even? No, not that, whatever else her mother ever did, there was always a purpose, and NEVER anything for a joke.

Finishing the conversation with her mother with "OK, Mummy, we'll be over in about half an hour", Pamela called up to Carla to let her know that they were going to pop over to Crowford to see Grandma and Granddad.

"That's what YOU think", shouted Carla rudely as she ran down the stairs and slammed out of the front door, not even stopping to find out why her Gran had sounded strange on the phone.

A moment later, there was a timid knock at the back door. Pamela walked briskly through the kitchen, assuming that it was Carla, having forgotten her key, coming back in to apologise and to ask why they were to pay an unexpected visit to her grandparent's house, something she was well aware that her mum was reluctant to do even when a duty visit was planned.

Pamela opened the door and started at the sight of an older woman with shocking pink spiky hair.

"Um hello" said the owner of the spiky hair

"Yes?" asked Pamela abruptly.

"Um, hello, I lives next door, sorry I 'aven't said hello before, only I've not been well. I seen you arrive with the removal van an that the other day..." Pamela said nothing, the conversations with her mother on her mind, along with the knowledge that she had promised to go to her mother's and that Carla had slammed out of the door, just as this spiky haired creature had come round the back – oh it was all too much, then "I err, just wanted to say – please tell me to mind me own business if you want, but the last two days I seen your girl walking along the ring-road in the direction of them big 'ouses, an I thought she may have been confused bout which bus to catch to school. Only it's a bit dangerous, you know, walking along that ring-road…."

Pamela flushed and said "Yes you bloody well will mind your own business, it can't possibly be my daughter you think you have seen, I've shown her exactly which bus to catch and where to catch it, now go away and leave me alone"

At that, the spiky haired neighbour shrugged and left, muttering that you can't help some people. Pamela closed the back door, absolutely appalled at what she had just done. Pamela rarely if ever swore, and had never ever in her life sworn at another person. She paused and considered – was it possible that Carla may have walked along the road? If so why? Pamela decided immediately to go and apologise to the neighbour, who, after all, only seemed to mean well. If Carla returned and had in fact forgotten to take a key as she had flounced out of the house, Pamela would see or hear her return. The strange, unbelievable problem regarding her parents would have to wait a while.

Taking a deep breath Pamela knocked on her neighbour's back door, 'Spiky hair' opened it almost immediately, as if she knew that Pamela would come round. This was odd in itself, because just as Pamela had never sworn at anyone ever before, neither was she in the habit of knocking on neighbours' doors.

Before she had a chance to begin to apologise she was told "Come on in ducks, they calls me Spike, but me name's Marian, if you prefer - you've 'ad a lotta work what with the move an all, and it looks like it's just the two of you – not that that's none of my business – there I goes again sticking me nose in".

Pamela cut in with "Please, I've come to apologise to you, I've not come to you for an apology!" Spike/Marian laughed shyly, and Pamela introduced herself, explaining briefly that she was, in fact, alone there with Carla, but she didn't explain why, because although she found herself feeling comfortable with her new neighbour, she didn't feel ready to start sharing confidences.

Marian put on the kettle, saying, confusingly, that "a good cuppa never did no one no 'arm", and insisting that Pamela sit down for a few minutes at least. Pamela explained that Carla was finding the move hard, and had slammed out of the door just a few minutes before, adding to the confusion of Marian's having come to Pamela's back door just when she did.

"Er, I have to go to visit my parents" Pamela told her, choosing not to explain why "and I don't know where Carla is or how long she will be out"

"How far away are they, ducks?" Marian asked, kindly.

"It's about half an hour's drive. That's why I am worried. Carla is not used to the area, she has no friends here yet so I don't know what to do, I don't know how long I will be with my parents."

"Might your girl have gone to see her Dad?" Marian asked tactfully.

Pamela stiffened, thinking of the bed-sit that Michael was staying in and shuddered, and without explaining why she said "I think that is most unlikely. After talking to my mother on the phone I told Carla we were going to see her grandparents and that's when she shouted something and flounced out of the door. Oh, I don't know, this isn't really like my old Carla at all"

Marian suddenly became practical "Tell yer what, ducks, hows about I sit in your house and wait for Carla, you let me 'ave yer mum's phone number and I'll call yer when she comes in. What d'yer think?"

Swiftly deciding that she had little choice, considering the calls she'd just received from her mother, Pamela accepted her offer. Marian was soon settled in Pamela's house armed with Pamela's parents' number so she could get in touch if necessary, while Pamela walked around the corner to the parking space allotted to her house.

Driving almost on auto-pilot, Pamela allowed herself to go over the two bizarre conversations she had had earlier with her mother. No, she mused, they were not conversations at all, just one sided statements issued by her mother – the first one stating that 'Daddy' had been having an affair – that in itself unbelievable – the acquiescent, compliant husband and father – but the next call from her mother was to say that Daddy had been arrested! Arrested? People just don't get arrested for having affairs, Pamela tried to say to her mother, but her mother was obviously very upset, so Pamela had said that she and Carla would come over.

Pulling into the familiar sweep of drive that was the entrance to the property her parents had inherited from her maternal grandparents, Pamela shuddered involuntarily, wondering what changes were ahead for her parents. Heaven knew, she had been through enough upheaval herself, with the break-up of her marriage, and she couldn't envisage either of her parents functioning without the other. Theirs was not an easy, nor even a particularly happy marriage, but it was a relationship in which both seemed to thrive, the dynamics of which Pamela rarely questioned, having been used to them since childhood. However, she thought, something extraordinary must have taken place to spark off the two very odd and out of character telephone calls from her mother.

Daphne appeared at the door having heard Pamela's car draw up "Oh, it's you, darling, we are expecting the Fotheringtons any minute – Leticia Fotherington's brother is staying with them, he's taking a break from his contract in New Zealand"

"But Mummy – what about…"

"Not now darling, see – here they are" as a dark BMW glided in next to Pamela's little old car. Pamela looked on in amazement as her mother began to greet her guests – was this the distraught woman Pamela had spoken to an hour or so ago?

Pamela went on through the house to see whether she could get any sense out of her father and finding him in the kitchen slicing lemons as though nothing had ever been amiss she wondered whether she'd imagined her mother's phone calls. "Daddy, what is going on"? Pamela asked him.

"Oh hello sweetie, what are you doing here? Where is my favourite granddaughter?" (Normally this faintly irritated Pamela, as she was an only child, as was Carla)

"Daddy; Mummy called earlier sounding extremely distraught, saying all sorts of strange things…"

"All a silly business, sweetie, it will soon be sorted out, no need to trouble your pretty head about it all. Now, will you stay and have a drink with us with the Fotheringtons? Leticia's brother…"

"Daddy, I've heard about all that from Mummy, I came over because I thought something was terribly wrong, I can't stay because Carla chose to stay at home with a neighbour keeping an eye on her…"

At this point Pamela heard her mother calling her loudly and found her waving to her from the hallway telephone table "Darling – there is some creature asking for a Pammy, must be a wrong number….Pamela took the phone from her mother just as Leticia Fotherington swept into the hallway calling loudly to Pamela's mother

"Daphne dear…"

Pamela turned away from the din and tentatively said "Hello" and there was Marian on the end saying that Carla was home. A wave of relief spread through Pamela, and gratitude that Marian had taken the trouble to call her and let her know. "Thank you so much for letting me know, the crisis here seems to be a storm in a teacup, so I'm coming straight back – I'll be about half an hour, and thanks again".

Pamela popped her head round into the lounge just as her father came through from the kitchen – "oh, there you are poppet – what will you have to drink?"

"Nothing thanks, Daddy, I really must get back to Carla,,,"

She was cut short by her mother saying loudly "Oh come along, darling, you MUST come and see the Fotheringtons for a few minutes.."

"Mummy – NO, please listen to me – I came over here because you seemed to be having some sort of crisis. And Carla is on her own and I have work tomorrow...".

"Steady the buffs, there" (this was Daddy)"no crisis here, just a silly misunderstanding". Leticia Fotherington caught sight of Pamela and boomed

"Pamela dear, do tell us all about this mysterious new life of yours….."

"Not now dear, Pamela has to get back as she only popped over due to some silly confusion and has to get back" Ushering Pamela out of the front door Pamela's mother hissed to her "I don't want Leticia to know you've moved into a council estate, as well as taking that awful job" then, in a softer tone "you

8

know Daddy and I would have been happy to have you and Carla here, sweetie" Driving home Pamela tried to shrug off the familiar feeling that her parents were living in a different century. She put the car radio on to reassure herself that is was still 1993!

*

The alarm clock interrupted Pamela's dream – but as she began to wake up she couldn't quite recall the dream – other than to feel slightly disturbed by it. She looked at the clock and saw that the alarm must have gone off at least twice before and she must have pressed "snooze" without even realising it. She quickly got up before she fell back to sleep again and went through the routine of waking Carla for school and getting their breakfast. This morning was different for Pamela, though. She had taken a few days annual leave for the house move; today she was to go back to work.

Pamela had only started the job a few months before the move, but had explained to her new employers at interview that she was in the throes of moving house and they had been understanding about her needing some time off for this. She didn't, however, tell them about her marital split and the real reason that she now needed full time work, i.e. that she wanted to be able to support herself and Carla with as little help from Michael as possible. Unfortunately, Pamela's office manager was less sympathetic about Pamela's needing the leave, and Pamela braced herself for the onslaught of sarcasm as she pushed her way through the stiff outer doors that led past the reception area and along the corridor to her office.

Pamela nodded gratefully to Rob as he had made a 'C' with his hand. Pamela slipped off her jacket and wondered, briefly, why it was that the team had accepted her and been quite helpful while Sandra, the office manager, seemed to resent her for some reason. As Pamela logged on to her computer Rob handed her a coffee and asked "Good couple of days off?"

Before Pamela had time to reply, Sandra came bustling into the office, gave Rob a sickly smile and asked him whether or not he had work to do. She then rounded on Pamela and said: "I can't think why they said you could have time off willy nilly. Please in future book all leave through me. I had to close down the purchase ledger myself for month end – that was the whole point of getting someone in to fill this position, to take the pressure off me – but, oh, you seem to be a special case, to be able to swan off whenever it suits you. Well, please be aware, I am your line manager, so I am the one who will authorise any time off you require".

Pamela just politely said "OK Sandra, thank you for making that clear", and she started to sort out the piles of invoices and statements that had been left on her desk. Pamela had never discussed her awkward relationship with Sandra with the other team members, but it was tacitly understood that Pamela usually only made coffee for the team when Sandra wasn't around, so as not to draw attention to herself.

Mid morning when Sandra went off to get some paperwork signed, Pamela gathered up everyone's cups and went to the small rest room to put the kettle on. As she rinsed out the cups and waited for the kettle to boil, she contemplated the previous evening's events. So disturbed had she been by the strange events that she hadn't even thought to tackle Carla about her behaviour. She was just pleased that Carla had come home and had even done her homework. Pamela had heard all her mother's arguments and pleas before about 'coming home' as she put it, and however kindly it was meant she had been away from 'home' for far too long to contemplate moving in with her parents. When she realised that her marriage was definitely at an end, she had not even considered it as an option. Although very hurt by everything that had happened regarding Michael, Pamela didn't want to ruin Michael's chances of his new business succeeding, so had agreed to the sale of their home in order to finance separate homes for them both as well as Michael's new business. Her solicitor told her she was mad, but Pamela was adamant, she may be the 'wronged party' as it was put to her, but she had no intention of insisting on staying put in the family home once they were no longer a family. She wanted a home that she owned outright (or at least, with the mortgage company!) with no ties to have to unravel once Carla finished full time education.

As Pamela poured tea and coffee into mugs as diverse as the team members themselves, she smiled to herself as she remembered her spiky haired neighbour's easy good natured comments as she left the other evening. When Pamela thanked her for her help she was told "tis nothing, ducks, when you're straight maybe you'll have time to sit an "ave a cuppa an' a proper natter". She wouldn't have minded having 'a proper natter' with Rob and the others as they drank their tea, but they never knew how long Sandra would be out of the office, and Pamela didn't want to give Sandra any excuse to have a go at her. Instead, she placed the drinks on her colleagues' desks and went back to the kitchenette to collect her own.

As she walked to her desk, Pamela's phone started to ring – "OK, I'll get it for you" – that was Maureen - as she picked up her own phone and dialled the group pick up code and took the call for her. As Pamela sat down and put her coffee on the desk, Maureen transferred the call to Pamela saying "I'm afraid it's Walkers again for you". Maureen wasn't to know, but Pamela had done a lot of work on the Walkers account, and had, in fact, managed to get a lot of their invoices approved, so she wasn't worried about taking the call as for once she had good news for them. She had been able to tell them that there would be a sizeable payment for them on the next payment run; she put down the phone with a buzz of satisfaction and must have been smiling to herself.

"Well, I don't know what you're smirking at, Pamela" Sandra had returned "It's all very well swanning around getting yourself coffee and letting other team members answer your phone. Maureen isn't your secretary, you know! And I want to know why you've gone over my head and dealt directly with the warehouse – I have just been extremely embarrassed in my meeting – having to hear what you've been interfering with behind my back"

Pamela had no idea what Sandra was talking about "Sorry?" she asked. "Don't play the innocent with me – you've been to the warehouse and gone through their goods received notes" Annoyed this time rather than intimidated, Pamela cut in with

"Oh, you mean the Walkers account – I can assure you I didn't go through any paperwork in the warehouse without permission – I had just called to ask whether there were any GRN's available so that I could clear some of Walkers invoices for payment as they were chasing as it's their half year end….." before she could finish, John Meredith, the finance director came in, and said to Sandra

"Well done with the Walkers account, they are very pleased with us".

"Oh, that's OK," fawned Sandra and she went back to her desk. Before leaving their office, John looked expectantly at Rob, who said

"Yes there are some" and John went to the communal biscuit tin and helped himself. Sandra scowled at Pamela a couple of times after that, but the rest of the day went reasonably smoothly for Pamela, and it was soon time to tidy her desk, log off the computer and go home for the day.

Chapter 2

Donald woke up with a start, feeling rather uneasy. As he came to, he remembered that today was the day of his court appearance. As he slowly got up and got dressed, the uppermost thoughts on his mind were to do anything he could to keep Daphne happy, and also to avoid any unpleasantness for Pamela and Carla. He still found it hard to believe that he had committed a criminal offence, despite the fact that the duty solicitor, when he had attended the police station after his arrest, had told him that that was, indeed, the case.

Thank heavens, he thought, that they had been entertaining the Fotheringtons on the evening of the day of his arrest, and that Pamela had come over in answer to her mother's two phone calls just as they arrived – both those things taking Daphne's mind off the events of that day; and Daphne had then proceeded to drink rather too much gin, as she often did these days in order to blot out what she considered to be the many let downs she had suffered in her life. Donald was aware that he disappointed her; that she felt that she deserved better, so he always tried to do his best to keep her as happy as he could. He was a kindly rather avuncular man but rather ineffectual in most areas of his life; for example when it came to contributing to the family finances and to making decisions about major changes.

His army career had come to an abrupt halt in Cyprus in 1967; just before he was due to receive a promotion which could have resulted in a posting to the Far-East – something that Daphne had had her heart set on. As soon as Daphne had understood the seriousness of Donald's being asked to resign, she set to and arranged for them to stay with her parents in the UK while Donald looked for work. He had been in the army for all his adult life, and all he had to show for it was the title of Major which he had been allowed to keep. That was all well and good for obtaining membership at the local golf club; the committee had soon welcomed Major Donald Fielding into their circle, but it was not a lot of use for gaining employment. He had tried his hand at several things including selling encyclopaedias, and had eventually managed to find a position as an insurance salesman. It didn't bring in a lot of money, but it did at least satisfy Daphne in that she felt it wasn't too beneath her to be married to someone who 'dealt in insurance' as she liked to put it to her friends.

As he waited for the kettle to boil, Donald thought back over the last couple of weeks. The whole crazy episode had begun with his going round to Peggy's to console her and her daughter Maisie over the death of their little Jack Russell. He had been outraged when Daphne told him that Peggy had turned up on her day off to tell them that someone had thrown poisoned meat into their garden to stop Buster from yapping. Donald poured boiling water into the teapot; Daphne insisted on the use of tea leaves and a tea pot, and Donald wondered again what sort of tortured mind could poison a little dog, rather than calling round and asking them to quiet the dog or take it indoors.

Peggy was what Daphne called their 'help', and she came in three mornings a week to do the heavy housework and the ironing. Daphne had inherited Peggy along with the house when her mother had died after a long illness. The idea when Donald and Daphne had returned from Cyprus had been to stay with Daphne's parents for just a short while, but Daphne's father's health had always been poor, in fact it had been ever since he returned from the Front at the end of the First World War, but it was especially bad at that time, and he had died within a year of their return. As Donald wasn't earning much, they stayed with Daphne's mother and helped to run the big house. When she died the inheritance tax had been considerable, and to Daphne's dismay they had had to sell off some adjoining land in order to pay the tax.

Donald poured Daphne's tea and took it upstairs. He knocked gently on her bedroom door and waited patiently. He then knocked a little more loudly and went in. When they had had to sell off the land to pay the taxes they raised money to make some improvements to the old place, as well as making some repairs and renewing the gravel drive, the sweep of which Daphne was particularly proud. Donald had thought that maybe Daphne was in her en suite bathroom, one of the improvements that they had had done. However, as he placed Daphne's tea by her bedside, Donald saw that she was still asleep, with her mouth partly open and her makeup smeared across her face and on her pillow. He was fond of her, but thought how unattractive she was beginning to look – probably the effect of drinking rather too much alcohol, he mused. In her younger days she had always clung rigidly to a beauty regime that included removing all make up and thoroughly cleansing her face before retiring to bed.

As they were never flush with money, Donald had taken to pouring himself a tonic for each gin and tonic that Daphne wanted, and often asking for a tonic only at the golf club where he was treasurer, using the excuse that he needed a clear head to work on the finances. This way he kept his bar bills down at the club, and saved on bottles of gin when they did the fortnightly shop. Daphne didn't acknowledge that it was she who was drinking a lot of gin, each time they needed more she would look a little startled and say that they must have been entertaining a lot. This would have probably annoyed someone less good natured than Donald, but he was used to Daphne and her little self-deceptions.

As he closed Daphne's bedroom door quietly behind him, the thought occurred to him briefly that it was possible that she would need all her powers of self-deception if his court appearance were to make the local papers. He shrugged away that thought, totally unaware that his name had already appeared in one local paper under 'pending court appearances'. Donald still believed that all that was required was just a quick appearance at the magistrates' court to clear up this little misunderstanding, as he saw it, and he was convinced that nothing untoward would come of it. The police officers who had arrested him had been almost deferential and apologetic. This, more than anything, had encouraged Donald to believe that this was all a silly mistake on the part of the social worker who had made the complaint against him.

Not wanting to draw attention to his visit to the court, Donald parked in the multi storey car park and walked to the court. Not knowing how long the whole business was going to take, Donald had taken the precaution of telling Daphne that he had a meeting with one of his insurance clients and had said he didn't know how long he would be out. Donald had been to the building housing the Magistrates Court before; to the planning office which was also situated there, but had never before had occasion to visit the court, unlike one of the other golf club committee members who had successfully contested a speeding ticket. It was with a certain amount of trepidation as he entered the court that Donald suddenly remembered that at least one of the prominent members of the golf club was, in fact, a Magistrate; Donald hoped that it wasn't going to be he who dealt with his 'little misunderstanding'.

Some three hours later Donald walked dazedly through the town centre, the words he had heard going through his head like some dreaded mantra; his case was to be 'referred to Crown Court as the offence of which he was accused was too serious to be dealt with at Magistrates Court level', and that he was still to be the subject of the police bail conditions;

he was not to be allowed within a three mile radius of the address where the so called (as he thought of it) offences took place. The duty solicitor was in a hurry to attend another case, so Donald had to wait until the following day for an appointment with him to discuss what was likely to happen next.

Unable to think straight and not knowing what to do with himself; Donald walked through the park in the opposite direction to the multi-storey car park in order to give himself time to think. His immediate worry that his case would be heard by the golf club member who was a Magistrate hadn't happened, but Donald was beginning to realise that he could no longer delude himself; before long everyone would know what he had been accused of, and his life and, of course, Daphne's could change again in the most awful manner. His stomach contracted at this thought, oh, and Pamela and Carla. What on earth would his beloved daughter and granddaughter think of him when they learned about it all? How had it all come to this, he asked himself? He had gone in all innocence to see Peggy and Maisie, to offer his condolences with regard to the vicious poisoning of Buster, and finding Maisie at home alone had accepted her offer of a cup of tea. Donald had followed Maisie into the little kitchen and watched as she took the tea making paraphernalia from the wall cupboard in the little kitchen. Maisie made tea in chunky mugs putting a tea bag in each mug and then pouring boiling water into the mugs. Donald had watched, fascinated, as Maisie spoke softly to herself as she did so, reciting the necessary steps to herself, like a poem or times tables learned. Donald had not seen much of Maisie as she grew up over the years, but he was aware of her ways, ways which had her labelled as 'with learning difficulties' when she was taken out of mainstream school and educated at one which catered for special needs children. Now about twenty years old, Maisie still lived with her mother, Peggy in their council house, and they lived on the money Peggy earned as 'help' to Daphne and Donald, and a disability living allowance Maisie was awarded as she was considered unemployable.

Maisie invited Donald into the little sitting room to drink their tea. She indicated that he should sit on the sofa beside her (she was finding it difficult to speak as she had begun to cry when Donald said how sorry he was about what had happened to Buster) as the only other chair in the room was piled up with what looked like clean washing just brought in from the line. Maisie put down her mug and cried with hearty sobs; not being a demonstrative man, Donald put down his mug and rather clumsily put his arm around Maisie's shoulders. Peggy had tried not to bring Maisie to work with her when she was a baby and then a young child; instead she had worked out a routine with a neighbour where she could leave Maisie with her on the mornings when she worked, and in return she would care for her neighbour's young son whenever his mother needed to go out. Consequently, Donald had never really got to know Maisie. Peggy would talk about her with pride if asked, but otherwise would not volunteer information; she seemed to want to keep this part of her life away from Daphne and Donald, almost like a secret she hugged to herself in the same way that she had the early pregnancy about which she had apparently told no one at all.

Gradually Maisie's noisy sobbing slowed down and then stopped. Donald gave her a handkerchief as she didn't seem to have one. When he had arrived Maisie had just said that Peggy was out – so now he asked her at what time she expected her mother to return home. Maisie said she didn't know, but that she was 'over Shirl's' and had indicated a rough direction with her arm – as though expecting Donald to know who Shirley was and where she lived. Donald had wanted to ask whether the body of the dog had been disposed of or whether his help was required in some way but as Maisie's sobbing had stopped Donald had decided that a change of subject was in order.

Donald sat down on a wooden bench in the park as he tried hard not to think about what had happened next – instead he focused on how he was going to deal with the immediate future – surely, he thought, once he had his meeting the following day with the duty solicitor all would be able to be put straight? In the meantime, he had a real appointment back at his office at home with one of his insurance clients, so he pulled himself together and set off back to the car park.

Chapter 3

Pamela sat in the kitchen drinking coffee. It was the third Saturday that she had been in the new house, and she was just contemplating where to start with all the tasks that still needed doing when Carla came downstairs smiling and put her pink holdall on the floor by the door. "Dad's picking me up at 8.30" she told Pamela

"OK, any idea what time he's bringing you back?"

Pamela forced herself to relax. She didn't want Carla to see how much it hurt; the fact that Michael was carrying on with his new life with "HER" and taking Carla to George's party, an event planned months ago in honour of George's birthday. Pamela had always been fond of Michael's brother, George, and she got on well with her sister in law, Carol. She couldn't help feeling a sense of betrayal that Michael's new partner was invited so apparently easily instead of her. This was to be Carla's first outing with Michael and "HER" as a couple to a family event. She pulled herself together and turned to Carla and asked (as calmly as she could) "Have you got everything?"

"I think so, Fee has said that I can try on something of hers if I like", Carla told her mum casually. Carla realised that this was a difficult time for her; Carla's cousins Paul and Fiona (Fee) were twins, two years her senior. The two families had lived quite close to one another until George's job had taken his family abroad for six months when the twins were three. On George's return he found it hard to settle, so to both Michael and Pamela's disappointment they moved on again to Cambridge where, much to everyone's surprise he took up a professorship and settled into the life as though he'd known no other. It was now no longer possible just to visit on spec, but the closeness that had developed between the two couples in the early days had continued despite the fact that visits had to be planned in advance, and, due to their all having busy lives, tended not to be as frequent as both couples would have liked.

Pamela busied herself with the kettle while she was mulling over these things. Carla opened the fridge door and taking out the orange juice asked "Do you want some, mum?" She forced a smile and said no, she'd just have a coffee.

"I'm going to tackle the garden this weekend" she said brightly "I know we still have a lot to do indoors, but while the weather is nice I'll try to do something with the wilderness". The old couple from whom Pamela had bought the house had suffered increasingly bad health and had sold in order to move to a sheltered bungalow. Old Mr Benson had been very apologetic about the state of the garden, which had been his wife's pride and joy; she had been very ill and he had had to nurse her and had no time or energy to spend in the garden. Sadly, Mrs Benson had died just before the contracts were exchanged so Mr Benson moved reluctantly alone to the sheltered bungalow.

Pamela had never really felt involved with their garden; Michael had seen to most of it just leaving the pots and troughs for Pamela to plant and care for. As their house was new when they had bought it soon after their marriage, Pamela had concentrated on the soft furnishings inside, while Michael had planted a few trees and bought a mower to keep the lawn that the developers had laid tidily mowed. Pamela had never had any interest in it.

Her grandparents' home in which her parents now lived had a garden that went all the way down to a river. It was an interesting place that had an old wooden shed at the bottom which had always seemed to Pamela as though it could tell many tales; almost too many, she had found it rather spooky when she had first moved there as a child until her grandmother had become frail and seemed to have a particular attachment to the place. When Pamela wasn't at school she would often ask her to help her to a seat nearby.

Once married, Pamela had been happy to concentrate on keeping house, caring for Carla once she arrived, and helping with various charitable causes as Carla grew and started school. Michael's salary as an accountant was plenty to support their lifestyle without Pamela needing to work.

"I'm off now, mum, Dad didn't say what time we'd be leaving tomorrow, sorry" Carla's words brought Pamela out of her daydream

"OK, love, see you tomorrow. Please try to finish most of your homework; you really won't feel like doing it tomorrow evening if you are back late".

"OK, I'll try, I expect Paul will help me".

Pamela watched Carla toss her pink holdall into Michael's car. She was pleased to see that "That Woman" wasn't in the car, but she noticed that Carla got in the back, so she realised that Carla knew that Michael was about to pick her up from somewhere. Carla turned and gave Pamela a quick wave, and Michael put his hand up in polite recognition. Pamela turned away after waving to Carla, she felt her stomach tighten uncomfortably and wondered whether everyone felt this way when their marriage failed and whether there should be a sort of etiquette for split couples. She had loved Michael (or, thought she had) and she realised that she and he had to work together on certain decisions regarding Carla as whatever happened they both had her best interests at heart, but she didn't yet feel ready to be civil to Michael's new partner, never mind being civil to her, she couldn't even bear to think of her by name!

Pamela had put on some weight in recent years. She hadn't noticed that it had crept on, she had just complained (along with several of her friends who were in the same boat) that clothes sizes were no longer the same and she had just bought bigger sizes, mainly in comfortable tops and stretch leggings.

When she made the radical decision to buy a modest house and get a job she had borrowed a skirt and jacket from Sylvie (without telling her exactly what she wanted it for) and when she was taken through the office to the room where the interview was to take place she took note of what the other office workers were wearing and once she was offered the job she bought some cheap but serviceable skirts and tops in a similar style. Pamela smiled to herself as she put these things in the washing machine along with Carla's school uniform so it would all be ready for the week ahead. She had wrought quite a transformation on herself already; most of her former friends would hardly recognise the person she had become in such a short time.

Pamela glanced at the kitchen clock. The wash load would take about forty five more minutes. She knew that there was an old rotary washing line in the shed; the question was would she be able to cut the grass and find the spike that the rotary line fitted into in the forty five minutes? She finished her coffee, rinsed her mug and Carla's breakfast things and went to find the key for the shed.

Pamela wanted to keep busy so she wouldn't brood on the things that would be going on at George and Carol's once Michael, Carla and Monique (there, she had at last thought of "HER" by name!) arrived there. She hadn't discussed with Carla the fact that Michael and Monique would most likely be sleeping together. She surprised herself by almost smiling to herself as she thought "sleeping together" was one of the silliest euphemisms she could think of! Pamela and Michael had been sleeping together, just that, nothing more, for several years now. Pamela had become resigned to this and assumed that it was normal in a fifteen year marriage; her own parents had had separate bedrooms since returning from Cyprus, but when Pamela noticed changes in Michael's demeanour she eventually guessed that he was having an affair and suddenly the term 'sleeping together' took on a whole new meaning!

Obviously Carla must realise that Michael's relationship with Monique was a full one, but Pamela didn't feel that at nearly thirteen Carla would be interested in the implications of this, and anyway, as George and Carol were welcoming Monique into the bosom of their family no doubt Fee and Paul would fill any gaps that there may be in Carla's knowledge; they usually did.

Carla had been careful not to express any opinions about Monique in front of Pamela, but as Monique was slim and fit (Michael had met her at the gym where she worked) and didn't have any children she seemed quite "cool" to Carla even though she had very mixed feelings about the end of her parents' marriage. Some of her peers had "extended" families due to their parents break-ups; at least she felt that hers hadn't embarrassed her totally by turning gay or picking partners whose ages were decades different from theirs. Carla had, in fact, met Monique when her friendship with Michael was just that; an innocent friendship. She had run him home after he had sprained his ankle playing squash and Michael had asked her in for a coffee. Pamela had been out at the time and Michael and Monique had found a lot to chat and laugh about despite Michael's painful ankle, and Carla had not thought much about it at all but had just found Monique quite lively and entertaining. Once she'd gone and Pamela had come home there was all the kerfuffle of sorting out how to collect Michael's car from the gym, arranging the evening meal around taking Michael to A & E for an X-ray, Carla noticed how fussy and serious her mum seemed in contrast with Monique.

Pamela plugged the cable of the little electric mower into the socket nearest the back door. She felt clumsy and nervous; she'd never used an electric lawn mower before and was worried about slicing through the cable. She soon found that there was a knack to it and trimmed most of the central area of the little garden. It was hard to see where the lawn ended and the flower beds began as it was all so overgrown. Pamela soon found the blue plastic cap that kept the metal spike insert clear of muck that the rotary washing line fitted into, but she couldn't get the cap off. Pamela didn't have any tools, but Mr Benson had left a few screwdrivers and a hammer and his gardening tools (including the mower) for her as he had said his sons didn't want them and he wouldn't need them in his sheltered home.

Pamela decided to take a look in the shed to see whether she could find anything with which she could prise off the blue cap. She didn't find anything thin enough so went back into the kitchen to try a knife. As she went back into the house the wash load was just on its final spin.

She caught sight of her reflection in the glass of the back door as she walked past it and grinned to herself: There she was with a dirt streaked face, a tiny garden, a tiny kitchen with all its domestic machines in it as there was no utility room and she had become so engrossed in what she was doing that she had forgotten to worry about Carla's weekend and was beginning to enjoy the autumn sunshine and the smell of the cut grass. She began to feel a small sense of achievement. Maybe her mother and her former friends would never understand her agreeing with Michael to sell their home and for her to buy this modest terraced house (The estate never had been built as council houses, not that it would have made any difference to Pamela if it had, but Pamela's mother insisted on referring to it as "Pamela's little council house" with undisguised distaste) and take a job to support herself so that all she needed from Michael was support for Carla.

They had, in fact, come to a fairly amicable agreement over this as they had heard horror stories about couples battling through the courts and felt that they were civilised enough to sort such things out for themselves. Michael actually had a lot of respect for what Pamela was doing but on the couple of occasions that he had tried to say so Pamela had bitten his head off and told him not to be so patronising. Her mother had been horrified that Pamela was buying the house and taking the job (a mundane low paid job according to her mother) but it was bringing in enough to support herself. The couple of employment agencies Pamela had contacted had made out she was unemployable when they discovered that she hadn't been in paid employment for almost twelve years.

Luckily, she had kept her computer skills up to date due to her involvement in the charity work that she gave up so abruptly on discovering that most of her so called friends knew about Michael's affair and had been gleefully discussing it behind her back.

Her mother had said "Sweetheart, you MUST come to Daddy and me.....Pamela shuddered at the thought of this; what her mother called "home" was the house she herself had grown up in and had inherited from her parents. Something had occurred in Cyprus; something that was never spoken of in front of Pamela but this "something" was the catalyst for all the changes that happened around Pamela's tenth birthday. Her father left the army and the three of them moved back to England and went to live with Pamela's grandparents in the large house. This had been a time of great upheaval for all of them and her mother had worked hard to settle Pamela into a local school and had thrown herself into 'good works', as her father called them, in the local community while he tried his hand at many different jobs. Pamela's mother had Peggy to help in the house Peggy had worked for Pamela's parents as a general help for many years. Peggy wasn't very bright, and her daughter, May, who was referred to as 'Maisie' by Peggy was diagnosed as having learning difficulties. Maisie had appeared in June 1973 after what seemed to everyone concerned a very short pregnancy but, in fact, Peggy had either kept her pregnancy a secret, or had not understood what was happening to her body. It was hard to tell with Peggy, sometimes she appeared to be quite stupid; at others she could display quite amazing cunning. But, whatever, it soon became apparent that something had occurred during a week-long visit to Rhyl that

Peggy had paid to a distant relative the previous September.

Pamela found an old kitchen knife and went out to prise off the blue plastic cap. She put up the rotary line, pegged out the washing and went back into the house to clean herself up before nipping out for some shopping. Whilst in the shower she quickly worked out how much she could afford to spend this weekend. Determined to be self-sufficient she planned not to use credit cards but to wait until she could pay for things before she bought them. She had opened a separate account into which Michael paid the agreed allowance for Carla so that it was easy to keep track of whether it was sufficient for Carla's needs. Thinking that in order to keep within these financial boundaries that she had set herself she would be better off not going into town where she might be tempted to buy some of the things she would like but that were not necessities. Instead she decided just to go to a small local supermarket where she could just get enough groceries to see herself and Carla though until the end of the week. She also needed to get Carla a new protractor, as Carla had already managed to lose the new one Pamela had bought her to start the school term with.

The interior of Pamela's new house was surprisingly well kept considering the poor health of Mr and Mrs Benson but they had been a very organised couple and had kept the house in good decorative order, so, even though the décor wasn't quite to Pamela's taste, she found it mostly "liveable with". The weekend after they had moved in Pamela had painted the bathroom white and Carla's room lemon and bought her a matching duvet cover and curtains and a lampshade of her choice. Pamela felt that it was important that Carla had a room she felt that she had personalised. The rest could wait until Pamela not only had enough money to be able to redecorate, but also until she could decide how she wanted the place to be. She had always prided herself on being good at choosing furnishings, but she had wrought great changes in herself, and found that her tastes were changing, and she didn't want to rush into anything. She had brought a lot of the things with her from the family home; Michael had moved temporarily into a furnished bed-sit several months before their house was sold. They had found the strain of living under the same roof once the split had been agreed too much and it was too confusing for Carla. Once the decision to part had been made, the arguments stopped and an uneasy peace had prevailed, occasionally Pamela and Michael had even found they could laugh about something and if Carla was around she would look at them wistfully as if hoping there would be a reconciliation. Quite a lot of the furniture was far too big for Pamela's new home, so Michael had suggested that she choose the pieces that she could make use of and he would put the rest into storage.

What Pamela didn't want was for her new home to become a smaller replica of her former home, but to start with it was hard not to, and she had found herself hanging pictures and grouping ornaments in a similar way to the way she had had them in her old home. Carla found this home from home quite comforting, but Pamela hadn't even realised that she had done it until Carla commented on it when she came in from school on a couple of occasions.

Pamela tried not to dwell for long on regrets and bitterness. She would be the first to admit that there had not been much passion in their marriage during the last few years, but they had still been close and had felt very comfortable with each other, snuggling and cuddling together in bed naked there had been no prudishness between them. However, Michael's last promotion and subsequent stress at work had drained him; Pamela would have responded sexually had Michael shown any interest, but he had always simply fallen into bed companionably but exhausted, that's what had made his betrayal even worse.

Pamela was aware that Michael used to wake in the early hours and creep downstairs and work on his paperwork. She used to find half-empty coffee cups on the kitchen table the next morning. Initially he was trying to make sense of the accounts the previous finance director had left in such a mess, but once he met Monique, he used that time to compose and send romantic and funny messages to her. Michael had always had a dream of running his own business; he had worked his way up from financial accountant to finance director in a large company selling gym equipment. He felt that the company had lost its way somewhat, and felt that there was a niche in the market that he could fill and he was planning to set up his own company with his share of the equity out of the family home.

Pamela dried herself off and planned where to shop as she dressed. She really didn't want to bump into anyone she knew; so rather than going to Waitrose she decided to try the little Somerfield just up the road. The previous Saturday she had gone to one of the bigger supermarkets where she had always used to do the family shopping. She hadn't been there for months, as she had been avoiding her old haunts but had decided to "brave it". That had been a mistake, as several people had stopped her and asked where she had been, and she found herself explaining, all over again, that she and Michael had parted and that now she had bought a small house for herself and Carla. She found it emotionally exhausting having to go through it all again.

Today would be different, she told herself as she parked her car and walked into Somerfield. She didn't need much as Carla was to be away all weekend, but she shopped for the week so she wouldn't have to worry about buying anything during the week after work. She managed to get everything she wanted apart from Carla's protractor. She wondered whether Carla would be able to borrow one for this week, as she would have to go into town the following weekend to buy a birthday present for her father.

Pamela felt quite hungry as she parked the car and walked back to her house. She remembered she'd eaten no breakfast so she put the shopping away and put some ham and mustard in a crusty roll as she put the kettle on. She glanced out of the window at the garden. The sun was still shining and it showed

Pamela how dirty the window was. She decided to clean it once she'd eaten her lunch, then she would carry on working in the garden while the October sunshine lasted, anything to try to keep her mind off Carla's weekend with Michael.

Pamela worked for hours without noticing the time pass. She liked the smell of the fresh earth and the freshly cut grass, and there was also a familiar smell that she couldn't quite place but that reminded her of the first summer she was back in England at the age of ten. She began to notice the lengthening shadows, and realised that if she didn't take the washing in soon it would become damp.

Feeling that she still hadn't thanked Marian for coming over to sit and wait for Carla when she had made her unnecessary visit to her parents, Pamela had bought two cakes when she shopped, as well as some Jammy Dodgers to put in the office biscuit tin, having intended to take them round to Marian's house and to either invite Marian to join her for a "cuppa", or to have one at Marian's house with her. As Pamela went indoors to clean herself up prior to taking the washing in, she realised it was rather late, and resolved to see Marian the following day, Sunday. Doing anything of this sort was alien to Pamela; there had been a certain formality regarding their social activities with any of their friends – the only easy friendship she had known was the one with George and Carol, and that had had to change once George made his career change and they moved away.

Pamela changed back out of her dirty gardening clothes. As she walked back towards the kitchen door, Pamela looked at the work she had done to the flower borders. There was quite a transformation, she felt quite pleased as she realised that she would be able to finish the job the next day.

Later that evening Pamela sat down in front of the television, and contemplated her day. She was feeling quite relaxed, and that without having resorted to alcohol. She couldn't remember a Saturday evening when she was still with Michael when they hadn't had at least a bottle of wine between them. With her new carefully worked out budget, alcohol would only be something she would have on special occasions. She had eaten a 'ready' meal that she had bought at Somerfield; something she had never done in her previous life. Being through choice a 'stay at home' mum she had promised herself she would never use convenience foods, but now as she was working and also as she only had herself and Carla to cook for, sometimes if Carla was away it would be more cost-effective than cooking for one.

*

Pamela woke up later than she normally did on Sunday morning. She had slept all night and not had any disturbing dreams. After looking out of the bedroom window to see what the weather was like, she put on her gardening clothes and went downstairs. After a quick coffee she went outside to finish clearing the flower borders.

As she worked her way along the last remaining border, Pamela remembered what the familiar smell was, that she had noticed the day before – she believed that it was the smell of marigolds, although her grandfather had called them calendulas, telling her that marigolds were different. She smiled as she remembered him, her mother's father. Pamela had barely had time to get to know him, but had quickly become fond of him and his gentle ways. As in her own parents' marriage, it was her grandmother who was the stronger personality. Thinking of her parents, she briefly wondered whether she would ever find out what had taken place when her mother had phoned twice. Maybe she would find out when she and Carla took her father his birthday gift.

After changing back out of her mucky clothes, Pamela decided to go round to see whether Marian was in. She knocked on Marian's door and suddenly felt very nervous. She needn't have worried because Marian soon came to the door and, seeing Pamela smiled broadly and asked her in. "I came to thank you for what you did the other week" she said

"Lovely ter see yer, ducks, I'll put the kettle on" said Marian "What's that yer've got there?"

"Oh, I brought us a cake each" said Pamela, suddenly feeling very embarrassed that it would seem that she had assumed that she would be asked in.

"That's nice ducks" said Marian, immediately making Pamela feel comfortable again. Marian busied herself making the drinks and getting plates out to put the cakes on and Pamela sat herself down at the kitchen table where Marian had indicated for her to sit.

The two of them spent a very pleasant hour chatting about what Pamela had done in the garden; what she planned to do in the house, and about her job, Pamela even told Marian a little about work and how although she got on well with her colleagues and the directors who had interviewed her, but how Sandra the office manager seemed to resent her. It wasn't until later after they had said their goodbyes and Pamela was back home that she realised that they had only talked about herself, and that she still hadn't learned anything about her neighbour with the pink spiky hair.

Pamela wasn't sure what Michael's plans were for the journey back from Cambridge. Not being sure whether Carla would have eaten a hot meal during the day, Pamela had decided to roast a small chicken, aiming for it to be ready about 6 o'clock. If Carla had eaten by the time she came home, they could use the chicken for sandwiches in the week and have cold chicken Monday evening for their dinner. She busied herself through the afternoon cleaning the house and cooking the chicken. She wasn't at all sure how Carla would feel coming back after her weekend away with Michael and Monique so she kept busy so that she would not dwell on it. It turned out to be good timing and good planning as Michael's car drew up at about a quarter to six, and Carla quickly hopped out and ran up to the front door.

Chapter 4

Sylvie had promised herself that she would spend most of Sunday going through her paperwork and sorting it out and, more importantly; actually throwing away the stuff she didn't need to keep. Why was it, she asked herself for the umpteenth time, that she found it so hard to get round to her assorted paperwork? She always paid any bills on time, but allowed other things to accumulate; and usually hid it all in her bedroom. There was a semblance of tidiness and order in the parts of her house that other people might see, but things such as letters and cards from friends, bank statements and information regarding her endowments and insurance etc., as well as the many offers of loans and credit cards, she tended to shove behind the curtains on the windowsill. However, this time the piles of correspondence had almost taken her bedroom over, and she could no longer ignore it.

The day started well. She awoke reasonably early and had some fresh orange juice. The weather was nice so she decided to go for a run before she could find an excuse not to. She put on her sports bra, trainers, shorts and top and set off along her favourite route. As she jogged along she pondered the fact that although she was fairly fit she was still a size sixteen to eighteen. Oh well, she thought, maybe if I didn't exercise I'd be as big as a house! Sylvie generally went out for a run like this about three times a week in the nice weather; in the winter she tended to go swimming a couple of times a week. She wasn't worried about her size; in fact, Sylvie was comfortable with herself in most areas of her life. At thirty six, she was settled in her career, had a nice home, and friends she could rely on even though she did not always see a great deal of them. The reason for the running and swimming was not so much for keeping fit, but to combat the stress that her choice of career as a probation officer inevitably brought with it. Sylvie was well aware that if she wanted to lose weight, she would have to cut out the comfort foods such as chips and chocolate, but Sylvie found these foods also acted as "stress busters", so had no intention of changing her diet.

As Sylvie ran past the familiar gardens she took pleasure as ever in the diversity of them. She didn't know any of the people who lived in these houses, but enjoyed trying to guess what sort of people lived there by the way the gardens were laid out and cared for. She had intended to get straight to work on her paperwork when she got back, but having seen how much nicer the gardens looked when freshly mowed she decided to cut her grass before showering. As a consequence it was late morning before she was ready to start on the paperwork, and, as ever, she felt less inclined to start on it than had it been first thing. At least, that's what she told herself; the truth was that it was a job she disliked so much, that any excuse usually prevented her from tackling it! Sylvie decided instead that she needed chocolate after all that exercise, so she walked to the paper shop to get some to have with a coffee.

Sylvie chose her chocolate bar and picked up a magazine. She didn't buy magazines very often, but a headline caught her eye that looked interesting, and, of course, if she had something to read with her coffee she wouldn't have to start going through the paperwork just yet. She had, however, brought the paperwork down from her bedroom windowsill and dumped it on her sitting room floor in an effort to make herself start on it once she got back from the shop. She had a plan – she would tackle it logically – she would sort the items into things that required replies, things that just needed filing, and stuff that could be thrown away, but not until she'd had chocolate and coffee!

An hour later Sylvie rocked back on her heels to survey the neat piles of paperwork. She was pleased to see that the biggest pile was the rubbish, and the smallest was the "to do" pile. Top of the "to do" was the notification from Pamela of her change of address. She smiled as she remembered the skinny sun tanned girl she first met at junior school – both she and Pamela were new to the school, and as everyone else seemed to know one another, the two new girls soon bonded in a way that was to last, despite their differences in personality and family background.

Sylvie straightened up, rubbed the backs of her legs and took the rubbish out. She returned with writing paper and envelopes – she had wished she'd thought of getting Pamela a card at the paper shop, then thought better of it deciding that a letter would be better. It had been ages since she had heard from

Pamela when she contacted her out of the blue and asked whether Sylvie would mind lending her something smart to wear – she hadn't explained what she wanted it for and Sylvie had sensed that Pamela wasn't ready to be asked. Such was the bond between the two that they knew when to delve and when not to. At that point Sylvie hadn't been even aware that Michael was having an affair. As Sylvie had remained happily single, the two had seen less of one another as Pamela had done all the conventional 'married' things; Sylvie secretly felt that Pamela was wasting her talents by just being a homemaker, but it was not in her nature to tell her so.

Sylvie had simply given Pamela the run of her wardrobe and let her try things on and to choose what to borrow. A few days later when Pamela had returned the jacket and skirt she had told Sylvie that she and Michael were splitting up and selling their house and that she had found herself a job. Pamela had said it all in such a "matter of fact" way, that Sylvie was at first astounded, but soon realised that it was just Pamela's way of dealing with it, that she was actually quite emotionally fragile – Sylvie was reminded of the way Pamela had dealt with various difficult times early on in their friendship – so she just followed Pamela's lead by not asking probing questions. Sylvie was, in fact, at that time dealing with a lot more difficult cases at work than usual – one of the other probation officers, Ralph, was on sick leave, and Sylvie had had to take her share of his cases. She felt almost permanently exhausted, and was rather glad that Pamela hadn't needed to turn to Sylvie for support.

Ralph's ulcer was now on the mend, and he was back at work and had taken his case load back, so Sylvie was able to give her own cases and clients a little more attention. She tried hard not to think about work at all at weekends, as she knew that that was how many of her colleagues succumbed to stress. Being a probation officer entailed getting involved in peoples' lives in a great deal of depth, and sometimes Sylvie would feel as though she could almost drown in some families' distress – when she dealt with a client from the start this usually meant a pre sentence report would be the first point of reference – and this would mean getting to know both the client and his or her immediate family and his or her friends to start with. Sylvie had worked at the same probation office now for over five years, and had a couple of clients who for various reasons she had an ongoing association with for that time, and in one case (as he would only be released "on licence" once out of prison) would quite probably continue to work with for the foreseeable future.

Sylvie decided to have a snack before writing to Pamela. Returning from the kitchen with a can of coke and a cheese sandwich, she picked up a local paper from the 'rubbish' pile and idly turned the pages. The paper was one that was delivered free and normally Sylvie put them out with the rubbish as soon as they arrived but this one must have got caught up with some of her paperwork. As she always tried not to think about work at a weekend, she tried to miss the page which held any reports that the reporters had managed to glean from the local police station and courts, but found that it had been moved from page two to further inside the paper, and she almost dropped her coke in shock as she saw the name Major Donald Fielding under the heading of *Pending Court Appearances*. It couldn't be, could it? Major Fielding was how she had been asked to address Pamela's dad as a child when she first went to play at her house that autumn all those years ago when they had been new to Addington Junior School, and she still thought of him as Major Fielding, although she hadn't seen him for years. Surely it had to be him? Sylvie put down her coke and reached for the change of address notification from Pamela to see whether there was a phone number on it – there was and as Sylvie reached for the phone she hesitated for a moment.

Her sense of never wanting home and work to mix kicked in and that moment of hesitation proved to be her undoing with regard to contacting Pamela. She decided to wait and see what she could find out at work on the following day before getting involved. Guiltily she thought what her mother's reaction would have been to her action (or, as she thought of it almost cowardly "non action") "Hmm, no wonder you have no social life and no boyfriends, my love" she would say…….and no doubt would say something along those lines this evening, thought Sylvie, when she went over to her mum and dad's for dinner. This was something she had done out of duty to start with, once she'd bought her own house, going for a Sunday meal every other week with her parents, but as time had gone on she found she really looked forward to an evening of family chat and her mother's lovely cooking. She was pleased, though, that it was always in the evening, giving her the whole day free; luckily her dad liked to work all day at something without the interruption of a heavy meal at lunchtime – he would either do some DIY or gardening, then relax in the evening afterwards. Sylvie decided to put the problem of Major Fielding from her mind and finished her snack and did a few chores before setting off to her parents' home.

*

The following day Sylvie hurriedly put her last two clients' files away in the secure cabinet and prepared to leave for the day. She had phoned her friend Jo, who worked part time at the magistrates court, at lunchtime to find out whether she had been working that morning as she was eager to prove herself wrong that the Donald Fielding listed in the local paper was anything to do with Major Donald, Pamela's father. She, however, got the news that she didn't want – that it was definitely the Major Donald she knew and that it was not a motoring offence he was up for. Jo recognised Sylvie's 'worried' voice and suggested they meet for coffee after work.

Making her way to the town centre Sylvie looked forward to seeing Jo for a chat and sincerely hoped that Major Donald's court appearance was nothing to worry about, and promised herself that she would contact Pamela straight after her coffee with Jo.

Sylvie's case load was still rather too high for comfort, but not almost unmanageable as it had been when Ralph had been off sick. Perhaps it was something in her nature that meant she could only get close to those people she had known and trusted for many years, or perhaps it was the effects of having been a probation officer for so long – there were many things that were confidential, and she would never ever be able to discuss with anyone other than her line manager and colleagues and this meant that unlike someone who had work stresses in a different type of working environment she was unable to share work stress confidences outside of work. With Jo, however it was different, as in many cases Jo would be aware of what Sylvie's clients were accused of, even if she did not know the details. She also would see the clients in their best clothes standing before the magistrate – and often would have seen the apparently 'angelic' side of an offender – and see what perhaps that person could have become under different circumstances. In many cases, Sylvie could become quite fond of her clients, whatever they had done, once she was aware of their circumstances and personalities – especially when they were able to follow advice and maybe embark on one of the programs available such as anger management or alcohol counselling or drug rehab. She had had some successes, and counted as one of those a young couple with a toddler who had, with help from the various agencies, sorted themselves out and now had a nice home and would call out to her and give a cheery wave if she saw them in town, and would expect Sylvie to do the same should she see them before they saw her. This was in stark contrast to other clients as it was part of her training not to acknowledge clients in public unless they acknowledged Sylvie in order not to breach any client confidentiality.

Sylvie spotted Jo through the window of the burger bar where they had arranged to meet; she was sitting at a table and there were two large paper cups in front of her. "You're not going to like this" Jo said as Sylvie sat down, and she wasted no time telling Sylvie that Major Donald had been accused of a crime that had now been referred to Crown Court and that the bail conditions had not been lifted.

Sylvie considered herself un-shock able when it came to human nature and what people could do, but when something hit close to home as this did, she could still feel rattled – and she felt very uncomfortable indeed as Jo told her what she'd been able to find out. Talking it through with Jo, she soon realised that confidentiality could become a problem if she were to contact Pamela at all at this stage, so she decided to wait and see what the outcome would be and to monitor the progress of the case. She realised that the CPS must be confident of their case, they had been slated enough of late for wasting public money on cases that had been thrown out for lack of evidence.

Chapter 5

As Pamela drove home from work, she reflected on her weekend and the previous evening. Her two days at work this week so far had gone quite smoothly. She had managed to make coffee for her colleagues while Sandra was in her Monday morning manager's meeting; she'd caught up with the work that had accumulated over month end while she had been moving house; she'd worked out a system with the warehouse regarding delivery notes that even Sandra should be able to find no complaints about (especially as she had taken credit for Pamela's work on the Walker's account) and the Jammy Dodger biscuits she'd replenished the office tin with had been gratefully received.

Carla had obviously enjoyed her weekend away with Michael but was tactful enough not to say too much about it – this gave Pamela mixed feelings – she was proud of Carla's grown up ease of acceptance of the situation, but at the same time could feel the child in Carla slipping away from her. However, Pamela was realistic enough to be aware that this would happen anyway as Carla grew up and with all going as well as it was maybe her new life in her little house and her office job would be something she could actually enjoy, rather than just endure, as it had seemed to her would be the way to deal with it all at first.

Pamela smiled as she pulled into her parking space; Carla had actually asked whether there was anything that she could do for her when she came in from school prior to her arriving home from work, but although it had pleased Pamela immensely to be asked, because she had cleaned and tidied the house over the weekend and washed and ironed the clothes and tidied the garden there was nothing she could think of to ask Carla to do. There was little preparation required for their evening meal, either, as they were having grilled fish and frozen vegetables, having finished the cold chicken and salad Monday evening.

Humming gently to herself Pamela opened the front door and called out to Carla – but there was no reply and the house seemed strangely empty. Puzzled, she wondered whether she may have forgotten something Carla may have mentioned about what she planned to do after school – despite the fact that she had offered to do something for her mother she may have 'double booked' herself and forgotten that she was taking part in something after school, or seeing one of her friends. Pamela set about getting dinner ready, but when there was still no sign of Carla by six o'clock Pamela began to worry. She thought about what Marian had said to her the first time they met, and realised that the mystery hadn't been resolved. She decided to pop over to Marian's; for one thing there was a slight possibility that Carla could be there, as they had seemed to get on well the evening that Marian had waited in for Carla when Pamela had gone to her parents' house and also Pamela decided that she would ask Marian whether she could shed any light on what she had said before about believing she had seen Carla walking along the ring road.

"Oh, "ello ducks, c'mon in" was Marian's first response – but seeing Pamela's worried look she asked "wassup, ducks?". Pamela hadn't realised she looked so worried so she said to Marian that it was probably nothing at all to worry about, but that Carla wasn't home and she wondered whether Marian had seen her. "Well, yes, ducks, she was brought to the house in that car that picked her up at the weekend; Carla went in the 'ouse and then went back out with a couple of bags. Is everything alright – I thought p'raps she was going to stay with her Dad for a bit?" Seeing Pamela's face, Marian steered her to a kitchen chair, made tea and, roughly shoving the clutter that always seemed to adorn her table, she put a mug of tea in front of her.

"Well?" prompted Marian.

"I, I d don't know..." said Pamela feebly, "no arrangements were made, I can't think why, and no note was left, I am just truly puzzled." Apart from anything else, thought Pamela, Michael was currently staying in a bed-sit, and there was nowhere there that Carla could sleep.

"Drink up yer tea an' try telephonin'" suggested the ever practical Marian. "C'mon, me phones over there, get on and do it now and solve the mystery, it's obviously botherin' yer".

Pamela dialled the number of the payphone at Michael's bed-sit; it rang several times before being answered by a vague sounding young man; "Who? Oh, Michael, no I haven't seen him" on being asked whether he would mind enquiring whether any of the other residents knew where he was he called out "Anyone seen Michael?"

Pamela heard voices then there was a lady on the phone "'e come in with a young girl, dear, an" packed "is stuff and then went back out wi' 'er". After thanking the lady, Pamela put the phone down; went to sit back down and explained to Marian what had been said. She also explained that she had no idea where or why they could have gone. Marian carefully asked whether Pamela believed that Carla could come to any harm with her dad, but Pamela said firmly that although her marriage had ended, and that she felt it was Michael's fault, she had no worries concerning his love for Carla. However, Pamela was at a loss as to what was going on, so she thanked Marian for the tea and said she'd better go home in case Michael was trying to phone her to explain.

Not knowing what to do with herself while she waited for the phone to ring, she wandered upstairs to Carla's room and stopped in amazement; totally shocked by the emptiness of the room. She stood still for a moment, trying to take it in, remembering that Marian had said that Carla had left with 'bags' plural.....

Pamela was upset and confused. Feeling unable to wait around for the phone to ring, she decided to phone George and Carol to see whether anything had been said over the weekend that would shed any light on the situation.

George answered the phone and immediately he realised who it was Pamela felt that he was being defensive. Initially hurt as she assumed it was because they had really taken to Monique, the hurt feeling turned to alarm as she listened to what George was saying:

"I'm sure it's for the best for now, Pam,……………"

"But WHAT is for the best?" shouted Pamela into the phone, as she had no idea what George was talking about.

"You mean you really don't know?" asked George gently, "Are you quite sure? Then you MUST speak to Michael…."

"But that is exactly what I am trying to do" Pamela's voice was strained with emotion "But I can't get hold of him – I've tried ringing the bed-sit – I don't have any other contact number for him".

"Ah, I believe he has gone to Mom and Pop for a few days..."

"WHAT?" Pamela sank down onto the chair nearest the phone. Michael was no keener on visiting his parents than she was hers. She felt even more confused. Thanking Michael she slowly put the phone down. What was going on? Mom and Pop as Michael and George referred to them lived in Eastbourne and if Marian was right and they had called in for Carla to pack bags at around four thirty they would still be en route, so no use calling him there just yet.

Feeling that she owed Marian some sort of update, Pamela slipped out of the back door and round to Marian's. Marian must have been looking out for her as she opened the door as Pamela approached it. "Come on in ducks, sit yerself down, I'll put the kettle back on." Pamela told Marian what she had been able to find out so far, but Marian found it as mysterious as she did, especially when Pamela said that 'Mom' and 'Pop' lived far too far away for Carla to be able to attend school, and that Michael was just as adamant as she herself was about their daughter not missing school unnecessarily.

Marian put a cup of tea and a packet of biscuits on the table in front of Pamela. She assumed that Pamela hadn't eaten anything since lunchtime, and that she wouldn't be interested in preparing a meal for herself. Pamela drank some of her tea and absent-mindedly ate a couple of biscuits. Marian asked her what she planned to do next. Pamela had never felt so unsure – even when she discovered that Michael was having the affair she always seemed to have positive things to do – thinking about that now she realised that all those positive actions revolved round Carla: Keeping everything as 'normal' as possible for Carla became paramount, so even if she felt like a sloth after many sleepless nights she would ensure that Carla had clean ironed clothes to wear to school and that her routine remained as much as possible as it had before the revelation of Michael's perfidy.

Marian seemed to realise that without Carla to consider, Pamela was rather like a boat without a rudder. She had become very fond of Pamela in the short time she had known her – they made quite an unlikely pair of friends, but since the strange start they had quickly become comfortable with each other. Marian understood that Pamela had never had a close friendship with a neighbour before, and smiled at the thought that Pamela seemed to consider that Marian had.

In fact, Marian had had many difficult times in her life, and had purposely never got close to any of the neighbours since she'd moved into her present home. She smiled to herself as she thought about their apparent differences; Pamela spoke with what Marian's family would call 'a bleedin' plum in her mouth', but Marian had learned some hard lessons over the last few years, and one of those lessons was that she couldn't always rely on old ties and family in deeply stressful situations.

Marian decided to take charge temporarily. "Come on ducks, let's go back to yours' now, then we can see about phoning to see if we can find out what's going on". As they walked back through Pamela's garden, Marian chatted the whole time about inconsequential things; she admired the garden, remarking on how smart it looked again, saying it had once been the smartest garden in the street and looked to become that way again. She guided Pamela through to her sitting room.

"Shall I cook the stuff here for you, or make you a sandwich?" Marian asked as she viewed the things on Pamela's worktop.

Pamela shook her head; she was behaving like someone sleepwalking.

"What about phoning your in-laws?" Marian asked.

Pamela explained that she had never really got on with them particularly well; better to wait until Michael arrived there – then surely he would contact her to tell her what this was all about?

Marian had liked the look of Michael the couple of times she had seen him, and it was obvious that although Pamela was extremely puzzled and upset, she didn't think Carla was in any sort of danger.

Marian spotted a highlighted date on the calendar which Pamela had left on her dining table. "Someone's birthday, duck?" She asked, wanting to keep Pamela talking.

"Oh, yes", replied Pamela dreamily "It's my Dad's birthday a week Wednesday, but we'll have to go over on the Thursday as there is a 'do' on at the golf club that he will be expected to attend."

That gave Marian an idea "What about ringing your parents?" she asked "Might they have any idea what Michael is up to?" Pamela shuddered slightly

"Are you cold, ducks?" Asked Marian and when Pamela didn't answer Marian decided to go take Pamela upstairs and find her something warmer to wear. Pamela stirred herself at this and realised she was still in her work skirt and top. It always seemed hot to her in the office, so she dressed lightly for work, but as autumn was approaching the evenings were becoming cool.

"It's OK", she told Marian "I'll nip upstairs and get changed". While she did this, Marian decided to put the kettle on and make another cup of tea for them both.

Pamela dropped her top into the wash-basket, put her skirt on the bed and found a pair of leggings and a sweatshirt. She went to the wardrobe to get a clothes hanger for her skirt. These actions had long been engrained into her – she'd never been one to drop clothes on the floor, her mother had taught her to be tidy and she had never been a rebellious teenager.

Hanging her skirt up she automatically moved the top she planned to wear the next day to work to the front of the wardrobe. Doing this jerked Pamela out of her dream-like state and made her realise that whatever was happening with Michael and Carla she would, in fact, have to keep going to work if she was to keep the payments up on the house and keep Carla's home ready for her to return to. Pamela wasn't one to feign illness to avoid going to work; she would just have to get through the next couple of days until Carla returned home.

Marian noticed with approval that Pamela didn't look quite so pale and was a little less dream-like as she descended the stairs and gratefully accepted the cup of tea "This'll warm yer up ducks" Marian said to her.

When the phone rang it startled them both. They looked at each other; Pamela put down her tea and picked up the receiver. "Hello?"

Relief swept over her as she heard Michael's voice, but that relief rapidly turned to dismay as she tried to take in what he was saying. "…..and to spare her too much explanation at present I just told Carla when I picked her up from school that her Granddad had been taken very ill and that you will be very busy helping out and that Carla was to come and stay with Mom and Pop and myself while it is touch and go…."

Marian was afraid that Pamela was going to pass out as she put the receiver down and went to move towards her but she stepped out of the way as she rushed to the bathroom and she heard the sound of Pamela upstairs being sick. She went to the kitchen to get her a glass of water and went upstairs to the little bathroom. Gently she helped Pamela clean up, persuaded her to drink the water and took her to her bedroom and sat her down on the bed.

"Well?" she asked, kindly. Pamela was very white and shaking and seemed on the point of passing out, so Marion encouraged her to put her head down and take her time. After a few minutes Marion strained to hear what Pamela was saying, but it didn't make much sense to her except that it seemed to be connected to the apparent misunderstanding that her mother had phoned about the other week, and Marian had waited in Pamela's house for Carla to return.

Haltingly Pamela managed to explain that it was all to do with an apparent sexual offence of which her father was accused, and that there was something written about it in the local Monday evening paper. Marion decided that the best thing to do was to nip to the shop and get a copy of the paper, so she set about settling Pamela for a few minutes while she went down to the paper shop on the corner of the next road.

Marion had a quick look at the newspaper shelves and when she couldn't see what she was looking for she asked at the cash desk she was told: "No, love, they've all sold out this week already – but they may still have some over the garage". Marion hadn't thought about the garage, she quickly checked her watch and as she'd only been away about fifteen minutes she decided to try it.

When Marion got back Pamela opened the door. She had a little more colour back in her cheeks. "Oh, thanks, you've got one, but you are all out of breath – I remember your saying you'd not been well when I first moved in, you really are very kind". Marion flopped down into an armchair and handed her the paper. Pamela sat at the table and slowly turned the pages until she found what she was looking for. There it was – in the court and police section on page six: The small headline read: Ex Major referred to Crown Court, and all the small article said was: After attending the Magistrates Court today charged with a sexual offence committed locally, Major Donald Fielding was served with an injunction preventing him from going within three miles of the location of the alleged offence. The case has been referred to Crown Court. Pamela felt a mixture of horror, confusion and somehow, shame. "What on earth do you think he can have been accused of?" She asked Marion "Heaven forbid, do you think he's been 'flashing' or something?" Pamela felt sick again at the very thought of her father doing anything remotely like that.

Pamela wasn't to know, but Marion had quite a lot of experience of the justice system and gently explained that he wouldn't have had his case referred to the Crown Court for something like that. "I'm afraid that he will have been accused of something far more serious than that, love" She told her gently.

Marion could see that Pamela was looking very pale, indeed, again and tried to encourage her to put her head down until the colour returned. "No", said Pamela fiercely, suddenly standing up "I HAVE to find out what this is all about, however disgusting it may be. It sounds like Michael knows more than what is written here in the paper. I will go over to my parents' house and try to find out what is going on. Something is obviously amiss, as I had those strange calls from my mother the day we met" Pamela's colour returned, though her cheeks now had unhealthy red patches, but Marion was no longer concerned that Pamela was going to pass out.

"Thank you so much for everything you have done for me. I will drive to their house now and won't be fobbed off by any silliness; I'll not leave until I have an answer" Pamela kissed Marion on the cheek as she saw her out and promised to let her know more as soon as she was able to.

Chapter 6

Opening the car door Michael asked "Would you like anything?" as he took his wallet out to pay for his petrol.

"No thanks" Carla muttered. She was puzzled, as they were on their way to Eastbourne, to go to stay with Grandmom and Grandpop, but she still didn't really understand why, as what Michael had explained to her didn't really seem to make sense, as though he were leaving something important out.

Getting back into the car Michael handed her a packet of Maltesers. Muttering a thanks Carla just put them down. "Dad, I still don't understand why I can't stay at Rachel's; I know they would put me up. There is so much going on at school I really don't want to miss....."

"Just accept it, will you?" Michael told her "Mrs Francham was quite willing to let you have the time off when I explained that your granddad was in hospital and your mum had to be with him. You won't be in any trouble."

"Uhh" Carla let out an exasperated sigh, a sigh that made her sound much older than her twelve years. "I just don't want to miss anything, you just don't understand!"

"I'm sorry you are so upset. You know Grandmom and Grandpop will be very pleased to see you, and I know you like staying there."

"Yeah, I spose" she agreed grudgingly "OK if we listen to Radio 1?" she asked

Michael was relieved as he felt it signalled an end to the awkward questions Carla was asking. The truth was that he hadn't sorted things out in his own mind – he had taken Carla out of school and away from Pamela's as a knee jerk reaction to George's analysis of the newspaper article that Michael had read to him over the phone. Having idly picked up a local paper that someone had left in the services where he'd stopped for a coffee between calls Michael had seen the article about Major Donald.

Puzzled by the vague references he'd called George at work as he knew that George had a close friend who was a magistrate and would be able to find out why the Major's case was being referred to Crown Court. When George called back he told Michael that the most likely explanation was that Major Donald must have been accused of a sexual offence with a minor. Michael was so shocked as he felt that Carla was at an impressionable age, and that he must protect her. Firstly from any knowledge of what he may have done, but then his mind started to work overtime and he began to imagine scenarios with Carla and he made his mind up to take action.

All he could think of was to put as much distance between Carla and Major Donald as possible. The bed-sit he was using as a temporary measure while sorting out how much of the capital he needed from the sale of their family home to use for his new company was not suitable for Carla to stay in, he couldn't take her to Monique's as there was not room for the three of them and he couldn't expect Carla to stay with Monique on her own, although he thought with a wry smile that they did seem to get on, they certainly had at the weekend they spent at George and Carol's.

Thinking of Monique helped clear his mind a little of the confusing emotions he'd been suffering since reading the shocking article, he loved her so much it almost hurt – he only felt whole when in her company, it was an emotion he'd never felt before. Michael had never been a rebellious teenager; he'd always been very diligent with his studies and when, in his late teens, he had met Pamela their relationship had started as a steady friendship and then gradually grown into something deeper until settling down seemed the right thing to do, and with both of them – and both their families - being rather conventional it was natural for them that marriage and a mortgage came first followed fairly soon after by Carla. He had felt some guilt during the time he was falling in love with Monique, but it happened so quickly in a tumble of emotions that each moment of time snatched with her felt like heaven rather than a betrayal of Pamela. He felt only admiration for Pamela, and the way she had handled things, but when he tried to express this he felt he unfairly had his head bitten off and Pamela accused him of being patronising. He was aware that he was very lucky indeed, as Pamela could have insisted on staying in the family home and prevented his dream of running his own small company, but, instead, she had been willing to find a job and buy a small house for herself and Carla. Thinking of this again he decided to look out for a callbox, as the payphone at the garage had been out of order, and he hadn't yet told Pamela that he was taking Carla to Mom and Pop's in Eastbourne while things were sorted out re Major Donald. He had wanted to leave Pamela a note, but then couldn't think what on earth to write, and anyway it would have been difficult to do so having told Carla it was because her granddad had been taken ill.

Telling Carla that he had to phone one of the gym's he had been planning to visit the following day, Michael pulled over in a lay-by where he had spotted a phone booth. Much to Michael's relief Carla had just nodded and said she'd stay in the car because when he got through to Pamela he soon realised to his amazement that she had no knowledge at all about Major Donald's offence, and she became extremely agitated and upset. He tried his best to calm her and promised that he'd call again once he had settled Carla with Mom and Pop in Eastbourne.

Chapter 7

Pamela drove to her parents' house almost on autopilot. As she pulled into the sweeping gravel drive she could barely remember how she had got there. Pulling on the handbrake she walked with determination up to the door and let herself in.

"Mummy, Daddy, where are you?" she called out.

"Oh, hello, Pamela darling, what a lovely surprise" said her mother as she strolled out of the living room with a glass in her hand. Noticing the rather glazed look in her mother's eyes Pamela decided not to launch straight into asking about what was going on.

"Hello, Mummy, where's Daddy?" she asked

"He's pottering in the garden, I think, darling. He's been on the phone a lot, seems to have something on his mind...." Pamela heard but didn't want to discuss it with her mother so she strode out into the back garden to find him.

Pamela found her father sitting on an old chair at the back of the older of the two greenhouses. "I suppose you've seen the newspaper?" was how he greeted her, rather uncertainly.

"Yes I have. So it's true, then? What Mummy phoned about the other week – you've done something shocking and been arrested for it?" As her mother had looked unconcerned but just pleased to see her she was still hoping that maybe it wasn't true or that her father was falsely accused of whatever it was.

"Well, yes love, something has happened, but it is all a silly misunderstanding and it should all blow over soon…"

Pamela cut him off "Blow over, blow OVER – Michael has taken Carla away from me because he believes you to have been involved in something sexual with someone young"

Pamela couldn't believe she was speaking like this to her father – even saying the word sexual made her shudder as she and her father had never ever discussed anything remotely concerning bodily functions. On the odd occasions that he had looked after Pamela when she was young he had been embarrassed when expected to help her with getting ready for bed or going to the loo. As her parents had had separate rooms ever since moving back to England when she was still young she was shocked when she learned from Sylvie that some people's parents still 'did it', especially once they had worked out from science lessons and from books what 'doing it' involved.

"Oh, Pamela" he started, dropping his head into his hands. She had to strain to hear what he was saying, although she was terribly afraid of learning embarrassing details. "Something did happen, but it's not what everyone thinks….." "What other 'everyone' knows about this then – I seem to be the only one who had to go and buy a paper…" "Oh, sorry, sweetie…" Pamela recoiled as he reached out to touch her: "Don't call me sweetie, and don't touch me" she shouted. "I don't want to know about whatever disgusting thing it is you've done, but why is Mummy walking about sipping her drink as though nothing has happened?"

Sighing heavily he began to explain "Your mother has a hospital appointment tomorrow. It is for tests for something potentially serious that she doesn't want to talk about. I managed to fob her off when the police arrived and I chose to go to the station with them rather than answer awkward questions in front of her. I have also made sure that she hasn't seen a copy of the paper."

Pamela thought she was impervious to any more shocks – this was the first she'd heard of any problem regarding her mother's health but the next thing her father said shocked her even more. "And, of course, what with Peggy no longer coming; it's hard for Mummy to cope with all the household jobs that she used to do…"

"What? Why on earth is Peggy no longer coming – she's been coming for donkey's years – surely she's not reached retirement age yet? I thought she'd carry on long past retirement age anyway, she's always worked here – how will she manage?"

"Just now it's more worrying how Mummy will manage, I've started to try to do some things; I tried some ironing. I told her I'd give up the Golf Club so that I could help more"

"Give up the Golf Club? Mummy won't like that, you know."

"I'm afraid I have no choice, they have read the same article and read into it what you have." Pamela struggled to pull her thoughts together. She wasn't sure that she herself had 'read anything' into the newspaper report – she had, after all, been directed to read it by Michael, who had the benefit of his brother, George's, analysis.

She remembered how this greenhouse used to smell of tomato vines when she was a young girl and had first come to England. Her father wasn't interested in growing vegetables, unlike her grandfather who had grown all his own fruit and veg. Thinking of him now and remembering her first few months in England when they had come to stay here with her grandparents was calming: She decided that she didn't want to know what her father stood accused of, she felt as though once she knew any details she would never be able to 'unlearn' them and if, as her father was trying to tell her, it was all some misunderstanding (she was worried but quite impressed that he wasn't telling her that nothing had happened at all) then the less she knew the better.

The Major could feel that she was struggling to come to some decision, so he took his head out of his hands and tried to straighten his shoulders and back and gave her time to speak.

"OK, Daddy, my main concern is to get Carla back home, I think I understand Michael's wish to get her as far away as possible, but she should be at home with me and able to attend school. I want you to speak to Michael if he will speak to you and reassure him that Carla is in no danger from you or whatever it is you have done. If you choose to tell him that is up to you but I don't want to know…"

"Sweetie…"

"Don't interrupt me and don't call me Sweetie. I am struggling here and want to say my piece before I change my mind and go running in to Mummy and tell her I never want to see you again. I am sorry Mummy has to have hospital tests tomorrow and I know how much she hates anything like that. We will just tell her I came to see what you would like for your birthday and we will keep things as normal as possible for Mummy. But this doesn't mean I shall always feel this way, it depends what happens, but as I said, my main concern is to get Carla home – do you know Michael has told her that you have been taken very ill and she must stay with him while I sit with Mummy at your hospital bedside. Whatever it is you've done has turned us all into liars and it is going to be very difficult to sort out when I get Carla home."

Pamela had been sitting on an upturned box whilst talking to her father. She got up and slowly walked towards the house. She saw that her mother was waving from the sitting room window; she had obviously been looking out for them to return from the garden. Pamela was worried that her mother would ask whether she had found out what was troubling her father, but she needn't have worried, she found her mother rather vague and glassy eyed as though she'd had rather too much gin – she supposed that her father had poured her a strong one to take her mind off the hospital visit. She forgot to ask why Peggy was no longer coming, as her mother wanted to know how Carla was and why she hadn't popped over with her to see what her granddad wanted for his birthday. Pamela realised at once that it was going to be very hard to keep her mother in the dark until she had the all clear regarding her health, as she couldn't tell her that Michael had taken Carla away without telling her why.

Refusing a gin and tonic because she was driving, Pamela allowed her mother to busy herself with the kettle and make her a cup of tea – despite the fact it was the last thing she really wanted as she'd had enough tea for one evening. However, it made it easier to chat about seemingly inconsequential things while Daphne followed the ritual she insisted upon with tea leaves, a tea pot and a tea strainer. All the time she did this Daphne made her usual speech about 'those people' who used mugs and tea bags – Pamela said nothing as it was easier in the circumstances just to let her talk. Usually her mother's dreadful snobbery irritated her and she would argue that you couldn't judge a person by mugs and tea bags but she often wondered why she bothered as it was an argument she would never win.

"Is Daddy coming in for a cup?" her mother asked.

"I don't know. He seems to be busy with his chrysanthemums. I can't stay very long" Pamela told her "Let's go and sit down while I drink my tea and then I must go home" The tea making ritual meant that Pamela had to go and sit down properly to drink it. She couldn't just drink up, put the cup down on the kitchen work top and go after her mother had gone to the trouble. She sometimes wondered whether people with time on their hands invented these rituals not only to give themselves something to do, but also as a kind of guilt trap to keep visitors for longer.

Eventually Pamela drove home. She glanced at her watch. Not bad, she thought, she would be home by nine thirty. She hoped that Michael hadn't already tried to call her.

Chapter 8

Marion had been listening out for Pamela and as she heard her walk up the front path she slipped round the back and tapped on the door. "I'm not gonna intrude ducks, I just want to know yer OK" she said as Pamela let her in.

"Well, it still doesn't make any sense, but that's because I made it clear to Daddy that I didn't want to know any details. He has managed to keep it from Mummy so far, mainly because she has to go into hospital tomorrow for tests and doesn't want her worrying." Just then the phone rang and when Marion heard that it was Michael and could see that Pamela wasn't on the point of collapse she let herself out of the back door and went home.

Pamela was at first relieved and then outraged. She had never gone in much for thinking of herself as the 'wronged party' as her solicitor had described her when she had first gone for advice when Michael had said he wanted a divorce. Now, however, to find that Michael was trying to explain that he was in an emotional turmoil, after it was he who had taken Carla out of school without first consulting her, she was furious. Here he was complaining that Carla was upset, his parents didn't understand him and Monique was furious with him! Pamela felt like saying something really sarcastic, but realised that Michael sounded very upset and stressed, indeed, and all she really wanted was to get Carla back home as soon as possible.

She did understand why Michael had not told Carla about the accusation against her father, and she realised that if she couldn't bear to hear any details about it she, even more strongly, didn't want Carla to know anything about it at all. Pamela suggested to Michael that he tell Carla that they had been mistaken about the seriousness of her granddad's illness, that he had had a mild heart attack, and that he would be allowed out of hospital the following day but would need to be kept calm and quiet at home for a while.

"But what will I tell Monique?" He asked.

Now Pamela did get angry "You tell her what the hell you like. That is most definitely NOT my problem!"

Pamela, surprised by how calm she herself felt after her outburst, and shocked by the way Michael sounded, had forgotten to tell him that her father was willing to speak to him about what had taken place that had lead to his being accused of a crime. Michael's next retort was to say that she needn't think that just because she'd visited her parents and found them behaving in a manner she believed to be normal that he would be bringing Carla home.

"After all," he said "there was always something odd about the way your father's army career just ended when you all returned to the UK from Cyprus, so as far as I am concerned anything is possible, and the moral safety of my daughter is more important to me than anything else!"

This bald statement really shocked Pamela. She realised that there was no point telling Michael that her father would speak to him, as he had never had a great deal of respect for him, in fact he had never really liked her parents at all. She was aware that her mother was a terrible snob; that she was somehow disappointed with her father, that it was only her parents' property – and having sold some of the land off - that gave them the lifestyle that her mother enjoyed. She herself had, in fact, had not had a close loving relationship with them over the years, only making 'duty visits' when she felt it was necessary. This, in itself, confused her with regard to Michael's decision to take Carla away; it was not as though she was forever spending time with her parents. Carla had never been there to stay on her own. Pamela didn't want to analyse the reasons for that now, but deep down she was aware that in fact she'd felt more comfortable on the occasions that Michaels' parents had had Carla stay with them, than she would have felt leaving her with her own parents. The problem now was that Mom and Pop had retired to Eastbourne, so any time Carla spent there would mean that she couldn't attend school, and up until today both Michael and Pamela had always been in agreement that school attendance was important at all times. They had never taken her out of school in order to take advantage of lower cost foreign holidays.

*

It was Carla that was to Michael at the same time both a brake and a catalyst with regard to his decision to ask Pamela for a divorce so that he would be free to be with Monique. He had never loved Pamela in the all consuming passionate way that he loved Monique. However, once Carla had been born he learnt to feel a different sort of love, a protective wondrous sort of love. As time went on and she grew he did what he had habitually done with other areas of his life and filed that love into a compartment deep in his brain. Once he met and fell in love with Monique, while he was deciding what to do he re-examined his feelings for Carla, and was torn between keeping the 'status quo' for Carla by staying with Pamela in a complacent marriage and tearing that apart in order to be with Monique. He found he had to face a new side of himself he had never known before and realised that by leaving Pamela he could only hope that in time Carla learn that there was more to life and love than a compromise of complacency.

When he first fell for Monique he felt as though he was on a roller coaster, or on the big water slide he used to be taken to as a child that gave a feeling of enormous excitement and fear at the same time as it hurtled his young body towards the water. This love for Monique had grown into something more adult, but was still far more passionate and all consuming than the affection he had felt for Pamela. Carla had glimpsed this other side of Michael's life at the weekend when the three of them had gone to George and Carol's for George's birthday celebrations. Monique was not only accepted immediately by

George, Carol and the twins, but she seemed to bring their company alive in a way that her mother never had.

"How far away is the gym?" Carla asked as she helped wipe up and put the dishes away. Not wanting to use his parents' phone for his call to Pamela, Michael had used the excuse that he wanted to visit the local gym to determine whether he could do business with them. Carla liked her Grandmom and Grandpop, but she had overheard them quietly saying to one another that it seemed rather callous of Michael to be thinking of his new business at a time like this with her other granddad being so ill and she had also thought it was an odd thing for her father to want to do as they were likely to be in Eastbourne for a few days, so surely Michael could attend to his business in the days to follow.

"Now what would I want with a gym" asked Grandmom with a chuckle. Carla laughed too, and felt herself relax for the first time since her dad had unexpectedly picked her up from school. Michaels' parents were the epitome of Jack Spratt and his wife from the old nursery rhyme – his mum, Eileen liked to be described as 'comfortably cuddly' a description that Michael's very thin dad, Edward, who liked to be known as Ted when he wasn't being called 'Pop' or 'Grandpop' was very happy to use. That's just what they were; a happy uncomplicated couple and Carla felt comfortable with them. "Now why don't you go and make yourself at home" Eileen said to Carla "Just unpack the bits you need as we don't know how long you'll be here, of course, we'd love you to stay for ages but we know you don't want to miss too much school. I'm sure your dad won't be much longer, and I expect your mum will phone as soon as she can."

As Carla went upstairs Eileen mused about the sad circumstance that had brought them the pleasure of Carla's company so unexpectedly. She had never really got to know Major Donald, as they found that they had nothing in common with Pamela's parents, so after the initial meeting before the wedding and after the wedding itself neither couple had made any effort to see one another. However, she was a kindly soul and didn't like to think of anyone being ill. She wondered again why it was that Michael had decided it necessary to visit the local gym on business, but then she had never really understood her serious child. She herself was a cheerful optimistic woman, easily pleased and happy with her lot, as was her husband. They loved Michael dearly, but both their sons had come along after many years of happy marriage; they had begun to think they would remain childless and as they were so content in each other's company that didn't bother them at all. However, although having children in later life was like the 'icing on the cake'; they both found that Michael, the younger of the two was rather more seriously minded than his brother George, or either of them had ever been, and he didn't seem to have much of a sense of fun as they did. They were pleased that he had always been very diligent with his studies, but would have enjoyed him better if he had had a sense of humour and would even have been pleased if he had been a little wild in his teens.

Eileen thought now that his marriage to Pamela had been typical of all his earlier years: Plodding and thorough. If she and Ted had been closer to him they would have perhaps been able to better understand the changes that had taken place when Michael fell in love with Monique, as it was they were just confused by his leaving Pamela and very worried about the effect that it could have on Carla. Most of all they were very worried that they may see even less of Carla than they did now. They had never been close to either Michael or Pamela, but in Carla they found a kindred spirit with a wicked sense of humour – they used to joke between themselves that she must have been a 'changeling' as she was so unlike either of her parents. Not many people saw this side of Carla, though, as she had learnt to be rather chameleon-like, and had been conditioned to act quite seriously around her parents and school teachers. A couple of her friends knew the 'real Carla', as did her cousins, Paul and Fee.

Carla unpacked a few things she thought she would need over the next couple of days. She knew that her dad had spoken to her headmistress about her absence and although she had worried about it initially, as she settled in, like Eileen, her Grandmom she began to see it as an unexpected bonus. Briefly she wondered how her other grandmother was coping with her granddad so ill, but she couldn't imagine as she had never felt particularly comfortable with her; she was quite fond of her granddad but had never really had the opportunity to spend any time with him and get to know him, as she always felt she had to be on her best behaviour whenever she was visiting them, as her grandmother had a range of monologues she would lecture Carla with about the correct way to do things, and Carla had always found this tedious and rather intimidating. When she thought about it, she couldn't remember a time at all when she had ever had a normal two way conversation with her maternal grandmother. Thinking about this, and how warm and cuddly her Grandmom was she smiled as she slipped back through to the living room to see whether her dad was back. He was, and he looked, Carla though, quite stressed.

"Isn't it time you were in bed?" asked Michael.

Carla looked shocked so Mom intervened quickly with "She was just waiting for you to come back to see whether you'd managed to get any new business from the gym, love. Shall I make us all a nice cup of tea then Carla can go to bed after you've told her how you got on?" Michael resented being told what to do by his mother but realised he and Carla were relying on their hospitality so he forced himself to smile and said

"Yes; that would be nice."

In fact, Michael was still smarting from the roasting that Monique had given him when he called her to try and explain why he had really brought Carla to Eastbourne. She was furious with him when he explained that he hadn't told her the truth to start with and then even more furious with him when he told her the real reason. He now felt that no-one understood him; when Pamela had given him a way out with regard to explaining things to Carla and his parents he hadn't taken it – he had just been annoyed with what seemed to him her laissez-faire attitude towards her father's alleged crime; when he tried to explain his reason for this to Monique he made a mess of explaining himself and she rang off having told him to 'sort his head out' and now as he arrived back at his parents' home he could see what appeared to him to be conspiring looks passing between his mother and his daughter.

Chapter 9

"What'll we do first today, then, old girl?" Donald asked Daphne as they buttered their toast.

"I do wish you wouldn't call me that" she said, but she smiled. Daphne was relieved that the previous day's hospital visit was behind her, but she would have to return in a couple of weeks to see the consultant to get the results. She was also relieved that Donald was helping her around the house with the chores now that Peggy had decided that she was no longer able to continue working for them. Daphne still felt rather puzzled about this; she had thought that Peggy would continue working for them as long as her health permitted her to, but as Donald had apparently accepted the fact of her leaving so easily and had also slipped into the role of helpmate she supposed she should also just accept it. Donald, of course, was grateful that Daphne hadn't asked too many questions about Peggy's decision.

Daphne realised that they couldn't afford to employ someone else, as they had never really increased Peggy's wage in line with the cost of living and anyway neither Daphne nor Donald relished the idea of letting someone they didn't know into their home. What Daphne was worried about, however, was what she was going to tell the Fotheringtons should they find out that they were doing their own household chores. Donald had said that if they couldn't manage to do the ironing themselves that they could take it to the Sainsbury ironing service, but Daphne had recoiled in horror and said that they mustn't be seen coming and going in Sainsbury's with their laundry! Donald had told her to 'steady the buffs' and said that he had always been able to iron his army uniform, so he was quite sure he could get back into the swing of things.

"How about if I tackle the ironing while you load the washing machine?"Donald suggested. As they only ever dried their washing on the washing line – or to be more precise, Peggy had only done washing on fine days and had always been the one to use the old washing line in the garden Donald suggested they look into the possibility of buying a tumble drier. Daphne wasn't keen on new electrical things, but felt she should take the suggestion in good part and agreed to look into it. She was pleased with what she felt was a positive attitude from Donald. He had always been kind and helpful; since she had begun to find it harder and harder to get up in the mornings he always brought her a cup of tea and waited patiently for her to get up and 'perform her ablutions' as he put it before they breakfasted together. This was unless, of course, he had an early meeting with a client – the excuse he had used on both mornings of the week he'd had to appear in the magistrate's court: the Monday because he had to appear in court, and the Tuesday for his meeting with Andrew Farrar, the duty solicitor who had been called to officiate in his case.

Donald had been disappointed with his meeting with Andrew Farrar. Having hoped that the solicitor would sympathise with him, just as the arresting Police officers had seemed to, and assure him that the referral of his case to Crown Court was all a big mistake or misunderstanding he had taken great pains to explain that such matters were taken very seriously indeed, especially as at no time had Donald denied that 'an incident' had taken place with the young lady concerned. In fact, the solicitor had acted very formally, indeed, with Donald; calling him 'Major Fielding' throughout the interview, when Donald would very much have liked to be on first name 'man to man' terms as he felt this would have enabled him to be a little more forthcoming with his explanation of 'the incident'. Donald was even more disappointed when Andrew Farrar explained that, as duty solicitor, he had been obliged to attend the police station when Donald was taken there for questioning, but had not been obliged to attend the magistrates court; he had just attended to see what the outcome would be and he was not obliged to defend him when he went to Crown Court. He explained to Donald that he had a couple of options. He could either plead not guilty and choose a solicitor to represent him, or he could plead guilty to the charge and hope for a lenient sentence. "Sentence…?" began Donald, his voice quavering "But I haven't committed a crime, why should I plead guilty?" The duty solicitor began to wonder whether the Major had been listening at all, either the first time he was accused of the crime at the Police station, or for the previous hour when he had explained yet again to the Major why what he had done was a crime. He tried again:

"Major Fielding, while you have admitted that an act of a sexual nature took place with this young woman…"

"But I've told you, she started it and she is at least twenty years old…"

"Please don't interrupt me Major. I have explained, as did the Police Inspector, that under the Sexual Offences Act, in order to protect the more vulnerable members of our society, it is an offence to take advantage of a person with learning difficulties. You know this family, so you knew that the young lady had been diagnosed as such – yes, and I know, you've told me, you claim that she started it. As I say, you have two choices. You can either plead guilty, and hope for a lenient sentence; a community order or a suspended sentence: Or you could plead not guilty, and find yourself someone to defend you."

"Would such a defence prove costly?" asked Donald.

"Not if you were to be found to be entitled to legal aid, but I must warn you that the rules have been tightened up with regard to legal aid in the last few years" the duty solicitor told him.

"What do you recommend, and how long would the court case be likely to take" Donald had asked him. The duty solicitor explained that should the Major decide to plead guilty, he would have to do so at Crown Court and then he would be called there again to be sentenced once all reports were complete. He explained that there would be a pre-sentence report prepared by a Probation Officer, and the case details would be read out in court as a formality and sentencing would follow. "Do you mean it would be all over in one day?" asked Donald

"Yes, that is likely, if you follow the route of pleading guilty" "and if I plead not guilty?" he asked

"Then it could be anyone's guess. It would depend, of course, on your counsel, and on the prosecution team, but it could take anything from days to weeks"

"and would be reported in the newspapers?" asked Donald.

"Very likely", said Andrew Farrar "but the young lady's name would be withheld in order to protect her identity".

So it was that Donald decided to plead guilty, and to take his chance with a community sentence of some sort. Having asked what form this might take, the duty solicitor had explained that he would be sentenced to spend a certain amount of hours doing something useful for the community; perhaps assisting with a local furniture project, where articles of unwanted furniture were collected from donors and distributed to those in need of such items, or possibly putting in a few hours at a charity shop. The duty solicitor said that it would depend on the judge; that he may not get a community order he could get a suspended sentence, and, in fact, he couldn't guarantee that the Major would not get a prison sentence, but he thought that unlikely in the circumstances.

Andrew Farrar did, however, recommend that Donald engage the services of a barrister to speak for him at the sentencing. Donald asked how much this would cost and when Andrew Farrar told him he realised it was almost the entire sum of his little nest-egg he had managed to keep after leaving the army. Andrew reminded him that there was a chance of a custodial sentence and offered to arrange for him to see a barrister so Donald decided that it could be money well spent, rather than shut his mind to that possibility, and pin his hopes on a suspended sentence, or at worst, a community order. All he had to do then was keep the local papers away from Daphne and home life could continue on very much as before.

He, too, was enjoying the new spirit of togetherness with Daphne in Peggy's absence. He felt that there was absolutely no reason for Daphne to ever learn the real reason that Peggy had left – just because of what Donald felt to be over zealousness on the part of a social worker who had informed Peggy of what had taken place between Maisie and Donald; making it sound like Donald's fault and reporting it to the Police and explaining to Peggy that Maisie as a vulnerable person had a right to be protected. He had sometimes felt that Daphne had the wrong attitude with regard to Peggy, that an occasional friendly chat would have been better than the way she treated her, but Daphne had continued in the same way that her parents had before her, treated her as a Victorian or Edwardian family would have treated the 'help', but now he was glad it had been that way, otherwise Daphne may have wanted to seek Peggy out and make awkward enquiries.

Donald suggested that they continue doing chores for the morning, he would iron all the dry washing that there was up until lunchtime, then they could take a light lunch and go into town and look at tumble driers. He had measured a space in the corner of the utility room, and assuming a drier would be approximately the same size as the washing machine it appeared that it would fit in the space.

Chapter 10

Pamela's day wasn't going well. She hadn't eaten or slept properly for two days and was not coping well with Sandra's black mood. Instead of meekly following Sandra's instructions she had disagreed with her because she was sure that Sandra was just using her authority for the sake of it and what she insisted Pamela do was unnecessary and a waste of time. Now there was an atmosphere in the office and instead of Pamela backing down for the sake of the others she confronted Sandra once again. "No, I won't photocopy all the backup papers for the mobile phone bills that I am sending out to the reps, I know there is a tax implication but the mobile company have sent a back up disc, and should we find we do at some point require paper copies at all we can obtain them from the disc!"

Sometimes Pamela felt it was Sandra, not she who had been out of the workplace for many years. It seemed that Pamela had kept abreast of technology better than Sandra had – she was furious at Sandra's insistence with regard to the unnecessary photocopying, and Sandra was furious with Pamela for defying her. Maureen slipped down further in her chair and looked studiously at her paperwork, but Rob perked up at this unusual confrontation and watched with interest what would happen next. He had never heard Pamela raise her voice before,

Sandra was always doing it, but Rob couldn't believe that Pamela was standing up to her. He was pleased, as he believed Sandra to be a bully where Pamela was concerned, but Maureen and the others, although they felt sorry for the way Sandra treated Pamela they had worked for Sandra for a lot longer and they knew that once Pamela had stood up to Sandra it was possible that Sandra would look elsewhere for someone to pick on, as she had in the past. Rob was not worried about this, as he had been brought in for his IT knowledge, and despite the fact that he often did tasks to help Sandra, he didn't report to her, but directly to John Meredith who didn't seem to notice that Sandra's managerial skills were often wanting.

Rob had been brought in earlier in the year on a temporary basis to guide the company through an upgrade of the accounting software package, and when Sandra had had a computer related problem when she had come to compile the P11D's Rob had been asked to help. He had found her somewhat unpredictable then – sometimes defensive and sometimes fawning, but never really interested in how she could develop the system and move forward with the available technology. When he had pointed out to her that there was no need to manually enter each journal line to get the monthly payroll records (which were kept on a separate system) into the main accounting database; that he could prepare an interface which would enable the necessary records to be fed in automatically and thus save half a day's work per month she had told him to mind his own business and that she would manage HER staff's work as she saw fit.

Before he had had this run in with Sandra, John Meredith had decided to make the position Rob had been filling permanent; Rob had applied for and been offered the post. He mused now, that if he had been aware of how much of an uphill struggle it would be dragging Sandra and her team into the present he may have reconsidered taking the position. That last run in with Sandra had stopped that particular area where he had felt he could help, but he now watched the interaction between an emboldened Pamela and an enraged Sandra with interest, as he was also well aware that the photocopying of the backup documents was a task that had been unnecessarily performed each quarter when the bill for the reps mobiles came in.

"Don't you dare defy me when I tell you to do something" Sandra's voice was becoming strained

"I am not defying you" Pamela said in a calm but firm voice "Just opening a discussion in which we can look at the necessity of this photocopying. Please could we discuss this somewhere away from the main office, and include Rob in the discussion." At this, Rob froze, as he had been turning his head looking from one to the other rather like a spectator at a tennis match. He was loath to get involved, but he needn't have worried, as, almost on cue, John Meredith appeared and asked whether there was a problem.

"No, not at all" said Sandra. We were just having an interesting discussion with regard to a disc sent to us by the supplier with whom we have our mobile phones. In fact, we were just about to find a quiet area in which to carry on the discussion, so as not to disturb the rest of the office."

"I'll make us a drink while we discuss it" said Sandra, putting on the kettle. Pamela and Rob dared not look at one another, but were happy to allow Sandra to regain her composure. Rob popped back to his desk to get a note pad and Pamela grouped three chairs around the small table in the corner of the coffee area. This was always a problem in their open plan office, there was nowhere private to discuss things. No doubt the others in the office would be straining to hear whether the argument was continuing, but they would have to be disappointed today; having made her stand, Pamela was more than happy to allow Sandra to regain control of the situation.

Rob needn't have worried. Without realising she was doing it, Pamela guided the conversation calmly and Sandra was now willing to listen. Rob explained how he would take a backup of the disc and store it somewhere safely, as part of Sandra's previous argument had been that computers were unreliable and such data had been lost to them in the past. The three of them talked on well past lunchtime without realising it, and Pamela having had no sleep until the early hours had had enough trouble getting up and dressed when the alarm went off; she had not even thought about preparing a sandwich as she had been in the habit of doing. Rob usually walked to the pub up the road to have a bite to eat with some friends who worked nearby, but he said he'd walk to the corner shop and get himself a sandwich. Sandra went to the fridge to get her yoghurt and turned to Pamela and asked "Oh, where is your little sandwich, have you already eaten it?" Pamela ignored the sarcastic tone and said with dignity that no, she hadn't made one that morning. She had no intention of letting Sandra get under her skin again today, she was aware that the small victory would probably cost her dearly in snide comments from Sandra whenever she got the chance to speak to her alone. This did not bother her; Pamela was aware she had gained Rob's respect and probably that of the other people in the office. She had quite enough worries outside of work not to let Sandra's manipulating ways trouble her. Luckily Pamela had an apple in her bag from the previous day, so she ate that at her desk while she got on with her work, pleased that she did not have to waste time on unnecessary photocopying as she had plenty of things to do that were essential.

Later, when she was driving home she mused at the human capacity to focus on daily trivia when something momentous was happening elsewhere in their lives. As theirs was a busy environment, no one in the office chatted much about personal issues. She knew that one or two of the others in the office had been there many years, and were friends outside work, but other than knowing whether each other had children, whether grown up or still at home, she and the others did not discuss their home lives. This wasn't only due to the busy environment; Pamela had known other, friendlier places that were just as busy, but Sandra ruled the office by dominance and bullying and in the main they all preferred not to give her any personal details which she could use as ammunition when it suited her. In the present circumstances, Pamela was pleased that she didn't have to pretend that all was well at home.

Chapter 11

Monique stood back and admired her tidy studio flat. It had served her well for the last four years after she had left the accommodation which had been tied to the teaching job she left at the same time. She and Michael were going to rent a house until his business was established. Monique was awaiting the arrival of a prospective lessee; she didn't want to sell the little flat until she and Michael had decided how much they were to spend on a house once they were ready to buy, she just wanted to be able to cover her mortgage for the time being.

That morning Monique had viewed a three bedroom property on the outskirts of the town; Michael had assumed that she would not go as she had been so angry with him for not telling her at once the real reason that he had taken Carla stay with his parents. However, she loved Michael deeply, and after she put the phone down the previous evening having told him exactly what she thought of him she decided that she would, in fact, still go to view the property as it was for a definite six month let and if she thought it suitable she would explain that there was a family illness and that Michael would check it out later. It was up for rent for a reasonable price and available immediately, and Monique felt she had waited long enough to live with Michael. The weekend with George and Carol had been a great success, and she and Carla had got on well; Monique was eager for Michael to give up the bed-sit and for them to live properly as a couple and to have Carla to stay occasionally. She hoped that the person who had arranged to view her flat would not be late; she had told the agency that she had to be at work by two thirty and the chap from the agency assured her that the prospective lessee was on her lunch break so they would be on time as arranged.

Monique checked her watch and decided to make a fresh pot of coffee and eat her lunch. She wondered how Pamela was coping; she had a lot of respect for her, although she realised that they could never be friends, but she had never intended to fall in love with a married man, let alone one with a young daughter. In fact, Monique had been quite happy with her life and hadn't been looking for a partner at all. She had left her small rural village in Brittany to come to England as a student-teacher of French and had loved it so much she decided to stay, but to qualify as a PE teacher rather than teaching languages, as she had always been very interested in physical fitness rather than academic subjects. She had, however, found that teaching PE in a comprehensive school was rather restrictive what with the working conditions, union unrest and the subsequent in-fighting and back-biting between the staff which she had no time for, and she had then found that there was a niche for her in the private fitness sector.

Michael knew that Monique didn't have to be at the gym until two thirty, so he decided to try phoning her at the flat. She thought he might, which was why she had been happy to make the arrangement with the property letting agent for the lunch break. He didn't know whether she would want to talk to him but he needn't have worried; she had a fiery temperament and had had plenty of time to cool down since shouting at him on the phone the evening before. She smiled as her phone rang; sure it would be Michael. She cut across his tentative enquiries "'Allo, cheri, I was hoping you'd call now. I've seen the house and it will be good for us for six months. I have someone coming in a few minutes to see the apartment, so I hoped you'd call so I know what to tell the property agents."

Michael was stunned but very pleased "Wow, so you went to view the house on your own?"

"Yes, and I'm told it can be ready to move into at the weekend, but the agent would like an answer and a deposit from us by this evening, if we are to take it"

For the first time in his life Michael made a snap decision, and to Monique's surprise and great pleasure, he said "Yes, we'll take it"

"Without your seeing it?"

"Yes" said Michael, laughing at his own recklessness "if you like it we will have it!"

"Right, then, if this person likes my flat they can also move in at the weekend!" Monique was thrilled. It would mean a lot of work for her over the next two days to get everything out of her flat and ready to take to the rented house and in her excitement she had forgotten to ask when Michael was planning to come back from Eastbourne, but she had a couple of good friends who would help her.

Michael walked back to his car feeling happier than he had for several days. Here was the solution; the rented house had three bedrooms, Carla could move in with them to keep her away from Major Donald. He would have to call Monique back later to arrange to get enough money to her to pay the deposit to the property agents but in the meantime he could tell his parents that they were only staying until the weekend and that Carla would be able to attend school again the following week. He knew his parents loved having Carla there and, as she was very fond of them she loved being there too, but she was uncomfortable about missing school and his parents, although saying a week away wouldn't ruin her education, realised she needed to go back as soon as possible. He wasn't sure, though, whether to tell them that he was going to rent a house with Monique; they had not been understanding about his divorce and they had not yet met Monique, although he was sure that George would have told them about their successful weekend. George had always had an easier relationship with them than he had himself. Michael had still allowed them to think that Major Donald was in hospital but he would tell them that they were returning because he was responding to treatment; he couldn't imagine telling them the real reason he had brought Carla away from Pamela!

Thinking then of Pamela he decided to pull over by a call box and give her a call but then realised he didn't have the phone number of the company she worked for. It would have to wait until the evening after he'd spoken to Carla and his parents about their going back; he'd have to find another excuse to pop out later to use a call box again. He didn't like acting like this, even when he was seeing Monique whilst still with Pamela he tried not to do anything he considered dramatic or 'cloak and dagger'. He and Monique had fallen in love and he had a genuine reason to be at the gym so they were able to see one another quite freely and they didn't strive to be alone together at every opportunity in the way that some of Michael's colleagues had boasted about when they were conducting affairs. He had always considered that sort of behaviour rather sordid, so poor Pamela was very shocked indeed when he told her he had fallen in love with someone else.

Although Pamela had called it 'his sordid affair' when she was upset and angry, he had never considered it as such and had tried to apologise to Pamela but that just made her even more angry and upset. Pamela simply believed that Michael was experiencing a mid life crisis with which he had dealt very badly and that by becoming involved with Monique he was simply temporarily running away from his problems; problems that she would have helped him work through and their marriage could have become even more solid and affectionate. Pamela didn't believe in mature adults simply falling in love with someone else and changing partners in the way a lot of people seemed to do these days.

Michael pulled into his parents' road and parked his car. As he walked into the kitchen he heard laughter and the smell of fresh baking. "Look dad, I've made scones" Carla said to him. She looked at him with her fresh open face and it made his stomach constrict to think how many lies he was telling to protect her from whatever it was her other grandfather had done. He decided then to try to phone Pamela from there and have a guarded conversation with her if Carla and his parents were listening. He guessed they would, as they were all concerned about Major Donald and the illness that Michael had invented, but he couldn't face telling any more lies that day and hoped that Pamela would go along with what he was saying, and it was time Carla talked with her mum, anyway.

Chapter 12

As Pamela let herself into the house she was feeling slightly sick and thought it was probably because she hadn't eaten. She looked in the bread bin but the bread didn't look appetising. She threw it out and looked in the freezer. There was a sliced loaf in there so she took the loaf out, lifted a couple of frozen slices off with a knife, put them in the toaster and put the remainder of the loaf back in the freezer. She made herself a cup of tea and put peanut butter on her toast. As she started to eat the phone rang. She let it ring a while as she finished her mouthful and gathered her thoughts as she expected it to be Michael. "Hullo darling" it was her mother "I wondered what we are going to do for Daddy's birthday? He is out in the garden so I thought you'd be in from work and I'd catch you before you and Carla sit down for supper". Pamela wasn't ready for this conversation! She'd prepared herself to argue with Michael and insist he brought Carla home; she began to slowly realise that it wouldn't be as easy as she thought to keep Carla away from her father while she was colluding with him (this was the first time she admitted to herself that this was what she was doing) with regard to the offence of which he was accused and keeping the whole thing from her mother. She couldn't see what else she could do while her mother had health issues, but she resolved to sort things out properly once her mother had been to her second appointment with her consultant. She also realised that she wasn't supposed to know that her mother had been to the hospital at all – "oh", she sighed "What was that, dear?" asked her mother – and Pamela realised that she hadn't been listening to a word her mother was saying.

"Sorry, I've only just got in from work, I was a little distracted" she said quickly.

"I was just saying that you haven't asked us over to see your little house yet, and I was wondering whether you'd like to cook Daddy a meal for his birthday..."

"Ah" said Pamela, trying to think on her feet "We are not very straight yet; I think it would be better to take Daddy out for a meal somewhere nice, or perhaps you and I could cook him something special at home?" Daphne was amazed, Pamela had never before offered to do something like this

"Oh, that's a lovely idea, darling, we could have a few gin and tonics and really spoil him. Would you and Carla like to stay the night?

"Oh, no, Mummy, I have work the following day and Carla has school – in fact I think that Carla may be rehearsing for a play that evening and may have to stay with a friend, but you and I can do something nice for Daddy and I can drink one glass of wine and still drive home"

"That's settled, then" said Daphne, "but I do hope that Carla will be able to come". They said their goodbyes, and Pamela put the phone down slowly contemplating the deeper web of lies she was spinning.

As she took another bite of toast and a sip of tea the phone rang again. This time it was Michael.

"Hello, just ringing to see how your dad is, and Carla would like to speak to you" Pamela guessed that he was ringing from his parents' home, and that both they and Carla were listening.

She spoke quietly so that she couldn't be heard the other end: "So you didn't take my advice and tell them all that he had improved and been allowed to go home, then?" but she said it more kindly than she had first intended as, after the conversation with her mother, she realised that keeping Carla away from them wasn't going to be simple as she had first thought.

Picking up on Pamela's softer tone he hoped she was willing to go along with him so said "Oh, that's good, there is some improvement, then?"

"There is if you are bringing Carla back" she said quietly.

"Yes, we'll be back on Saturday morning then if that's OK with you" he told her. He didn't, however, tell her that he intended Carla to live with himself and Monique and, in fact, he hadn't told that to either Monique or Carla as yet. "I'll put Carla on" he said, handing the phone over.

"Hi, Mum, what an awful couple of days you must have had" she said.

Pamela thought that she had never said a truer word! "Yes, it has been difficult" she said "But I have really missed you and can't wait to see you at the weekend. Big hugs and kisses, and I'll see you soon, love you."

"Love you, too, mum" Carla said, putting down the phone.

"So, that's good, sounds like he's off the danger list." This was Michael's father. "Is dinner ready yet?"

"Trust you" said his mother, laughing "How come you always think about your belly but never put on an ounce of weight?" She went off out into the kitchen to put the finishing touches to the evening meal. Since retiring they had been used to eating their main meal at lunchtime, but as Michael said he was taking the opportunity to visit all the gyms in the area to promote his new business and some of them were a couple of hours drive away his mother had been cooking them all an evening meal. Carla was more used to this too, as she had a snack at school and an evening meal with Pamela.

As Pamela put the phone down she contemplated her cold tea and toast. Not fancying it she put it in the bin and tidied the kitchen. She was so looking forward to having Carla home she decided she would worry about the evening of her father's birthday as it came closer, at least she had appeased her mother with the promise of spending the evening there, and had averted the possibility of their first visit to her little house, as her mother called it. She had sounded rather half hearted about coming to see it, anyway, and Pamela felt it would not be too hard to put her off again when the subject arose in the future. She could, at last, make some use of her mother's snobbishness. She decided to pop next door to see Marian and let her know what was happening. As she closed her back door and walked towards Marian's, Pamela realised that it wasn't only because of her father and whatever he had done that she didn't want her parents to come to her house. She wouldn't have minded just her father coming as things had been before her finding out about his alleged offence, but she was proud of her home and what she had achieved there in a short time and had become fond of Marian. The thought of her mother's attitude towards either the home or to Marian if they should meet filled her with something akin to dread.

Pamela realised that most people liked their families' approval and encouragement in most areas of their lives, but she had spent her lifetime in the strange dynamics of her parents' relationship, and at a very young age had developed her own standards in the face of, and probably because of, her mother's snobbishness.

Marian saw her coming and opened the door. "Cuppa?" she asked, waving the kettle.

"Yes please, I made one but it went cold while I was on the phone". Pamela told her friend the gist of both phone calls as Marian made the tea and put the biscuit tin on the table.

"Good, so Carla is comin' 'ome on Saturday" Marian said "What are yer going to do about yer dad's birthday then?" she asked. Pamela told her that it had sounded as though Michael had calmed down a lot since taking off with Carla so suddenly. She wondered if she just might take Carla and say nothing to Michael. "But Carla thinks that 'er granddad's just come out of 'ospital, won't she think it odd to find 'im looking so well? Won't she ask awkward questions?"

"Oh, heck, I'm no good at this business" said Pamela with a heavy sigh "Whatever am I going to do?"

"Well, I think yer'll 'ave ter talk ter yer dad again and find out more of whas's going on an then see" said Marian "

Pamela drank some of her tea and ate a couple of biscuits. "At this rate I'll have to buy you more biscuits" she said to Marian "I seem to eat more of your biscuits than you do yourself!"

"Never you mind about that" said Marian, kindly "Tis nice ter see yer looking a bit brighter than yer did the other day. I've not bin well lately and I've 'ad a few troubles meself. Iss nice to be able to think on someat else for a change, but I don't mean it's good you got troubles, though" she said.

"No, I know what you mean" Pamela said then told her a little about her day at work and how the argument about the photocopying took Pamela's mind off things.

"Thassit, thass just what I mean" Marian told her. Pamela asked her whether she realised that since they had met they had only ever talked about Pamela

"You must tell me a bit about yourself" Pamela told her.

"It'll keep, ducks. Yer got enough to think about an' we got all the time in the world to be friends." Pamela thought about this as she made her way back through Marian's back gate and into her garden. She had never had a neighbour as a friend before, and she found that she felt comfortable with Marian.

Pamela was both relieved and worried about Carla returning on Saturday. She had never been in a position where she needed to be untruthful before and she was finding it hard. She remembered a friend she had had at college; a very good looking lad who had a string of girlfriends, each one thinking they were the 'one and only'. He always used to say to her that you had to have a very good memory to be a liar. She smiled as she remembered him, but her smile soon faded as she thought again about the reason for not telling the truth. She had, at least, prepared the ground, almost automatically with her mother by saying that Carla may not be able to come when they cooked Daddy's birthday meal, but she would also have to find an excuse to tell Carla that she couldn't come. She decided to cross that bridge when it came nearer, and proceeded to write a shopping list for Saturday. She knew it would take a couple of hours for Michael to drive back from Eastbourne, so she decided that she would get up early Saturday and be in town waiting for the shops to open.

In the meantime, she realised that Marian was right, she needed to find out some sort of time scale – how long before her father was due to appear at the Crown Court? When would her mother's follow up appointment at the hospital be? Providing her mother didn't have to have any medical treatment would her father then tell her mother about the pending court appearance? And, she wondered, as she wrote her shopping list, what on earth does one buy for one's father's birthday when he's been accused of an apparently serious sexual offence? She had always been extremely fond of her father, but it had still been difficult to know what to buy for him for birthdays or at Christmas as, like most men of his generation, he seemed to have most things he needed. Pamela always tried to get something reasonably original, and had only had to resort to 'comedy' socks on a couple of occasions, but now, as she wondered whether she'd ever have any respect for him ever again, she couldn't get motivated with regard to something nice to buy for him. What was making it more difficult was the fact that she'd used the excuse that she had popped over last time she went to ask him just that – what he would like for his birthday, when, in fact, they'd sat in his oldest greenhouse discussing his pending Crown Court appearance! Then it came to her: Chrysanthemums! She had explained away his not coming back to the house for a cup of tea by saying that he was involved with his chrysanthemums, so she decided to buy a garden centre voucher and tell her mother that he had suggested a particular new strain of chrysanthemum but that she was afraid of getting the wrong one. She knew that he would be so pleased that she was there at all and pretending that all was well that he would go along with anything she said. This made her feel rather uncomfortable again, as she felt she was almost colluding with him, but, like him, she wanted to know that her mother was well before making her aware of the shocking facts.

Chapter 13

Sandra was in a foul mood as she let herself in the door. What a cheek that blooming woman had! She was still smarting from her defeat; she would find a way of getting her own back. She felt that Rob and Pamela had become far too 'pally'; she would find a way of putting Pamela back in her place.

It was bad enough that John Meredith had ignored her pleas and made the new position of Systems Accountant report straight to him – she had warned him it was the thin end of the wedge and would affect discipline in the office. How could he expect her to be office manager successfully if he was going to start employing people who reported straight into him? His argument at the time was that it was a trainee position, that Rob was still studying accountancy, although his IT skills were very good, indeed. He tactfully pointed out to Sandra that she herself had no accountancy qualifications and that it would be difficult to expect someone part qualified to report to someone unqualified. Tactfully put or no, this had infuriated Sandra at the time and Sandra had always been wary of Rob; considering him to be John Meredith's pet, and when Rob had first started to bring packets of biscuits to the office to share she tried to stop him, telling him that the tea fund didn't work that way, that it had never been done that way.

To her further annoyance, Rob had told her that this was precisely why he had been brought in, that he had a knack for changing hearts and minds when clerks thought there was 'no other way' and his pet hate was, in fact, the phrase 'it's always been done this way'!

He couldn't have alienated her more if he'd have been trying, as he didn't even acknowledge her 'Office Manager' status but included her in the coverall term 'clerks'. He hadn't at that point realised how status conscious she was; he was attempting to be jolly and make a joke of the biscuit packet issue, but much to Sandra's ongoing fury (Rob would have called it paranoia!) the others in the office backed Rob up by taking it in turns to buy packets of biscuits, then John Meredith found the biscuits and started munching them happily and so that he wouldn't have to remember to buy packets too often he bought a large tin of 'Tea Time Assorted' and the team had been topping the tin up ever since. Sandra never ate one on principal so she would never have to buy a packet. This wasn't because she was mean with money, but was because she felt that this was a way of showing she wanted nothing to do with it.

As she was crossly thinking about Pamela now, she remembered that Pamela had pleased John Meredith by buying Custard Creams and got even more annoyed at the thought of his being pleased with her. It was like when Pamela had improved things with the Walkers account; it was only by thinking on her feet that Sandra had managed to take the credit for it. As she remembered this, she also thought about the near miss with John Meredith this afternoon. It wasn't her fault that she got so angry with Pamela; it was the way in which 'miss high and mighty', as she thought of Pamela, nastily, had refused to do the photocopying. She felt pleased with herself, though, remembering how quickly she had managed to take her hand off her hip when John Meredith appeared and smile sweetly and explain that they were simply having a discussion. She hoped that Rob was wrong, that he wouldn't be able to reproduce copy backup from the disc, so that she could prove that her fears were correct and that Rob and 'miss high and mighty' were wrong.

Sandra jumped as she heard the door bang. "Oh, bloody hell, look at the look on your mug – I can see we're in for a good evening, (not!) What's for dinner?" this was her son, Simon.

"Oh, I'm fine, I was just thinking…"

"Thinking who you could stab in the back, it looked like to me" Simon interrupted her

"Oh, no" Sandra fawned, "just thinking. I've only just got in from work and am just sorting out dinner."

The door banged again and Sandra's husband, Malcolm, came in. "What's for dinner then, I'm starving?" he asked.

"Fuck knows; she's in a mood and hasn't even started to cook yet!" this was Simon.

"Well, that's no good, is it, what have YOU got to be in a mood about?" Malcolm asked Sandra.

"I am fine, I'm not in a mood, and I've only just got in, I'll find something in the freezer for dinner – it won't take long" Sandra told them.

"Oh, great, so we work all day and come home to crap convenience food out of the freezer just because you can't be bothered to cook properly for us, whatever next?" asked Malcolm

"Sorry, I'll cook us something really nice at the weekend. Do you mind if we have pizza, salad and oven chips this evening?" she asked.

"Looks as though we have no choice, why can't you get in from your silly little job earlier, so that we can eat properly?" asked Simon.

Chapter 14

Pamela had left the alarm to go off as though she was going to work. She awoke feeling slightly disorientated before remembering, thankfully, that it was Saturday. It hadn't been as bad as she'd feared at work the day after the disagreement with Sandra, although she could tell that Sandra was wary of her, and the other team members were keeping a low profile as though they feared getting on the wrong side of Sandra. Rob, however, had been his usual noncommittal cheerful self; he had shown Sandra the saved files on his screen from which he assured her he could reproduce the backup paperwork if necessary, but she still shook her head and muttered things about it 'all being very well, but computers had proven unreliable in the past.

Pamela stretched comfortably and put away thoughts of the office; she had quite enough to think about without worrying about petty office politics. She was just thankful that her actual work wasn't too onerous and that her salary was enough to cover her mortgage.

Having decided to buy the garden centre voucher for her father for his birthday, Pamela had no real need to go into town, but as she didn't need to do any housework before Carla returned she thought a trip to town would take her mind off everything. She wasn't sure whether Michael would want to come in and talk to her about her father, nor was she sure about how to tackle the problem of her father's 'illness' as explained to Carla, so a quick trip into town would keep her occupied until the need to face them arose. She could buy the protractor Carla needed for school, pop into the small town centre supermarket for a few bits and check out a couple of the sports shops to look at prices of trainers as Carla was going to need yet another new pair before long.

Not feeling hungry and wanting to get going Pamela just had a quick drink of orange juice before going into town. It was getting chillier as autumn approached; so Pamela had looked out an old pair of jeans and a thick sweater, as she would then not need to put on a jacket. Autumn was Pamela's favourite season, and she always tried to avoid wearing a winter coat or jacket too soon as, to her, it seemed to make winter come more quickly.

To her surprise, Pamela found that the jeans were far too large – thinking about it now she realised that her new work clothes had become a little large on her – she had assumed that this was just because they were inexpensive and the fabrics had stretched, but now she thought that maybe she had lost some weight. She didn't have any scales, had never really worried about weighing herself in the past so wouldn't have known what she weighed before anyway. Instead of the jeans, she put on one of her thicker pairs of leggings and a jumper that used to be too tight to wear out anywhere, and was pleasantly surprised with the result, apart from her hair which she noticed needed some attention, when she looked in the mirror before driving into town.

Pamela wondered whether she had time to get her hair cut. Parking in the multi storey car park, she walked quickly into town, taking a path that she knew would take her past a hairdresser's shop which advertised good quality cuts without an appointment. She hadn't been to a hairdresser's for years; within her circle of friends (hah, she thought, briefly, 'some friends', as they had all seemed to know about Michael and Monique) there was a hairdresser, Sharon, who used to do their hair at home, and Pamela hadn't had her hair cut since Sharon had last cut it.

It was just nine o'clock, and Pamela was the first customer: "Would you be able to fit me in, and if so, how long would it take?" asked Pamela

"You are our first today, it depends on what you would like done, and whether you would like your hair blow dried or not" said the friendly girl at the reception desk.

"Well, I could do with a new style, but I am not too worried about a blow dry, as it's not so cold today and it will soon dry naturally" she told the girl.

"Well, you are lucky, if I left mine all I would get is a big frizz!" the girl told her "Take a seat over there by one of the sinks and I'll get someone to do you a wash and restyle, if that's OK". Pamela asked how much it would cost, and deciding she could afford it she took a seat as instructed.

Just half an hour later Pamela walked quickly to a well known stationers' to buy a protractor. After shopping in the small supermarket for a few essentials she looked at her watch and decided there was just time to check out a couple of sports shops – she wanted to have time to pop into the garden centre on the way home and she also needed to buy her father a birthday card as she had not seen any suitable cards in the stationers'. Her stomach contracted as she thought of this – would she ever feel any love or trust for him again, she wondered? She was just doing all this for her mother's sake, and she wasn't even supposed to know her mother had been to the hospital!

Not having seen any of the sort of trainers Carla liked Pamela walked quickly out of the shop and almost bumped into someone trying to come in. "Oh, I'm so sorry" they both began to say; and then "Oh, my goodness, hello" as Pamela realised it was Sylvie. "Heavens, have you been avoiding me?" asked Pamela with a chuckle. Sylvie looked first slightly guilty, then concerned and serious. "I was joking" said Pamela awkwardly "but, of course, you must know about Daddy, oh, how difficult for you!"

Sylvie's heart nearly melted as she thought how typical this was of her friend. She had been very concerned, indeed, as she learnt the details of Major Donald's alleged offence, and when she heard he was going to plead guilty and that a pre-sentence report would be required from Probation she had fully intended to contact Pamela and ask her if she was all right. However, Ralph, had just been taken ill again and her workload had increased terribly, although there was no chance of her having to do Major Donald's report as she knew the family so she would

115

have to declare that fact and would not be allowed to do it as it would be considered that she may not be able to be impartial.

"Oh, Pamela, I've been so worried about you, but I've been inundated at work as Ralph is ill again, I've been meaning to contact you – are you alright?" "You do know, though, don't you, that I can't talk to you about his case?" Sylvie lowered her voice as she said this, and they both realised they were blocking the shop doorway. "How about a coffee, I was after a new swimming cossie, but I'm not desperate to find one right now?" asked Sylvie;

"I don't think I have time…" Sylvie cut her off

"The burger bar is just round the corner. The burgers may be revolting but their tea and coffee is good and they serve quickly. Come on, there will be very few people in there as yet so we can have a quick chat, at least".

Pamela was so pleased to see Sylvie, and quickly deciding that she needn't look in any more sports shops – she could do that with Carla; it would make more sense, and she could buy the garden centre voucher on Sunday, she followed Sylvie to the burger bar.

Sitting down in a quiet corner Pamela quickly told Sylvie that, of course, she was aware that Sylvie couldn't talk about the case, but she wanted to tell her that she didn't want to know any details anyway; that she didn't think she could bear to know exactly what he had done.

"So, where's Carla…"

"So, how are your parents?" they both spoke at once "You first..." they both said. Sylvie made a 'zip' sign across her mouth and pointed to Pamela to allow her to speak. "Well, here is our first difficulty" Pamela told Sylvie, and went on to explain how Michael had reacted to what he had seen in the paper, and, holding up a hand to stop Sylvie speaking she said quickly "I know we can't discuss it, but I needed to tell you why Carla isn't here and why I am in a hurry to get back home as soon as we've finished our coffee"

Sylvie was appalled but not surprised by Michael's taking Carla to Eastbourne. She could see how he had worked out that Major Donald may have been accused of a crime involving a minor and she remembered enough conversations around Pamela and Michaels' dinner table before she had begun to turn down invitations to their dinner parties. Michael liked to draw her into conversations about her work – but she soon realised it wasn't because he was genuinely interested; but so that he could start a conversation about his own views either of offenders in general, or especially about sex offenders.

Michael had very fixed views, as do many people, and didn't understand how complicated the judicial system is, and that even if popular thinking was that the public would be safer if a particular offender were locked away for life that the law didn't actually allow for this.

Carefully skirting around anything to do with Pamela's parents, she and Sylvie caught up with each other's news, and Pamela amused Sylvie by telling her a little about her new job and the office politics which she had found herself involved in recently. Sylvie was pleased that Pamela was working now and apparently enjoying the work, although she was sorry that it had taken the break-up of her marriage to force her into the workplace. Saying that she would love to see Pamela's new home, and both promising to keep in touch more regularly they parted; Sylvie going back to her shopping and Pamela heading back to the car park.

*

Sylvie turned back to look at Pamela as she hurried away. She had seen that Pamela looked haggard and strained, but she had lost weight, and her hair looked nice – making her look very attractive and a little like the endearing girl she had met when they were both ten year olds. She hoped very sincerely that all would turn out all right for her.

*

As she drove home Pamela thought through what she would say to Carla about her granddad. She had also prepared herself emotionally for a chat with Michael, as she intended to invite him in when he returned with Carla. She had even bought the biscuits he liked when she had popped into the supermarket. She smiled wryly when she thought that she had never intended to be friendly towards him or invite him into her new home, but this problem with her father wasn't going to go away just yet, and it had given her something far worse to think about than Michael's perfidy.

Pamela parked her car and took the shopping indoors. She glanced at her watch and decided to put the kettle on as she felt sure that Michael and Carla would arrive any minute. She had picked up a magazine when she bought Carla's protractor so she sat down and started to glance through it. Starting to feel chilly, Pamela checked the time again and was surprised that half an hour had gone by. She only had the central heating set to come on for an hour in the morning and a couple of hours in the evening, with the idea that if it became cold enough at the weekends she would just over-ride the time switch and set it going. Thinking that perhaps Michaels parents had insisted they have a full breakfast before they leave she decided to make a cup of tea for herself, and to put on the heating.

Checking the time once again after she had drunk her tea, Pamela began to worry that perhaps Michael had left earlier than she thought he might and that he and Carla had come back while she was on her way home from town. She decided to pop over to Marian's to ask whether Marian had seen Michael's car. She was disappointed, however, as Marian was not at home. She wondered what to do. She couldn't think where Michael might take her if she was right and they had come back whilst she was still out; there was no one she could think of to phone and ask.

Chapter 15

Carla had enjoyed the journey back. Michael was happy and they had sung silly songs together, as they used to when Carla was very young, and they both laughed when one of them couldn't remember the words. Michael had explained to Carla that he and Monique had arranged to rent a house together and that she, Carla, could help them to move in. He told her that she would have her own room for when she comes to stay with them, and that she could help prepare it and maybe stay a while whilst Pamela was busy helping out at her parents' house. "OK, Dad, that will be nice" she had told him "But I do want to see Mum as soon as possible."

"Of course you do, love" he had told her "we'll see how the day works out".

Monique had had to work the early morning shift at the gym; she had started at six and was due to finish at eleven thirty, but as she was moving out of her flat the colleague coming on the next shift had offered to come in early, so Michael had arranged to pick her up at eleven o'clock. Michael still hadn't told Monique that he was planning that Carla should stay with them for the foreseeable future; this was something he wanted to do face to face rather than on the phone. He wanted to find out as much as he could about whatever it was that Major Donald had been charged with, and he had had enough trouble trying to explain to Monique why he had felt the need to take Carla away from Pamela. Monique assumed, just as Pamela had, that he would take Carla straight home to Pamela once he got back from Eastbourne.

Michael pulled into the gymnasium car park and drove by the door to see whether he could see Monique. She was just coming out so he pulled up and she jumped in, having said hi to Carla, and telling her to stay where she was in the front; that she would get in the back. Michael explained to Monique that Carla was going to help them as Pamela was busy but Carla interrupted

"Dad, are you SURE Mum's not at home today? We haven't spoken to her since we told her you were bringing me home, won't she be worried?"

"You are quite right", he told her; "we'd better not call round with Monique, though, that'd not be fair on either of them, would it Monique?" he asked her, turning slightly to the back seat as he manoeuvred out of the car park.

"No", said Monique, but we could call her from my flat if we are going there first – or should we go and get the house keys first from the property agent?"

"Oh, yes, said Carla, I'd love to see the new house; how about if we get the keys and phone Mum from the new house – is it far?" Monique told her that the house was not far from the gym, but that they would have to double back to the estate agents' in order to collect the keys.

"That won't take long" Michael told them and he did a quick three point turn (he had been headed towards Monique's).

"Oh wow, that looks nice" Carla said as they pulled up outside. It was a three bedroom detached house with an open plan front garden and, although it was a relatively new house it had double glazed windows with leaded lights, and was built with old looking faded yellow brick. Michael opened the front door and they went in. The kitchen was fully equipped, and the rest of the house was sparsely but tastefully furnished. Monique and Michael explained to Carla that they were lucky to get the rental; that the owner had been offered a contract to work in the United States for six months, and that suited them ideally, as they should know within six months how successful Michael's business was going to be, and, therefore, how big a mortgage they could manage when they were ready to buy a house. However, Carla was very eager to see her mum, so she reminded Michael that he had said they could phone her from the new house.

"The phone is over there" said Michael, pointing, "go on; give her a call".

Carla was disappointed that there was no reply. She had picked the exact moment to call her mum when she had popped over to see Marian and found that Marian was out. Michael was very relieved that there was no reply. "There", he said, "I told you she'd be out"

"Why don't I ring Grandma's to see if they are there?" Carla asked.

"You can if you like" he said "but what if Mum and Grandma have popped out shopping and Granddad has to struggle up to answer the phone?"

"Oh, I didn't think of that" she said, disappointed.

"I tell you what" he said "We are having the biggest bedroom, but why don't you pop upstairs on your own and decide which one of the other two you would like for yourself? Then we can go to Monique's and collect her things, then on to my bed-sit for mine and somewhere along the way we can get a few things for lunch and I'm sure we'll catch up with Mum sooner or later. Carla agreed to this. She still felt uneasy as she hadn't spoken to her mother since saying they'd be back Saturday morning, and she didn't think her mum knew about Michael and Monique's new house, but she didn't see what else she could do. She had wondered about phoning Marian, but she knew neither Marian's phone number nor her surname. She smiled as she thought of Marian – what a strange lady, she thought! She'd found her sitting patiently in their house the day she had got cross at the thought of having to go over to Grandma and Granddad's the evening her mum had received that strange phone call. She knew who Marian was, as she'd seen her in the house next door, but, up until then she had never spoken to her.

Marian had made her feel comfortable in her company straight away; she had not made her feel guilty for running out and slamming the door on her mum. When Carla had started to apologise to Marian for her behaviour Marian had simply told her to save that for her mum, to apologise to her as it was her she had been rude to, not to Marian, and she went on to explain that Pamela didn't think Carla had her key, so that was why she had offered to wait in for Carla to return.

Carla had never seen hair like Marian's before, it was red and it stuck up in spikes. Marian spoke with a very marked accent which Carla didn't recognise; sometimes she had to listen carefully to understand what she was saying. However, the thing that had surprised her most was that after telling her why she was there, Marian had said to her "Now, sit down a minute, ducks, I wants ter talk to yer" and she proceeded to tell her that she'd seen her walking along the ring road early in the mornings and wanted to know why she was doing it.

Carla was shocked, she'd not mentioned it to anyone and didn't realise anyone had seen her. Marian had encouraged her to tell her why and where she was going, and Carla found herself explaining tearfully that she didn't want some of the girls who would be on the bus she now needed to catch to know where she lived. Carla didn't want Marian to think she was ashamed of where she was now living, especially as Marian lived there too, but these girls could be particularly nasty and would love to be able to taunt Carla about moving from the home she grew up in to the estate of terraced houses where she was now.

Marian talked it over with her, really with her, not lecturing her in the way Carla found most adults did when they thought they knew better than a child. Marian asked her questions about the girls; where they lived themselves (Carla didn't actually know) whether or not Carla was afraid they would hurt her physically, or whether it would just be taunts, and Carla found herself feeling real relief in discussing it all with Marian. She hadn't wanted to bother her mum with it as she knew she was struggling to cope with the marriage break up and the new home and new job, but also because she sometimes found that her mum's glib solutions to such things were not the answer she required.

Carla agreed with Marian that the ring road was dangerous, and Marian told her that she had mentioned the fact that she had seen Carla walking along it to her mum, but that her mum had thought she was mistaken. Marian agreed to say no more about it to Pamela, so long as Carla promised not to do it again, she had managed to convince Carla that she was in physical danger from the traffic, but in no danger at all apart from her feelings from the girls on the bus who probably had more hang ups and problems than Carla had ever thought about. She had even been able to laugh with Marian when she had acted out various scenarios of imaginary conversations between these girls and their own parents and had listened when Marian had told her that not everyone was lucky enough to have a loving mum as she had. Marian had pointed out that Pamela would never forgive herself if something happened to Carla specifically because she had chosen a house here that she could afford.

Michael called out to Carla that they were off to Monique's now to get her stuff. Carla had chosen which room she would like for when she came to stay, but had then gone out into the garden to see what was behind the little shed she could see from her chosen bedroom window. It was just another area of lawn, but while she was there a serious looking little face poked through a gap in the fence and said hello and she was just smiling and saying hello back when she heard her dad call her. "Bye bye", she said to the little face and gave a wave as she went back through the house and out to the car.

Carla thought there was a bit of an atmosphere between Michael and Monique, but thought maybe it was just because they had a lot to do to move their belongings in. She hadn't heard the hushed argument they had when Michael had told her that he wanted Carla to come and live with them properly until such time as he could find out exactly what it was that Major Donald had done.

There was no furniture to move, as all Michael's stuff was in storage to be moved once he bought a house, and Monique was leaving her small amount of furniture in her studio flat as she was letting it furnished. The back seat of Michael's car could be split so that half the boot area could be extended, and as Monique strode off purposely towards her flat Carla waited awkwardly while Michael fiddled around with the back of the car. She hadn't felt she should just follow Monique, although she was happy to help with her boxes and cases, but she had never been to Monique's flat and she felt in some small way that she would be betraying her mum if she went in. Carla had become fond of Monique, as she was fun and had brought a side of her dad out that she had never seen before – he was very relaxed and happy in her company, but Monique had seemed stressed on the way here in the car and Carla did not know why.

Carla asked Michael when he thought they could try to phone Pamela again. He swung round, surprised that she was there, as he thought she had gone to help Monique "Oh, for heaven's sake, don't keep on" he said to her. She struggled to keep back the tears that had been threatening since they got back from Eastbourne. She had so enjoyed the journey back, singing songs and laughing with her dad, but now it was hours after she thought she would be going home. She was hungry and fed up with travelling around and she did not know what to say. At this point Monique arrived at the end of the path carrying two boxes and pulling along a suitcase on wheels. Michael managed to get the back of the car sorted and turned to help her.

Monique could see that Carla was upset. She wondered what Michael had said to her. She herself was still reeling from the news that Michael wanted Carla to live with them. She liked Carla, but wanted Michael to herself – she didn't think it was a good idea to set up home together for the first time with a twelve year old in tow, however nice the girl was. Monique didn't want to ask Carla what the matter was, so she pretended not to notice that she was upset but just said "I don't know about you two, but I am starving. Why don't we pop to the shop on the corner and buy some sandwiches and have them with a cup of tea before we do any more?"

"Good idea" said Michael, pleased that there was something to distract Carla from keeping on about phoning Pamela. In fact, Michael didn't know what to say to Pamela and it was only luck that she hadn't been there when Carla tried to call her before. He was disappointed that Monique was unhappy about his wanting Carla to stay with them for the time being, they had, in fact, had an intense hushed argument while Carla was upstairs.

Quite apart from not wanting Carla with them for selfish reasons, Monique also felt that it was extremely unfair on Pamela, as it was not Pamela's fault that her father had been involved in some sort of sex crime, but when she had tried to say this to Michael she had not explained it very well and trying to hear Monique's hushed but angry words Michael had thought that she was making light of Major Donald's crime and he was very annoyed with what he felt was her laissez faire attitude towards it.

Monique suspected that Michael hadn't really thought through what to say to Pamela but she didn't know what he had said to Carla to make her close to tears. She knew, however, that Carla wanted to speak with her mum, so as they went into her flat with the sandwiches and pork pies they had bought at the shop she asked Carla whether she would like to try her mum again on the phone while she made them all a drink. This made Carla a lot happier about coming into Monique's flat, but she decided that she wouldn't tell her mum exactly where she was phoning from but she would allow her to believe it was the new house.

Pamela answered the phone on almost the first ring. "Oh, I'm so glad to hear it's you. I was beginning to think you had had an accident, I was so worried"

"We've been doing stuff" Carla began to tell her, then, suddenly feeling the relief of hearing her mum's voice she realised it wasn't her place to tell her mum that Michael and Monique were renting a house and moving in together "We tried to ring you earlier but you weren't in" She then put Michael on the spot by saying "Dad can tell you all about it and he can tell you when he will drop me off" and handed him the phone.

Monique had to smile and look away: This girl had her head screwed on, she thought, as Michael stammered his way through an explanation of how he'd wanted to show Carla the new house that they were going to rent and trying to explain why he had neither brought her straight home nor phoned as soon as they got back to let her know that he was going to show Carla his new house first. He was stumped when Pamela said "So, where are you now?" as, like Carla, he didn't think it a good idea to say they were at Monique's. He hedged his way round giving a straight answer and said he would see her in about half an hour or so. He had said it quietly hoping that Carla wouldn't hear exactly what he said, as a plan had begun to formulate in his mind as he was speaking to Pamela.

Michael said to Carla and Monique as they finished their lunch that they would make a trip to the new house and perhaps Monique wouldn't mind starting to put things away while he dropped Carla back home. Monique was very suspicious of this, as she doubted that he had changed his mind about wanting his daughter to stay with him.

Monique's suspicions were proved right when, once back at the new house, Carla was busy helping carry some boxes up the stairs and Michael called out to them that he had just thought of something he needed to do and would be right back. Carla looked in amazement at Monique as they rushed back down the stairs and saw her dad's car disappearing along the road.

Chapter 16

Pamela had mixed feelings as she put the phone down. She was extremely relieved that all was well, that there had not been an accident, but she was shocked that Monique and Michael were going to move in together, she wasn't really sure why she was shocked; Michael had never made a secret of the fact that that was what they intended to do but she most certainly didn't like the fact that Carla had already been involved and had seen the house. She felt rather betrayed again, as she had when she had first found out about Michael and Monique. She thought then that Carla must have known about the rented house, and was disappointed that Carla hadn't mentioned it when they had spoken on the phone, or that Carla hadn't asked Michael to bring her straight home and told him that she wanted to go home to mum and that she'd rather see the new house another day.

Michael drew up outside Pamela's house. She heard his car and decided to pull herself together, as before she'd known about the house, she'd decided she would be civil and ask him in and offer him tea and biscuits. She knew there was still a need to discuss her father so she forced herself to relax a little and opened the front door saying "Come on in" and trying to look welcoming. She was very eager to see Carla, anyway, and as Michael walked in the door Pamela was still looking towards his car for her.

"She's not here, and she's not coming" Michael told her.

Pamela was stunned. "What do you mean, not coming?" she asked him.

"I've decided she's safer with us for now, until we can find out exactly what it is your father has been doing" he told her.

"But how does Carla feel about it; what have you told her?" she asked. Michael wavered a bit as he thought of telling Carla that she wasn't going home. He hadn't thought that bit through, but he wasn't going to tell Pamela that he hadn't even told her. Pamela began to feel even more betrayed, if that was possible. No wonder Carla passed the phone to Michael to let him speak to her, she thought. Pamela suddenly realised Michael was speaking again:

"Carla has chosen her bedroom and is quite happy with the idea of staying with us. You know she has never been keen on her grandmother and doesn't like the idea of having to spend loads of time there with you while you visit your father during his convalescence."

Pamela didn't think this sounded like Carla; it was true that she wasn't keen on her grandmother, but she did love her granddad and Pamela was sure she would, in fact, want to visit him to ensure he really was on the mend. However, she realised that as his illness was not real but a fabrication and that she didn't know either what it was her father stood accused of that maybe just for the time being it would be easier not to have to explain why she was being kept away from him.

Pamela couldn't help wondering how differently they would have been dealing with this had they still been together as a couple. She put those thoughts away before she said something she would regret; she realised that she and Michael needed this 'fragile peace' as she saw it, she also felt disgust at whatever it was her father had done and wanted Carla protected from it, but she did, however, feel that Carla had agreed to it rather readily without talking it through with her. She felt that Carla was slipping away from her, but she decided resolutely that she wouldn't try to change Carla's mind for the time being, after all, it wouldn't be for long, she thought: "OK, she will need her school uniform and all her books and school bag and sports clothes and things; she will need to come and get those things herself".

As Pamela said this Michael could see a way of explaining things to Carla. He would bring Carla home; make it seem like he was having a quiet word with Pamela and then tell Carla that, unfortunately, her granddad had taken a turn for the worse and that she was to come to stay with him for a while. He knew that Pamela would not contradict him; as they had agreed, albeit reluctantly on Pamela's part, that Carla should go and stay with Michael for a while. He would advise her to go and pack whatever she needed for school for the week and tell her that that would enable Pamela to see her father whenever she wanted to.

Michael wasn't comfortable making up these lies; not for the first time he felt very angry again with his father in law; not just because of the crime he had committed (Michael was sure he was guilty – he'd always wondered what had been behind the family's return to the UK and the end of the Major's army career) but because of the knock on effect of the lies they were telling Carla. Michael didn't really want to take her away from Pamela, neither really did he want her there with him as he and Monique set up home for the first time together.

As Michael drove back to his new house he was thinking that the hard part had been achieved; all he had to do now was appease Monique and get Carla briefly to her mothers and back. He also realised he needed to explain to Carla and Monique where he had been, so he made a quick detour to the nearest supermarket and bought a bottle of Champagne and a box of chocolates. He would tell them this was to celebrate moving into the new home. He would suggest a takeaway later, once Carla knew she was staying as well and they could make a pleasant evening of it.

There was still a lot to do, though, if they were to settle in this weekend properly. Monique's belongings had been moved; clearing her flat had been important as Monique had explained to him that her tenant was moving in the following day. Monique had already packed her things and cleaned the flat once they had agreed to take the rented house, but they had made a bit of a mess bringing the bags and boxes out to the car, and Monique had wanted to go back and clean it properly, as she'd arranged with the property agent that it would be left in a good state for the tenant to move in. She had been furious when Michael shot off in his car as she had wanted him to drop her back to the flat so she could do the final touches and collect her own car, which she had left in its parking bay. She also wanted to say goodbye to her flat; it had served her well and although she loved Michael dearly, and was looking forward to their life together, this business with his father in law had begun to change things a little – fond though Monique was of Carla, she didn't like the idea of the three of them setting up home together.

Monique couldn't help wondering how Carla would react when Michael told her she had to stay with them, she also was wondering about practical matters; at George and Carol's Carla had spent most of her time with the twins and had brought enough clothing for the weekend. Monique wondered how much day to day care a twelve year old required; did she need a baby sitter or could she be left alone? Monique worked shifts at the gym, and as Michael's business was selling and leasing gymnasium equipment he was often working in the evenings when he would make presentations and demonstrate his equipment.

Monique also had a lively group of friends, with whom she still kept in contact. It was a long time before she told her friends that she was involved with a married man; they knew she was seeing someone and she had changed and saw a lot less of them, but she made a point of going out at least once a month with them when they were doing something special. Monique wondered now whether Michael was going to expect her to act as a mother and chivvy Carla to get her homework done and to wash her clothes etc. she didn't like the idea of it, she liked Carla but didn't feel ready to be anyone's mother, let alone a ready made child of twelve.. She decided to tackle Michael about it all as soon as she got him alone, whenever that might be. That was another thing; they had a very lively sex life, but Michael had been shy at his brother's in case someone heard them – she was worried that Carla's presence in the room next to theirs would put a damper on things.

As well as these considerations Monique did genuinely think that Carla should be with Pamela, it was thinking about the mothering side of having Carla with them that made her think again how unfair it was on Pamela. She wondered when Carla's school broke up for half term, and the small seed of an idea began to form in her mind. She had intended to berate Michael for having gone off in the car without an explanation but was still smiling slightly to herself when Michael pulled up outside and came back in. Instead she just said "Where on earth did you shoot off to?"

Michael smiled and showed her the Champagne and chocolates. "Is Carla ready to go home? He asked, confusing Monique totally.

"I thought…"

"Where is she?" Michael quickly asked. Monique explained that she had found a very small boy who she had described as 'cute' next door and was out behind the shed talking to him through the fence.

Michael soon explained where he had been and what he had told Pamela. "I'll take her there now" he told Monique. She realised she would have to be forceful if she was going to get anywhere today:

"No. Only if you take me to my flat first so I can do what I need to do there and collect my car." Michael wasn't keen to do this as he didn't want to delay; he was too worried that Pamela would have time to change her mind, he wanted to get Carla there and back with her things she would need for school as soon as possible. However, he was well aware that Monique was a very strong character and he needed her agreement to have Carla with them, so he agreed and went out to the back garden to let Carla know he was back.

This didn't go well; Carla was furious with him; she really wanted to get home now. She had a bag full of dirty clothes that she brought back from Eastbourne, she felt she had been travelling forever and hadn't intended to get caught up with her dad and Monique and their new house. She was worried about her mum, she thought the strain of having had her dad so ill must have been awful for her; she wanted to get home and give her mum a big hug and then phone one of her friends to see what had been going on at school for the week she had missed. Carla couldn't see why going out to buy Champagne and chocolates could possibly be more important than taking her home. She was very frosty with Michael

"OK, but I want to go home to mum NOW" she insisted.

When Monique walked towards the car too, Carla looked askance at her dad but he said nothing. She could sense an atmosphere between them and she was pleased. She felt they had been stringing her along for hours, she assumed that Monique just wanted to come along for the ride and that they would just drop her off with her holdalls. However, Michael didn't head straight towards Pamela's so Carla asked, quite rudely for her

"Oh for heaven's sake, NOW where are we going?"

Monique answered her "I'm afraid I insisted that your dad drop me off at the flat first. I must give it a quick clean through and collect my car, I am working the early shift again tomorrow at the gym, it seemed to have slipped your dad's mind that I started work at six o'clock this morning and will be doing so again tomorrow and will need my car"

Carla sighed heavily but sat back. For the second time she found herself feeling rather helpless. There was nothing she could do but wait until Michael had dropped Monique off; she just wanted to go home but realised that they would soon be on their way and she could give her mum a big hug soon enough. She wanted to sort through her bags. Her Grandmom had offered to do her washing, but she had declined, saying she had brought plenty of things with her. She had not been too particular about what she had packed where, as she had intended to tip it all out on her bedroom floor and give the dirty washing to her mum. Pamela liked to do it on a Saturday morning, but Carla was sure Pamela wouldn't mind doing it now, but she was concerned that the things that didn't need a wash would be all creased up as they had now been in the bag so long. She was fed up with travelling, she had only been back from George and Carol's for one night when her granddad was taken ill and her dad came for her at the school and took her home to pack her bags. She had had to find stuff she hadn't worn for ages as her favourite things she'd taken to her cousins' were in the wash basket.

Chapter 17

Sylvie cut the labels off her new swimming cossie. She chuckled as she thought of her morning's swim; it had been a little while since she had been swimming, but the weather was changing and she knew she couldn't rely on jogging for her exercise for much longer, she needed to get back into her early morning routine of swimming a couple of times a week. The evenings would soon be too dark to go out jogging, but she would still do the occasional Sunday morning on a nice day. Luckily she thought that no one else had noticed how transparent her old swimming cossie had become. It looked fine when she put it on, but when she stepped out of the communal shower she noticed that it was showing a lot more of her body than she liked! The people already in the pool were all busy swimming up and down the lanes so she kept her back to the changing rooms and quickly made her way into the water. She swam her customary thirty lengths and then swiftly got out taking care not to face anyone as she got her clothes out of her locker and went into the nearest changing room. Once dressed Sylvie decided not to go back home but to go into town and replace the transparent costume which she had thrown away so she wouldn't be tempted to wear it again.

Sylvie loaded the damp towel into her washing machine and went off in search of other things to put in to make a full load. As she was doing so she mused over her unexpected meeting with Pamela in town that morning. She had thought that although Pamela had been very stressed when she was explaining about Michael and Carla she had not seen her looking so lovely for years; her hair was swinging like it did when she was a girl, and she had lost weight. Sylvie wondered whether getting out of what she considered to be a rather pedestrian marriage and facing such things as buying her own house and finding a job to support herself had something to do with the 'new Pamela'. She hoped so, and she hoped that this matter with Major Donald would not affect her too seriously. She would not be able to discuss the case with Pamela until the facts of it were in the public domain. Pamela understood this and had said so to Sylvie.

However, Sylvie was worried about the fact that Pamela said she didn't want to know what her father had done; she would find out sooner or later, whether she wanted to or not. With Ralph ill again they were short staffed, and Sylvie wondered who would compile the report. If it was to be one of the colleagues she got on well with they would ask her questions about the family, as she could be of help, but if it was to be done by someone drafted in from another office they may not feel comfortable involving her at all.

In the compiling of a pre-sentence report the probation officer would usually like to meet all the members of the accused's family, and also some of his friends to ensure that a balanced report can be submitted to the judge who will sentence the offender. Sylvie hoped with all her will that the case would not drag on too long – all sorts of things could slow a case of this sort down, not least their own offices' lack of staff. Once Pamela was aware of the facts, either because she will have been interviewed by a probation officer or because more details will have leaked out to the press then Sylvie could discuss things with Pamela.

Having sneaked a look at the case notes submitted; Sylvie was not surprised that the Major had pleaded guilty. There was no doubt about whether he had taken part in the act with the young lady concerned; his defence had been that he was not aware that he was committing a crime, but, unfortunately for him, ignorance of the law is no defence under English and Welsh law. Sylvie had never met the social worker who had reported the alleged incident to the police; she didn't think that she would have known the family she was supporting for very long, she must be fairly new, as most of the local probation officers and social workers had met one another in the course of their work or at inter-disciplinary seminars and meetings. Sylvie found herself wondering how long Ralph would be off sick this time as she would like to be able to talk to him about the case; he had more connections than she did among the social worker network as he had a sister in law who, although retired now, had worked locally as a social worker herself and still kept in touch with the colleagues with whom she had worked.

Thinking about Ralph now, she hoped he would soon recover as she really missed him, apart from his being able to tell her about the personality of the new social worker he was a good and experienced probation officer with a quick wit and a dry sense of humour. She thought it a real shame that he had the ability to make his colleagues see a balance in all the things they had to deal with, and yet he was unable to avoid the stress getting to him, as it had again recently causing him to be ill again with his stomach ulcers.

There was, however one area in which Ralph had very fixed views: that of Probation Volunteers. Ralph felt strongly that by encouraging the use of them, it 'watered down' the service itself, that the very need for them suggested a stretched service into which the government was not putting enough money. Other officers did not feel the same way; quite a few tended to make use of the volunteers and sometimes had them working alongside them.

Sylvie had tended to keep out of the heated debates that sometimes raged around the office re their uses, she had been grateful for Ralph taking her under his wing when she had first come to this office and, although she didn't have a strong view either way, she had not been to any of the meetings as she didn't want to antagonise Ralph. Thinking about it now, Sylvie wondered whether a volunteer could be of any help in the situation she now found herself; worrying about Pamela but unable as yet to be of any help herself. Guiltily, she remembered a memo and small green booklet entitled *Volunteers Handbook* recently making its way round the office with its customary list of typed names paper clipped to the front. Sylvie had simply written her initials next to her name to say that she had read both, but in fact she had been too busy.

Turning her attention to her wash load and the other domestic chores that needed doing that weekend, Sylvie decided to track down the memo and booklet as soon as she could on Monday morning.

Chapter 18

Pamela stood stiffly by the door as Michael and a very pale looking Carla passed through it with bags to load into the car. She didn't know what to think. She had been feeling very betrayed; believing that Carla had wanted to spend the morning with Michael and Monique but by Carla's comments and manner it seemed that this wasn't the case, that she had really wanted to come straight home. Pamela now realised, however, that not only had Carla really wanted to come home as soon as she got back from Eastbourne, but that until Michael quietly took Pamela to one side and asked her to back him up Carla had known nothing about the fact that she was expected to stay with Michael and Monique in their new house.

Carla wouldn't look at Pamela. It all seemed very sudden that her granddad was ill again and that she was to go back with Michael. She had tried to say that she was grown up enough to stay for a while at home alone; she had even offered to do some practical tasks such as loading the washing machine and preparing meals while Pamela was with her father but Pamela had said adamantly that she should go with Michael and that if she could have the phone number of the new house she would call as soon as she knew how things were with her parents.

Michael could sense Carla's confusion and his heart went out to her. Apart from everything else she was obviously worried about her clothes that needed washing as she had mentioned it several times whilst going up and down the stairs. Pamela had said that she was sure there must be a washing machine at the new house and Michael confirmed that there was a small utility room with a washer and drier in it. Carla didn't get a chance to spend any time at all with Pamela alone and was far too embarrassed to mention to her dad that some of her knickers were marked and she didn't want anyone but her mum to see them. Carla wondered whether the washing machine would be difficult to use.

Michael helped Carla carry her stuff up to the room she had chosen. Carla was very relieved to see that Monique wasn't back yet, and she said she was going to go into the garden to see whether the small child was in the garden next door. She didn't really like small children, but this child with the serious little face had interested her. However, it was just an excuse to go through the utility room and linger by the washing machine to determine whether it would be easy to use. She was in luck, having had a quick look at some labels on some of the things she had just brought from home, she saw that they had numbers on them. This washing machine had a diagram on the front showing which letters of the alphabet on the control knob referred to which label number. "Sorted!" she said to herself, and slipped back upstairs to her bedroom. She emptied all her bags and sorted through the items that needed washing, including the lovely top that Fee had given her to wear to George's party the previous weekend.

Carla smiled as she thought of her cousins. She was quite sure that some of the things Fee had given her would still have fitted her, but Fee had so enjoyed Carla's enjoyment of trying on the clothes that she had been generous and given her several things. Carla was not sure how much would fit into the washing machine in one go, but she had seen her mum load the machine often enough to have a rough idea. She gathered a bundle of light coloured things together as she had seen Pamela do and she headed for the utility room. Saying nothing to Michael she put her things in the machine, ensuring that she put her knickers in last. Next problem: washing powder or liquid; her mum used a liquid and had a ball with calibrations on the side. Carla had seen Monique carry boxes of things into the utility room earlier, so she opened a couple of cupboards until she saw a box with a familiar logo on it. She opened the box and found inside little wrapped blocks. She was hoping to be able to put some washing liquid onto the stains on her knickers – she was never embarrassed with her mum as her mum had explained it was all a part of growing up, the first time she noticed it, and that once her periods began properly she would get into a monthly routine. Carla stuck her head round the door to see where Monique and her dad were and as there was no sign of either of them she took the bottle of washing up liquid from the kitchen sink and, listening carefully in case her dad or Monique were approaching she took out each pair of knickers and applied a little washing up liquid to the gusset of each pair. Popping them back in, she put a washing tablet in as instructed on the box and set the machine going.

Feeling satisfied that at least one of her problems was sorted Carla went up to her room to organise her things and put some stuff away in the cupboards. She wanted to call a couple of her friends to find out what had gone on during the week she had missed, so once she had arranged things in her room to her satisfaction she went downstairs to make a few calls.

"What on earth have you put in there" Monique was just asking Michael as Carla came down the stairs.

"In where?" he asked.

"The washing machine, look at it, it's gone mad" she said, and slipping into the utility room to see what Monique was talking about Carla saw, to her horror, that not only was the machine full of foam, they could see it through the glass, but also the foam had started to creep out of the drawer where the fabric conditioner went in. Michael explained that he hadn't started the machine off, that it must have been Carla. They both turned to look at her and she blushed. Carla had forgotten to put the washing up liquid back on the kitchen sink. Monique spotted it straight away, but, as she was so impressed that Carla had obviously made an effort to do her own washing she said nothing about it and suggested that Michael leave them to it and that they would sort it.

Carla thought she would die of embarrassment as Michael walked back out to the kitchen, but Monique just said "Don't worry; we'll turn the dial to rinse and then start it off again with another washing tab in. If you are worried about anything very dirty just put in two tabs – never mind what it says on the box. I'll not say anything to your dad, just don't use washing up liquid again, it froths up too much". Monique then replaced the washing up liquid on the sink and went back to rearranging the kitchen cupboards.

Satisfied that no embarrassing questions were going to be asked, Carla went out into the garden to see whether the small child next door was outside in his or her garden. As all Carla had seen was a very small earnest face she was not even sure whether it was a little boy or girl that she had spoken to briefly earlier in the day.

*

Pamela sank into a chair after Carla and Michael had gone. That was the hardest thing she had ever had to do since leaving Carla at playgroup for the very first time. Pamela had never ever lied to Carla. Even when she had any medical treatment Pamela had always warned her when something was going to hurt; her view was that it was better to know beforehand, however young you were, so you could brace yourself. Her own mother had been of the old 'this won't hurt' school even when she pulled a plaster from a scabby knee and knew it would hurt. Pamela had spent twelve years building up trust with Carla and now, because of something her own father had done, she was in a position where she felt she had to lie to protect her. She began to feel angry rather than upset. She realised, not for the first time; that she didn't even know exactly what she was protecting Carla from; as she had felt far too embarrassed to want to know what it was that her father had been accused of. She decided that her relationship with Carla was more important than her own feelings regarding her father, so she resolved to find out what it was he had done as soon as she could. However, she couldn't face actually asking him, so she would have to do some digging, and not through Sylvie, as that wouldn't be fair. She decided she would telephone the newspaper office when they were open and ask whether they had any extra information, or whether they could suggest to her how she could find out what she wanted to know.

Getting up from the chair, Pamela decided to organise herself in such a way as to pass the rest of the day as quickly as possible. When they had moved in she had not had a great deal of time to spend on organising cupboards, so, in order that she didn't have a lot of time on her hands until Monday morning when work would occupy her mind again she decided to start in her bedroom and reorganise her wardrobe and chest of drawers, at the same time checking what actually fitted her now and what didn't.

Feeling quite satisfied that several hours had passed and she had spent the time doing useful things, and she had found a couple of outfits reasonable enough to wear to work, Pamela went into the kitchen to prepare herself something to eat. Moving her handbag out of the way she found a small flat bag underneath it – Carla's new protractor; she had forgotten all about it!

Having been brave and sensible since Carla walked past her, stony faced and pale, her strength and resolve left her and clutching the protractor she started to cry, heaving heavy dry sobs as she thought about all the things she wanted to be doing with and for Carla just now: Making her dinner; putting out her school uniform for tomorrow; checking she had everything she needed, like her protractor, and ensuring she had a quiet calm evening before starting another week of school.

*

Monique smiled to herself as she thought of Carla and the washing up liquid. Maybe it wouldn't be so bad her being with them for a while after all; at least she saw to her own things and didn't expect Monique to do her washing. She was hoping it wouldn't be for long, anyway; she had a plan for half term and she had contacted an old friend when she had gone back to her flat to run the vacuum through, and that old friend had come up trumps and agreed to what Monique had asked. All she had to do now was to convince Michael that it was a good idea. Half term was only one week away and Monique felt that if her plan worked then Carla would be back with Pamela, where she believed she belonged, once they had spent half term week together. It also rested, Monique realised, on Pamela's being able to get the week off work at short notice, and she had no idea what the arrangements were in Pamela's office.

It was getting colder, the small child was not in the garden so Carla had gone in and asked Monique whether she knew how to operate the tumble drier. They went to have a look at it together, and Monique showed Carla how to set it to know when the clothes were dry. This could either be dry enough to iron, or dry enough to wear and when Monique explained that if she set it to dry enough to wear and hung her stuff up straight away it probably wouldn't need to be ironed Carla said "Sorted!" for the second time that day. Carla then explained to Monique that she would like to call a couple of her friends and see what they were doing the following day and meet with them if possible and wear something new that Fee had given her. Monique reminded Carla that she was working in the morning, so suggested she ask Michael whether he could arrange to take her to see her friends. Pleased though she was with how things had gone so far, Monique balked at the thought of having the house full of Carla's friends so hadn't suggested she ask them round. Monique wasn't to know, but Carla was already worried about explaining her new circumstances to her friends, as it all seemed bizarre enough to her and she didn't want to answer too many difficult questions.

Michael was happy enough to agree to drop Carla at the leisure centre at ten the following day once she had contacted her friends to see what they were planning to do. Emily had skating lessons every Sunday morning, and she often persuaded the others to come and watch so they could all have a coke and a gossip together afterwards. Carla was pleased with the arrangement as it would allow her to find out what had gone on at school in her absence, not in lessons, luckily she was quite bright and would soon catch up with all that; but with everyone's social life.

Both her parents had gone to single gender schools; her dad never talked much about his school days but Carla and Pamela had often chatted about the differences; Pamela had told Carla how all the girls had crushes on the science master; the only male under the age of forty in the whole school, and Carla often entertained Pamela with tales of the interactions between the various groups of young people.

Chapter 19

Locking her car, Pamela turned to walk into the office and noticed that Sandra's car was not yet in its customary space. There were no designated spaces in the work's car park but Pamela smiled as she thought what creatures of habit human beings were, everyone in her office usually parked in more or less the same place each day. Pamela had a lot of work to do, as she wanted to prepare a payment run but had to get all the invoices onto the system first, so she made straight for her desk and logged on to her PC. It was half way through the morning before she felt the need for a mug of coffee and realised that Sandra was not there. "No Sandra?" she asked as she went to put the kettle on.

"No, apparently not, and no explanation from anyone" said Maureen. That makes things awkward, thought Pamela. She needed to ask for a week off, but was reluctant to ask John Meredith after Sandra's reaction when she returned from her leave after moving house.

Pamela made coffee for everyone and Rob passed round the biscuit tin. As Pamela gave Maureen her coffee she asked whether she had any idea why Sandra wasn't in. Not only did Maureen have absolutely no idea, she also said that it had never happened before. Sandra was never off sick; rarely took her holiday entitlement and had never ever just not turned up for work before. Then Maureen really surprised her by saying "And when she does come back, we'd better all mind our P's and Q's, as she is likely to be in a foul mood as she hates being away from here". Pamela was most surprised, and Rob looked quite startled as Maureen almost never expressed any opinion; in fact she was generally a very quiet person who just got on with her work.

Joan looked up from her desk and muttered quietly to no one in particular that she didn't think Sandra had a very easy time of things at home. Pamela hadn't been planning to mention the fact that she needed a week off to anyone other than Sandra herself, but hearing these things said she plucked up courage to say to the rest of the team that something very important had come up at home and she had been hoping to ask Sandra for the half term week off, so she was disappointed to find that Sandra was not there.

"If it's very important to you, my advice is to ask John Meredith and worry about Sandra when she returns" Maureen suggested. She then surprised Pamela further by saying that as it would be the run up to month end, just as it had been when she had the time off to move house; that she and Joan could help out with the invoices if Pamela were to show them what needed to be done, so that Sandra would not have cause to complain about having to do all the month end work herself. "I'm sure it will be OK, Lauren has the week after off; so there will only be you away."

Pamela was so pleased that she could have hugged herself. She had no idea that the rest of the team could be so accommodating. Obviously they had all suffered Sandra's bullying at one time or another, but they were willing to put themselves out to help her even though she had only worked there for a short time and had needed to take a few days off near the end of the previous month. What Pamela wasn't sure about, however, was whether or not she was entitled to a week's leave yet as she had only been in her post for a few months. This week off was very important, indeed, to her, so she decided to go and see John Meredith straight away and offer to take the week off as unpaid leave.

Walking back to her desk from John's office she saw the others glance up at her questioningly so she nodded and told them he had given her permission to take the week off. She began to prepare the payment run. When Sandra had first showed her how to do this she thought she would never be able to do it without referring to her notes, but after the first few times she found the sequences quite logical and today, as she typed in the parameters that would define which suppliers would be paid she thought about the unexpected phone call from Michael the evening before.

She had been feeling weak but no longer tearful when the phone rang: she had sobbed until she could cry no more after finding the protractor that she had forgotten to give to Carla. It was getting dark as she had struggled to the kitchen to put the kettle on when the phone had rung. Hearing Michael's voice on the other end she was wary; what now, she had thought?

Michael launched straight into the question "What are the chances of your getting next week off work?" Pamela wondered what he had in mind as the following week was Carla's half term.

"I don't know, I can try – why, what are you thinking?" she asked him. He hesitated and Pamela again wondered what was coming. She asked tentatively "Have you found out more about Daddy?"

"No, it's not that" he told her

"Then what? Haven't you confused Carla enough already – didn't you see how dreadful she looked as she followed you out of the door?"

"Yes, I did, and I hate lying to her and I know she should really be with you, but I don't want her anywhere near your father…"

"Yes, I know all that; please get to the point" Pamela was beginning to feel angry.

"Sorry, this is hard, as I am sure you are going to tell me you don't want any favours from Monique, but it's not like that…"

"WHAT is not 'like that'?" she demanded "Just tell me what you have to say and I will be the judge of how I feel about it, not you"

"OK, it's like this. Monique has a friend whose parents own a little old cottage near the sea in Brittany and you and Carla could go there for half term if you like, I will pay for your ferry crossing" Pamela was stunned. She had never been on a cross channel ferry; had no idea how difficult it was to drive on or off one, in fact she had never driven in Europe, so had never driven on the right. As all these difficulties went through her mind she knew it was a chance to spend a whole week with Carla. She didn't know whether her old car would cope with the journey so she asked him

"Which channel crossing would it be, and how far a drive is it the other end?"

"Portsmouth to St Malo" he told her "and the journey from St Malo to the cottage is about 150 miles…"

"HOW many?" she asked "Will my little car do that OK?"

"Yes, it should do if you take it steady, it's not much further than to George and Carol's and we used to do that in the little car sometimes

"Yes, used to, and the trip across France is half as much again - I'd like to do it though, but I don't want to break down anywhere"

"OK, I'll arrange full break down cover for you as well, but you won't need it, she's a sturdy little car. When will you know whether you can take the week off?" That, of course, was the sticking point for Pamela, she didn't want to antagonise Sandra, but this was extremely important to her.

"I'm sure I will be able to, I'll know by mid day tomorrow. Have you mentioned any of this to Carla?" she asked him.

"No, and I'm ringing from a call box, so she doesn't hear our conversation" Pamela bit her tongue, as she wanted to say something nasty about his being used to call boxes since he started his clandestine affair with Monique, but she didn't want to upset him as he was offering a way for her to be with Carla.

Instead she said "I could ring you at mid-day if you give me a phone number" Michael didn't know where he would be at any given time as he was still travelling round the gyms to get business, so he asked whether he could phone Pamela at work.

"OK then, I'll give you the number" she had told him.

Pamela glanced up at the office clock and saw that it was 11.45. She wanted to be by her desk to await Michael's call at mid-day but she wanted to get her payment run signed off before that as John had told her he would be out of the office for the afternoon as he had an off-site meeting to attend. Quickly she assembled her paperwork and took it to John's office. In Sandra's absence Rob was going to do the 'mysterious' part of the payment run, the connection to the bank that would allow the suppliers to be paid by BACS, the part that Pamela had not been shown how to do.

However, if Pamela thought she was going to be in and out of John's office quickly she was mistaken. Sandra usually initialled the paperwork before taking it to John to be signed, and although Pamela knew that Sandra never looked at it before she signed it, it was obvious that John didn't know this. He checked almost every page, and Pamela, having asked whether John would prefer her to go away and come back, kept very still so he wouldn't feel her impatience as he had said "No, no, this won't take long, but I must check it or Sandra will be after me when she comes back if I've missed something" Pamela wondered, not for the first time, about why John was so sure Sandra was so good at her job. Even his reference to her being 'after him' was said in a pleasant, jovial manner.

Just as Pamela made her way back to her desk her phone rang. "It's OK, I'm back; I'll get it" she told Maureen as she saw Maureen reach for her phone. It was Michael, as she had hoped it would be. Pamela thought she heard relief in his voice when, after telling him she could, indeed, have the following week off. He asked whether it would be OK to call on her one evening in the week and give her the ferry tickets and the details for the car cover and the directions to the cottage. Putting the phone down, she remembered that she hadn't mentioned the protractor that Carla needed for school. Suddenly it didn't seem important as she considered the adventure that she and Carla were to embark upon on Friday evening. Michael had said that he would book the ferry for the overnight crossing Friday night, and the return trip on the day crossing a week the following Sunday. He had then said that Pamela could drop Carla back to his house on the Sunday evening.

That's what he thinks, she had thought to herself, but she hadn't said anything. Pamela had intended to try to phone the local newspaper office to see what she could find out, but she decided instead to drive quickly into town and pay the office a visit as it would be easier than trying to talk softly and worry about people overhearing what she was saying in the office.

Pleased that she'd found somewhere to park straight away Pamela walked purposefully towards the newspaper office. She put her hand on the door handle and looked in through the glass as she did so. She saw a friendly looking lady sitting at a low counter who looked up and smiled as she saw through the glass door. Pamela smiled back hesitantly then hurried away in panic. What on earth was she thinking of? What would she say? That she was the daughter of an alleged sex offender and wanted to know more about what he was accused of? Pamela walked swiftly away and didn't stop until she got back to her car. Shaking she unlocked her car and slowly got in. She realised now that she couldn't even telephone the paper office. She really hadn't thought through what she was going to say; the newspaper people would not be bound by any sort of client confidentiality as Sylvie was; Pamela sat in her car shaking as she imagined the paper gleefully writing an article about her father and his 'concerned daughter'.

Backing slowly and carefully out of her parking space, Pamela made her way back to work. She'd not thought to get anything to eat and she felt quite light headed. She made it back to the office within the hour so she went straight to the kitchenette and put the kettle on. A cup of tea and a couple of biscuits would have to suffice; she didn't even fancy that, but she could feel a headache coming and she knew she must have something. Rob had put the completed BACS paperwork back on Pamela's desk and gave her a thumbs-up sign as she looked up at him when she saw it, indicating that the payment run had gone through. Pamela was pleased, as this meant she could busy herself printing off the remittance advices and putting them in envelopes; a time consuming but satisfying task that she didn't have to think too hard about. Having taken a couple of headache tablets with her cup of tea and eaten two biscuits she settled down to the task in hand.

Chapter 20

Not wanting to start another lively discussion on the rights and wrongs of the service's using probation volunteers, Sylvie had gone in to work early and had rummaged through the paperwork where she had last seen the little green volunteers' handbook. She was in luck; she had found both the memo and the booklet in a pile of non urgent paperwork awaiting Ralph's return. Sylvie had popped them into her bag to read when she got home.

Once she'd cleared away the potato peelings Sylvie popped a pizza into the oven and the chips she'd cut into the deep fat fryer and, checking the time, she leaned against the worktop and began to read the memo before reading the booklet. Sylvie was aware that their probation area had a new local Chief Probation Officer; this was why there had been even more memo's than usual circulating the office.

Once she began to read the memo Sylvie was pleased to have this opportunity to do so. She never liked to get involved in what she considered to be the politics of her job, but, in fact, politics played a very large part in the Probation Service. Whenever there was a public outcry about an incident involving an offender, whether it be someone on early release from a custodial sentence, or an attack by a known serial sex offender, the government would be pushed by the press to make announcements with regard to what they were going to do about whatever the issue was. However, it takes a lot of time to make changes to the law, so often a policy change would be required within the service, so that the government could be seen to be doing something.

Like most of the staff at her office, Sylvie just did her best for her clients within the parameters of the law When the prisons were deemed too full and some offenders released before their sentences were fulfilled they would be busier than ever with extra clients released 'on licence', and whenever funding was found for a new program of courses for such things as anger management, drug or alcohol rehabilitation or resources for the families of offenders, the probation officers would endeavour to sign up the clients most in need of these services and try to ensure that they attended their courses.

As Sylvie began to read the memo about the use of volunteers in the service, she did so with a certain amount of cynicism as she knew that not all extra funding promised by a new senior officer would ever find its way to the project it was meant for in the long term, but she read with interest what his intentions were and she felt that if she explained her reasons to Ralph for looking into the use of a Probation Volunteer to support Major Donald's immediate family that he may understand and be supportive.

It was not necessary for Sylvie to get Ralph's permission to do this, but she had a tremendous amount of respect for him and was also very fond of him. She did not want to alienate him, especially as he was still off sick; she did not want him to return to work and feel that she had done something he felt strongly against while he was not there. She felt the need to do something, however, as Major Donald's case had arrived at the office that morning. It hadn't as yet been assigned to a particular officer, but with Sylvie unable to take the case on as she knew the Major, and with Ralph absent, that left only three other officers to whom it could be assigned; one of whom may be willing to discuss parts of the case with her, but the other two Sylvie knew were sticklers for the policy of confidentiality when an officer knew a client personally.

Sylvie took her pizza out of the oven and put it on a plate tipping the crispy chips on top. Taking salt and ketchup with her she went into her sitting room and settled in front of the TV, so she could switch herself off altogether for a short time while she ate, before phoning Ralph to see whether she could pop round to see him.

After stacking her plate and cutlery in the dishwasher Sylvie phoned Ralph's number. She hated housework of any sort, she felt it all to be a waste of time, so, much to her mother's amusement; she had bought herself a dishwasher. Sometimes it took all week before it was full enough to run, but she felt it was a worthwhile investment as, living alone, she didn't make much mess in the house and so long as she ran the vacuum cleaner and a duster around everywhere once a week her home usually remained clean and tidy.

Sylvie was in luck; June answered the phone "Oh, hello, Sylvie love, I'm glad it's you, how are you?" Sylvie proceeded to tell June that she would like to run an idea past Ralph, but didn't want to cause him stress or tire him. "No problem at all, my love" June said to her "Ralph is feeling a lot better but you know what he's like, the doctor has signed him off for at least a month this time, and he's chomping at the bit to know what's going on at work; you pop on over and I'll put the kettle on"

Chapter 21

Pamela had popped home from work to pick up the garden centre vouchers and the card she had bought for her father's birthday. She had intended to go straight from work but had forgotten the vouchers and card when she had left for work that morning.

The arrangement was originally to have been for the Thursday, the day after his birthday, as there was a function on at the golf club which he had been expected to attend on his actual birthday, but as he had been asked to resign as treasurer, obviously he would not be attending. Daphne, of course, was unaware that he had been asked to resign; he had used the excuse of Peggy's no longer coming to say that he had resigned in order that he could spend more time helping with the household chores.

As far as the Major was concerned this was working well, so far. They had bought a tumble drier and installed it in the corner of the utility room, and finding that it had a 'minimum iron' setting they found that everything no longer needed to be ironed. Daphne was still worried that her friends would look down their noses because they had not replaced Peggy, as they all had 'help' as they called it, but Donald had reassured her that they could hold their heads up and say that as Peggy was of the 'old school' and the only available 'help' seemed to be young people, that they were still looking for someone suitable now that Peggy had decided to retire.

Pamela did not want Michael to know she was going to see her parents, so when he had asked whether he could pop round one evening with the ferry tickets etc. she had just said that would be fine, she just hoped he would phone first to check whether she was at home.

Just as she was going back out of the door with the vouchers and card in her hand she heard the phone ringing. Concerned that it might be Michael she went back in to answer it. It was and he apologised for not having called sooner but explained that he was very busy and asked whether it would be OK for him to pop over the following evening. Extremely relieved that she didn't have to tell him she was about to head off to Crowford she agreed and after asking him how Carla was and whether she was looking forward to the trip to France she put the phone down and set off for her parents' house.

Driving over to Crowford, Pamela wondered what it would be like to drive on the right hand side of the road and she wondered yet again how her little old car would cope with the long journey to the holiday cottage. Although she was beginning to look forward to the break, she cursed her father once again for whatever it was he had done. Whatever it was it was the cause of all the lies told to Carla and it was keeping Carla from her. Having initially not wanted to know what it was he had done, common sense began to make her see that she would have to know sooner or later. Like Michael, she desperately wanted to protect Carla from any knowledge regarding her father's alleged offence, but unless she knew what he stood accused of she would not know what it was that she was protecting Carla from.

Knowing that she could not mention it until her mother had the all clear with regard to her health; she remembered that she was not supposed to know that her mother had been to the hospital for tests. This was something that Pamela was determined to bring out into the open. She would make some seemingly innocent remark to her mother in front of her father about their good health, possibly when toasting her father's birthday and attempt to force her mother to tell her about the hospital visit. Pamela had only promised her father not to upset her mother by telling her about his alleged offence, and she would not break his confidence, instead she would find a way of putting her mother into a position where she would have to tell her about her hospital appointment and what the tests were for.

Pulling into the sweep of drive that her mother was so fond of Pamela fixed a smile in place and went in to deal with one of the most bizarre situations she felt she had ever had to face. She made straight for the kitchen and found her mother there preparing vegetables. "Hi, Mummy" she said giving her a kiss on the cheek "What would you like me to do. Where is Daddy, does he know I am coming?" "Daddy is in his study doing a crossword. Yes, I did tell him you would be over because I told him Carla couldn't come; I didn't want him to be disappointed that he wouldn't see her this evening".

Pamela wondered what her father would have made of the fact that she wasn't bringing Carla. She thought of going to see him in his study but she couldn't bring herself to do so. She had felt brave on the drive over; imagining herself getting him alone and asking him straight out what it was he was accused of, but she found that she couldn't bring herself to. So much for innocent until proven guilty, she thought to herself, but when she had come over to try to find out what was going on the night that Michael took Carla to Eastbourne he had said that 'something had taken place' and that confirmed to Pamela that he had done something. If Marian hadn't said to her that it must have been something more serious than flashing, she may have thought that her father had suffered some awful late life crisis and been caught doing something of that nature, but she couldn't imagine her mild mannered father doing anything of that sort. Yet he had said those words 'something had taken place', so that was an admission of sorts that he had done something.

"Funny that Daddy hasn't come out to find you" said Daphne as she peeled potatoes and Pamela sliced beans "he must have heard you pull into the drive. Why don't you go and find him to say Happy Birthday?" Pamela assumed her father was as reluctant to see her as she was to see him. Suddenly she felt angry that he had caused all this trouble somehow and now was too timid to come out and speak to her. Turning her back so her mother wouldn't see her face she wiped her hands and mumbled that she'd pop along to see him now.

"Well?" she said as she stood in the doorway of her father's study.

"Oh hello, I was doing the crossword, I didn't hear you arrive".

"You are holding the newspaper upside down and you are not wearing your reading glasses" she said to him stonily. "I am not going to say Happy Birthday, not when we are on our own, anyway. I shall keep up the charade in front of Mummy for a while until I know what is supposed to be wrong with her"

"OK, Sweetie, I don't deserve a happy birthday…"

"Don't say that" she said, softening a little "One is supposed to be innocent until proven guilty under our law" she closed the study door and went to sit on the edge of her father's desk "I still don't want to hear anything embarrassing, but Michael is still keeping Carla away from me in case I bring her over here, so you had better tell me a little bit of what you stand accused of so I know what it is that we are supposed to be protecting Carla from. It is breaking my heart having her staying with Michael and Monique, but I do agree with Michael that we ought to know what it is that you are supposed to have done"

"What shall I tell you then; I don't know where to start" he said very quietly.

"Come on, where is my sous chef?" Daphne called out happily as she opened the study door "You must have said Happy Birthday by now, we can all have a good chinwag over dinner, if we ever get it cooking!"

luckily she went back out before she noticed their serious expressions.

"Later, Daddy, let's just get through this and maybe we can talk later" Pamela slid off her father's desk. "I do want Mummy to admit she's been to the hospital and to tell me what's wrong. I will say something about her good health and I want you to make some remark about it that will make it necessary for her to tell me.

"OK, if that's what you want" he told her quietly.

"Goodness knows what's up with Daddy" Daphne said as Pamela finished preparing the beans. "He has been very quiet. I wonder whether he is missing the golf club." "It was kind of him to resign so that he could help me more around the house now that Peggy has retired, but there was no need for him to miss the function tonight, it had been planned for at least a year and he would still have been able to go even though he resigned as treasurer"

Pamela didn't know what to say. If she glossed over her father's behaviour now it would be worse when her mother found out about it and found that Pamela had known before she did. She didn't have her father's faith that 'it would all blow over' as he put it. She was well aware from her chats with Sylvie that anyone accused of a crime of a sexual nature almost never recovered from the accusation as people's attitude invariable tended to be 'there is no smoke without fire'. She was also aware that men in some professions such as teaching were automatically suspended while any investigation took place, whether the man ended up being found guilty or not.

"...colour of your front door" Pamela suddenly realised that her mother was talking to her.

"I'm sorry, Mummy, I was daydreaming, what did you say?" she asked

"Your little house, dear, have you had your front door painted yet?"

"What are you talking about?" She asked, rather abruptly

"I know it was just a little council house before you bought it, so I thought you should have your door primrose yellow. My mother, your grandmother, always set great store by a primrose door" Daphne told Pamela. Pamela began to wonder whether coming here had been a good idea. In fact, her grandmother, when she had become unwell, had liked to spend time on a bench she had had set near the old boathouse door where primroses used to grow in the early springtime. Her mother had always grasped the wrong end of the stick where this was concerned. Pamela gritted her teeth and tried to think of a suitable reply but, luckily, before she could reply at all:

"Well, that's everything cooking nicely" said Daphne "For heaven's sake where is Daddy? I am sure the sun is over the yard arm" Pamela wondered how much longer her parents would call each other 'Mummy and Daddy'. It certainly seemed incongruous in the circumstances. She knew that her mother's expression of the sun being over the yard arm meant that she wanted a drink, but she had seen her mother sipping from a glass with clear contents; a bit early for a gin and tonic she thought, but maybe it had been water.

"I'll go and see; I expect Daddy will be ready for an aperitif too" said Pamela

Donald was still sitting in the same position in his study. He was no longer pretending to do the crossword but just staring into space. "Mummy would like a gin and tonic, and I would like a diet coke if you have any and you'd better pour yourself something or she will really start asking questions" Pamela told him as she popped her head round the door and Donald got up wearily.

"OK, Sweetie, I'm coming. Could you bring me Mummy's glass and I'll refresh it" he told her "Oh, so that was gin and tonic Mummy was drinking, then?" Pamela asked, surprised. Donald had not intended to mention that Daphne already had had a couple of gins so he said

"Oh, just a small one. She usually likes a drink while she is cooking"

The evening was as successful as it could be in the circumstances. Pamela gave up trying to get her father alone but did force the issue with regard to her mother's health, and as Daphne was enjoying herself being 'just the three of us as we always were when you were young, Pamela' as she said several times throughout the meal, she hadn't minded filling Pamela in about her hospital visit. Pamela realised that her mother was playing it down, having just said it was a bit of digestive trouble, but at least the hospital tests and the awaited visit with the consultant for the results were out in the open.

Donald, of course, didn't ask any questions about Carla's whereabouts, and when Daphne began to ask about what it was Carla was doing Pamela cleverly deflected the conversation away by telling her parents that she and Carla were going to Brittany for the half term holiday. Naturally she didn't mention the fact that they were being lent the holiday cottage by a friend of Monique's; that would have needed some explanation and anyway, Pamela was trying not to think about Monique's connection to it all.

"Oh, sweetheart, what fun!" was Daphne's immediate reaction to the news, so the conversation for a good part of the meal revolved round the various aspects of 'Pamela and Carla's adventure'. Daphne asked whether Pamela thought her little car was up to it, so she told her that Michael was helping with the arrangements and that he was paying for full European cover just in case. "Hm, after all he's put you through, sweetheart I should have thought he would buy you a new car" was Daphne's retort to this, but before Pamela could think of an answer she added, much to Pamela's surprise "Still, at least yours is a reasonably amicable split; Leticia Fotherington was telling me some real horror stories when she came over with her brother a few weeks ago" as she said this, Daphne's brow furrowed as thought she was trying to remember something.

"More wine, old girl?" asked Donald rather smartly "I think it rather compliments the wonderful spread you two have put on in my honour" he added as he poured his wife another liberal glassful.

"Oh, we only wanted to please you, didn't we, sweetheart?" Daphne told him, nodding to Pamela. She then went on to tell Pamela how good he had been resigning from the golf club and helping around the house with Peggy no longer there to help. She told Pamela how afraid she'd been of telling the Fotheringtons that they were doing their own housework but said how marvellous her father had been in suggesting that they only say they are still looking for someone suitable.

Pamela would usually be getting totally exasperated with her mother's dreadful snobbery by this time. She usually found that after about three hours in her mother's company she was clock-watching and wondering how long she could hold out before telling her mother what she really thought of her shallow friends. Tonight, however, was different as Pamela found herself thinking that her mother would have something far worse to worry about once she found out about her father's alleged sex offence; that would not be something she could explain away to any of her friends. Pamela shuddered.

"Feeling chilly?" her father asked. Pamela realised he had been watching her closely throughout thy meal.

"No, I am fine, thanks" she told him. "I was just thinking that I'd better make a move in a minute, as I have work tomorrow, as you know, and Michael is coming over tomorrow evening to let me have the paperwork for the extra car breakdown cover" she didn't want to say any more, as her father was well aware that, in fact, Carla was staying with her father, but she didn't need to as her father said

"Righty ho, then, you and Carla will be wanting to pack and all that as well if you are leaving on the Friday evening ferry"

"Will you have some more coffee before you go?" asked her mother

"No, thanks, I need to get a good night's sleep, as Daddy is quite right, Carla and I need to pack and I want to sleep well tomorrow night before our big adventure. We'll be sleeping on the ferry Friday night before our long drive, and I don't know how well we will sleep in the cabin; I expect we will both be excited"

This started Daphne off again on the one hand worrying about Pamela and Carla but on the other saying what fun it would be for them. Pamela was just thinking how much her mother really did care for them and that she was really very fond of her but she went on to spoil the moment by adding "and of course, I'll be able to tell Leticia all about how you and Carla are off to Brittany to a little cottage by the sea for the half term holiday."

Pamela swiftly said her goodbyes, brushing her cheek against both her mother's and her father's and as she left she pointedly asked her mother to let her know as soon as she received the date for the appointment with the consultant. She glanced at her father as she said this, he nodded to her in silent agreement that he understood that she was only keeping quiet while she was concerned about her mother's health.

Driving home Pamela felt exhausted. She had to drive with a window open and the radio on so that she stayed alert. Once she arrived home she went straight to bed and fell asleep almost immediately.

Chapter 22

Sylvie cleared a small space on her desk before setting down two cups of coffee. Bernice was on her way for a chat, but she had stopped at her own desk to take a phone call and now was talking on the phone and simultaneously trying to find something buried amongst her paperwork and make apologetic gestures to Sylvie.

Sylvie was relieved that Major Donald's case had been assigned to Bernice; during her visit to Ralph the other evening they had discussed the other team members to whom his case may get assigned, and although Bernice was the newest recruit to the office and Sylvie didn't know her very well she knew that she was an experienced Probation Officer and felt that she was approachable.

June had been very pleased that Sylvie had come to visit Ralph; she had complained that he was like a bear with a sore head being signed off work for a month. Sylvie had been apologetic about bringing Ralph her dilemma but he was quick to tell her that he was very pleased to have something concrete to think about; and he promised he wouldn't get stressed and make his condition worse. Sylvie had looked at June for assurance and she had smiled and said that he was probably just as stressed fretting about might be going on in his absence and that the chat with Sylvie would do him good.

Sylvie explained about Major Donald's case; and about her friendship with his daughter, Pamela. Without beating about the bush she simply said:

"I know you have strong feelings about the use of volunteers, but I wondered whether you might think that in this instance it could be justified". Sylvie waited for a reply from Ralph with baited breath, as she knew Ralph felt strongly against the use of volunteers.

"Possibly, but let's take the situation apart and look at it from all angles" he surprised her by saying. They then spent a couple of hours discussing the various scenarios and possibilities and Ralph had Sylvie in fits of laughter a few times as he was a very good mimic, and gave a couple of very convincing impressions of the other team members.

By the time Sylvie was ready to go home she felt a lot better about it all. Ralph had enabled her to take a step back and look at it like any other case, reminding her that one of the reasons he had so much respect for her was that she was good at her job and had a real empathy with most of her clients just as he had. She laughingly told him as she was leaving: "Much good that's doing either of us: You are too ill to work and I, as my mother constantly tends to remind me, have no room in my life for a partner or prospective husband!"

June had heard Sylvie's parting shot and as she gave Sylvie a hug she had said "You all work too hard and not many people realise how stressful your work is. If the right person were to come along you would find time, but there's nothing wrong with being single;

you just remind your mum occasionally that it's better to be alone than in an unhappy relationship"

As she drove home Sylvie thought about what June had said. She knew that June was right; she and Ralph had a great marriage and the fact that June had been a social worker when they had first met had meant that they had a great deal in common with regard to client confidentiality and the stresses that go with their type of work. June's sister had also been a social worker and was now retired, but she had worked locally and Ralph had promised to find out what he could from her with regard to the social worker who had reported the incident with Major Donald.

Sylvie herself didn't long for a partner; she was quite content with her life, it was just her mother that felt that life was passing her by, as she hadn't done the marriage and children thing. She knew her mother only meant well, but Pamela wasn't the only recent divorcee that Sylvie knew personally and Sylvie decided to remind her mother of this the next time she saw her.

Bernice finished her phone call and made her way over to Sylvie's desk. Sylvie had followed Ralph's advice, and the morning following her visit to Ralph she had come into the office, announced to everyone who was listening that she knew that she wouldn't be assigned Major Donald's case, as she is his daughter's friend, but that she was going to read the case notes anyway before they were assigned, and that if whoever they did get assigned to wanted to chat with her about what she knows of the family then she was willing to do so. That way, Ralph told her, she would shock the couple of officers who would not agree that she should see the notes, but she wouldn't be doing anything wrong and she was being up front to everyone there about what she was doing. Ralph even suggested that one particular officer he was not keen on would, in the same position, have sneaked a look without telling anyone she was doing so, and, much to Sylvie's amusement, he had performed a wonderfully accurate impression of her appearing to be horror struck at Sylvie's openness.

"I'm afraid I think our coffee's gone cold" Sylvie chuckled as she told Bernice

"I don't care" Bernice said and sat down with a big sigh and began to drink the luke-warm coffee "Let's drink it first before we get too involved; then you can tell me what you know about the family. I am due to contact the client this afternoon in order to arrange a meeting with him. I understand why some would prefer to have the first meeting without any prior knowledge to get in the way, as it were, but you've been a friend of the family since childhood, and I'd like to hear your views"

For the next forty minutes or so Sylvie told Bernice what she knew about the family; from first meeting Pamela at school and her first visit to their home when they had not long settled in after their return from Cyprus, to the last time she had actually seen the Major, which had, in fact, been more than twelve years ago at Carla's christening. Sylvie explained the family dynamics as she saw them, but without making judgemental statements about their personalities. Bernice was interested to know the reason for the families' return to the UK and why the Major's hadn't continued in the Army, but Sylvie couldn't help her with that as she had been too young at the time to want to know, and Pamela had never said why they had come to the UK from Cyprus. As two ten year olds new to the school they both had enough to occupy themselves, both with getting to know one another and with settling in, without worrying about why they had found themselves there.

Sylvie explained that although she hadn't seen the Major for years, she had kept in touch with Pamela, so in the normal course of her friendship with Pamela they had kept abreast of any news regarding their families.

Bernice didn't interrupt while Sylvie was talking, but as she finished Bernice went to get them both another coffee, promising not to answer her phone again if it were to ring when she walked past her desk.

As they sipped their coffee, Bernice asked Sylvie a few questions, mostly about whether she'd felt comfortable with the Major when she had visited the house as a child, and again later as a young adult. Sylvie had been asking herself such questions since she had first seen the newspaper article; she didn't find it any easier to answer Bernice, than when she had questioned herself. Bernice was happy with Sylvie's explanation of this, however, and taking the empty mugs to rinse out she went back to her own desk and thanked Sylvie for her time. They had also discussed the possibility of engaging the services of one of the probation volunteers, and Bernice said she'd make the offer to the Major when she saw him.

Chapter 23

Pamela was pleased to be busy as she was very nervous about driving the car onto and off the ferry and even more nervous about having to drive on the right hand side once she and Carla reached France. There was a curious atmosphere at work, but Pamela was just too busy to worry about it. Sandra had returned to work the previous day, Thursday, and Pamela had immediately explained to her that John Meredith had granted her a week's leave at short notice and that she, Sandra, wouldn't have to prepare for month end alone as a couple of other team members had offered to help with the invoices. To Pamela's surprise, Sandra just said quietly "Yes, I know, John told me about your leave next week on the phone while I was off sick, that's fine by me"

Pamela gathered up the invoices that she had been unable to deal with that morning in order to hand them over to Maureen and Joan. She had attached a post-it note to each one explaining what needed to be done during the week she was away. As she passed Sandra's desk she asked her whether she would like to check them but she just waved Pamela away. Sandra was looking very pale and had a bruise on her left cheekbone and everyone assumed it was the result of the fall she said she'd had the previous weekend. As Pamela approached Maureen and Joan's desks, Joan got up, gave Pamela a wink and said "Won't be a minute, why don't you tell Maureen what you want us to do with those, I have some business to sort out with Sandra, we know you want to get away sharpish this afternoon for your adventure"

Gratefully Pamela did just that, and before long she headed off to the car park. She grinned as she saw the GB sticker on the rear of her car that Michael had stuck there for her the previous evening. She had, in fact, had quite a pleasant chat with Michael as he brought her the ferry tickets and apologised that he hadn't managed to get them a cabin. They were all full as it was half term. He had explained that they would have a reclining seat allocated to each of them and that blankets were normally provided, and claiming their seats by puting a blanket onto each one would be a good idea before going to eat at one of the on board restaurants She wondered at first how he knew all this, then briefly annoyed, she realised that Monique would have had a lot of experience of the cross channel ferries. She quickly shook off her annoyance, however, as she realised that this was a chance to be with Carla.

Pamela considered how she would manage to deal with any awkward questions she would have to answer when Carla started to ask how her Granddad was recovering, and, of course, why it was that Pamela could suddenly spare a week away from him. Tentatively Pamela had asked Michael what he had been telling Carla about her Granddad, but he said that, curiously she hadn't really asked. The time had gone quite quickly, with Carla at school each day, and she also had seemed to have made friends with a very small boy next door, to whom she had taken to communicating with through a hole in the fence behind the shed. Michael had added that the little boy seemed a monster, as every time he was taken out anywhere he seemed to have tantrums and screamed the place down, but that Carla seemed to have a way with him. Pamela thought it odd that a child so young seemed to spend a lot of time at the bottom of his garden alone, but she didn't say so to Michael as there were other things to discuss, such as where to find the key to the little house they were to stay in, and what Carla would need to pack to bring with her of the things that she had with her at Michael and Monique's.

Slipping next door quickly to say goodbye to Marian, Pamela went through a mental list to try to ensure that she hadn't forgotten anything. Their previous holidays as a family had normally been as a package trip to somewhere warm and sunny, and they had always asked one another as they left the house "Tickets, passports money?" to ensure that they had the essentials with them. Money was interesting for this trip, as it was nearing month end and Pamela wanted to stick to her 'no borrowing' rule. She had not even thought about getting currency – but Michael had given her a wad of French Francs the previous evening, telling her not to get too carried away, as with about nine Francs to the pound it wasn't as much as it looked. He also told her that there was a bureau de change on the ferry if she wanted to buy some more, so she had cashed some of the money from the account she kept just for the allowance Michael paid in for Carla so that she could spend it on Carla if necessary.

"Oh 'ullo, ducks, you off tonight, is it?" asked Marian as she opened the door and ushered Pamela in.

"Yes, that's right, I'm afraid I can't stay for a cuppa, I don't have time. I just called in to say goodbye and see you soon and to thank you for everything".

"You don't 'ave to thank me for nothing" Marian insisted. I'm only sorry I wasn't 'ere the other weekend when you was so upset and all that".

"Don't start that again" laughed Pamela, we did nothing but apologise to each other when we first met; let's not start that up again!" Marian chuckled too.

"Orright then, you just have a great time and don't you worry about nothin' 'ere. That lovely girl of yours must be wonderin' whether she's on her 'ead or 'er 'eals, with all to toin' and froin'."

Pamela hugged Marian and hurried home to change and pick up her bags. She decided to travel in something comfortable, with the thought in mind of sleeping on a reclining chair, and she hoped that Carla had done the same, as advised, rather than wearing one of the fashionable tops she was so excited about that her cousin Fee had given her. Michael was dropping Carla off, as Pamela had drawn the line at coming to get her from Michael and Monique's. They had estimated that it would take about an hour and a half to get to Portsmouth, and they needed to be there forty five minutes before the sailing time. Pamela wanted to build in as much extra time as possible as she was very nervous about finding the ferry port and getting into the right part of it.

Carla called out "Hi, Mum, I'm here – where are you?" just as Pamela was pulling on her leggings.

"Up here, just coming" she answered. As Pamela reached the bottom of the stairs she stopped in her tracks as she saw Carla standing there not only in rather tight jeans and one of Fee's sparkly tops, but she was also wearing makeup and her hair looked different. Pamela was almost speechless, it was really only a few days since Pamela had last seen her, but she seemed to have grown up in those few days. It wasn't just the clothes and hair and makeup; Carla seemed to have poise about her and she looked stunning. Pamela had initially intended to tell her off for not dressing comfortably, but she looked so radiant, and she was so pleased to be spending an entire week with her and leaving all her troubles behind that instead she said

"Wow, you look good!"

It was the best thing she could have said as far as Carla was concerned, and she seemed to grow another couple of centimetres as she did a twirl to show off. "Come on you" laughed Pamela, "we'd better get going, the sooner I've driven us on to that ferry the sooner I can stop worrying about having to do it" "Oh, did Dad explain to you that it's best to pack a separate bag to take on the ferry as there's no access to the car decks during the crossing?"

"Yes, mum, I've got this backpack ready for the ferry" Carla replied. In fact, it had been Monique who had told Carla all about the crossing, about where they were going to stay and about how much she had loved it there herself as a child, but Carla didn't want to push things with her mum and make too much of the fact that she was beginning to get on rather well with Monique.

The bags safely stowed in the boot and the duvets and pillows on the back seat with the bags to go on the ferry easily accessible they set off with Marian waving to them. Monique was concerned that if there was any bedding at the house it may well be damp, so through Michael, she had advised that Pamela take her own.

Pamela needn't have worried about Carla asking about her Granddad's health; she seemed to Pamela to be almost avoiding the subject. However, Pamela thought that perhaps it was just because Carla was excited about the trip, as she told Pamela at least three times on the journey to Portsmouth that the ferry had two restaurants, a couple of bars, one with live music and a disco. Pamela began to worry that she had underdressed, being comfortable in her leggings and baggy tee-shirt, but she had her make-up bag with her and could dress it up a little with the scarf she had popped in her bag.

By the time they arrived at the ferry port Pamela was infected by Carla's enthusiasm, and, whether that was the reason or not she stopped feeling nervous and just followed the instructions of the ferry crew and they were soon parked up and walking up what seemed to Pamela to be a never ending staircase clutching their overnight bags and a pillow each. It was Carla who had suggested the pillows – Monique had told her it was a good idea as the reclining seats are not very comfortable – but again, Carla didn't want to upset her mum, so she just made a joke of it and said that if she's going to be dancing at the disco she would need a good night's sleep. Pamela was thinking more about the long drive ahead of them on the 'wrong' side of the road, so she didn't need too much persuading to bring a pillow.

The ferry was very full; it was a struggle for Pamela and Carla to make their way to the reclining seating area, especially carrying pillows and bags. They managed it, though and despite being disappointed that their reclining seats were not next to each other, they 'staked their claim' to their allotted seats and left their pillows and some of their belongings on them.

"Phew, that's easier" Carla said, as they proceeded to explore the ferry with a lot less baggage in tow. They spent the next half hour or so checking the menus and prices at the restaurants; initially the great long queue at the self service one had put them off, but quite apart from it being a lot cheaper than the piano bar restaurant there seemed to be more things that Carla fancied at the self service.

It seemed for a while that the queue was not moving at all; then suddenly Pamela and Carla were struggling to find a table with their plates balanced on trays on which the plates took on a life of their own. Carla would have liked a window seat but she was afraid of dropping something and when Pamela spotted some people leaving a table she was happy enough to put down the tray.

Once seated, Pamela began to relax. She had chosen a small bottle of wine to go with her dinner, and as she unscrewed the little metal top and poured some wine into her glass she sighed an enormous sigh. Carla chuckled and lifting her cola glass up in the air she said "Cheers, Mum, well, this is a bit different to flying out to an apartment with all facilities included, I wonder what the cottage will be like, Monique says that the coast is very pretty and the beach is sandy" as soon as she'd said it she wished she hadn't, she'd been trying not to mention Monique, especially as Monique had helped her with her hair and make-up, and she wasn't sure what Pamela really thought. Michael had rushed back from one of his meetings to pick her up and take her home to Pamela's and hadn't noticed that his daughter was looking about two years older.

She mused then about Monique's behaviour through the week. Carla realised that Monique hadn't expected to be setting up home with her new lover with his twelve year old daughter in tow, and she had ranged from being almost childish and sulky to being extremely helpful to Carla, especially with regard to using the washing machine and tumble drier the previous weekend and then to offering to let her use some of her make-up and showing her another way of doing her hair. Carla supposed that she was glad that she would be away for a week. She wondered then whether she would be going back to stay with her mum as she wanted to, or whether her dad would find another excuse to keep her with him. She had been very confused about this business about her Granddad's so called illness, as she had begun to think of it until she had come into the living room quietly one evening and found her dad on the phone to her Uncle George talking about court hearings and probation officers and the like. She wouldn't have taken any notice except that when Michael saw her he immediately changed the subject in that way that adults do when they want you to think that there is nothing going on, but of course that just made Carla aware that maybe the conversation was important and was in some way connected to her.

Carla glanced up at her Mum. Pamela was quiet but had let the reference to Monique go as she was grateful to her for this opportunity to be with Carla. So much had gone on in the preceding weeks that she no longer felt bitter; she had other things to worry about now and she couldn't see the point of blaming Monique for the split with Michael. Maybe it would have happened anyway eventually.

"I'm looking forward to exploring the area around the cottage too" Pamela told Carla "But first we must get there in one piece and that means my getting used to driving on the right and navigating what will seem the wrong way round roundabouts and junctions. We will take it steady, I don't want to push the car too hard, and judging by how full the ferry is it looks like a busy time for tourists. We will take plenty of breaks and try not to get lost. Anyway, never mind tomorrow, what would you like to do once we've finished eating, try out the disco bar?"

That's just what they did do, and a couple of hours later they made their way back up to the reclining chair lounge. It was just as well they had followed advice and checked the seat numbers beforehand, as it was crowded when they got there. Some people were fidgeting, trying to get comfortable and trying to work out how to recline their seats and some were already snoring. A couple of families were trying to settle young children and despite the fact that they were both tired and pleasantly relaxed, Pamela wondered whether either of them would ever get to sleep. Quietly saying "Night night, love, I hope you can get comfy" Pamela made her way to her seat while Carla did the same. They could just about see one another in the soft light if they bent forward a little, and as they were settling down Pamela bent forward to look in Carla's direction and put up her thumb. Carla did the same, so Pamela laid her head back against her pillow to try to get some rest. She tried to let her mind go blank in order to ignore the rustles and snores and whispers going on around her; she knew that if she started to worry about not sleeping then she definitely wouldn't drop off; she reckoned that so long as she could remain very relaxed for at least a few hours she would be fit to drive.

Carla, however, was finding it harder to settle. In the seat in front of her was a mother with a young child who seemed to be about the same age as Benjamin, the little boy next door to Michael and

Monique's. They were not disturbing her at all, quite the opposite in fact; she felt the soothing tones of the mother very pleasant as she tried to stop the little boy who she called Harry asking many questions in a high pitched voice. What was disturbing her was the contrast between the way in which Harry's mother spoke to him in pleasant soothing tones, while all she had ever heard Benjamin's parents do was shout at him in response to his throwing tantrums. She smiled as she thought about what an odd little boy Benjamin was. He had first called her 'fence lady' until she told him her name was Carla Matthews and now when he wanted to summon her to the hole in the fence he always called out 'Carla Maffoos' in full, rather than just saying Carla. Carla thought then about her friend Emily, to whom she had spoken about Benjamin; Emily had said that perhaps Benjamin could be autistic, like her little cousin. Just then, the big chap on the recliner next to Carla turned slightly and began to snore loudly and Carla grinned as she imagined telling her friends all about the trip once she got back to school after the half term holiday.

Pamela heard the large chap next to Carla snoring, so she looked across towards her. The large chap shifted once more in his seat and Carla jerked away from him and stood up rather unsteadily. Pamela watched as Carla scrabbled around for her shoulder bag and rushed out of the recliner lounge. Pamela quickly followed her as she headed to the ladies, and, finding her clutching a wash-basin with her shoulders shaking she was concerned that Carla was ill. Putting her arm round her shoulders, however, she was very surprised to find that Carla was shaking with laughter "Mum, he farted right in my face" she told Pamela "Can you believe it – right in my face!!" and instead of laughing silently she could contain it no longer and was laughing her head off. Pamela, initially shocked and surprised, soon saw the funny side of it and started to laugh as well, but she put her finger to her lips and tried to laugh silently, as did Carla, but the more they tried to be quiet, the harder it was. "D d don't ask me to go back in there, p p please" Carla spluttered between heaving with laughter "If it's not one end with that man it's the other making a noise – there's no way I'm going back next to him".

"I'm not at all sure I could settle down again in there" said Pamela once she controlled her laughter "I tell you what, let's go and see if we can find a vending machine that does hot chocolate or something and then see if there' s somewhere else we can sleep."

They picked their way past people lying on the floor in sleeping bags, each time they heard someone snore or snuffle they found it hard not to start laughing again. Eventually they found a vending machine and got themselves a hot chocolate each. As they were sipping it, Pamela spotted an area between some fixed seats where she thought they might be able to lie down and get some sleep. She suggested to Carla that she sit down there and finish her drink while she, Pamela, went back to the recliner lounge and collected their pillows and things.

When Pamela returned she only had one of the pillows; she told Carla that she couldn't reach Carla's pillow without disturbing the large man and this started her off giggling again. They decided to snuggle down together between the seat and the wall, as it was a little darker there, as the ferry lights were on everywhere except in the recliner lounges. Pamela wrapped her body protectively around Carla's as she had used to do when Carla was very young and couldn't sleep for some reason or another. Carla snuggled her backside into her mum's curve so they were like two spoons and as she sighed sleepily she said "Oh, I do love you, Mum. I don't care what on earth it is you've done, I want to be with you and I will always love you whatever it is." Before Pamela could ask her what the devil she was talking about Carla was sound asleep. Pamela lay awake worrying about it for a while, and wriggled about a bit trying not to feel the hardness of the ferry floor biting into her hip and shoulder; then she snuggled further in towards Carla and fell into a fitful sleep herself.

Chapter 24

Donald fussed around in the kitchen making Daphne a pot of tea. He had met a probation officer the previous day; she had phoned him on the Thursday afternoon and had wanted to make an appointment to visit him at home. The Probation Officer, who introduced herself simply as Bernice, explained to him that she had been tasked with preparing a pre-sentence report, and he, worried that Daphne would wonder what the phone call was about cut her short and said "Yes, I do know about it, but to save you trouble I can come to you". Bernice guessed that there was someone there with him, so she gave him directions to the probation office and arranged for him to come the following day at two pm. Donald just told Daphne he had a client to see and that he had made the appointment to see her at home.

Donald had been extremely nervous before meeting Bernice; he was aware that they would have to discuss the details of his case, and that had been hard enough with the duty solicitor; he felt that it would be even harder and more embarrassing and humiliating to discuss it in detail with a woman.

He was, however, in for a surprise. He was shown through from the reception area into a small meeting room and asked to wait a few minutes. Nervously he'd walked up and down the small windowless room until the door opened again and a pleasant faced, petite, dark haired woman strode in, introduced herself, shook his hand and asked him to be seated.

Immediately Bernice made Donald feel at ease; she smiled at him as she sat down, putting the file she'd carried in with her on the table in front of her. She patted the file, smiled at him again and looking him straight in the eye, she said "I have the advantage over you, as I have read this file, which, incidentally, holds all we have been told about your case. However, it tells me nothing about you, as a person, and as you know I have been tasked with writing a pre-sentence report to submit to the sentencing judge. In order to compile the report I need to get to know both you and the people around you; some of them, your wife, for example, I will need to meet in person so that I can build up a full picture of you for the judge. This will, out of necessity, be as unbiased a picture of you as it is possible for me to produce, as it will, as its name suggests, form the basis on which the judge will sentence you for the crime to which you have pleaded guilty." Donald had been about to say something but Bernice stopped him saying "Yes, I purposely said you had 'pleaded guilty' not that you were. I know there are many reasons a person would plead guilty, so please could you tell me all about yourself, from before the offence was committed. I will not interrupt you unless I really need clarification on something." She smiled straight at him again and told him "I won't take notes, not yet; anyway as I believe there is nothing more off-putting than speaking to someone who is writing.

Donald hadn't known where to start, and said so to Bernice. He didn't feel so at ease now that he had to start speaking about himself. "OK, start by telling me why you have the title 'Major', what you do now for a living, how and when did you meet your wife, what it is like where you live – I have your address, but have never been to Crowford – do you have any children, if so what do they do?" Bernice suggested.

"Goodness" said Donald "I didn't think you'd want to know that sort of thing" he glanced at his watch. Bernice laughed; Donald was surprised; he had expected this to be a very formal meeting, indeed, and this probation officer had a wicked sounding laugh!

"Don't worry" she told him, "I've only booked the interview room for an hour, we don't have a great deal of space here at the office, that's one of the reasons we prefer to meet clients for the first time at home, when possible. I gathered from our telephone conversation yesterday that someone was with you, and you did not want that someone to know about your meeting with me. Would you like to begin there, and tell me who it was that was there with you, and tell me why you did not want them to know you were speaking to me?"

When Bernice stopped him, Donald was amazed to discover that their hour was almost up. He had started by explaining that it was Daphne, his wife, who had been there when Bernice phoned and that he had made out he was talking to one if his insurance clients, so that he could pretend that he was meeting with a client this afternoon. Bernice was no stranger to the lengths clients would go to in order to keep their families unaware of the fact they were in trouble of some sort. With a little gentle encouragement, Bernice had prompted Donald to tell her about himself and about his relationship with those people closest to him.

What surprised Donald most, however, was that Bernice had managed to convince him that, in fact, Daphne had a right to know what was going on. She hadn't made Donald feel in the least cowardly or in the wrong for having wanted to shield Daphne; on the contrary, she agreed that she could see why he had done so, but she had said to him that because he held her in such esteem, and because she had been so strong in their relationship that she deserved to be told. Donald had explained to Bernice what took place at Peggy's house with Maisie; he had even gone into some detail and explained how it had made him feel at the time – something he'd not even admitted to himself before.

Bernice had suggested that he tell Daphne at an appropriate moment over the weekend, and to tell her that she, Bernice, would like to make an appointment to see them both the following week.

Donald had explained that Daphne was unwell and awaiting a hospital appointment, and Bernice had said that was even more reason to be honest with Daphne. "What would you say to her if your court appearance for sentencing coincided with her hospital appointment, and you were then unable to take her, how would you explain then?" she'd asked him.

Donald had realised that she was right; and here he was now on Saturday morning, with Daphne's tea tray ready to take upstairs to her, and an envelope with the local hospital's logo franked on it had just dropped through the letterbox.

Leaving the envelope from the hospital on the kitchen table, Donald made his way heavily up the stairs. He tapped on Daphne's door, but as was customary with her these days she was still asleep. He left the tray on her bedside table and went back down the stairs, muttering to himself "Oh, Daphers, old girl, whatever are we going to do? What and how I am I going to tell you?" He knew she had been unwell again during the night. He had heard her flushing the loo in her en-suite bathroom several times in the night and had, rightly, assumed that she had had a recurrence of the problem that had driven her to see her doctor in the first place: severe indigestion followed by bouts of vomiting.

Back in the kitchen, Donald made himself a cup of coffee and a piece of toast. He put Daphne's letter from the hospital on the table and sat down to have his breakfast. He wondered how Pamela and Carla's ferry crossing had gone, and hoped, guiltily, that their little car would get them safely to their destination on the south coast of Brittany. He realised that it was because of him that they were making this trip; that if it wasn't for his having got involved with Maisie in the way that he had Michael wouldn't have taken Carla away. He thought about some of the things that Bernice had said the previous day. Donald had no idea whether it had been her intention to do so, but she had, in fact, made him feel better about the whole thing.

Bernice's attitude was a simple one: the 'event' as she called it had taken place, it was deemed a crime; Donald had pleaded guilty to it. Now they had to move forward and give the person who was to judge the case, and subsequently sentence Donald, the best information available in order for that judge to do his or her job in the fairest manner. Put that simply, it helped clear Donald's mind, and helped him make the decision to tell Daphne all about it this weekend just as soon as she seemed well enough to take it in

Guiltily Donald realised that, particularly of late, he had been encouraging Daphne to drink more gin (not that she needed much encouragement, he though wryly) so that she wouldn't remember to ask awkward questions about the day the police arrived and took him to the police station. Her drinking, coupled with her constant tiredness due to her bouts of sickness had made it relatively easy to pull the wool over Daphne's eyes. Donald realised now that this weekend he would have to gently remind her and face up to telling her what it was all about.

Chapter 25

"Oh, Mum, have you ever eaten anything soooo delicious?" laughed Carla as she tried to pick up all the pastry crumbs from the little patisserie box in which the lady in the bakery had put the two strawberry tartlets. Pamela's mouth was too full of crumbly pastry and strawberries for her to answer. She looked at Carla's happy face and then laughed too as she took a drink of water from the plastic bottle Carla held out for her.

Pamela had gained in confidence as they had disembarked from the ferry at St Malo and then driven straight out of the ferry terminal and over a small roundabout. She had intended to pull over for a while somewhere in the ferry terminal itself in order to give herself a breather before tackling the traffic, but she had found herself in a long line of traffic and it was easier just to follow. She had felt cold and stiff when she had woken up, still curled protectively round Carla just as they had eventually fallen asleep after their rapid exit from the recliner lounge. The first thing she remembered was the remark made by Carla as she fell asleep, but Carla was so interested in everything on the ferry again as soon as she woke up that Pamela knew it was not the right time to tackle her about it.

After tidying themselves up as best they could in the Ladies washroom they retrieved the rest of their belongings from the recliner lounge, or rather Pamela did, while Carla hid a way down the corridor worried that she would start laughing helplessly if she were to see the big man again who had emanated noises from both ends the night before. They then breakfasted on chocolate croissants plus in Carla's case fresh orange juice and coffee for Pamela before making their way back down to the car deck.

Pamela had a good look at the map while they were waiting to disembark, and she showed Carla the route they needed to take and asked her to check the town names as they passed through to ensure they were going the right way. Carla was happy to do this and together they made good progress until they both began to feel hungry and Pamela realised she needed to take a break. Carla said that the next town marked on the map was called Loudeac, so Pamela followed the signs to the town centre and they found a small but friendly looking bakery where they bought the strawberry tartlets. Pamela had studied French at school, but hadn't been very good at it. She had had so much on her mind and so little time to prepare for this trip that she hadn't even considered the language. She knew enough to be polite, and, in the shop she smiled at the lady behind the counter and pointed to what she and Carla had chosen and said "Deux s'il vous plait"

Carla had been impressed. "I didn't know you spoke French" she told Pamela.

"I don't" she laughed "It doesn't get any better than that!"

When they'd eaten their 'tartes aux fraises' as the lady in the bakers shop had called them, and washed them down with bottled water, Carla mentioned that she could do with the loo. Pamela said she felt the same and that she would like to wash her sticky hands, too, so they locked the car and left it in the little car park they'd found behind the bakers shop and went off in search of one. Finding a small stone building marked 'Toilettes' they tried to work out if it was for ladies or gents. There only seemed to be one entrance and so, bravely, Pamela pushed the door. She was startled to see that there was in fact no toilet there at all, just a hole in the floor with sort of raised places either side as though to put ones feet there, and the smell that came from it was dreadful! "Are you desperate?" she asked Carla,

"not that desperate" she laughed on investigating what Pamela had seen.

"I tell you what" Pamela told her, "we shall need a bit of shopping. Let's get back on the road and next time we find a bigger town we shall see whether it has a big supermarket with a loo."

That is just what they did, and three hours later an exhausted Pamela pulled up outside a long low grey building that Carla was pointing to excitedly saying "I'm sure that's it!" Carla had done a sterling job, not only checking the main towns on the map to ensure that they didn't stray from their intended route, but also guiding Pamela through the small lanes of the last ten miles or so once they left the main thoroughfares. She realised her mum was stressed with driving on the right, although she'd soon settled to it, and also that she was tired having slept fitfully on the floor of the ferry.

"I can't leave the car here" Pamela said, but it was too late, Carla had hopped out and was excitedly moving large flower pots looking for the key. Pamela climbed out of the driver's seat and stretched. Looking around Pamela saw that there was a break in the stone wall that fronted the building, and there was a patch of scrubby looking grassy gravel. She couldn't leave the car in the road as it was not wide enough for two cars to pass, so she got back in and moved the car onto it, hoping that it did belong to the property. There were no other houses around; there had been a few in a small hamlet they passed to get to this one, but this seemed to be on its own.

Pamela walked to the door which Carla was valiantly trying to open with a large key. Pamela caught hold of the large door knob and pulled it towards them as Carla turned the key, and slowly it turned and they pushed the door open.

"Oooh" they both said, at the same time. It was very dark inside, the only light coming in from the door by which they had just entered. Then Pamela spotted a window and they realised all the windows had shutters, which they opened by first opening the cobwebby windows. What they then saw was very basic, indeed, as they had been told it would be; but all the essentials were there. There was a stone sink in the corner of a large room which had a wood burning stove at one end with two easy chairs in front of it and a wooden table with four chairs round it in the centre. There was an old fridge which was propped open and unplugged and a white enamel cooker that looked huge, but on further investigation they saw that this was because there was a gas bottle stored in one side of it. There was a lot of dust everywhere and quite a few cobwebs.

Carla plugged in the fridge but nothing happened, then Pamela remembered that Michael had said she would need to turn on the big electricity switch located above the door. This she did and immediately they heard a strange sound coming from a door at one end of the room. On investigation they found a small shower room, the noise had been the electric pump which activated normally only when the lavatory cistern was flushed, or the shower tray full, but they guessed, correctly, that their turning the power back on had activated it.

They decided to explore the rest of the little house. At the far end of the large kitchen there was another door; this lead to a room with two beds in it; one, a high bed that looked like a small double, the other, set against the wall, a bed that looked more like a sleigh. Both beds were piled high with bedding, some looking like home knitted blankets made of squares, some like large old curtain material. There was a big brown wardrobe at the foot of the sleigh bed, so Pamela suggested they take off all the bedding and fold it up and put it in the wardrobe.

Once they'd wiped the inside of the fridge and the table top and swept through the house Pamela and Carla brought in their bedding, bags and shopping from the car. It was very cold in the house, and beginning to get dark. Pamela had thought to bring a few things from home: pasta, salt and pepper, washing up liquid and a couple of clean cloths and tea towels, and they had stopped at a supermarket and bought some onions, garlic, lardons and tomatoes but she had not thought about anything with which to light the fire. She was very tired by now, and a little dispirited. Carla found a small wooden box next to the wood burning stove, and in it was a box of matches and some kindling wood. "Well done" Pamela told her "Could you scout around outside before it gets too dark and see if you can find some logs or something while I try to get this cooker going?"

Carla came back into the kitchen with an arm full of slightly damp logs. She set to and tried to lay a fire, but it was something neither she nor Pamela had ever done before. Pamela was having no success either with the damp matches and the cooker. Together they searched the little house to see whether they could find any sort of heater, or a drier box of matches. While they were doing this, the door opened and an angry looking man stood there and shouted at them "Que'est-ce que vous faites ici?" and when they looked at him and said nothing, he shouted it at them again, but louder, this time. Pamela's French and her nerve deserted here, and she burst into tears. Carla went to stand by her protectively, but she said to the man, hesitantly, in answer to his asking what they were doing there

"Nous sommes les amis de Monique" but he just said

"Qui?" which Carla assumed was 'who?" and she racked her brain to remember Monique's friend's name, the daughter of the owners of this holiday cottage.

"Monique, les amis de Monique" she tried again. Then she remembered, Michelle, was the name that had eluded her. She said slowly "Nous sommes les amis des Michelle et Monique" and this time a big grin spread over the man's face.

"Ah, les petites, Monique et Michelle" and then he took in the scene, a cold kitchen, Carla with dirty hands and face where she had been trying to light the fire, and a despondent tearful Pamela standing by the cooker with a damp box of matches. "Alors, je prends les choses pour vous-aidez" he said and then he was gone. Carla and Pamela peered out of the door in time to see him jump in his tractor and drive away.

"Well, what was all that about?" wondered Pamela.

"I think he has gone to get something for us, now he knows we are supposed to be here, at least I hope he has" said Carla, trying to cheer her mum up. In fact she was right; just as they were still talking about him the man reappeared in his tractor. He came in to the kitchen with a basket. Setting the basket down he went over to look at the cooker and showed Pamela that she had to turn the gas on at the gas bottle under the cooker before attempting to light it. He lit one of the rings with an

"Eh, voila" and a flourish of his hand, and Pamela set the pan of water on to it. They hadn't found anything that looked like a kettle, but had filled a saucepan with water in order to make tea. Next he gave his attention to the wood burning stove. Taking a bundle of dry sticks and a pack of firelighters out of the basket he showed Pamela and Carla how to build small bits of kindling wood above the firelighter and set a match to it. With another

"Eh voila!" he shut the glass door of the wood burner and stood back as it began to blaze. Soon the kitchen began to warm up and the man, who had in the meantime introduced himself as 'Serge' showed Carla how to operate the air vent at the front that let extra air in when it was needed.

"Merci, merci" said both Pamela and Carla, and after lots of handshaking and smiles Serge left them. The pan of water began to boil, so Pamela made them both tea. Carla didn't often drink tea, but she was cold enough to want a cup now. Although Serge had very kindly left the rest of the dry sticks and the firelighters and dry matches for them, rather than risk not being able to light the cooker ring again, Pamela started to make a tomato sauce to go with the pasta she had brought with her and, once it was bubbling nicely Carla gave her a big hug and asked her if she was OK.

"Yes, love, I'm fine now. Sorry I lost it when Serge shouted, but what with the driving and the cottage being dirty and cold..."

"Enough Mum" Carla interrupted her. "Let's have dinner and an early night and tomorrow we can explore. I think we are quite close to the sea here, and we should be able to walk back to that little village we passed through with the bakery on the mini roundabout if there is anything we need. Then we won't need to take the car out at all for a few days and you can have a proper rest." Pamela agreed and realised that she really was exhausted. She hadn't even noticed the last little village they'd passed through.

Chapter 26

Daphne had come down to the kitchen looking pale and shaky. She had put her tea tray on the worktop and Donald made her some toast and handed her the letter from the hospital as she sat down at the table. "Here you are' old girl" he said "Let's see when your appointment is and we can soon see about getting you feeling better."

With shaking hands Daphne had opened the letter. The appointment was for two week's time and Donald knew then with a heavy heart that he could no longer delay telling Daphne about the business with Maisie; Bernice would certainly not be willing to wait that long to see him and Daphne together, she had made that quite plain. However, Donald wanted Daphne to be feeling a little better before he told her, so he decided to take good care of her for the day, try to pour her weaker gin and tonics that evening and try to get her to eat a little more than she usually did.

Donald decided he'd better come clean and tell her everything, even about Michael taking Carla away and that leading to Pamela and Carla's trip to France. He knew it would upset Daphne all the more, but it did, however, give him a lead in to the subject as he would be able to start off by saying he was wondering how they were getting on, and then explain that there was a reason that they had gone away together.

Unknowingly, Daphne made this easier for him the following morning. She had drunk less than she usually did the previous evening and Donald had said he fancied a dessert so Daphne had made a banana custard and eaten some herself. She had a better night's sleep and was feeling a little better than she had the day before. "I'll have to let Pamela know when my hospital appointment is as she seemed most concerned about my health when she came for your birthday – she made me promise to tell her when the appointment comes, but, of course she and Carla are away, aren't they?"

"Yes, they are away, and it's my fault they are, there is something very serious that I must tell you about..."

"What on earth are you talking about?" Daphne interrupted him.

"Don't interrupt, old girl, this is going to be hard for me. Do you remember when the police came to talk to me and I went with them and you phoned Pamela and she popped over just as I came back home and the Fotheringtons arrived?"

"Of course I do, but every time I asked you about it you just told me it was nothing and it was just a silly misunderstanding. Are you going to tell me now that I DO have something to worry about?" she asked him.

"Yes" he told her "I will tell you everything but please, you must promise not to interrupt until I have finished speaking."

"OK" she said, hesitantly "but I don't like the sound of this – is it Cyprus come again?"

"Oh, don't say that Old Girl"

"Don't 'Old Girl' me until you have told your story, I won't interrupt; get on with it then" she told him, sitting bolt upright and with her face almost rigid.

So he began. "The day after Peggy's dog was poisoned I went to their house to see whether there was anything I could do. Knowing Peggy and Maisie are on their own I didn't know whether they had a friend who would be willing or able to dispose of the dog's body for them. Peggy was out and Maisie was alone. Maisie invited me in and made me a mug of tea but, understandably, she was very upset about having lost Buster and was very tearful whilst making the tea. She took the two mugs into the sitting room and indicated that I should sit on the sofa as the only other chair was piled high with laundry. She started to cry properly then, so I put my mug of tea on the floor and put my arm around her. Soon after that, the most amazing thing happened. She stopped crying, put her mug of tea on the floor too and then she unzipped my trousers and got my old boy out! I'm so sorry, Daphers, but I feel I must tell you it all exactly as it happened. While I was still startled she did no more than put her face in my lap and take him in her mouth. There, I've told you how it happened. I'll not say I'm not to blame as I didn't fight her off, and I couldn't help what happened as a consequence." He paused here, looking at his wife. She took that as leave to speak:

"Well, naturally I find it totally disgusting, but the girl must be twenty if she's a day, so why the police, why the trouble?"

"Because, according to the law, she is diagnosed as 'with learning difficulties', and I know now to my cost that it is an offence to engage in any sort of sexual activity with such a person, whatever their age, just as it is with a minor"

"But can you not explain that she took the initiative, that it was she who started the, the um, activity" Daphne was struggling to find the words. "Well I did try that, but, you see, Old Girl, but I err, went back to see her again, and it was after that her social worker found out and all this kerfuffle started."

Now Daphne became angry "You stupid, stupid man" she shouted at him. "You could have been forgiven for the once, but you just had to go back for more. You filthy, dirty creature! After all you put us through in Cyprus; you have let me down again." She stopped for a moment and took a breath. She was pale and shaking "My God. So who else knows about this?" realisation began to dawn: "You, you beast – this is why Peggy left – and what about the Golf Club? I presume that's why you left there too – nothing to do with 'helping Old Daphers around the house' Oh, you, you, Animal!" she took a few deep breaths and Donald got up and poured her a glass of water and put it on the table in front of her. She ignored it: "and Pamela, she must know then – why has she taken Carla away – what is to happen to me, to our friends, oh my God, it really IS Cyprus come again, but this time we have nowhere to run to…"

Donald tried to speak calmly: "No, it isn't like what happened in Cyprus. That cost me my job. I will have to appear in court to be sentenced for this..." this time Daphne did interrupt him

"Sentenced, why? Is one not still innocent until proven guilty in this country?" So Donald explained the whole thing, why he had pleaded guilty, that he was hoping for a community sentence and that this way it should be kept out of the public domain as it wouldn't be interesting enough to appear in the papers, apart from that article that had alerted Michael and someone at the Golf Club. He explained also that Bernice, the probation officer, wanted to come and speak to them both and would be phoning on Monday to make an appointment to come to the house and see them.

Daphne rallied a little after this, but she was still very pale and shaky. She was less angry now but still very upright and stony faced. She asked Donald a lot of questions, and, once she was satisfied that he had told her the truth and told her everything she told him she needed time on her own to think. She couldn't resist a dig, though: "Well, in the past I'd have packed you off to the Golf Club to give me some time alone. I don't care where you go, but just go out. I need time alone to think."

Donald tried to ask her whether she'd be OK, but Daphne just gave him a withering look and so he put his coat on and went out. He didn't feel up to driving as he was feeling very emotional. He knew he'd let the whole family down. It had been very hard explaining to Daphne about Michael taking Carla first to Eastbourne and then to his new rented house with Monique and that he'd only let Pamela be with her by virtually sending her out of the country. She'd reacted very badly to this news "Oh, so THAT was why Carla didn't come on your birthday – because they all believe you to be a pervert from whom even your own Granddaughter isn't safe!" That last sentence rang in Donald's ears as he walked along the path through the fields. He didn't know where he was going, but he just put his head down and walked.

Daphne sat at the table for quite some time, until she began to get indigestion. Once the discomfort of that began again she thought about her hospital appointment. She had never been one to dwell on her health; until this problem had begun a few months ago she had always considered herself to have the constitution of an ox. She got up from the table and took one of the tablets the doctor had prescribed. She then put on her coat and went out to walk around the garden. This is something she had always done when she had something on her mind. She loved this big old house and garden; it was where she had grown up. She had lived there until her marriage, and, as a young girl had never imagined that she would one day live here after the death of her parents. It was something she'd never thought of when she was young, but circumstances had brought them back here, and she had established a circle of friends she thought of as her equals: this was something very important to her. She had been very disappointed when Donald's career had ended abruptly in Cyprus; she had been hoping he would be promoted and posted on after Cyprus but she had made the best of things on coming back to England and had grown quite content with life as Pamela had grown up into a fine young woman and made a good marriage and given them a lovely granddaughter.

As Daphne walked round the garden and looked up at the house she considered all these things and forced herself to think calmly about what she and Donald could do to minimise any damage to their social standing. She was fond of Donald in a strange way although she didn't have a great deal of respect for him and it didn't occur to her to want to leave him or to throw him out. The garden went all the way down to the river and Daphne spent the next hour or so considering their options and what to say to family and friends as she walked slowly down to the river and sat down on the wooden bench under the trees. The bench was slightly damp but Daphne had far too much on her mind to worry about that. She would normally go into the old boathouse and fetch a dry cloth to wipe it with and a cushion to sit on, but she was so deep in thought that she barely knew what she was doing.

Chapter 27

Grateful that she had been advised to bring her own bedding, Pamela had fallen straight into a deep sleep on the soft bed. Carla had woken first and crept out into the kitchen so as not to disturb her mum. She had intended to boil a pan of water, but was a little afraid of the gas stove, so she filled the pan ready and laid the table for breakfast. She'd had to turn the light on in order to see what she was doing, as she knew the windows and shutters creaked and she didn't want to wake her mum up just yet. Carla poured herself some orange juice and sat down at the table. She didn't have long to wait, as she had just sat down when her mum appeared, yawning, from the bedroom.

Pamela took in the scene; a grinning Carla sitting at the table with her juice, the pan filled and the table set and said "Oh, you angel! I'll just pop to the loo and freshen up and I'll be with you in a moment" Carla opened the shutters in the kitchen and as the natural light flooded in she turned the light off and then went into the little bedroom to do the same. It was a warm morning; it felt warmer outside than in the small stone house so Carla left the windows open. Pamela reappeared, lit the gas and popped back into the bedroom to get dressed.

Carla was keen to explore in the direction of where she thought the sea might be, but once they'd finished breakfast Pamela said "There's a few things we could do with and I know that the shops here may not be open today, Sunday, but, if you don't mind I suggest we walk in the direction we came from last night and see what they have in that little shop you spotted if it's open." Carla was happy to do this. She was so pleased to be with her mum again and she felt rather protective towards her and agreed that her mum shouldn't drive again until she was properly rested and felt confident to do so.

"OK, good idea, I don't think it's all that far away."

In fact it was a lot farther to the little village than it had seemed in the car the evening before, and it took them half an hour to reach it at a fairly brisk pace. However, they were pleased to find that the little bakery was, indeed, open but only until mid-day on a Sunday, and they were pleasantly surprised by how well it was stocked; it had everything they needed except fresh milk, and laughing, the lady produced a litre bottle of sealed non refrigerated milk when, giggling, Carla and Pamela made themselves understood by making mooing noises and gestures. "Du lait" the shop lady had said when she produced the milk. Carla had remembered 'pain' for bread but hadn't known the word for milk.

The two laughed almost all the way back as they carried the bags between them and made mooing noises. Pamela hadn't felt so carefree for as long as she could remember, and when they got back to the little house she suggested they make up a picnic and take it in the direction of the sea.

They put the picnic things in Carla's rucksack and Pamela carried it as Carla ran on ahead. Suddenly

Carla shouted and ran back towards her mum. "Look, look, I'm sure 'plage' is beach – there is a sign that says 'Tahiti Plage' just on that corner up there by that stone wall. Have we woken up in a parallel universe?"

"Well, I don't think so" said Pamela laughing "but let's follow the sign and see what we find."

As they rounded the corner the road narrowed and scrubby looking trees grew along each side of it. They walked on and it widened out again and this time they both stopped and stared; they could see the sea down below and the view was absolutely breathtaking. The road was a dead end and it just widened out into a large car park. A few cars were parked here and Carla and Pamela picked their way through them, past an enclosed area for bins and on along a sandy path. They passed a wooden building and found a path that lead to a bench on the edge of a sandy cliff with grass growing on it. There was an elderly couple sitting on the bench and when Carla excitedly asked her mum whether she thought they could get down to the beach from here, the gentleman on the bench turned to them and smiled and said "Zat way", pointing to the side of where they were standing. Pamela thanked them and they investigated the area where he had pointed and saw a path running all the way down. It took them a few minutes to get down to the beach and when they did they stopped and stared again, as it was a beautiful sandy beach and, apart from a couple of people walking dogs and a young family flying a kite they had the beach to themselves.

"Wow" was all Carla was able to say. "Oh, my, it's fantastic" Pamela agreed. Carla looked at her watch

"Do you realise, Mum, it's only taken us ten minutes to get here; we can come here EVERY day!"

"We can come several times a day, if you like" laughed Pamela. "What would you like to do now?" Pamela asked her. "It's a bit early for lunch, and although it's warm we may get chilly if we just sit still"

"I'd like to walk further that way" Carla told her mum. "See that island that looks as though it's sort of joined to the rocks? And look, there's a spooky looking tower thing up on the cliff" Pamela laughed

"Well, we are here for a week, we don't need to see it all in one day, but let's walk in the direction of the rocks and see how soon we get hungry.

"Done deal" said Carla and happily set off in that direction.

It was quite tiring walking on the sand; and Carla didn't get as far as she thought she would before wanting to stop for a while. The distance to the rocky island was deceptive. Pamela indicated a small cove cut into the rocks and suggested they settle there and have their picnic. There were a few rocks and they selected one to perch on Pamela dug out the baguette and goat's cheese. They shared it and washed it down with lemonade out of the bottle. "That was lovely. Now what's all this..." before she could finish and ask her mum what was actually going on, Pamela cut across her saying

"I wanted to ask you what you meant when you said what you did when we snuggled up on the floor of the ferry to go to sleep"

"Ah, well" said Carla hesitantly "It's pretty obvious that none of this is about my Granddad being ill, as of late everyone even has stopped pretending to give me updates on his progress." At this Pamela looked away, ashamed that they had colluded to lie to Carla, even though they had felt it was in order to protect her. Carla felt that this gesture reinforced the version of events that she had come to believe so again she said "Look, Mum, I don't care what it is you have done, I love you and I will stand by you whatever it is." Pamela looked puzzled

"But what makes you think I have done something?" she asked

"Well, Dad has done his clumsy best to keep me away from you, last Saturday was horrendous and I felt something was very wrong. I just wanted to come home and hug you and see how Granddad was and Dad kept coming up with bizarre reasons not to bring me home and even Monique was puzzled, especially when he almost kidnapped me and made me stay at their new house. Then you just let me collect my stuff and go and a few days later I came in from the garden and heard Dad on the phone talking about probation officers and sentencing so..."

"Good God, you poor thing, I can see why you thought what you did" Pamela said

"Well, what is it then, if not that?" asked Carla beginning to sound strained and tearful.

Pamela realised she would have to tell Carla something close to the truth. Then she realised she still didn't know exactly what her father had done, so she resolved to tell Carla everything that she did know, as it wasn't too shocking and Carla had shown such maturity that she felt she owed it to her to tell her exactly how the present state of affairs had come about.

Apart from the odd snort of disapproval, Carla didn't interrupt, and the snorts of disapproval were not on the subject of what her Granddad may or may not have done, but on the way her dad had reacted by taking her out of school and off to Grandmom and Grandpop's and then the bizarre actions of the previous Saturday. When she did speak she said "My God, mum, so Dad thinks he is protecting me from something obscure that Granddad has done, but I have to lie there listening to him shagging his fancy woman night after night!"

Pamela was too shocked and surprised to tell Carla off for her use of language; not surprised that Carla had heard bedroom activity but surprised that she had that attitude. She didn't like the idea, obviously, that her ex husband who she had truly believed that she still loved when he admitted to his love for Monique and had left her, was enjoying an active love life, and she began to feel angry that he had not realised that Carla would hear them and not considered Carla's feelings.

Carla spoke again "So, we really don't know what it is that Granddad has done?" she asked yet again.

"No," said Pamela "but, as I understand it, it must be something quite bad if he has to go to Crown Court to be sentenced."

"Then I think the most important thing to do is for us to find out, somehow" said Carla. "There must be someone we can ask; what about Sylvie, isn't her job something to do with all that?"

"Yes, it is" Pamela replied, and told her about their meeting accidentally in town. "Anything Sylvie finds out from work is confidential, and she wouldn't be allowed to discuss it with me" Pamela told her. Carla shivered and Pamela thought they'd sat still long enough and were both starting to feel cold. "Come along, lets walk some more, which direction shall we go in now?"

"I could do with spending a penny" Carla told her mum. They packed the cheese wrapper and bottle into the rucksack and walked back in the direction from which they had come. Carla looked thoughtful: "Do you really think Granddad would have touched a child, or forced someone to do something sexual?" she asked.

"I really don't know, anymore" Pamela told her honestly.

"Well, I don't know much about these things" Pamela glanced at her at this, she was hoping her daughter didn't know anything about 'these things' as she put it, she had shocked her enough with her talking about Michael and Monique 'shagging' as she'd put it, but despite being shocked she was secretly amused at her daughter's indignation about it "but Granddad has always been so gentle and kind, I can't imagine his being unpleasant at all, let alone making someone do something they didn't want to do. The only thing that's ever annoyed me about him is that he doesn't stop Grandma nagging me and being horribly snobby and everything – oh, sorry," she said to her mum "That's your mum I'm being nasty about!"

"Oh, that's OK, I've always known what she's like, don't worry" she told Carla "You never know, you see, with a relationship like that what someone pleasant and mild might be tempted to do. I just didn't know what to say; I was so, so shocked when Granddad sort of admitted to me that something had 'taken place' as he put it that I stopped him talking. I just couldn't bear hearing about what he had done, not from him himself. He was a nice dad to me when I was growing up, but he never, ever talked about anything remotely to do with body parts, and, unlike your Dad he never bathed me or even took me to the loo when I was very small. And he and my mum slept in separate rooms for as long as I can remember, certainly they have done so ever since we moved back to England from Cyprus."

"Oh, Mum, I'm so relieved" said Carla for about the fourth time since Pamela had explained everything. "I really thought that it was you who had done something awful and that you were going to be put in jail or something. Can anyone really make me stay away from you because of what Granddad has done?" she asked.

"Well, I don't see how they could, it's just that the whole thing has been such a shock, and Dad sort of whisked you away and we both felt, wrongly, now, I know, that you should be protected from the knowledge of what may or may not have gone on, but I still would like to find out what it is Granddad stands accused of, and I don't propose to tell you all the details when I do find out" Pamela told her.

"No, that's OK, I feel like you do, I really don't want to know exactly what he's done, but I don't know about you, but I think the most horrible thing to have to bear would be if he has done something with a child. In that case I am very sure that I would never ever want to see him again."

"I feel the same way" Pamela told her. "It was most strange spending the evening there last Wednesday for his birthday, pretending to Grandma that all was well and all the time not knowing what it was he had done."

They carried on walking until they reached the little wooden building they had passed on the way down. Carla was delighted to see it was a loo, but sent Pamela in to have a look first before venturing in. "It's OK, said Pamela "A bit smelly, but it is a china loo as we know it!"

They walked on back to the little stone cottage and Pamela put a pan of water on so she could have a cup of tea. Carla took off her trainers and wiggled her feet and groaned and Pamela remembered that she needed a new pair as she had almost grown out of these. "So," said Carla, as Pamela sipped her tea "You do now want to know what Granddad is supposed to have done, and I want to live with you all the time and just occasionally visit Dad and Monique – even if it's just to see how that funny little Benjamin next door is getting on; I think I have a cunning plan" Pamela nearly dropped her cup:

"A cunning plan, where on earth did you hear that expression?" she asked, chuckling.

"Oh, Paul kept saying it that weekend we went to Uncle George's" she told her mum. "Ok, then what is this plan?" Pamela asked, thinking wryly that Carla's cousins had been busy teaching Carla more than just sayings about plans.

"Well, what about my phoning Granddad and Grandma to tell them we've arrived safely and how lovely it is here and to wish Granddad a belated Happy Birthday and apologise for having missed it, and depending on whether he or Grandma answers the phone I can pass you over and you can see if you can ask him about it?" Pamela looked dubious but at the same time was impressed with her daughter's inventiveness.

"Let's just enjoy our holiday for now; there is no phone here at the cottage so we'll have to find a call box. You need a new pair of trainers so we'll have to venture out with the car before too long. If, after thinking about it for a day or two we still think that contacting them is a good idea, we will do so."

"I see your point, Mum, and I know you're not keen to drive over here unless you have to but we're both refreshed now and I may chicken out if I have too long to think about it – Granddad won't think it odd if we phone this weekend to say we've arrived safely."

Pamela took a deep breath "You're right, love. I don't really want to brood on it for days – goodness knows, I've been doing that since I came home that awful evening and you weren't home. Let's walk back to the village with the bakery; there should be a call box there, hopefully.

Chapter 28

Daphne sat on the bench facing the river until she began to feel really cold and she realised the bench was damp. She was feeling a lot calmer now; she had been thinking through an imaginary conversation with her late mother and she grimaced as she felt she could hear her mother admonishing her for sitting on the damp bench. Her mother had been strict and not very easy to talk to, in fact Daphne had never told her mother the full story about why they had come back from Cyprus and asked to stay with them in Crowford; her mother had understood that they had little or no alternative and had welcomed them warmly without asking for explanations.

Daphne's mother, Elizabeth, had inherited the house and grounds from her parents who had at one time despaired that their only daughter would never marry. Elizabeth was an unattractive girl who grew into an awkward young woman more at home with horses and rural pursuits than with the opposite sex. Being what they themselves considered several cuts above the common working men sent out to be killed in the trenches during the First World War, their main worry about the war was that the men good enough to marry Elizabeth were also sent away, lessening Elizabeth's chances to meet someone suitable.

Daphne's father, Captain Charles Brooker, had been wounded and had never completely recovered from his injuries. Like most young men at that time he had been eager to fight for his country and he had shown much bravery and risen to the rank of Captain before being badly injured and sent back to England. Daphne's mother had always been friendly with Charles and was delighted when he eventually recovered from his injuries enough to propose to her and when Daphne came along Charles and his family were thrilled and Elizabeth happily spent her entire marriage caring for him. He was never able to work, but he became passionate about gardening and took great delight restoring the grounds over the years.

Despite her father never having worked, money had not been an issue during Daphne's childhood. The farm abutting their land, known as Home Farm, had brought in some rent and her father had been the youngest of three children but had, nevertheless, still inherited a reasonable sum of money when his parents died within weeks of one another in a 'flu epidemic, and that, added to his war pension gave them enough to be able to maintain a reasonable standard of living. They were not practical people, however; when it came to financial matters, and, unlike many others in their position had neither invested wisely nor made provision for death duties. When Daphne and Donald returned from Cyprus it was to find her mother even more distant and eccentric than she had been during Daphne's childhood, and her father kindly and bumbling as ever but with his passion for his garden dampened by ill health.

Daphne's father had died soon after their return from Cyprus, in 1967. Her mother had lived on for another five years and after her death it had been necessary to sell off Home Farm and the adjoining stables in order to pay death duties. Like her mother, Daphne had been no beauty in her youth, and her parents had been very pleased when Lieutenant Donald Fielding started to show an interest in her. Daphne thought that this was probably why they asked no questions when they returned from Cyprus.

Daphne looked around her now as she stood up and was saddened as she looked at how much smaller the garden was now; it still came all the way down to the river, but she and Donald had sold off a strip from the road to the river in order to fund repairs and alterations to the house, and there was now a high hedge running along the new boundary and a new house the other side of it. But then she thought that they hadn't been able to afford any help, other than Peggy, and Donald hadn't been interested enough in it to keep that part even tidy, let alone pretty, so ruefully she thought it was probably just as well that it was a lot smaller now. It was odd, she thought then; Donald was 'daft' about his chrysanthemums but he grew them in one of the greenhouses, and so long as that didn't fall down he was happy as far as gardening was concerned. Daphne assumed that was typically male; she didn't have a very high opinion of men in general, as her experiences of men had not been altogether very good.

Shivering slightly Daphne dragged her thoughts back to the present and tried to concentrate on deciding how to handle the news that Donald had shocked her with earlier. Her first priority was to ensure that as few people as possible would find out about it, her second priority then was to be ready with a plausible story for those who thought they did know something about it. She had always believed in confrontation rather than running and hiding whenever possible where any sort of gossip was concerned. She felt it was a shame about the golf club, but Donald had resigned and she realised that there was no going back on that. Family, however, were a different matter, and as there was no under-aged person involved she resolved to make contact with Pamela as soon as possible so that she could, in turn, contact Michael in order to let him know that there was nothing to worry about with regard to Carla.

There was, of course, no need as far as Daphne was concerned for anyone to know the sordid details, as she thought of them. She walked purposefully back up towards the house as she thought of this. She resolved to drop into the conversation with anyone that she felt needed to know that there had been some 'unpleasantness' with the daughter of their 'help', the upshot of which Donald had volunteered to plead guilty and was simply awaiting the outcome.

When Daphne stepped into the kitchen she was surprised to see that a couple of hours had gone by since she had asked Donald to go out and leave her to think and she wondered how much longer he would be out. She wished she had some way of summoning him back so she could speak to him now. Once

Daphne made her mind up about something she liked to spring into action straight away; she had never been a particularly patient person. Still feeling rather chilly she decided to have a cup of tea and, sitting down at the table with it she spotted the letter with the hospital appointment again. The appointment was for two weeks the following Monday, and would be with the consultant, who would explain to Daphne the results of her tests, and to talk through any choices regarding either medication or surgery, depending on what the tests had shown.

Daphne got up from the table and wrote the appointment on the wall calendar. She then took the letter into the study to put it in her bureau so she could take it with her when she went to see the consultant. Daphne had always been a controlled, organised person, and she saw no reason to change just because Donald had been involved in something rather sordid. Her experience of men hadn't been very vast, and her mother had had a rather distant attitude to bringing Daphne up, so she had learned the facts of life from the husbandry she had witnessed at Home Farm and at the stables. She hadn't enjoyed the activities she believed a bride was supposed to indulge in with her husband, so after Pamela was born she avoided such contact whenever possible and once she and Donald returned from Cyprus to live in England she told her mother they required separate bedrooms. Her mother never questioned this; the house was plenty big enough and she herself had slept apart from Daphne's father for as long as anyone could remember.

Realising that it could be some time before Donald came home and wanting to keep busy, Daphne decided to pass the time by doing the chores she would normally have done when she first got up. She went upstairs, checked Donald's room which he had left tidy as usual, and then went to make her bed and organise a wash load to put on. She thought then, crossly, about the reason that Peggy no longer came to help out, but she realised that they were, in fact, saving money and that with the new drier, and Donald helping, they were no worse off.

Taking the laundry to the utility room Daphne checked the time and decided to take something out of the freezer for their supper. On doing this, she remembered she had not had any lunch but as she hadn't had a recurrence of the indigestion she decided not to bother. She thought a light supper would be best, so once she'd put the washing in the machine she took some plaice from the freezer and took it to the kitchen. Glancing at the calendar as she passed it she noticed that the only other item showing was Leticia Fotherington's birthday. She knew that the Fotheringtons were going to be away on a cruise for Leticia's birthday, so she decided that she could use the forthcoming birthday as an excuse to invite them round beforehand, and ask a few other friends at the same time. The sooner 'this business' as she had begun to think of was out in the open the sooner it would diminish in everyone's eyes, so she resolved to arrange one of her 'little soirees' as she liked to call them. She would not have them thinking she had not known about it when Peggy had left and they had changed their domestic arrangements to suit. She would drop 'the business' into the conversation as soon as possible when she got them onto the subject of 'domestic help' and would make it sound as much Peggy and her daughter's fault as possible.

Making a mental note of who to invite, Daphne started to clean some small potatoes to cook with the plaice for supper.

Donald had trudged for miles, first as far along the river path as he could go and then towards one of the small villages. When he reached the village pub he realised he hadn't brought his wallet; he'd just grabbed his old waxed jacket as he went out of the door and had neither his wallet nor his keys. He wondered what Daphne would decide to do. He knew she found anything vaguely sexual rather disgusting; she had 'submitted' to it occasionally both before and after their marriage, but Donald didn't have a high sex drive and as Daphne didn't really join in he gave up trying after Pamela was born. He wondered whether he could have explained things any better, but, on reflection, he thought that he had probably explained well enough. Daphne had obviously understood exactly what he had meant as she had asked relevant questions once he had stopped talking.

He turned back towards Crowford. He had considered it to be home for the last twenty five years or so, since returning from Cyprus. He wondered where he could go if Daphne should decide to throw him out. The only friends they had were the people Daphne considered to be their equals; he was aware that she was a dreadful snob but he had always humoured her in such matters as it was very important to her and when she was happy life was peaceful, and a peaceful life was always what Donald wanted. Donald's parents had died many years ago; he had one brother with whom he had never been close; they no longer exchanged Christmas cards and he doubted whether he still had his address. The parental home had been sold and the proceeds shared between him and his brother, but that had been long before property prices had risen, so neither of them had inherited much.

As Donald walked along the path that led back home he contemplated his fate. If 'Old Daphers' should throw him out he would understand; after all he did feel dreadfully ashamed about what had taken place. It had been so long since he had experienced any sort of sexual arousal at all that when Maisie did what she did he was taken completely by surprise. He didn't even think he had had an erection, but, nevertheless, soon he had experienced that wonderful feeling and didn't even want to think about ejaculating into Maisie's mouth. It was with a mixture of both disgust and excitement that he had gone to see Maisie again a few days later, knowing this time that Peggy definitely wouldn't be there as he had chosen to go on one of the mornings that she was at his house, working.

Maisie had simply led him to the sofa and repeated what she had done on Donald's first visit. This time Donald did have a sort of semi erection, and Maisie stroked Donald's penis lovingly before taking it in her mouth and making him come. On Donald's previous visit, when he had gone to see about Buster, the dog, he had left the house abruptly after what Maisie had done. This time, Maisie made tea afterwards, and once they'd had their tea and a couple of biscuits had said that her mum would be home from work soon and that it would be better if she didn't find him here saying; "You're Maisie's special friend, not Peggy's". He had been happy to leave, as he was very confused about his feelings. He felt that what had taken place was wrong, but he had felt compelled to visit again just to see what would happen. The first time he had visited he had parked his car as close to Peggy's house as possible, as although he had not mentioned the fact to Daphne that he was going there it was, in fact, with the best of intentions. This time he had parked his car a couple of streets away, and even that had added to his sense of anticipation. Now, of course, as he walked back towards his home and contemplated the shame he felt and how it had affected the family; both Pamela and Carla were his pride and joy, never for a moment when he went back to Maisie for that second visit did he think that anyone would find out. He had wanted to explain things to Pamela when she had confronted him in the garden but she was too embarrassed to want to know any details, then when she had tentatively asked about it on his birthday Daphne had interrupted them before he could explain. He didn't like the idea at all of Pamela knowing exactly what had happened; he cringed at the thought of that, but he would have explained that something had taken place with a young woman in her twenties, just so that Pamela wouldn't think that he had done anything with a child. The thought of this horrified him, as did the fact that Michael had thought him capable of such a thing.

He wondered again where he could go. Perhaps it would be better for them all of he just disappeared; maybe he should head for London? Perhaps he could go to an ex-serviceman's club, he still held the honorary title of Major, and he had resigned in Cyprus when asked to do so. He doubted whether any records still existed after all this time that would have details of why he was asked to resign; maybe this was the answer? He could go and find somewhere to stay that he could afford with his meagre pension. But then, what if old Daphers insisted on a divorce? He had heard that divorce was very expensive and, apart from a very small share of an inheritance from the sale of his parents' home, his pension was all he had.

Not having taken a key, Donald walked round to the back door with a heavy heart wondering what frame of mind Daphne was in and whether he would have to pack his bags and leave immediately. He did not think about any legal rights he might have with regard to his home; he knew it was Daphne who had inherited it and did not feel that it belonged to him in any way. As he hesitated with his hand on the back door handle Daphne turned to get a saucepan from the rack and said "Oh, there you are, old thing. I didn't know what you'd want for supper so I've got plaice out and thought we'd have peas and potatoes, is that OK?"

Donald was amazed. Daphne seemed really chipper as she put the potatoes in the pan and bustled round the kitchen. "I've decided it's time we had a little soiree and you can help me decide who we should invite. How about you pour us a couple of substantial G&T's and we can sit and discuss it." Donald hung up his old coat in the utility room and went off to get the drinks. He didn't have his customary tonic only, wondering whether this was the lull before the storm, or whether old Daphers had finally gone off her rocker. He decided that, either way, he needed a stiff one himself so did as she had requested and poured two large gin and tonics.

"Here, I have the ice and lemon ready" Daphne told him taking the glasses off him and adding the ice cubes and a slice of lemon to each glass. "Now, sit yourself down and have a drink, you look exhausted" she told him. He didn't know what to say. He had been contemplating a very bleak future, indeed, and here was Daphne acting as though nothing untoward had happened at all. "I've had plenty of time to think, and we must act normally and face this out" Daphne got a packet of cheesy biscuits out of the cupboard and sat down at the kitchen table with Donald. "I don't suppose you had any lunch, so let's nibble these while we wait for an early supper to cook" she told him. "Mummy always said if one can't run one must fight, so fight we will. We will invite all our friends, and drop a version of 'your little business' into the conversation, indicating, of course, that it is Peggy and Maisie's fault that it happened. We all know that Maisie is illegitimate and, obviously, Peggy has not brought her up in a decent manner."

Donald's face was flushed with the warmth of the kitchen, after his cold walk, and with the effects of the unaccustomed large gin. He didn't know what to say. Daphne bustled about the kitchen setting the plaice to grill, checking the potato pan and boiling the kettle to add water to the pan of peas. He could tell by the set of her shoulders that she was, in fact, still distressed and he wondered how he could reach out to her. He was still trying to think of something suitable to say when the phone rang. Not at all sure that Daphne's idea of a 'little soiree' as she liked to call it was a good idea, and worried that it could be someone from Daphne's circle of friends calling he tried to get to the phone to answer it before Daphne did. She got there first, however, as she was closer to it and moved faster.

"Oh, hello sweetie, yes he is here" he heard her say "but is mummy there with you? Oh good, could I speak to her first, please, and then you can wish Granddad belated birthday greetings in a minute." Donald sat transfixed, wondering what Daphne was going to say to their daughter about what had taken place.

Chapter 29

Carla handed the phone to Pamela. She didn't say anything, just pulled a face. Not knowing what to expect, Pamela said "Hello?" tentatively.

"Hello, sweetie" said her mother "I know Carla wants to speak to her Granddad to wish him a belated happy birthday and she can in a minute, but Daddy and I have been talking about this silly business that he was involved in and we wanted to put your mind at rest and get you to contact Michael to do the same for him so that he doesn't worry about Carla any longer" Pamela was stunned.

"So, you know all about it then? She asked her mother.

"Oh, yes, and I have my hospital appointment, it's for two weeks on Monday and I did promise to tell you, didn't I?" Pamela then realised what had happened. The letter for the appointment had come through and her father had felt compelled to tell her mother, but her mother seemed to be taking it all surprisingly well. Pamela didn't know whether she wanted to hear any details, but if she was to sort everything out with Michael, and have some sort of a version to explain to Carla herself, then she would have to know.

"Go on then, Mummy, what is it I need to know?" she asked.

Carla stood waiting patiently while Pamela listened for a while without speaking. Then Carla heard her mum asking some questions about court and probation and she tuned herself out and watched two old men walk across the little village square towards each other, greeting one another with smiles and hand shakes they tottered off into a dark-looking bar. Then Pamela was handing her the phone and saying "Here, Granddad is on the line for you".

"Hullo sweetie" her granddad said, "I hear you had a safe journey and that you like it there in Brittany?" she thought he sounded rather strained, so she told him she liked it a lot, wished him a belated happy birthday and asked him if he wanted to speak to her mum again. "No thanks, you two just have a great week and we will see you soon when you come home" he said and then he had hung up. Carla looked askance at her mum.

"Come on, let's get back to the cottage" Pamela said to her. Carla noticed the tight set of her mum's jaw and decided not to ask any questions. Pamela would explain what she needed to know when she was ready. Carla was just happy to be with her mother and staying in such a nice place.

Pamela was quiet as they walked back. She had said as they walked out of the phone booth that they would relax and enjoy their holiday in the little stone cottage by the sea and that she would tell Carla what her grandparents had said about 'the trouble' later that evening when they sat down after their evening meal. Carla was curious about what it was her granddad had done, but was happy to wait until her mum was ready to tell her.

It was turning quite cold again as they reached the cottage. Carla was laying the basis for the fire as Serge had showed her the previous evening and Pamela was looking in the cupboard deciding what to cook for their tea when Serge walked in having tapped on the door shouting "Bonsoir, c'est moi, Serge" as he pushed open the door. "Oui, oui comme ca, c'est bien" he said approvingly as he watched Carla light the end of the kindling with one of the long matches he had left for them the previous evening. "Et, maintenant, venez avec moi pour prendre un aperitif avec ma famille" he said to them with a big smile. Pamela and Carla looked at one another but neither of them had understood what he said. Serge waited a while for the fire to flare up and then settle down; then he put on a couple of logs for them, shut down the little vents at the front and tried sign language. He made them laugh with his antics and soon made them understand that he wanted them to follow him. He make quite a pantomime out of it and had them in fits of laughter as they realised he wanted them to climb up on the cab of his tractor with him.

"Well, there's a first time for everything" laughed Carla when Pamela said she'd never been on a tractor before. Serge laughed too as if he had guessed what had been said and showed them both where to hold on while he reversed the tractor, turned round and set off across the field behind their little house apparently into the middle of nowhere. It was beginning to get dark, and as Serge took a sharp turn a farmhouse could be seen the other side of another field and Serge indicated with his hand

"Ma maison, là-bas". Carla understood that; he had said that was his house, over there.

They were still wondering why he was taking them, but Pamela thought she had caught the word 'aperitif' when he had said the long sentence in their kitchen, and she was quite right, as when he parked the tractor to the side of the farm house and helped them down his wife came out and fussed around them ushering them into the large warm kitchen where there were bottles, glasses and dishes of crisps and nuts on the table. Serge introduced his wife by pointing to her and saying "Marie Therese" and then pointing to Pamela and Carla in turn and struggling with their names for his wife to repeat. Marie Therese was a tiny woman; very pretty with very black short hair. She had a loud voice, however, for one so small, as she turned towards the stairs and shouted "Eloise, Jean Pierre, maintenant, no invités sont arrivés". Suddenly footsteps thundered down the stairs and two teenagers appeared grinning hugely.

"How do you do" said the boy, with a smile and kissed them both on both cheeks. "I am called Jean Pierre and this is my sister Eloise" and Eloise also kissed them both on both cheeks.

Pamela had thought the previous evening that Serge was much older, but she realised that his face and hands were roughened by hard outdoor work, and that he must only be in his forties. "Alors, Kir Breton ou limonade pour les enfants, et pastis pour les adultes" said Serge starting to pour generous measures of a clear dark yellow liquid into some long glasses. "Oui, Kir Breton, s'il te plait" said Jean Pierre. He then said to Carla "Eees very good, you like?"

"Uh, I don't know" Carla answered.

"Bon, you try" answered Jean Pierre.

Marie Therese indicated that they should all sit down, and Serge added ice and bottled water to the drinks for the adults and they turned cloudy whitish. He then poured a small amount of a dark red liquid into three smaller glasses and added something pale brownish in colour from an unmarked bottle and the drinks turned pink. "My fazzer make 'imself" said Jean Pierre trying to be helpful "Iss very good" but neither Pamela nor Carla could make out what either drink was. Pamela and Carla shyly took their drinks as they were handed them. Marie Therese was bustling round preparing things in the kitchen and Pamela hoped that they were just there for the before dinner drink and not for dinner itself. She was relieved that Jean Pierre and his sister spoke a little English, but she suspected, rightly, it was limited to what they were learning at school, and wouldn't stretch to a great deal of translation.

Once they all had drinks in front of them Marie Therese sat down, and Serge lifted his glass and said something that sounded like "Yermat" but they later found out it was the first Breton words they had learned and was actually "Yec'hed mad" and literally meant 'health good'. Once they had all clinked glasses and repeated the Breton words they began to drink. Pamela quite liked hers; it tasted of aniseed and reminded her slightly of ouzo, something she'd had many years ago when she'd gone on holiday to Crete with Sylvie when they were still at college. Carla liked her drink; it tasted rather like apples and blackcurrants and felt pleasantly warm as it went down.

They had a very enjoyable hour. They all had two drinks each, were encouraged to eat lots of the crisps and nuts that were on the table, and managed to have a conversation of sorts with the help of Jean Pierre and his sister Eloise. Serge managed to explain, partly through Jean Pierre and Eloise's translations and partly through Serge's amusing sign language that he had always lived in this house and that he remembered with great fondness the visits Michelle and Monique used to make to the holiday cottage when they were all children.

They found that they were honoured, as Serge had been sent to find them at mid-day, the preferred time of the family for eating their main meal on a Sunday, but, as they weren't at the cottage the family had put off having their meal until the evening so that they could share their 'apéro', as Eloise called it, with them.

Serge helped Pamela and Carla back up on to the tractor and drove them back across the fields. This was after much handshaking and kissing and many "Au revoirs" and "Mercis" and then "Kenavo", which they were told was Breton for 'au revoir', from Pamela and Carla. He saw them safely back into the cottage and nodded approvingly when he saw that the little wood burning stove was still burning. With a friendly wave he drove his tractor back home across the fields for his dinner.

"Wow, that was fun" said Carla

"You can say that again" laughed Pamela "I think that pastis must be jolly strong, I feel quite squiffy, I hope you don't want anything too complicated to eat!" Carla plonked herself down on one of the chairs

"Well, I don't know what it was we 'enfants' were drinking, but it was not innocent like lemonade, I can assure you" she told her mum, laughing. "Goodness, you too?" Pamela asked.

"Yes, I haven't felt like this since that time Paul added vodka to the bottle of coke in the fridge for a prank three years ago. Actually, I'm not all that hungry, having eaten all those crisps and nuts." She told her mum.

"Well, we need to eat something to soak up all that alcohol" said Pamela as she checked the cupboard where she had stored their groceries "How do you fancy sharing a tin of beans and sausages with some of that crusty bread?" "Great" said Carla "Something very English after a very French experience, I'll lay the table and get the bread out while you warm up the beans and sausages"

They chuckled their way through preparing and eating their tea and followed it up with a couple of the yoghurts they had bought at the little corner shop that morning. "Oooh, much nicer than the yoghurts we get at home" Carla enthused. Pamela smiled. Carla's cheeks were flushed quite pink from the unaccustomed alcohol and from the warmth of the wood stove. Pamela hadn't forgotten that she'd promised to tell Carla what she had learnt from her phone conversation with her parents, but Carla seemed to have temporarily forgotten and she looked so sweet and innocent that Pamela couldn't bear the thought of reminding her. Instead she made them both a drink of hot chocolate and suggested an early night.

Chapter 30

Pamela woke up first on Monday morning and crept out to the kitchen closing the bedroom door as quietly as she could behind her. She wondered, not for the first time, how on earth Monique's friend Michelle's parents used to cope in this tiny cottage when they used to come for the summer with lots of friends. From what they understood the previous evening at Serge's, when the family used to bring loads of friends the children used to camp in the little back garden, but, even so, with such basic facilities, they would have had their work cut out managing. However, from what they learned from Serge it sounded as though the little house was always filled with laughter whenever the holiday makers were in residence.

Opening the shutters, Pamela saw that it was raining so she decided to light the wood burning stove. It was her first attempt as Carla had lit it under Serge's instruction the two previous evenings. She suspected that Carla would probably sleep for quite a bit longer, so she put the pan on and got out the books she had brought with her to see which one she would like to read first. Pamela didn't read very often but did really enjoy a good novel when she could relax and lose herself in the story.

This morning would be a struggle for Pamela as she didn't want to rush Carla; she wanted her to wake up in her own time but she had resolved to tell her a version of what her mother had told her on the phone the day before and then ring Michael to tell him exactly what her mother had said, and to tell him emphatically that Carla was to live with her as they had first agreed, and that she would visit him as often as both he and she wanted. Naturally, Pamela was eager to deal with these issues, but to help pass the time she would allow herself to become absorbed in one of the books. There were five to choose from; she had happened to mention that she would need something to read when Maureen had asked whether she was packed and ready to go and so Maureen had very kindly asked around on her behalf and about a dozen books appeared from people's desk drawers. Some she had already read, a couple she didn't fancy at all as she didn't like science fiction or anything with too much violence and she had ended up with five that she really thought she would like. She was sure that at least one of them would be absorbing enough to take her mind off the day ahead.

The wood burning stove was not burning very well, so Pamela opened the little grills at the front and put some more of the small dry twigs on. She made her cup of tea and settled at the table to choose her book. There were a couple by authors with whom she was familiar, the first book of a trilogy by an author she didn't know but whose historical novels had been televised and had been very popular about fifteen years previously, although she hadn't watched it, and a thriller and a court room drama which she had originally turned down as 'male reading' but Rob had suggested she might like them as his sister had not wanted to read them at first and when he got her to try them she found that she loved them. Not wanting to read something predictable today Pamela chose one of Rob's books. She checked the wood stove which was now going well and then settled down to read. She struggled at first as it was something she was totally unfamiliar with; it was fast moving and American but after a couple of chapters she was hooked.

Pamela didn't hear Carla opening the bedroom door and almost jumped as she said "My, you look cosy, excuse me, I'm dying for the loo!" as she nipped into the little shower room. She looked very sleepy when she emerged a few minutes later.

"How are you feeling?" Pamela asked her.

"Fine, thanks, a bit sleepy, but I don't think I have a hangover. I still don't think I want to make a habit of drinking, though" she told her mum.

"I should jolly well hope not, at your age" laughed Pamela.

"No, and I suggest we don't mention it at all to Dad when you phone him to talk about Granddad, and my coming home to live with you, we don't want to give him anything else to worry about!" Carla said to her. "I'm really thirsty and I don't fancy orange juice. Is it OK if I have some coke?" Carla asked.

"OK, just this once, but you know I'd rather you didn't have it for breakfast" Pamela said.

"Breakfast? Have you seen the time?" Carla asked.

"Good grief, how did that happen?" Pamela said as they saw that it was almost mid-day. "Are you hungry?" she asked Carla. Carla said she was starving, so Pamela made them both scrambled eggs and as the bread had gone hard she cut it into strips and held it over the gas flame until it toasted and she buttered it and served it with the scrambled eggs on top.

When they had both eaten, Pamela cleared away the plates and sat back down at the table. "Go on then, Mum, I'm ready" said Carla correctly guessing that her mum was ready to tell her about her granddad. So Pamela explained gently but in a faltering voice that her father had become 'involved' with May, the daughter of Peggy, but because May was diagnosed as having 'learning difficulties' this was against the law so it was an offence whether that 'involvement' was consensual or not. Pamela made sure that Carla understood the meaning of consensual, and Carla asked a couple of questions to help her understand the whole issue, and once they both felt the subject had been explored fully they decided that nothing was to be gained by going over it again.

"You will talk to me about it if you want to, won't you?" Pamela got Carla to promise.

"Yes, if I have a bad dream or something I will let you know. But I know how awful it is for you, so don't worry about me, just call Dad this afternoon and tell him what we now know and make sure he knows I am in no danger from Granddad and that I want to come home and live with you properly" she said "I don't ever want to go through another weird day like the day Dad and Monique moved in together.

"Don't worry, love, I'll try phoning him today and I will tell him what I've found out. I'm absolutely sure he had your best interests at heart, but by law he can't keep you away from me" she assured Carla

Chapter 31

"Oh, god, I love you!" Michael said to Monique as he looked at her lying languorously in the crumpled bed

"Mmm?" she asked, sleepily.

"Don't 'mmm' to make me repeat it – I know you like to hear me say it so; I love you, I love you, I love you" he said as he jumped back onto the bed on his knees and bounced up and down. "Come on, get up it's gone nine and we both need some fresh air and exercise!" he told her. "This is the first full day you've had off in ages and I suggest we go somewhere for a really nice walk."

"Mmm, OK" Monique said sleepily but she tried to snuggle back under the duvet

"Oh no you don't" Michael said as he tried to dig her out from under the duvet. But as his hand brushed her breasts he became aroused as he felt her nipples harden and she pushed the duvet out of the way, pushed Michael onto his back and sat astride him.

"You want to do what, today?" she asked

Two hours later they finally set off for Burnham Beeches, somewhere that Monique had never heard of, but was apparently a favourite haunt of Michael's family when he was growing up. Monique always tried hard not to ask questions about the places that Michael used to go to with Pamela, but she instinctively felt that this was somewhere he remembered as a boy and not somewhere he had gone much with Pamela and Carla. She realised from the things Michael said and the way that he acted that he had changed very much since he had met her, and she didn't like to push him into telling her about his life with Pamela unless he was in a reflective mood, and, even then, she would sometimes stop him as he did feel guilty about the end of his marriage and the effect it had on both Pamela and Carla and he would become quiet and a little withdrawn.

"Well?" Monique asked him "Is it how you remember it here?" Michael had parked the car and they were walking along a wide path.

"I don't know yet, it doesn't feel right yet. I want to find the places we can walk through loads of scrunchy fallen leaves, then it will feel like I remember it, rather than like a tidy tourist attraction" he told her. They started to walk briskly and at first they tried to walk in step, but Monique's legs were not as long as Michael's and she had to make a little hop every now and then in order to stay in step with him. Tiring of this, she playfully punched his arm and said

"come on, I thought you said you needed exercise?" and began to run. They were soon in amongst the big beech trees and Michael veered off the path they had taken from the car park and said

"come on, this is what I wanted you to see with me" and he shuffled through the crunchy beech leaves and picked handfuls of them up and threw them in the air.

"Tu es fou" Monique told him, reverting to her native French as she laughed with him enjoying his playful mood "You are mad" she repeated in English in case he hadn't understood.

"Oh, I understand fou, alright" Michael told her. Then he looked thoughtful and said that he wondered how Pamela and Carla were getting on in Brittany.

"Well, I know you said you weren't going to do any work today, but you could always check with your answering service to see whether Pamela has left a message for you – you did give her that phone number, didn't you?" Monique asked.

"Yes, I did, I didn't think it would be fair on either of you if she phoned and you answered" Michael answered. He looked at his watch. "I tell you what, lets walk for another half an hour or so and then we'll find a nice little pub and have some lunch, then we'll look for a call box afterwards and I'll make that call. You know, I've been wondering whether it would be worth my while buying one of those portable phones that you can have in the car. I know I don't want to spend too much out on the business as I am getting it going, but not actually having an office with staff to take any messages may turn out to be hampering my progress.

"Wow, is the great company man asking my advice, now?" Monique asked him playfully.

"Sort of" Michael said "After all, you have a lot of knowledge of the fitness business and you know how hard it is to organise calling people back within office hours, and the answering service I'm paying for only works during normal office hours. The fitness business is not something that operates within that sort of timescale."

"OK, I have quite a few suggestions to make, but I want you to take them seriously and think about them, so I suggest we enjoy our walk now, and discuss your new business over lunch." Michael was quite surprised. This was the first time Monique had let him know that she had some ideas about his new business and he was intrigued. He agreed, though, that it was a good idea to wait until they were ready to have lunch.

Monique was very pleased that Michael was happy to listen to her views. She understood that he had found a good niche in the market and she believed he was right to try to fill it, but she had misgivings about his ability as a salesman; Michael was a very good accountant, good enough to have been made Finance Director of the company he had just left to start up on his own, but Monique didn't know whether he had the right manner to gain the confidence of the people that he would need to impress with his business propositions in the fitness world. It was one thing having the ideas, and, at present, people were willing to see him to see what he had to offer as he was known to come from one of the big providers of leased, maintained and sold gymnasium equipment, but Monique knew that most people were currently agreeing to see him because he had 'novelty value' because of who he was employed by before, and she wasn't sure he had the right personality to keep gaining access in his own right to the people responsible for the purchase and maintenance of the equipment he was hoping to provide.

Monique tried to bring back Michael's playful mood by shuffling in the fallen leaves and teasing him about his level of fitness while reminding him that they had been very active in bed that morning, but he was a little quiet, despite her best efforts, and she understood that he was probably thinking about Pamela and Carla. She was just pleased that her idea had worked, and that they were now able to have some time to themselves, especially as they were now, at last, living together. She hoped vehemently that all was going well with Michael's ex wife and daughter; Michael wasn't aware, but, in fact, Monique had made a great sacrifice by suggesting that they stay in the little stone cottage by the sea where she'd spent so many holidays as a child. She had very much wanted to take Michael there and show him all the secrets that the place had to offer, but now she would always know that Pamela and Carla had stayed there before she could take Michael. Inadvertently Monique shuddered as she shook off the thought and told herself not to be so silly, but to enjoy the week alone with Michael and to hope that some agreement could be reached whereby Carla could go back to live with Pamela and just visit them occasionally. She liked Carla a lot; there was a lot of Michael in her and she loved Michael unconditionally but that didn't mean she wanted Carla with them all the time.

"Are you cold?" Michael asked her having noticed her shudder "Come on, let's speed up a bit, we're nearly back where we parked the car. What do you fancy for lunch – what sort of pub shall we look for?"

"I'm fine" Monique told him "But I am hungry – what about somewhere that does nice pasta – a nice lasagne, or something" Monique suggested.

"Good idea, I think I know just the place, unless they've converted it to one of those gaudy places that serves plastic tasting food!"

"Yes, and its half term, we don't want somewhere full of screaming kids" As soon as Monique said it she could have bit off her tongue. She needn't have worried, though, as Michael just laughed in agreement with her.

Half an hour later they were seated in a quiet corner of a nice old pub with half a lager each and a large notepad on which Michael was writing notes as they awaited their order of lasagne with a side order of chips for Michael and salad for Monique. Monique had teased him "What's the point of all that exercise if you are just going to eat more?" she'd asked him. But he had just said he needed his sustenance in order to keep up with all her energy and she said to him that she couldn't argue with that. Then Michael had said "Come on, then, let me have some of your ideas about the business. What do you think about my investing in a portable telephone for the car, for example?"

Monique then proceeded to surprise Michael by the depth of her interest in his new business and the extent of her knowledge of the fitness business. She put him through his paces with regard to his business plan projections and finances as though she were a prospective investor, and, in a way she was, as when she tactfully suggested he may not be as good a salesman as he was an accountant, she suggested that she could, perhaps, do less hours at the gym and become his representative on a part time basis until the business really took off. Michael was thrilled. He was well aware that he may not be the best person to promote his ideas, but he was fully confident, as was Monique, that there was a niche in the market for what he was promoting so he readily agreed that Monique should become involved straight away. "I have an appointment at a large gym in Beaconsfield tomorrow" he told her "What time does your shift start tomorrow?"

"Not until 3pm as I'm on until 10pm" she told him

"Good. My appointment is for 11am, how about we go together? I'll introduce you and let you start the negotiations, if you like?"

"Excellent, I'd love to" Monique said. "What are you hoping to sell them?"

"Not sell, this time. I know that the lease is almost up on some equipment they have, and they will be given the chance to buy it, but I can offer them a better deal on a new lease on some new equipment."

Their meals arrived and Michael pushed his notebook away so the waitress had room to put the dishes and plates down. "I tell you what" Monique told him "If we are successful tomorrow how about looking at prices of portable car phones? We could deduct the cost of the messaging service and see whether it would be worthwhile financially. It would certainly make contacting you easier and we could, maybe, have new business cards printed with our home phone number and the car phone number on"

"Don't get too carried away" Michael said "Don't forget we only have the house for six months; Dave the owner is only on a six month contract in the states – he won't want to come home to our business calls! You've got me thinking, though, I wonder whether we could have a second phone line put in with a new number, and then take that number with us when we buy our own house?"

"That's a good idea, so long as that doesn't cost too much. Now, let's enjoy our lunch and our day off together and stop talking about the business." Monique said as she tucked into her lasagne. She knew that Michael would check with the messaging service after lunch, in the first instance to see whether he had any business calls, but also to see whether Pamela had called. He had asked her to let him know whether all was well, both with the car and with the little cottage. Pamela had not promised to do so, though, as although she was grateful to be able to be with Carla she found Michael's apparent need to control the situation very irritating.

Wanting to try to lighten Michael's mood Monique asked him "So, how old were you when you last walked through the leaves in Burnham Beeches, then?" It did the trick, and Michael spent the rest of the lunchtime telling her about his antics with his brother, George, when they were small. George was far more adventurous, and she thought, reading between the lines, more fun loving than Michael while they were growing up. However, as she had now met George, and spent a weekend with him and his family she felt that George was the more serious of the brothers. It was since Michael had had time to tell her about his childhood and a little bit about his meeting Pamela and his life with her and Carla that she had learnt that the Michael she knew was not the Michael that the rest of the world knew.

Chapter 32

"I can either take a message or ask Mr Matthews to call you back" said the annoying voice on the end of the phone. Pamela tried again.

"I don't have a number that he can call me back on" she told the messaging service lady.

"Then what DO you want me to tell him?" she asked. Pamela wondered, wryly, what the messaging lady would say if she were to tell her all about her father and of what he was accused. Instead she told her

"Please ask him to ring me on this call box number at 4.30pm your time. I will endeavour to be here to answer it and that should give him plenty of time"

"And who shall I tell him he is calling?" she asked. Pamela seriously didn't want to sound like the ex-wife that she was so just said

"Pamela Matthews" allowing the woman to wonder whether she may be a relative.

"How did you get on?" asked Carla as Pamela came out of the call box.

"It was very frustrating" she told Carla "But, hopefully, your Dad will phone this call box at 5.30 our time, and hopefully there will be no one but us here when he does."

"OK, so we have a few hours" said Carla "What shall we do until then?"

"I don't know; what do you fancy doing?" asked Pamela.

"I don't mind, but if we are going to do much more walking I'll have to take these trainers off" Carla told her mum.

"Right, you've been patient enough" Pamela said. "We'll go back and get the car and find a large town with shops and we'll get you a new pair of trainers. If we time it right we can park near the phone box and await your dad's call"

Just half an hour later, having consulted the map, they headed for Concarneau, a town that Pamela decided looked big enough for a good 'retail therapy' session. She didn't have much to spend, but, luckily Carla wasn't like some of the girls she mixed with who always insisted on having the latest craze of designer label gear; like her twin cousins she was easily pleased. Though, Pamela mused now, she was looking more and more grown up as the weeks went by, and there was plenty of time for her to change into a demanding teenager! Taking care to check how long it took to drive to Concarneau so they wouldn't miss Michael's call on their return, Pamela headed for the town centre. She found a large car park opposite the quay and the two of them walked towards a large grey fortification which had grabbed Carla's attention as they drove past it.

Walking arm in arm they crossed over a bridge into what seemed to be old fortifications. They found themselves in a largish open area which narrowed as they passed through what looked like a very old gate and into a narrow way with shops on either side.

Some of the shops were open and there were ice cream stalls selling a multitude of interesting looking flavours. Seeing Carla's face light up Pamela just laughed and asked what flavour Carla would like. She took a little while deciding, as did Pamela, then they walked on, licking their ice creams and looking in the windows of the tourist shops. Many of them sold clothes; some of them too expensive to show the prices at all and Pamela laughingly said, between licks of her ice cream: "If we have to ask the price, we can't afford to go in!"

Carla surprised her mum by suddenly saying "You know, Mum, you seem to have lost a lot of weight; why don't you buy yourself something really nice from one of these shops? One that DOES show the prices, I mean!" and, having finished her ice cream she put her arm around her mum's waist and gave a friendly squeeze "See; there's a lot less of you than there used to be! You deserve something nice, Mum" Pamela was thrilled. After the previous weekend, when Michael had brought Carla home to pack some things and she had said nothing as a very pale Carla had walked out of the front door she had wondered not only when she would next see her, but also how damaged their relationship would be when she did see her again. Now, it was only a week later, and they were closer than they had been before. Carla was still so relieved that she had been wrong in thinking that her mum had committed a crime, and that she could come back home to live that she was looking at her mum as a person, rather than just as 'mum' and she found that she liked what she saw.

"Let's get you sorted first, with your trainers, and we'll think about me when we see what money we have left"

"OK, but let's window shop here for nice stuff for you, and then we can go looking for trainers – at this slow pace my feet will last another half hour or so" Carla laughed.

"OK, but this is obviously tourist stuff" said Pamela as they looked at the shops that were open "I bet this place is full of people in the summer when all the shops are open. I wonder where the best place would be to buy trainers?" Pamela wondered aloud.

"Well, we could either head inland towards the centre of the town, behind the Mairie" Carla suggested "Or out to one of the big supermarkets we passed on the way in" Pamela looked at her watch.

"OK, I suggest one of the big supermarkets, then, if they haven't got exactly what you want then maybe they will have something really cheap just to mess about in on this holiday, and we can buy something nice to cook for tea and be at the call box in time in case your Dad did get the message"

"OK, but promise we will come back here later in the week and you can try on some stuff and we'll get you kitted out" Carla said.

"I don't know about 'kitted out' I don't have much money to spare, but I'm certainly tempted to get myself something; it all looks so much more stylish than the stuff at home, especially those waterproof jackets"

Pamela found she was much more relaxed now, driving on the right. She did ask Carla to keep reminding her if it looked as though she was about to make a mistake, but provided she concentrated when doing less usual manoeuvres such as coming out of the car park onto a main road, she was finding it easier than she thought she would. Pamela missed the first large supermarket they saw, as the entrance was on the other side on the roundabout than she expected and by the time she realised where she should have turned in she was in the wrong lane. "Never mind, Mum, let's try the next big one, it's on the other side of this road, but I think you access it by leaving this road on the slip road and going under it to the supermarket"

So that's what they did, and they were pleasantly surprised how big the supermarket was; it had a good selection of a new range of clothes, shoes and boots for autumn and winter, as well as a selection of summer stuff that was on sale. Pamela saw that there were some things similar to the stuff she'd seen in the fortified town but that it looked even more reasonably priced than the things there.

"Oh, Mum, I don't know what to look at first!" Carla said as she saw the rows of nice new autumn wear.

"Just as well you're still easily pleased; there is no rush, it will take us about twenty minutes to get back to the call box, so as long as we are out of here by five we will be fine" Pamela told her

"Easily pleased, I thought I was quite fussy about what I wore?" Carla put her hands on her hips and pretended to look sulky.

"You know what I mean" Pamela said to her "Not wanting everything to have expensive designer labels and the like"

"Oh, don't" groaned Carla "We have plenty of girls at school like that, and now Emily is starting to get stuff like that and show off about it, just because some of the girls she skates with are like that. I really don't see the point, and neither does Fee; the nice tops she gave me came from somewhere called Mark One and were very inexpensive." Pamela laughed

"Inexpensive – now why not cheap?"

"because Paul told Fee 'never say cheap' just say that we have found 'an inexpensive version of the same thing, allowing us to spend our money on other far more important things' if anyone points out that he is not wearing a designer tee shirt, or Fee isn't wearing designer jeans!"

"Well, come on then, let's take a look at all this 'inexpensive' stuff then and see what we would like. Then we'd better decide what we want for dinner; maybe we could grocery shop for the next couple of days then we can concentrate on enjoying ourselves"

"Sounds good to me" Carla told her "And what about fresh milk and some more orange juice as well" she suggested.

Pamela checked her watch again as they stowed their shopping in the car boot. She was getting really nervous about the phone conversation with Michael; for a start she was worried that there might be someone in the call box at the appointed time, or, even worse, someone wanting to use it when they were waiting for it to ring. "Don't worry about that, Mum" Carla had said, when Pamela had mentioned her worry at the checkout in the supermarket "You can hold the receiver to your ear while surreptitiously leaning on the thingy and pretend to be talking"

"And just where did you learn to be so devious?" Pamela asked her

"Ah, I saw it done on a film" she told her mum. So Pamela just worried instead about how she would tell Michael a version of what her mother had told her, and how he would react.

Pamela could see that there was no one in the call box as she parked the car. So far, so good, she thought. Carla had elected to stay in the car while Pamela took the call; she suspected that her mum had given her a watered down version of events as told by her Grandma, and she didn't want to embarrass her mum further by being there when she told her dad. It was still five minutes before the appointed time when Pamela strolled to the call box and she immediately did what Carla had suggested by lifting the receiver and holding down the hook to make it look as though she was talking to someone.

She was still very tense and when the phone rang two minutes later she nearly jumped out of her skin. She hadn't realised it would ring so loudly. She let go of the hook and said, tentatively, "Hello?"

"Yes, it's me" Michael replied "What's up? Are you both OK? The messaging service lady just said to call you, are you OK, I've been worrying for the last couple of hours"

"Yes, we're fine, I'm sorry I worried you but I need to talk to you and didn't know how else to get hold of you"

"Oh good, I thought you'd had an accident or one of you was ill, or something?" He said

"No, sorry I worried you, it's nothing like that, but I've spoken to my mother and have found out what my father has done" Pamela told him.

Michael didn't answer for a moment. He knew that this was very difficult for Pamela and he knew she was distancing herself from both her parents by referring to them as 'my mother and my father' because, for as long as he had known Pamela, she had always referred to them as 'Mummy and Daddy', something he felt was terribly pretentious, especially as she was in her late teens when they met but that came so naturally to her that he had tried not to needle her about it, despite the fact he had always found it irritating.

Michael took a breath "OK, you say you know what he has done, rather than what he is accused of, does this mean he is guilty?" he asked her.

"In law, yes" Pamela said "I'm not saying that to excuse his behaviour, just to explain how it is. I can see how you thought he was involved with a minor; in fact he has been involved with a twenty something diagnosed with learning difficulties and the law protects such people just as it does those under the age of consent." Michael was puzzled

"So why are you phoning to tell me?" he asked her.

This was the hard part for Pamela. Before Michael had become involved with Monique she had trusted his judgement fully; and there had been very few occasions when they had disagreed over matters to do with Carla. Now Pamela felt she had to put her foot down and get this right as it was her best chance to make Michael see that Carla was in no danger from her grandfather and agree that her place was, as they had initially agreed, with her. "Well" she started "Do you know what Carla's interpretation of all this was?"

"No, and please tell me you haven't discussed this with her. We agreed to tell her nothing…" Pamela began to get angry at this and all her carefully constructed arguments went out of the window

"We agreed nothing. You spirited Carla away and told her a pack of lies before I knew anything about any of this" She retorted angrily "Do you know what the poor child thought?" Michael took a breath in order to reply, but she carried on "She soon worked out that you were lying about her granddad's being ill; she's not stupid. Then she came in one evening and heard you speaking on the phone about Probation Orders and Court appearances and she knew you'd been keeping her away from me and…"

"Oh no" Michael cut in

"Oh yes" Pamela replied "The poor girl thought I'd been accused of something and was going to go to prison and she was very distraught about it"

Pamela was close to tears of anger as she went over it all in her mind again. Michael was quiet as he took on board what Pamela had just said. "But why didn't she say something to me, I'm her dad" he said rather sadly. Pamela didn't feel so angry now with Michael, she had worn herself out emotionally, both worrying about this call beforehand and by getting upset as she was talking to him.

"Well, yes, you are her dad. But not the dad she grew up with, the dad she knew – you are a dad with a new relationship and a new house, albeit a very temporary one – not the person she has known so intimately all her life until now" Michael knew she was right about that, and he couldn't help feeling guilty. It had been a gut reaction that had made him take Carla from school and race across the country with her to Eastbourne – as though he could protect her from whatever it was her granddad had been involved in.

"OK, it sounds like you'd better tell me the whole story, from how Carla first broached the subject to how you found out what he's done to what it is he's done, if you don't mind" Michael said to her.

So she did just that, and she managed to do pretty well what she'd been planning to now that she had calmed down and that Michael was receptive to what she had to say. She told him all about the first night on the ferry, although she didn't tell him exactly what Carla had said that sent the two of them into fits of giggles when the man next to Carla had been both snoring and windy – now she was on track with what she wanted to say she didn't want to say anything light hearted. She told him about Carla snuggling in and saying "I love you mum, whatever it is you've done" and she told him about their heart to heart sitting on the beach. She then told him about the phone call to her parents and what it was her mother had told her and also told him what she had told Carla, so that they could explain should she have any further questions.

Pamela then went on to say that the reason for the call was that Carla wanted desperately to come home to live with her, and just to visit him and Monique at some sort of regular intervals to be agreed by them all. When to Pamela's surprise Michael readily agreed to this, before Pamela had even said that she would keep Carla away from her parents, she found it in her to tell him that she thought that Carla quite liked Monique and Michael said "Well, thank you for that" as he knew it was Pamela's way of saying that she, too, didn't think Monique was all bad! Pamela then assured Michael that she would keep Carla away from her grandfather for the time being, and that she would be in touch when she and Carla got back, and Michael gave her his home phone number and explained about possibly getting a car phone and/or a new line into the rented house.

Pamela felt that after all she'd been through that she wouldn't mind too much if Monique answered the phone, and although they said nothing about it to each other Michael thought that as Monique had accepted him as he was with his 'baggage' of separated wife and child, taking the odd call from Pamela wouldn't be too bad for her, especially after

Pamela's saying that she felt that Carla quite liked Monique, and his understanding that there was a subliminal message there regarding Pamela's own feelings towards her.

They said their goodbyes, and Pamela walked thoughtfully back to her parked car. "Well?" asked Carla as Pamela got in

"All's well, love" she told her "Dad understood and has agreed to your living with me again" Carla slumped back in her seat

"Oh, thank goodness" she said "I shall want to visit them, and to speak to that funny little boy next door – did I tell you he used to call me 'Fence Lady' before he knew my name and now insists on my full title of Carla Maffoos, as he can't say his th's?"

"Yes, you did say" said Pamela chuckling. Then she said "I don't know about you, but I'm exhausted. I don't know if it was all the emotion or the shopping trip, but I'm all in"

"Me too" said Carla, but we can just cook tea and then do nothing but sit in front of the wood fire until bed time. "Ooh, yes, lovely" Pamela said as she pulled off the road onto the space beyond the wall of the little cottage.

Carla went out the back in search of some more wood, and when she came back in with an armful she was animatedly trying to explain something about a set of stone steps out the back leading to a mysterious door! Tired though she was, Pamela was intrigued and went to have a look with her. "Well" she said "That explains how all those people used to stay here, there is another storey on top of where we are and we never noticed before! I wonder if the other key on that key ring opens that door?" Pamela asked

"I'll go and get it, shall I" Carla said as she nipped back round the front.

They did the same as they had the first time they'd opened the front door: Pamela pulled the door towards them and Carla turned the key. "Well" they both said at once, and laughed, as they had discovered a couple more rooms, with wonderful views from the roof windows across the back of the house. There not being any windows the other side they had not noticed before that the house had two storeys. They had a quick look round, then locked it back up and went down again to light the wood stove and cook their evening meal. They sat quietly, both reading books in front of the stove after they'd eaten and, when they both began to doze off they cleared away the dishes and went to bed, leaving the washing up for the following day.

Chapter 33

Bernice pulled into the sweeping gravel drive and said "Wow" to herself as she got out of her car and looked around. There was no sign of Major Fielding, but a stately looking woman opened the imposing front door as she approached it and introduced herself as Mrs Daphne Fielding saying "I assume you are Ms Bernice Liddel, with an appointment to see myself and the Major?"

"Yes, that's right" said Bernice, but my surname is pronounced Liddle as in Little, not Lidelle, with the emphasis at the end"

Bernice did not usually worry about the pronunciation of her name, but she felt that Mrs Fielding was trying to dominate the situation as she ushered her through the house saying "The Major and I are taking tea, would you care to join us?" as though this were purely a social visit and that they were superior in some way to their visitor. Goodness, she thought to herself, I am making assumptions quickly here; I'd better take a deep breath and go back to my usual professional self – I must have been shocked by the size of the ancestral home, despite the fact that Sylvie had warned me! So Bernice smiled at Daphne and said

"Oh, yes please, I'd love a cup of tea, then we must get on and talk about the reason I'm here"

"Quite so" said Daphne in her clipped manner as she went to the kitchen with Donald trotting along behind her to help with the tea things. Bernice had been asked to take a seat and now she had a chance to look around. The room she had been shown into had given her the feeling that it had not been decorated in a long time, but it was clean and cared for and the pieces of furniture looked to her inexperienced eyes as though they could be antiques.

Donald and Daphne came back into the room carrying trays with the tea paraphernalia and a plate of biscuits. These they placed carefully on a large table in front of them and Daphne began the process of pouring tea from a teapot, making use of a tea strainer while she did so. Bernice could see, by her movements, that this was something Daphne did regularly; it wasn't just a show for her benefit but, when Daphne began to say that she thought this was the only way that tea should be taken, Bernice decided that it was time she took the initiative, so she said

"That is very kind of you, Mrs Fielding. However, I believe you are aware of the reason that I am here today, so I should be very grateful if we can get down to business." To show that she meant it, Bernice bent down and pulled a reporters style notepad from her small handbag and explained to both Donald and Daphne that she just wanted to chat with them to start with, in order to get the feel for the relationship between them and that of their wider family and friendships. She also wanted to reiterate what she had said to Donald when she met him the previous Friday, as she didn't know quite what Donald had said to Daphne, so she said "Major Fielding, Mrs

Fielding, you both know why I am here. It is because Major Fielding has pleaded guilty to a serious sexual offence, and I have been tasked with preparing a pre-sentence report to be submitted to the judge in order to assist him when he comes to sentence him. In order to help me to compile such a report, it is customary for me to meet, in the first instance, the immediate family, and then if I feel it necessary to meet with other family members and friends…"

"Oh, I shouldn't have thought that would be at all necessary, do you dear?" Daphne cut in…"

"I'm afraid that that will be up to me to decide" Bernice told her "Now, why don't you start by telling me a little about your lovely home?" she suggested, looking carefully towards both Donald and Daphne. She knew from Donald's visit to her office that the home had been inherited by Daphne, but she wanted to see which of them would start to talk first; she needed to determine the dynamics of their relationship, and her training had taught her that it was easier to observe a relationship by giving a task, such as asking about their home, and then watching how they responded. It was easier to assess a person alone; the techniques for interviewing a single person were different to those when more than one was present.

Bernice was already forming an opinion that Daphne was the more dominant person in the marriage and she seemed to Bernice to be what she considered a snob, but she wanted to be sure that she hadn't jumped to those conclusions from a first impression. She hadn't taken to Daphne at all, so far, but she was too professional to allow personal like or dislike of a client or their family to get in the way of that professionalism.

Daphne surprised Bernice by looking to Donald, and waiting for him to start the conversation this time, and it was Donald who explained that they had come to stay at this house in 1967, when he left the Army; how Daphne had eventually inherited the house and how they had found it necessary to sell first Home Farm in order to pay death duties, and then a strip of land in order to make repairs and alterations. Donald sounded quite animated as he explained the improvements that they had done, such as changing the old scullery into a utility room, and having the en suite in Daphne's room installed. Bernice picked up on that, and after asking a few other apparently pertinent questions, she asked them how long they had slept apart, and for what reason.

This time Daphne didn't look to Donald to give an explanation. She started by asking Bernice "What right do you have…" but she tailed off and Bernice answered her

"I have every right, I'm afraid, to ask all such questions. You have a right not to answer, of course, but that is what I will have to write in my report, if that is the case; that I have asked a particular question and that you have refused to answer it. Now, it's up to you, but I would like to know the answers to certain questions. Some, like why you don't share a bedroom I have no other way to find out other than asking you. However, other questions, such as why you, Major Fielding, chose to resign your commission in Cyprus and return to the UK just when you did I can find out by checking Army records; another thing I have every right to do. You did tell me quite a lot about yourself and your family when you came to my office; but I felt that there was quite a lot left unsaid. It would be very helpful indeed, if you could fill in any details that you think will help me to help the judge understand what you are like as a person"

"Naturally, I do understand" Donald said calmly and quietly. "My wife has a natural reticence about matters which she believes are private. I realise that by pleading guilty, as I have done, in order to protect my family from unnecessary press interest I must answer your questions with honesty. Before I begin, would you like some more tea?" Bernice hadn't wanted the first cup, but accepting it had been a part of putting Daphne at ease

"That's very kind, but no thank you" she said to him.

"Right, then" Donald began, firmly, looking at Daphne as if to say 'let me speak and please don't interrupt' "I will begin with Cyprus, as, if you have never lived in a very hot country it will help me to explain to you why we have separate rooms. We had a large comfortable apartment in Cyprus, but it wasn't blessed with air conditioning and we soon found that it was difficult to sleep, but that when one of us did manage to sleep the other was awake and fretful trying not to disturb the other. It seemed natural in those circumstances to sleep separately.

"We left Cyprus for family reasons, nothing sinister there, I assure you. When Daphne's parents very kindly offered us temporary accommodation here on our return from Cyprus, they gave us the option of having separate rooms, as the house is big enough. They had in fact, themselves always had separate rooms, so it seemed natural to them for us to do the same. In fact, the main reason we accepted their kind offer was that there was no separate living room and we were very conscious of not wanting to impose, so by accepting a bedroom for each of us either one of us or our daughter could go to our room for a short while if we wanted a little time alone." Donald smiled shyly "And, of course, if we wanted to be, you know, intimate, we could always visit one another's rooms" Daphne looked quite startled at this, Bernice didn't know whether she was embarrassed, or whether it was something that had long been out of the question in their relationship.

Bernice thanked Donald for his explanation. She then went on to ask how it was that they had stayed at Crowford rather than looking for accommodation of their own.

This time it was Daphne who spoke. "My father had never had good health. He had been badly wounded in the First World War and had never been strong throughout my childhood. At first, when we returned from Cyprus the idea had been to just stay a little while as my husband organised his ongoing career, we had thought that my father was just his usual frail self, but it soon became clear that he was very ill, indeed. We stayed on to support my mother through my father's terminal illness and then after his death she asked us to stay here permanently, and as my husband had begun to be successful locally in the insurance business, and our daughter had settled well in the local school it seemed the best thing to do."

Bernice felt that the interview was getting away from her. These two had closed ranks as successfully as if they had done it with a physical force. She would learn no more about their return from Cyprus and their early life together, so she decided to ask instead about their daughter. "Ah yes; you say your daughter settled well in the local school, I suppose it must have been very different for her, coming back to the UK, what age would she have been then, about nine?"

"Just ten, and we came back here during the school summer holidays, so it was just right for her to start the autumn term of the last year in a local primary school. We were lucky. It was a good rural school, and they took an interest in Pamela. She had been to a good Episcopal school in Cyprus; and other good schools in my husband's previous postings and, while not being extremely academic, she was conscientious in her studies. After the primary school she went on to the grammar school in Wallingford and then on to college where she took a course in office management." Daphne was motoring now; try as she might Bernice found herself disliking her more and more. She wondered what it must have been like for Pamela, this upheaval at a young age followed not long after by the death of her grandfather. She had meant to find out about her as a person, not to get a straight academic record from her mother – as though Pamela's success in some way measured Daphne's success as a mother. There had been no mention in Daphne's educational listing as to whether Pamela was a happy child, and even the way in which Daphne pronounced her daughter's name was beginning to grate on Bernice.

Bernice tried again "That is a good achievement after several changes of school in early life. Was it a happy childhood for her? Was this her first taste of rural life? Was she fond of her grandfather; it must have come as a shock – to you all, of course – but especially to a ten year old, his dying soon after you moved back to the UK"

This time it was Donald who answered. Bernice was beginning to see a pattern. For straight facts and anything she felt was needed to 'set the record straight' as it were, Daphne would answer but something needing a little tact or thought tended to be answered by Donald. "Pamela didn't really have much of a chance to get to know her grandfather well, which was a shame as my own father died when she was very young, so she didn't get to know either of them properly. This was Pamela's first taste of living somewhere very rural, I believe she was rather daunted by it at first, as she had been within safe walking distance of other suitable children of her age in Cyprus, but here arrangements always had to be made should she want to visit a friend or bring one home. Her grandfather loved gardening, and Pamela would go round the garden with him to start with, before he became too ill to do so, as I believe she found the long garden a rather alien place when she was alone. It goes all the way to the river, you know"

"Yes, you did tell me" Bernice said to him.

She was struggling here; more than she thought she would. She never expected to like a client; this was her job and she always tried to distance herself from any emotional involvement, but with Donald's mentioning 'suitable' friends and Daphne's overt snobbery she almost felt like screaming at them 'remember why I am here'. Her own background was mixed, and she usually found herself comfortable in whatever surroundings her job as probation officer took her to, from the most humble rented flat to the wild chaotic households of some of her regular clients, where more than one family member was often on probation. Bernice had had clients from middle and upper class backgrounds before, but this was the first time she found herself bristling with dislike. She pulled herself together and told herself to be professional. "Would you like to show me the garden, if that is not too much trouble?" she asked in an attempt to gain control of the interview again "You can tell me more about your daughter as we walk, I will have to meet her, you know. You did tell me, Major Fielding, didn't you, that she does know about your offence?"

"Yes, she does know" Donald answered "But she doesn't know as yet that you will want to meet with her. It's all rather difficult, as she is away in Brittany for half term week at the moment"

Bernice wondered whether she would have to walk down the garden to the river alone with the Major, as his wife didn't seem to be moving. However, the temptation to show off the back of the house and the large garden got the better of her and, after taking the tea trays back to the kitchen they found that Bernice had followed them so, apparently to Daphne's dismay Donald said "Oh, we're all here now, we may as well go out of the kitchen door" Daphne's face was a picture; she obviously didn't feel it was the correct way to show a guest the 'grounds' as she called them.

"Well we normally would show someone around from the back patio doors, but I suppose as we are all here now we may as well go this way"

Donald sneaked a look at Bernice, but Bernice had managed to fix her face in a noncommittal pose and thanked him as he held the door open for her. She found herself wondering, not for the first time, how often the Major felt the need to rebel and whether, in fact, the offence he had committed had more to do with rebellion than sex. She had been very interested when he told her the reason for his initial visit to Peggy and May's house. He had sounded almost critical of his wife when he had explained that she wasn't in the least interested in their little dog being poisoned and that he had felt sorry and wondered whether they needed a man's help in disposing of the body of the dog. Bernice had listened to many lies, over the years, from her probation clients, but she felt that here Donald was telling the truth; that the first time he had visited the house and the young woman had performed oral sex on him he was totally astounded. She didn't feel dislike towards him as a person, just when he backed up his wife in her snobbery; then he seemed to her to be weak. She had found herself wishing that he hadn't been weak enough to go back to see whether the young woman would do it again. She doubted that there would have been a case to answer, however insistent the young woman's social worker, had the Major only gone there the once. It was after the subsequent visit that the social worker had found out, and brought it to the notice of the police.

Bernice didn't feel strongly either way about that first visit. She had not met the young woman in question but was acquainted with enough sexually promiscuous people of all ages and genders to know that someone who seemed almost sexually naive like the Major could easily be led. That didn't mean that Bernice thought that it was wrong to protect those with learning difficulties, as the young woman in this case was diagnosed, but she felt that there was a fine line between such a person's human rights and privacy, and the, sometimes, overzealous protection of a social worker. She did wonder, however, about the Major's pleading guilty. He seemed oblivious to the fact that he might get a custodial sentence, despite the fact that the duty solicitor had warned him it was a possibility. The Major seemed to think that he would just get a suspended sentence or a community order and then he and his wife could just sweep it under the carpet and get on with their lives. Bernice couldn't help wondering that if he had gone to Crown Court with it and pleaded not guilty, and had a good barrister defending, that the young woman could have been shown to be sexually precocious and the social worker's case discredited.

She suddenly realised that she was being spoken to. Luckily it was about some plants in the garden, so she was able to ask Daphne to repeat the name of the plant, saying "I'm not much of a gardener, I'm afraid, but I do like to see a lovely garden"

"I was just saying that that's a marvellous example of a Rubens Montana, it's magnificent in the spring" Bernice thought it sounded more like a famous painting, but she just smiled and nodded and asked

"So what does it look like when it's in flower?" Daphne answered

"Oh, it just drips with tiny pink flowers; I know it sounds daft to say it 'drips' but that is the best way to explain it. My father trained it to go up that pergola years ago; it is sheer delight in the spring." Bernice looked at Daphne and felt that she was looking at another person; this was the first time Bernice had seen her interested in something that wasn't some sort of artifice to show that she thought herself better than other people.

Bernice allowed herself to be led along the path all the way to the river. She was interested to see how the dynamics between the Fieldings changed as Daphne described various plants and explained alterations made over the years. There was still a ring of almost bitterness when any alterations made were for reasons of economy, or because the Major was not as keen a gardener as Daphne's father had been, but, on the whole Daphne was a different person out in her garden than she was in the house. As they passed a couple of greenhouses the Major told Bernice that he enjoyed growing chrysanthemums, and that the best of his collection were in the closer of the two "Would you like to have a look?" he asked Bernice.

"Yes, please, then we should go on down to the river and then back to the house, as I have another appointment this afternoon, and I must compile your report before I see someone else." She told them.

Back in the house Bernice accepted Daphne's offer of another cup of tea, saying "Yes, please I will. If you will excuse my making some notes while you prepare it. You may then ask me any questions you like and I must make arrangements to see your daughter when she returns from Brittany"

Chapter 34

Sylvie closed her front door behind her and walked to her car. She hadn't been in the office for a couple of days and she wondered how Bernice had got on with Major Donald. She knew Bernice had seen him in the office on the Friday; she had been around but kept away from the interview room as she didn't want any contact with him at this stage. Bernice had not raised the subject of using a probation volunteer as yet, but Sylvie knew she was considering it and would discuss it with her when they were both in the office. Sylvie had had a couple of days of client visits and a court attendance; she knew her paperwork would have built up during her absence but she was keen to have a chat with Bernice, if possible, before she got stuck in.

Finding that she was one of the first to arrive, Sylvie gathered some mugs together and put the kettle on. Bernice came in just as the kettle boiled so Sylvie made two coffees and called out to the others that the kettle was hot. "How did it go?" she asked and Bernice pulled a face "That good, eh?" Sylvie joked. Bernice told her how she'd struggled at first, feeling that she'd wanted to strangle Daphne until she saw another side to her in the garden. Sylvie chuckled "I know what you mean. The woman is a dreadful snob, but I believe there is some humanity under that exterior, somewhere"

"Mm, maybe, but at first I wondered why the Major wasn't up on a murder charge, rather than a sexual offence!" Bernice said. "Am I glad that you didn't tell me any more than you did, I struggled to remain professional as it was. By the way, did you know that the daughter and granddaughter are in Brittany for half term week?" Sylvie said that she hadn't known, but she felt very pleased that Carla was with her mum now.

Bernice told Sylvie that she had offered the services of a probation volunteer, and, predictably, Daphne had begun to say she thought it unnecessary, but the Major asked what sort of thing a volunteer might do for them. Bernice explained that volunteers were there to do all manner of things, from straight befriending of a client and their family, for those who needed help of that sort, to accompanying to court, arranging lifts and many other things that a probation officer would like to do but wouldn't have time to. She also told them that the volunteers work to the same code of confidentiality that the officers themselves did; that the volunteers were properly trained and that some clients found them very helpful, indeed.

Sylvie was surprised but pleased to hear that the Major had agreed that it could be very helpful to meet a volunteer; and Bernice had told him that she would arrange for someone to come and meet with him and his wife. "Do you know many of the volunteers that work for this office?" Bernice asked Sylvie.

"No, but I believe there is to be a volunteers meeting one evening next week, they seem to be open meetings, what about if we both attend?" Sylvie suggested.

"We could do, but I think we need to choose a volunteer before then; I want to interview the daughter (sorry, your friend) as soon as she agrees to see me when she's back from Brittany next week, I'd like the report finished as soon as possible so that a court date can be set. I am worried about the health of the wife, and the sooner he is sentenced the better." Bernice told her "Who is it that liaises with the volunteers, do you know?" Bernice asked Sylvie.

"It's Faith, but she doesn't get allocated any extra time on top of her case load in order to do so, that is why so many volunteer meetings get cancelled, and despite their knowing why, the volunteers do get frustrated. They are supposed to be allocated their work through Faith, but the system doesn't always work" Sylvie had been following up on her reading about the volunteer program and had discovered that it was Faith who had been tasked with leading the volunteer program, but like all other such programs that had been introduced there was little funding and no extra time allocated to it.

Bernice went to look at the message board that showed who was where; not everyone made proper use of it, Sylvie chuckled as she thought of Ralph's attitude to it "If I'm here I'm here, if not I'm either in Court or on a client visit" he'd say, infuriating the new Chief Probation Officer, who had initiated the system. They were in luck; Faith had kept up with the entries on the line showing her movements and she had been away on an ABPO conference, but was now back and she was down as in Court that morning at 10am but was due back in the office that afternoon.

Bernice and Sylvie decided to go their separate ways for the morning and meet back up in the office at 2pm, hoping to catch Faith in order to have a quick chat with her to see whether she could recommend a suitable volunteer to befriend the Major and his wife. Amongst other things, the volunteer would have time to explain Court procedure, offer lifts and generally explain anything to the client's family if they wanted information and describe the various projects that he may be assigned to should he be given a community sentence.

Bernice went out on another new client family visit and Sylvie got stuck into some paperwork as she had one of her regular clients coming to report in to her at 11am. Both Bernice's new client and the one Sylvie was expecting at eleven were in the more usual age range and social standing for probation clients. While their probation office dealt with all manner of people who had committed all sorts of different crimes and were from all backgrounds, the majority of their clients were between the ages of seventeen and twenty five and most of those from poorer backgrounds and most of their crimes were drug related. Sex offenders came in all age ranges and from all backgrounds, but apart from two young men currently on probation for indecent exposure and one middle aged man serving a long sentence for a more serious sex crime who would be out 'on licence' in another year or so, their office was not currently dealing with any other sex offenders. The Major didn't fit the profile of any offenders they were currently dealing with, so even if Sylvie hadn't known the family she would have found the case interesting and was looking forward to discussing it with Faith and Bernice. She was hoping that Faith wouldn't mind her joining in the discussion, but wasn't sure of her opinion regarding her knowing the family.

The rest of the morning went quickly, and suddenly realising it was almost one thirty, Sylvie decided to pop out to the nearest supermarket and get herself a sandwich. She decided to walk, as she had been frustrated by her eleven o'clock client and wanted a breath of fresh air. When she got back to the office with her sandwich she saw that Faith was in and that Bernice already chatting with her. "Put the kettle on" Bernice called out to her. "Faith has a few minutes to spare so we can chat while you eat your sandwich". Sylvie was pleased. Bernice had obviously filled Faith in and Faith was happy to talk to them both.

In fact, Faith had just returned from a very interesting conference and was keen to put across some of the things she'd learned to anyone who would listen. As Sylvie approached with mugs of coffee and her sandwich precariously balanced on the little tray they all used, Bernice pulled another spare chair over so they could all three sit down by her desk.

"I'll do a deal with you" Faith said to them both, smiling "I'm supposed to come back and spread the word about some very interesting stuff I learned at the conference – it has little to do with the subject of volunteers or sex offenders – but I will listen to what you want and see whether I can help you, so long as I can count on you two spreading the word about what I learned on the two day conference.

"You're on" said both Sylvie and Bernice at the same time.

"OK, you two start with the case you were telling me about, and I'll think about whether a volunteer would be appropriate, and if so, who to recommend" Faith said.

Bernice had already explained what Sylvie's interest was in the case, and Faith had agreed that she had no problem discussing the case with her. After Bernice had outlined the offence, she explained why the Major had pleaded guilty and given a shortened version of both the Major's visit to her here in the office and Bernice's visit to their house, Faith had quite a few questions.

"OK, so why do you feel that a volunteer would be appropriate, and what would you like them to do?" Faith asked to start with. She then went on to say "You do realise that apart from the van driver for the Furniture Project all our volunteers currently are female; and it is policy to only let them go in pairs to see a sex offender. Very often, if I can't find two volunteers who can go at the same time, I go myself." Bernice said that she hadn't thought of that and Sylvie was tempted to say that she thought that no one would be in any danger from the Major, but thought better of it. She didn't know Faith very well, she had only become a fully qualified probation officer about eighteen months previously, and this was her first posting. She explained that she had, herself, been a volunteer as part of her training, and this was one of the reasons that the new chief had asked her to be the new Volunteer Liaison Officer. Privately Sylvie thought it was more likely because no one else would have wanted to do it, but she said nothing.

Bernice began to explain why she, herself, believed that a volunteer would be appropriate in the Major's case, and Sylvie was pleased that she had kept quiet as she was quite surprised with what Bernice had to say. She had begun by asking Faith's opinion of the effectiveness of using volunteers to work with sex offenders and Faith had explained, quite animatedly, how she currently had two volunteers who regularly called on a young chap in his twenties who was on probation for indecent exposure, with the intention of befriending him and making him more socially aware and able to relax in the company of women. This, she told them, seemed to be working, and now the young man was able to invite the two ladies to sit down and have a cup of tea with him without stammering and blushing and he was beginning to be able to converse with them on a variety of subjects. Faith explained that this young man had a job and his own home, but that he'd been caught exposing himself after having been seen on a number of occasions and the judge had given him a suspended prison sentence but said that he must attend a sex offenders course. As usual, there was no place available on such a course for at least six months, due to funding shortages and waiting lists, so the probation service had set up the system of the volunteers visiting him until such a course was available for him.

Bernice explained why she felt that, in her opinion, the Major was as much a victim as the young lady whose social worker had brought the case, and that she was concerned about what sort of sentence he would get. "Don't get me wrong" Bernice said "I can't condone what he has done, especially as he obviously went back for more. But what you have just said enforces my view that the system isn't set up for the likes of the Major; he is, as far as we know, neither a serial sex offender nor, in my opinion, a danger to the public. If he is given a suspended sentence he will more than likely be expected to attend a sex offender's course, and if he is given a community sentence what are we going to find him to do? He is in his sixties – I don't suppose he'd be much use to the Furniture Project."

"What about the Motor Project?" asked Faith – does he know much about cars?" "What Motor Project?" asked both Sylvie and Bernice. Faith explained. It was one of the chief's newer ideas, and he had attended the last volunteer's meeting and talked about his plans for a drop-in centre where the young lads (and sometimes girls as well now) who were on probation because they had stolen vehicles could go and learn about engines and car repair etc. "What, so they can learn which cars are easier to break into?" asked Sylvie.

She was still recovering from the thought of the young client she had seen that morning who was on probation for breaking and entering. He had come to her all full of his new window cleaning round which one of his uncles had set up for him. He was very pleased that his uncle had bought him some ladders, buckets and cleaning cloths and he had excitedly told her about how much money his uncle had told him he could earn and that he would now 'go straight' and not get into trouble again. Sylvie had been quite depressed by this; mainly because the young chap's enthusiasm seemed genuine, but she had seen so many young people try this that it was almost a joke in the probation service – and, whether he knew it or not, she knew that his uncle had a record for petty theft and breaking and entering. Either his nephew was being very naive, or he was a good actor. Either way, Sylvie found it depressing, just as the thought of a motor project seemingly programmed to fail depressed her.

"No" said Faith, laughing. "You should have been there. It is actually rather a good idea, and the chief said that there would be funding" Sylvie could just imagine Ralph's comment to this; she wondered whether she was becoming as cynical as her friend and mentor. Ralph would say "Fine, funding for now – but what happens to the project when it's no longer someone's pet, or no longer required politically" Sylvie knew that this was the way that many projects went; there would be a public outcry about something that, perhaps, had been strongly reported on and picked up by the media, there would be pressure on the government to do something and funding would be found for a short while for the probation service to do something with, for example, domestic violence when new Anger Management courses would spring up around the country, or, as in this example many cars were being reported as stolen by young people and driven dangerously around housing estates. Sylvie sighed as she thought, as did Ralph, that there was no more car stealing and 'joy riding' than usual, but the media had picked up on it recently as news was slow, and here they were talking about a new project in which to interest the young people so as to stop them from wanting to steal cars.

Sylvie just smiled, as she didn't want to spoil Faith's enthusiasm and she did think that maybe Faith had a point. However, if they were tasked with finding something for the Major to work his community hours on, supposing he were given a community sentence they realised that they would not be able to recommend him to the Motor Project as he would not be able to work with young people as a sex offender. Bernice was questioning the policy of always sending two volunteers to work with a sex offender "So, does it always have to be that way, or, if, for example a volunteer was required to take Mrs Fielding somewhere would you send two?"

"No, in that case, if Mrs Fielding were definitely to be the one the volunteer was to work with, then one volunteer would be OK to go alone. Or, indeed, if the volunteer were to work with both the Major and Mrs Fielding, I am sure someone would agree to visit on their own." Faith said to them. Sylvie asked what arrangement Bernice had made with regard to contacting Pamela, and she said that the Major was going to ask her to call Bernice once she was back from Brittany in order to make an appointment, if she was willing to see her. Faith said she would contact a couple of her volunteers and see who had time to see the Major and his family. Bernice and Sylvie thanked her and went back to their own desks, promising to give Faith some time later that day so she could fill them in with regard to the conference she had just attended.

Chapter 35

"I don't know about you, Mum, but I can't BELIEVE we are already preparing for the journey home!" Carla said to Pamela as she was packing her bag and Pamela was sweeping the bedroom floor.

"I know, the time has flown by, hasn't it?" She answered "Still, we have the rest of today, and so long as we leave nice and early, as we've planned, tomorrow, we can enjoy the journey back to St Malo as well.

"Ugh, I don't call four o'clock in the morning nice and early, I call it the middle of the night" Carla said, laughing.

"Yes, but a day crossing on the ferry will be nicer than that night one with everyone trying to sleep in those reclining chairs" Pamela said.

"Oh, don't remind me, I agree, a day crossing will be nice, and then I'm coming home, thank goodness, rather than going back to Dad's".

They had been really lucky with the weather. Only one day of rain, on the Monday, and the rest of the time it had been sunny but chilly. They had taken to walking as far round the coastline as they could manage, usually with a picnic, and they had decided to do the same on this, their final day. Pamela was no longer afraid of driving on the right, in fact she had become used to it, but they really enjoyed walking and exploring the area, as they found they could see more and get to more interesting coastal places on foot than by car.

Once they had organised what was going to be packed in each bag, and Pamela had swept the floors, they set off in the direction of Rospico. They had found a little cafe there that overlooked the bay and were planning to have hot chocolates to follow their picnic. Pamela had bought chicken pieces at the supermarket the previous day to cook for supper; she planned to cook them slowly with leeks and potatoes in the one large cooking pot, so that was all organised, and Carla had walked alone to the little bakery in the village that morning for the bread for the picnic.

Both Pamela and Carla were feeling very relaxed and happy; Pamela realised this was the happiest she'd felt since the split with Michael, despite the problems with her father. Pamela now recognised the fact that she had lost a lot of weight; she had bought two pairs of jeans in the supermarket, a blue pair and a black pair. Luckily for her there was a changing room in the supermarket, in the clothes section, as she didn't understand the French sizes; and the first pair she'd taken to try on was far too large. Carla had talked her into buying two tops; at first she'd considered them far too skimpy, but Carla had said "Oh, Mum, you look really brilliant", so, as they were far more reasonably priced than the similar looking ones they had seen in the tourist area of Concarneau Pamela bought herself a couple. Carla had complimented her mum on her new hair cut; the morning after she'd bought her new clothes she'd washed her hair and let it dry naturally, as she had begun to do after the compliment Sylvie paid her the day she had it cut, and Carla had persuaded her to try on her new things and she had said "Oh, Mum, you look fabulous!" and had given her a big hug.

For the first time in a very long time Pamela realised that she was attractive, and she thought that maybe she also ought to revise her working wardrobe. Not that there was anyone at work that she was interested in; she wasn't yet up to thinking about going out with someone, but she had noticed that her work skirts were loose before she came away on holiday, and the healthy eating and all the walking had honed her body after the unintentional weight loss due to all the worry.

"What are you smiling about?" Carla asked her as they puffed their way up a steep incline.

"Oh, I was just thinking that some people go on very difficult diets, and here I am having lost weight without having noticed" Pamela told her "I may have to buy a couple of new things for work, if I don't want my skirts to slip off!"

"Well, you be careful what you wear when you come to see Mr Gregory" Carla told her.

"Why?" she asked

"Because he is a right old letch" Carla said.

"Carla, really, what have you been learning?" Pamela asked, laughing "He seemed quite nice when I met him last year at the parents"

"You fancy him, don't you?" asked Carla incredulously.

"No I don't" denied Pamela "He just seemed nice, that's all" she said.

"Mmm, you be careful, that's all. I just want you to have a word with him about my going to Dad's for a while, and why I didn't have a protractor – he was really nasty and sarcastic about it, and I did try to tell him about Granddad being ill and everything – we can still say that's what it was, can't we? I don't want anyone to know my Granddad is an old pervert"

Pamela let that go; she was concerned with the apparently easy way that Carla had accepted what had happened with her grandfather and she wondered whether it would affect Carla more as time went on. They were getting on so well and Pamela realised that it was partly due to the fact that Carla was still relieved that it wasn't her who had committed a crime. She didn't want to be continually reprimanding Carla about her choice of language. She was a growing girl; almost a teenager and she still had a lot to learn. This business with her grandfather was rather like a baptism of fire for one so young and inexperienced in sexual matters. She couldn't help wondering, though, where she had heard the expressions 'old pervert' and 'old letch'. She and Michael had never spoken like that.

"Hopefully no one that knows us will need to know about your granddad" Pamela told her "No one I work with knows my maiden name, and I don't suppose any of your school friends know your granddad's surname?" she asked

"No, we don't talk much about our grandparents – except, of course, I told all my friends I was away from school because Granddad was ill, and that's what Dad told Mrs Francham when he collected me from school early, that day. But when we do mention them, it's usually just 'my grandma said this, or my granddad gave me that, etc"

"I will make arrangements to come and talk to Mr Gregory as soon as we get back" Pamela told her "And, yes, I'll just confirm that your granddad was ill and you went to stay with your dad at very short notice and didn't have all your things. Are you struggling with the maths at all, or are you just nervous of Mr Gregory because of the way he spoke to you?" she asked. "Well, I don't know that I'm struggling any more than anyone else is, but I didn't do very well in that maths test but mainly because I was upset at his reaction to my asking to borrow a protractor. It made me nervous" Carla told Pamela.

"Does he ever treat other people like that?" Pamela asked

"Yes, I thought I'd said before; you can never tell who's going to have a go at next, or what will set him off" Carla told her

"Well, I can only talk to him about you, and how upset you were when already under pressure because you'd had to go to your Dad's so suddenly, but it's helpful to know he behaves like that to others as well. It will be interesting to see what he has to say when I challenge him. Right, now let's see which of us can get to the top of this hill first – come on!"

Pamela challenged, wanting to change the subject and make the most of what was left of their holiday.

Carla upped her pace and beat Pamela to the top. "Oh look, it looks even lovelier than it did the other day" she exclaimed as Pamela reached the top of the path with her. Pamela laughed breathlessly

"It is lovely" she gasped, beginning to regret having challenged Carla to a race. "But I'm exhausted, let's stop and admire it for a while" They stood and looked across the little hidden bay where the small river they had crossed earlier ran into the sea. Pamela started to chuckle when she got her breath back

"What?" Carla asked her.

"I was just thinking that this will ruin your street cred" Pamela said

"What will?" Carla asked "Not that I've got any, of course" she said

"Enjoying a holiday just with me and loving the scenery and even just liking buying the bread and all that" Pamela explained.

"Yes, but only we'll know what we've been through, with the worry of granddad and everything" Carla told her. "Anyway, what's wrong with it? It may not be as exotic sounding as the holidays we used to have as a family, but what adventures we've had, what with Serge and his family and our arriving and not knowing how to light the fire and the gas and stuff. We wouldn't have had fun like that in a posh holiday complex!" Carla said.

"Well, I am very glad you see it this way, I'm enjoying myself more than I could have imagined. How far do you want to walk before we have our picnic?" Pamela asked

Chapter 36

Pamela had been stunned when, on arriving at work, Sandra had told her that the ledgers were not yet closed for month end; that she, Sandra had required two days off the previous week and John Meredith had agreed that the ledgers could remain open until mid morning Monday. Pamela was very relieved that Maureen and Joan had dealt with all the items that she had given them before she went on holiday as she now had had a lot of invoices referring to the month end in the post and it would make a lot less work in the long run if she could get them on the system now, before they closed the ledgers. The trouble was that she had two important private phone calls to make; she had planned to do so quickly and quietly while Sandra was in her Monday morning managers meeting but with all this extra work she wasn't sure she would be able to do so.

Rob knew Pamela was very busy, as were the others, so he went to make their morning coffee as Sandra went off to her meeting. Pamela wondered which of her phone calls would be the quicker to make of the two. One was to the school to make an appointment to see Mr Gregory, Carla's maths teacher, the other to the Probation Office. Pamela's father had phoned the previous evening soon after they arrived home; ostensibly to ask whether they'd arrived home safely and whether they had had a good holiday, but also to let Pamela know that he and Daphne had seen Bernice Liddel, the Probation

Officer assigned to write his pre-sentence report and that Bernice wanted to know whether Pamela would agree to see her. Pamela wasn't sure how she felt about it at all, but she felt that as she now had Carla home with her she wanted to do anything that would help confirm that her father hadn't done anything wrong with anyone underage.

Pamela realised that she would be unlikely to be successful with either phone call in her lunch break, as the people she wanted to get hold of may also be at lunch. She decided that the school appointment was the more important of the two calls, so she lined up the invoices she was inputting so that she could carry on working while she spoke to the school secretary. She was in luck, her call was answered straight away, but the secretary was unable to make the appointment, she asked Pamela for a couple of days and times convenient to her and said she'd contact Mr Gregory, arrange one of the times suitable to Pamela, if possible, then phone her back later in the day. Pamela was pleased with that, she had promised Carla she would do it, and at least she had initiated things and hopefully would be able to tell Carla that evening when she was to see Mr Gregory.

Rob put her coffee on her desk and she looked up and smiled gratefully as she put the phone down. She had managed to carry on working while she made the call, so she decided she'd also make her other call and see whether she could get hold of Ms Liddel at the Probation Office. She wasn't so lucky this time. A very pleasant voice asked her what it was in connection with, and whether she could get Ms

Liddel to call her back, but a call back from the school was one thing, if a colleague answered, but she most definitely didn't want anyone to take a call from the Probation service on her behalf!

Pamela had been toying with the idea of getting in touch with Sylvie now that she knew the basics of her father's crime, so she decided that was the best way to go with regard to how to get in touch with Bernice Liddel. In fact it was Carla who had suggested, during their ferry crossing, when they were chatting about what they would do in the coming weeks at home that she ought to get in touch with Sylvie again. Carla had said "Never mind the business with Granddad, Sylvie is your oldest friend and is also single; maybe the two of you could go out occasionally, maybe to the cinema or something. I'd be fine on my own for a while, or if it's a weekend I may stay over at Dad's" Sylvie had been thrilled to see her when they accidentally met in town and Pamela was beginning to realise why Sylvie had backed away a little from the friendship as time went on when Pamela was still with Michael. Pamela was aware that Michael used to goad Sylvie rather when they gave a dinner party. Pamela herself didn't have strong views like Michael's with regard to crime and punishment; she supposed it was because she understood Sylvie's personality, and although Sylvie didn't ever talk about any specific cases she worked on, when she did defend the Probation Service on the couple of occasions Michael had spiked her up enough to want to do so, Sylvie's explanations had made a great deal of sense to Pamela, mainly because Pamela trusted Sylvie's judgement as she had known her for so long, and known her to be both practical and fair.

Pamela's phone rang; she hoped it would be the school secretary calling back but it wasn't; it was one of the suppliers wanting to know how much they would be paid on the next payment run. Pamela explained they were trying to close for month end, and promised to phone back early afternoon, when she'd have time to deal with the enquiry. Just then Sandra came back into the office from her meeting, so Pamela was pleased it hadn't been a private call she was involved with. She wasn't afraid of Sandra, and she felt fully justified in taking and making the odd private phone call as this was something she'd checked with John Meredith at interview. She had asked what the company policy was on the subject, and been told that it was fully understood that some calls had to be made during works time such as urgent family business or the odd call to make an appointment for something and that so long as advantage wasn't taken, it was acceptable to make and take the odd personal call. It was simply that with Sandra's unpredictable temperament it was easier to do nothing that would antagonise her.

Sandra did not, though, seem to be back to her usual abrasive self. The bruise she had had on her cheek when she returned from her sick leave after her fall had faded, but she was still quieter than usual and seemed to be allowing the office to work together more as a team than she normally did. This had been one of the reasons that Pamela wondered why John Meredith couldn't see that Sandra wasn't a good manager; she seemed to almost foster a bad atmosphere and stamp on anything that smacked of cooperation between colleagues and positively discourage teamwork. However, Sandra surprised her further this morning by now asking politely how the inputting was going and whether everyone was almost ready for the ledgers to be closed for month end. She then turned to Rob and asked "Once everyone has finished, would you be able to close the ledgers and open the current month, please? I have to go out to an appointment this afternoon and John Meredith suggested that I ask you to do the month end routine for me"

Rob looked very surprised but said "Of course I will, Sandra. Always happy to help" and Sandra said

"Thank you, I appreciate it." Both Pamela and Maureen looked down at their desks, not sure how to deal with this 'new Sandra' but Joan said, kindly,

"Sandra, we've all just had a coffee, but would you like me to make one for you?"

"Oh, no thanks, we had some coffee in the meeting, but thanks for the offer. I'll just sort my desk and make sure all my month end stuff is in order and then I'll pop home for a bit of lunch and then go to my appointment." There was more stunned silence. It was most unusual for Sandra to tell anyone anything. She did still look quite strained, despite being more open and friendly than ever before, and after sorting through her desk and stopping by Rob's desk with some papers and chatting briefly with him she said a quick goodbye and she was gone.

Maureen looked askance at Joan, but at that point Pamela's phone rang and this time it was the school secretary, telling her that Mr Gregory could see her the following day; either at 10am or 4.30pm. Pamela chose the afternoon, deciding that she'd bring in a sandwich and work through her lunch break and then she could leave in time for her appointment and go straight home afterwards. She was pleased about that; she would be able to tell Carla that the appointment was made.

Rob asked everyone whether they were ready for him to close the ledgers; they all said they were and logged out while he did so. Maureen and Joan worked on the Sales Ledger, while Pamela did the Purchase Ledger and Sandra the General Ledger. It was unusual to close all the ledgers at once, but obviously this is what had been agreed by John Meredith. Pamela wondered whether Sandra would be back later in the afternoon, so she could tell her she had an appointment at the school the following afternoon.

Pamela looked at her watch. She hadn't brought anything to eat as she hadn't been organised enough at home after arriving back from France the evening before. She'd had to take Carla to Michael's so she could pick up her school uniform and all the other things she needed now that she wasn't staying there. Pamela had been very cross to find that Michael hadn't thought about Carla needing her stuff clean for school and was very pleased to have Carla back home with her so she could care for her properly. She didn't have a tumble drier, so she just washed Carla's uniform in the washing machine and ironed one school shirt and then hung everything Carla needed in the airing cupboard to dry. She wondered what Michael would have done had she been dropping Carla back to live with him again that evening but she didn't ask Carla, as she really didn't want to be thinking about Michael and Monique's domestic arrangements. She was grateful to Monique for arranging for them to use the holiday cottage, but she didn't want any contact with her. She would only contact Michael if it were necessary to make arrangements for Carla, and then she was happy to go back to leaving it between Carla and Michael, just so long as Michael didn't get it in his head to take Carla away again.

It was just midday; a little early to take her lunch break, but other than a little filing Pamela couldn't do anything until Rob had finished on the computer. Pamela asked the others whether there was anything she could do for them, and when they all said no, they were in the same position as she was, she said she'd take an early lunch break. "Have you any plans for lunch?" Maureen asked her

"No" she replied "I was just going to get a sandwich from one of the local shops"

"Rob, how long will you be with what you are doing?" Maureen asked him

"Oh, only about fifteen minutes or so, providing, of course, everything balances as it should, is that a problem for you?" Pamela was watching this interchange with interest; it was just as well she was sitting down, as what came next would have stopped her in her tracks had she been walking across the office:

"We thought we'd go to the pub, if Pamela fancies joining us, we haven't been for ages; they do nice baguettes at the Pig and Whistle, you could tell us what to order for you and then join us when you've finished"

Pamela laughed; she'd never heard of a pub called the Pig and Whistle, she wondered how far away it was, she'd lived in the area quite a while but didn't know of it. She was glad to be able to tell the others this was why she'd laughed; it helped cover her confusion and pleasure about being asked to join them. Rob was pleased too and it was soon agreed that they'd drive round in one car, to save time and get the order in, and that Rob would walk through the path behind the offices that made a short cut and have a lift back with the others. Maureen explained that there was not much parking there and that they often used to walk over there, sometimes with John Meredith as well before the extra people were employed and John became too busy. In fact the route to the pub seemed quite long by car, but Pamela realised that they had turned enough corners in a largish housing estate to actually be not far behind their company warehouse. Joan confirmed that this was so, and that Rob didn't have far to walk. They chatted about inconsequential things as they parked the car then went up to the bar and placed their order.

Once the three of them settled at a corner table with their drinks and shuffled round a bit to make room for Rob when he arrived, Maureen raised her glass and said "To happier times" Joan gave her a bit of a funny look, and Pamela just said

"Cheers", not being too sure what Maureen meant, although she took it to be a comment about Sandra. They'd already asked Pamela whether she'd had a good holiday and Pamela was busily trying to think of something to say that would fill the uncomfortable silence between Joan and Maureen; she felt that Maureen wanted to say something about Sandra but that Joan didn't but at that moment not only did Rob approach their table but he had John Meredith with him. Both were smiling happily and John said

"Thought you'd come over here without me, did you? Just as well I popped out to see whether Rob had managed Sandra's duties successfully" Pamela was surprised and relieved. She liked John Meredith, he seemed a really fair 'no nonsense' sort of boss, even though she didn't understand why he let Sandra rule the roost they way she did. Surely, Pamela thought, this visit to the pub just showed that all wasn't well with Sandra as office manager?

No more was said about Sandra, or Rob's performing her duties. John had phoned ahead and ordered himself a baguette, so their order arrived together and they spent a companionable lunch break chatting, much to Pamela's surprise, mainly about Brittany. It turned out that John loved it, and as Pamela had never been there before John wanted to know all the ins and outs of Pamela's stay and what she thought of it and then he proceeded to tell them what he knew of the area and asked the others what holiday plans they had for the following year. The time went very quickly and once John had finished his pint he said he'd walk on back, but that they shouldn't hurry back. Rob said he'd walk back with John, and Pamela, Joan and Maureen felt that they shouldn't stay any longer, despite the fact that John had said they could.

As they got in Joan's car Maureen said "I know you won't like my saying this, Joan, but, Pamela, this is what the atmosphere always used to be like before Sandra was brought in as manager. We always used to pull together and were rewarded by the occasional pub visit with extra time when John came with us. Joan, I know that you know something about Sandra's home life; and, I have to say there is obviously something wrong at the moment, but we have just shown that we can, indeed, still pull together, and to manage without her. The atmosphere is just so much more pleasant when she's away, surely you notice it too?"

"Yes, of course I notice it, I just feel sorry for her, that's all. She does have a hard life at home, but, you are right, that's no reason for her to change the office so much. I'm sorry, Pamela, we do know she's been very hard on you at times. Rob too, but he can look after himself, did you know she was furious when John Meredith refused to have Rob reporting to him though her?"

Pamela thought carefully. She didn't want to criticize Sandra too much, but she was thoroughly enjoying this new camaraderie. "No, I didn't know that Sandra wanted Rob to report to her, but it doesn't surprise me, as she does seem to need to feel in total control. Maybe this is because she's not in control at home? This is usually the case with bullies, isn't it; because I do acknowledge that that is what she is, a bully. However, don't you worry about me; I too have plenty going on at home, but I could do without some of the battles with Sandra. Just knowing that you two will help me if I'm stuck, and that we all agree that there is something wrong in the way Sandra runs the office has made me feel much better. How about if we agree not to discuss this again (I know you'd rather we didn't, Joan) unless we have a pressing need? There is one thing that puzzles me though, and that is why John doesn't seem to realise what a pain Sandra can be."

"That's easy to answer' Joan replied "John and Sandra go back a long way; no funny business, I don't mean that, but Sandra was a junior at one of the places John was working while he was still studying. This would have been before Sandra was married and he remembered how efficient she was then, and how helpful she had been to him when he first started to work there. Now, let's stick to what Pamela has suggested and get on as best we can".

Joan and Maureen assured Pamela that they would help her out whenever she needed it, but Maureen added "Not that you seem to need much, you are so professional, just what we needed here" and Pamela was so pleased, especially when Joan agreed as she parked the car, and the three of them walked companionably back into the office. The rest of the afternoon went quickly, and Pamela was soon home with Carla, getting tea ready and telling Carla that she had the appointment the following day with Mr Gregory.

"Oh, good" Carla had said "He was OK with me this afternoon, but he had a go at Emily for no apparent reason"

"Well" Pamela told her "You know I can't talk to him about his attitude to anyone but you"

"I know" Carla said "But maybe you can find out what's up with him". Pamela just smiled. She only wanted to talk to him about his upsetting Carla. She had no intention of finding out what was 'up with him' as Carla put it.

Chapter 37

Sylvie was glad to get home. Why, she wondered, did Mondays always seem more tiring than the other working days of the week? She was glad that Bernice hadn't been in the office, as she had begun to wonder whether she had done the right thing with regard to speaking to her about Major Donald. Bernice was anxious to get the pre-sentence report written, that Sylvie understood, and she was hoping to secure a meeting with Pamela before she did so. Sylvie didn't know Bernice very well but she hadn't considered her to be a particularly nervous person. But on Friday she had asked Sylvie several times whether she thought Pamela would be willing to see her, and if so, how long Sylvie thought it would take Pamela to get in touch. It had begun to irritate Sylvie, as she was extremely busy and had told Bernice that she had no idea on either count.

Sylvie's weekend had followed the pattern that most of her weekends did and she wondered whether perhaps her mum was right. She had had dinner with her parents the previous evening and her mum had brought up her favourite subject of Sylvie's social life, or rather the lack of it. After her visit to Ralph and June a while ago and June's comments about it being better to be alone than in an unhappy relationship Sylvie had said this to her mother the following Sunday when she had asked Sylvie for the umpteenth time what she'd done to relax that week, this being a euphemism for what had she done about meeting a prospective partner.

Her dad had got the message and persuaded her mum to stop nagging her for a couple of weeks, but the previous evening her mum had had another go, and, although she was very nice about it, telling Sylvie that she was only concerned about her, Sylvie wondered whether she should stay away for a couple of Sundays. Maybe she really was in a rut, and maybe the first thing to change should be the Sunday evenings with her parents. The original arrangement had been for Sylvie to eat there every other Sunday but of late her parents had expected her to go every week.

Rummaging in her freezer as she mused on these thoughts she chose a microwavable spaghetti bolognaise and an individual cheesecake for pud. She did love her mum's cooking, but that was not the only reason for her weekly visit. It was mainly to see her dad, to whom she had always been close. She loved her mum, of course, she thought to herself, but it was the lively conversations with her dad that she enjoyed the most.

Sylvie set the microwave timer and put her ready meal in it. She stood the cheesecake on top of the radiator next to the sofa so it would thaw out. She picked up the TV remote control but before she could use it the telephone rang. She sighed as she walked slowly over to the phone and hoped it wouldn't be anyone too demanding as she felt so tired.

She picked up the receiver and said, tentatively "Hello?" there was a pause and an intake of breath and then

"Oh hi, it's me, Pamela. I have an idea what it is my dad has done now, so is it OK to talk to you?" she asked nervously. Sylvie perked up immediately

"Of course, oh, you don't know how pleased I am to hear from you. How are you?"

"I'm fine, thanks. Healthy and fit after walking miles of the southern Brittany coastline with Carla"

"Wow, that sounds great" As she said this Sylvie felt a quick stab of jealousy and immediately felt really guilty; poor Pamela had been through a lot recently. Sylvie heard the microwave ping and knew that she needed to stir her meal and reset the microwave for another couple of minutes. Her friendship with Pamela, however, was far more important than stuck together pasta, and Sylvie had hated the fact that she'd been initially unable to be supportive to Pamela "It's brilliant to hear from you" she told her

"was that a microwave ping I just heard – am I interrupting your dinner?" Pamela asked her "All I wanted to say was could you get in touch with Bernice Liddel for me, as I tried to call her today but she wasn't there, and you'll understand I didn't want one of my colleagues picking up a return call from the Probation Service, so I didn't leave a message for her to call me back"

"Woah there, take a breath" said Sylvie "you always were a chatterbox; you haven't changed, thank goodness. Yes, that was my microwave, I suspect my pasta will be soggy and I don't care, I'd much rather talk to you" she told Pamela.

"OK, then, I have an idea. Carla and I haven't eaten yet, I'm afraid I am a bit disorganised. How about you come over and bring fish and chips for three with you, that's if it's OK for us to see one another now?" Sylvie perked up even more. She realised she wasn't really tired, just dispirited.

"What a great idea – I haven't seen your new place yet. Is it just the other side of the big roundabout with the line of red 'thingies' on? What sort of fish would you like with your chips should I bring anything else with me?" Pamela laughed

"Steady on, calling ME a chatterbox! Just bring yourself and three portions of whatever the nearest fish and chip shop have ready, and yes, our end of the estate is the one just the other side of that roundabout. See you soon"

Sylvie just stopped long enough to move the cheesecake off the radiator and chuck her soggy spag bol in the bin, grabbed her bag and went out of the door. She didn't know Pamela's housing estate very well but estimated that it would take her about fifteen minutes to drive there. She decided to buy the fish and chips at her local chippy and then drive straight over. She was in luck, there was no queue and there were plenty of chips in the fryer and both freshly cooked cod and haddock to choose from. Sylvie wondered whether Pamela still liked the huge green gerkins they sold from a large jar in the chippy; she decided to take a chance and buy them one each.

Although Pamela had said 'don't bring anything else', as she had also said that she was a bit disorganised Sylvie went to the shop next door and bought a large bottle of cola. Sylvie hadn't had fish and chips for ages, and she did love to wash them down with cola.

Pamela was looking out for her, as she knew the house numbers were hard to see in the dark. As Sylvie pulled up Pamela pointed to a space where she could park, and Carla ran out to greet her and help her carry in the fish and chips. "My, you've grown" Sylvie said to her "I haven't seen you for ages" They went into the kitchen where Pamela had three plates ready. Sylvie unwrapped the fish and chips and put them on the plates; as she got to the gerkins Carla exclaimed

"What on earth are those gross looking things?" Pamela looked and laughed, especially when she saw the bottle of cola.

"You've thought of everything – remember when we used to have this after college as a treat when we could afford it?"

"Yes," said Sylvie, "I wondered whether you still liked the giant gerkins"

"God, is THAT what they are?" asked Carla, laughing

"Would you like to try a bit?" her mum and Sylvie both asked at once

"Certainly not, thank you" she replied. "Now, would you two mind if I go into the other room and watch TV with mine while you catch up on some gossip?" Carla asked

Pamela realised that Carla was being tactful as they didn't usually eat in the sitting room, Pamela usually preferred to eat at the little kitchen table. "No, of course not, you don't want to listen to us going on about college and gerkins; you go in the other room and watch TV"

"My, she's growing up. It's really good to see you, Pamela; you are looking great! What do you want to talk about first – do you want to tell me what you've heard about the business with your dad, or do you just want to relax and eat and tell me about Brittany?"

"Let's get the 'dad' thing over first. The trip to Brittany was because of that anyway, it was the only way I was going to get to see Carla, so if you don't mind I'll tell it all to you as it happened and then you can let me know if I've got it right. Is that OK?"

"Yes, of course it is; fire away" Sylvie told her.

So Pamela started at the beginning; Sylvie knew about Michael's taking Carla as Pamela had told her when they met in town, so Pamela's 'beginning' was Michael calling her to suggest the Breton holiday cottage, then the ferry trip with Carla's odd remark about 'loving her whatever she'd done' through to her explaining what she knew to Carla and then phoning her parents and getting her mother's version of what her father had done. Sylvie tried not to interrupt, but she couldn't stop herself when she realised what Pamela meant about Carla assuming it was she, Pamela, who was in trouble. Pamela's voice had faltered at that, showing Sylvie just how much of a strain it all was, despite the fact Pamela had made her laugh telling her about their helpless giggles about the big man next to Carla in the communal sleeping room.

Carla had popped back out to the kitchen for some more cola when she heard Sylvie and her mum laughing and had joined in the tale about the snoring man with wind. She realised, of course, that her mum and Sylvie also needed to talk about serious matters, matters which she had now put to the back of her mind; a trick she had learnt to do when she didn't want to think about something upsetting, or to discuss something with her friends at school. She could hear them talking, but not hear what they were saying. She knew that they were lowering their voices from time to time, but she waited for a lull in the conversation when she wanted to go and say goodnight. She took her plate out to the kitchen and said "That was lovely, thanks, Sylvie. I'm off to bed now, Mum, see you in the morning" Carla said

"Night night, love. Remember I am seeing Mr Gregory tomorrow afternoon – you don't have maths tomorrow, do you?"

"No, not on Tuesdays, thank goodness – the only day without that old letch!"

"That's enough of that, see you in the morning" Pamela said to her.

"What was that all about?" asked Sylvie "Oh, the maths teacher upset her while she was staying with

Michael. She didn't have a protractor – but there must have been more to it than that, she was really upset about it." Pamela told her

"But why did she call him an old letch? Did Michael not know she was upset?" Sylvie asked.

"I don't suppose she told Michael" Pamela said "It was very odd for her staying there, it was Michael and Monique's first week of living together" Somehow, despite their closeness, Pamela didn't want to repeat what Carla had said about her dad's 'shagging his new woman'. She did, however, tell Sylvie that even though Michael had initially wanted Carla to go straight back to him after the trip to Brittany, he had not washed her school uniform. Sylvie said that she believed it was much better for Carla to be back home with Pamela.

"And it is a lovely home you've got here, I know you said it was in a clean state and didn't need much decorating, but it really is quite lovely and just right for the two of you.

"It is, isn't it?" Pamela said, pleased. "Do you know, I've really missed you."

"Oh, I've missed you too, I felt so guilty not contacting you as soon as I knew about your dad, but…"

"I'm not talking about the past few weeks" Pamela cut in "I realise why you'd stopped accepting invitations to dinner with us; I know now that Michael just wanted you there to 'spike' you up and give him something to talk about. I've learned a lot about myself in these last few months. For instance, it was you I automatically turned to when I wanted a jacket to wear to interview, and I knew you'd ask no questions until I was ready to talk to you about the reason why. It's times like this that you learn who your friends are, and I'm not talking about what my Dad's done, I mean Michael's affair with Monique. Did I tell you that most of those old bats on the committee for whom I did the books knew about it?"

"Yes, you did" Sylvie said "I know what you mean about friends. My mum has been nagging again about my social life, or lack of it, rather. I'm not sure I want to find a partner to share my life with, but I know I should go out more. I was wondering…"

"I bet I know what you were wondering" Pamela said "and Carla has beaten you to it! "

"Beaten me to what?" asked Sylvie "Well, Carla talked me into buying some new clothes while we were away, and she said I looked nice in them and said I ought to start going out, and she suggested I ask you if you want to do something occasionally"

"Then great minds do think alike" laughed Sylvie "What about it; do you like the idea?" she asked

"I certainly do" Pamela told her "I wouldn't know where to start, though – what do you suggest?"

"Well I don't suggest we go out on a 'manhunt', I think our 'tarting' days are behind us; maybe we could go to the pictures then a drink afterwards?" Pamela laughed at that

"I agree that we are not man hunting! How about seeing what's on Sunday afternoon and this first time, if Carla doesn't want to see Michael maybe she could come with us?"

"Good idea, she is getting so grown up, we can have a laugh with her. You know, I was wondering about how to stop going to my parents' every single Sunday, you must be a mind reader!"

"Not a mind reader, just a good friend" Pamela said "It won't hurt your mum to be without you one weekend – and you can tell her it's the only day I can go"

"OK, but we'll have to be a bit cunning, tell her there's a film you really want to see, otherwise she'll be inviting you as well as me and giving you the third degree about your love-life too!"

"Actually, I'd quite like to see your parents again. We'd not have to mention about my Dad, would we?" Pamela asked, nervously.

"No, you need to understand about the confidentiality of Probation; this is what my Mum finds so hard to understand. I do have to be careful what I tell to whom, so I find it much easier to say nothing at all to anyone outside the service. She's given up asking me about anything she reads in the papers."

"That's good, then. I wasn't suggesting that I'd like to see your parents next weekend, though. I think it would make a nice change for both of us to go out together."

"That's settled, then. I'll have to get going now – I didn't realise how late it was! Do you know; I felt really tired and miserable when I got in from work;

now I feel I have a new lease of life, even though it's late. I'll tell Bernice you will see her any evening between five and six, apart from tomorrow when you are seeing 'The Letch' and I'll see you next Sunday." Pamela playfully punched her on the arm as she let her out. It seemed nothing could really harm their friendship; they just felt so comfortable with one another again.

Chapter 38

Pamela didn't want to get up. She had not eaten all the portion of fish and chips that Sylvie had brought for her, but what she had eaten had lain rather heavily on her stomach and she had had difficulty getting off to sleep. She had felt sleepily comfortable, though, as she lay awake and thought about the pleasant evening she'd spent with Sylvie. It had all seemed so natural, talking about her father and the situation he now found himself in. Reflecting on it now, as she got up and showered, Pamela thought that although it seemed natural talking it through with Sylvie, it was she who had to get through the days at work, the meetings first with Carla's maths teacher and then with the Probation Officer.

She hadn't realised that she felt nervous about the meeting that afternoon with Mr Gregory, but after showering she was having trouble deciding what to wear. Whatever she chose would need to be suitable for work and smart enough for her to feel confident in when tackling Mr Gregory, so she was searching in the back of her cupboard when Carla called out to her and asked whether she was OK. Pamela almost gave a grumpy reply, then she remembered why Carla was so concerned; it was less than a week ago that she found she'd been wrong and wasn't about to lose her mum to a prison so she said "Sorry, love, I can't make up my mind what to wear"

"Can I come in?" Carla asked her "Yes, love, do, perhaps you can help?" her mum said

"I'm not surprised you're having trouble" Carla said "You've lost so much weight that those things you bought to start the job just don't look right. Let's see, what about a pair of the dark trousers you bought on holiday and one of the new tops?"

"Oh, I don't know, I bought the stuff in France for casual wear" Pamela said, doubtfully.

"Well, try the black jeans and one of your older blouses, then – you'll have to decide soon, or you'll be late. I've had some cereals and will be off to catch my bus in a minute. Come on; let's see what you look like"

Not having left herself time to eat anything, Pamela grabbed a slightly stale croissant and an apple they'd brought back from France to take with her to work. She wondered if she'd have time to do a quick shop after seeing Mr Gregory, as she hadn't shopped since they had returned. She grinned as she caught sight of her reflection in the glass of the kitchen door. Carla had said "That's it; you look great, Mum" and Pamela had glanced quickly at the mirror on her wardrobe door and felt reasonably pleased with the effect. Carla had been right, the new black jeans, when teamed up with a very old red blouse that Carla had pulled out from the back of Pamela's wardrobe didn't really look like jeans, especially with the old red blouse worn on the outside, rather than tucked in. It was quite a cold day; autumn seemed to be ending quickly, so Pamela shrugged herself into her winter jacket which she took from the cupboard under the stairs.

Pulling into the office car park Pamela saw that Sandra's car was already there. She wasn't sure from what she had said the previous day whether she was going to be in the office this morning. So, deciding to take the bull by the horns Pamela hung her coat up and went straight up to her desk "Hi, Sandra, I hope it's OK, but I have an appointment with my daughter's maths teacher this afternoon, I plan to work through lunch and leave early – is that OK?" Sandra looked up

"Yes that's fine. Do you know whether all was well with the month end close yesterday?" she asked. Pamela thanked her and said that yes, Rob had managed the month end close and that, as far as she knew, everything had balanced. At that point Rob himself came into the office, so Pamela went to her own desk and left them to it.

Apart from the fact that Sandra was a little quiet; and that had the effect of making the office atmosphere a little heavy Pamela found that the day went by very quickly. She had eaten the stale croissant with her mid morning coffee and had forgotten about the apple until she realised it was almost four o'clock so she ate it while she tidied away her paperwork and logged off. She was quite nervous about seeing Mr Gregory and didn't want her stomach to rumble while she was with him. It was only because she had asked for the meeting that she was a little nervous; she had got on fine with him when she had met him at the parents evening, but because she had requested the meeting she wasn't sure quite where she should start as she wanted to get her point over about his having upset Carla, but she didn't want to sound as though she was complaining.

The traffic was heavy and it was exactly 4.30 as Pamela parked the car so she was a little late when she walked into the school reception and as she was saying that she had arranged to meet Mr Gregory he appeared, breathless, and apologised for having kept Pamela waiting! Pamela laughed and said that she'd been held up in the traffic and had only just arrived herself. He led her to a staff room and offered her a coffee which she gratefully accepted and then balancing both coffees rather precariously on a small tray with a couple of biscuits on a saucer he led her to a classroom where he said they would not be quite so comfortable but where they were less likely to be interrupted. He put the tray down and indicated for her to take a seat as he pulled another chair towards the desk. "Now, what can I do for you?" he asked, pleasantly. "Please, have a biscuit – I am going to have one because my stomach will rumble if I don't" he told her, laughing.

Pamela took a biscuit and told him that she had had an apple before leaving work for the same reason and he said that if either of their stomachs did rumble despite the precautions that neither of them should be embarrassed. Pamela felt comfortable with him so she launched straight into telling him why she had asked to see him, explaining that Carla had been very upset. He was very surprised, indeed, that Carla had been upset; he vaguely remembered speaking to her about not having a protractor and saying that she shouldn't need to disturb a classmate by asking to borrow one as it was for a test, but he hadn't meant to upset her. He looked intently at Pamela and asked her whether anything else was happening in Carla's life just now that would upset her "I know we had a 'change of address' form submitted for Carla fairly recently, may I ask whether that means anything?" he asked her.

"Oh, yes, my husband and I have separated" she told him "But, Mr Gregory..."

"Please, call me Matt" he interrupted "Do go on" so she told him that the separation had taken place some months ago and that Carla had accepted it, but she went on to explain that Michael had taken her to stay with him for a while, but despite the fact she felt comfortable with him she stuck to the story about her father being taken ill.

Matt went on to explain that there was a certain element in the class, mostly boys, who could be disruptive if allowed to be, and it was possible that on that day one or more of them had claimed not to have something that they needed for the test, and that perhaps that was why he had spoken more harshly than he had realised to Carla. Pamela wasn't totally convinced, especially as Carla had said that sometimes he behaved like that to others in the class for no apparent reason, but, she thought, perhaps it was with the more disruptive element that he was normally harsher. She thought that she should give him the benefit of the doubt, and, if Carla was unhappy again she could always ask to see him again.

Pamela tried to look surreptitiously at her watch and Mr Gregory (she couldn't think of him as Matt!) smiled and said "It's only just after five" as he saw that the cuffs on Pamela's blouse were too tight for her to see the time.

"Oh, I am sorry, I'm not trying to rush away, but we only got back from our holiday on Sunday and I haven't shopped yet; I was hoping to have time to shop on the way home"

"No problem" he said to her "I think we have cleared up the matter; but please don't hesitate to come and see me if Carla gets upset at all again."

"OK, I will. Thank you for your time, and thank you very much for the coffee and biscuit. All I have had today so far is a stale croissant and an apple. I will shop now quickly on the way home. Good bye"

"Good bye" and they shook hands and Pamela hurried back to her car.

She was deep in thought trying to decide what to buy at the meat counter when a voice startled her "I'm glad to see you're not a vegetarian!" and she swung round and said

"Oh, it's you"

"Yes, I realised I needed something for my dinner and hadn't taken anything out of the freezer. I hope you are having something substantial this evening after your stale croissant and apple?" Pamela laughed

"Don't forget the biscuit you gave me - that saved me from starvation!" she said to him. She looked up at him and saw that he was looking appraisingly at her. She smiled shyly, this was different to seeing him as a teacher; she'd not really thought about his having a home life at all, she'd just wanted to talk to him about Carla and then forget about him. She quickly chose some chicken pieces and some mince and put them into her trolley and glanced at him; he was wearing motorcycle leathers and looked very different. Pamela thought that he must be a little bit younger than her, she'd not even thought about his age; teaching a group of lively twelve and thirteen year olds must be quite hard for him at times. "Well, I must get on now, it was nice to see you again" she said to him.

"It was nice to see you too" he said "Perhaps we will bump into each other again sometime"

Pamela hurried round the supermarket thinking on her feet what they would need for the rest of the week. She'd been paid the previous Friday so didn't have to worry too much about what she was going to spend, although she did want to pay back to Michael what she'd spent on herself out of the holiday money he gave them; she was more concerned about not having to shop again until the weekend than about what the groceries were costing. She also wanted at least one meal that would be very easy and quick to prepare because it was likely that the Probation Officer, Ms Liddel would want to see her straight after work one evening. She was feeling very tired and as she straightened up after bending over the freezer to get a couple of pizzas she sighed deeply. Matt Gregory watched her quizzically from the next aisle. Pamela just had some fresh veg and salad to get and then she was finished. As she went to put out her hand to pick up a lettuce she touched a hand and withdrew hers quickly and looked up to apologise "Goodness, you again!" she said

"Yes, sorry, I just decided I needed a lettuce and there you were again! Perhaps we are destined to keep meeting" Pamela laughed and grabbing a pack of baby tomatoes and a bag of sprouts she made her way to the checkout.

When she got home Carla helped her put away the shopping and put a quick salad together as Pamela popped some oven chips and a couple of breaded turkey steaks in the oven she asked her mum how she had got on with Mr Gregory. Pamela told her that he had said 'call me Matt' and they both laughed. She explained what he had said about the disruptive element in the class but Carla was dubious about that. "I know who he means, but they were not playing up that day or I'd have realised why he was sharp with me. Never mind, now that you've been to see him I expect he will be OK with all of us for a while" Pamela silently agreed and decided not to mention bumping into him at the supermarket. Now she thought about it, it did seem a little strange, but it had seemed natural enough at the time.

Just as Pamela put the two plates on the table the phone rang. Carla went in to answer it and came back out and said "Sylvie for you" so Pamela went to take the call.

"Just a quickie" Sylvie said "If it's OK with you Bernice can come to your's at five o'clock tomorrow"

"Yes, fine, let's get it over with but could she make it five fifteen? That way I won't need to leave work early two nights in a row" Pamela said to her. Sylvie had explained the previous evening that the sooner Bernice could submit the report the sooner the court date for sentencing could be set. Carla had told Sylvie that Pamela had just put dinner on the table so Sylvie said

"bye then" and told her to go and eat her dinner. Pamela hadn't thought to ask Sylvie just how quickly the court appearance for sentencing would be arranged; her father had told her that her mother's hospital visit was to be the following week and she wondered whether everything was to happen at once. Then she thought about it and supposed that the judge would need time to read the report before sentencing could take place. She shuddered suddenly as she thought about it and Carla asked whether she was OK.

"Yes, love, I'm fine. This Probation Officer I told you about wants to come here tomorrow evening, and I've told Sylvie to let her know that's fine." Pamela then went on to tell Carla that Sylvie had also had the idea that they could go out from time to time, and that they were planning a trip to the pictures the following Sunday. "I don't know what's on yet, but you can come if you like, if you aren't going to your Dad's"

Carla was pleased "I think it's great that you and Sylvie are going out. I don't want to go to Dad's this weekend, I'd like to stay over at Rachel's on Saturday if that's OK with you because Emily has figure skating practice in full costume on Sunday morning and would like us to go and watch"

"OK, that's fine, so long as your homework is all done before you go" Pamela said. Mmm, she thought, full costume; and she found herself daydreaming about Matt Gregory in his motorbike leathers! She wondered what was the matter with her and pulled herself together so she could take in what Carla was telling her about the competition that Emily's coach had entered her for.

Chapter 39

Sylvie was looking forward to seeing Ralph at work again, and sang along to the car radio as she drove into work. She'd hardly been in the office at all so far this week, she had been attending court and making home visits, and one of the court attendances had been for a client of Ralph's. Ralph was not allowed to come back to work full time but his doctor had advised a couple of half days starting today, Thursday, so he would just have two before the weekend; then he had an appointment the following Monday and if the doctor was satisfied with his progress he was to be allowed two weeks of half days before going back full time.

The arrangement was for him to come in at nine and meet with the Chief Probation Officer, then spend a few hours sorting through his paperwork and catching up with his colleagues. He wouldn't be assigned any new cases until his doctor gave the OK for him to return full time, but he would see any of his clients due for morning meetings, and he would see whether there was anything he could do to help the other officers who had been covering his casework.

Bernice had seen Pamela the previous evening and she felt that she was ready now to write Major Fielding's pre-sentence report. She was also pleased that Ralph was coming into the office today as she'd been covering one of his more difficult cases and wanted to discuss it with him. The message board indicated that Sylvie was due in; she hoped she'd be able to catch her before she became too involved with Ralph as she hadn't seen her for a while but she was aware that she had irritated her the previous Friday and wanted to apologise. Like all the officers Bernice had too high a case load of her own work, without having to cover cases for other officers. She knew that stress manifested itself in many different ways and with her it made her anxious and inclined to repeat herself, not always realising that she was speaking out loud rather than trying to clear things in her mind. She hadn't been working at this office very long; her previous colleagues were used to this with her and would, without offending, just tell her she was 'at it again' and to shut up! She had spoken to Sylvie on the phone when Sylvie had made the arrangement for her to see Pamela, but she had not thought that the right opportunity to mention it.

Sylvie grimaced at the state of her desk. As well as the non urgent paperwork she had left there on a fleeting visit the previous lunchtime, there was an awful lot of stuff in her in-tray. She knew that what was not urgent the previous week would soon become urgent. She was checking through it when Bernice came up to her desk and plonked a coffee down for her "Oh, thanks" said Sylvie, surprised.

"Well, I want to thank you for arranging for me to see your friend, Pamela, and to apologise for being a pain in the arse last Friday" This was so unexpected that Sylvie laughed so loudly that several heads popped up from their desks to see what was going on

"Oh, you did go on a bit, but I wouldn't have put it quite like that myself" Sylvie told Bernice

"No, I know what I'm like when I get stressed – promise me if I do it to you again you'll tell me to 'shut it' just like my colleagues in Andover used to" Sylvie chuckled and said

"OK, I promise. So, how did you get on last night with Pamela, then?"

Bernice went back to her desk to collect her coffee and gave Sylvie a quick rundown of how the meeting had gone. She told Sylvie how she had got there before Pamela and that it was Carla who opened the door and asked whether she was 'Sylvie's colleague to see Mum' which Bernice had been very impressed with "What a sensible young lady that is. She put the kettle on, and when her mum came in she very kindly made herself scarce, giving me a chance to chat to Pamela alone." Sylvie said that Carla was, indeed, a very lovely girl and Bernice said that she had had a great chat with Pamela and was about to write the report on her father, Major Fielding. "I do need to catch Ralph, though, when he is through with the Chief, as I need to talk to him about Harry Wheeler..."

"That old rascal; is he up to his tricks again?" asked Sylvie

"No, not the father, the son..." Bernice told her

"But his Social Worker should sort him out, surely?" asked Sylvie, remembering him as a young teenager.

"No, he's come of age, and I'm afraid he looks to be following in his father's footsteps. I'd like to ask

Ralph's advice about him today, if I can." At that, Ralph appeared and Sylvie suggested Bernice collar him first, before any of the others did. She was happy to wait, as she knew she could visit him at home if she didn't manage to chat with him now. She was more concerned with his health than any of his cases she was covering, luckily, this time, she only had fairly routine ones, but she was very pleased, for his sake, to see him back.

Sylvie turned back to her paperwork, but before she could get stuck in Faith came over to her and asked whether she 'had a minute'. Sylvie waved her hand at her paperwork and said "I don't think one more minute will make any difference to this lot" but seeing the serious look on Faith's usually cheerful face she followed her dutifully out to the coffee making area. "What's up?" she asked Faith.

"Oh, you know how people can be" she began "I've arranged for a volunteer who is willing to work on this case to meet with Major and Mrs Fielding, and as I was about to come over and tell you and Bernice I overheard Josie say to Patricia 'look at them, I suppose Bernice will be getting Sylvie to write her friend's father's pre-sentence report next'. Now I don't usually sneak to people about what's said about them, but I know you've been professional through and through with this, but do you mind if I deal only with Bernice over this from now on?" Sylvie was very touched that Faith had told her this. She was not in the least worried about Josie and Patricia talking about her behind her back; it was what both she and Ralph would expect of them.

However, she didn't want to drag either Bernice or Faith into anything that anyone could construe as less than professional, and growing to like Bernice even more since her confession about being a 'pain in the arse' when stressed, she asked Faith whether she would act as go-between and explain what she'd overheard to Bernice so she would know why she, Sylvie was avoiding her for a while. Faith said "Of course I will, leave it to me" and went back to her desk turning to pull a face at Sylvie as she did so. Sylvie busied herself making a coffee she didn't really want so that it didn't look as though she'd been gossiping with Faith. Look at me, she thought, I'm acting like them because of them!

Sylvie did, in fact, get the chance to talk to Ralph; he came to her desk as soon as he'd talked with Bernice about young Harry. "Aren't you going to spend any time at your own desk?" asked Sylvie, laughing and indicating the pile of paperwork on it.

"No, I've been told emphatically both by my doc and by the chief that I mustn't get stressed, so I'm going to sit with you while you sort yours out and update me on what's been going on in your neck of the woods" Sylvie was pleased to have Ralph to herself for a while, but did ask him whether he shouldn't ask the others whether there was anything pressing they had to see him about but he explained that he had one of his long term clients coming in at eleven and as it was now ten minutes to, there wouldn't be time. "Anyway, Patricia has been seeing him for me, and I had a quick chat with her before I saw the chief, and she says there's nothing new to report. He only has a few more weeks to come in and he hasn't missed any appointments, so seeing him should be straightforward".

"OK, that makes sense" Sylvie told him. "How did you get on with the chief?"

"Well, along with the usual promises, he did seem genuine about trying to lower the stress levels in the office generally and he asked me my opinion with regard to the best way forward"

"Wow, that's a first" Sylvie said to him. She wanted to tell him about Patricia and Josie so she said "Oh, you know what you demonstrated to me at your house that evening? Well, you were quite right and it was witnessed this morning" Ralph knew exactly what she was getting at and was still chuckling as he made his way downstairs to meet with his client.

Bernice decided she would write the Major's report at home. She had had a hectic morning and realised that the afternoon would be no better; at least she could ignore the phone if it rang at home and she could get a clear couple of hours without interruption. She was just packing away her paperwork as Faith approached with someone Bernice hadn't seen before "Before you rush off, may I introduce Isobel?" she asked

"Of course, nice to meet you" Bernice said, shaking her hand. "You are going to meet with the Major and his wife?" she asked in confirmation

"Yes, that's right" Isobel told her "We have a policy of only going in two's to a sex offender, but we can't spare any other volunteers just now, so Faith has kindly offered to come and meet them with me initially" Isabel was in her late fifties, softly spoken with a faint Scottish accent.

Bernice took to her straight away; Faith had explained to Bernice earlier that Isobel was one of her best volunteers; a no nonsense older lady who just did volunteering out of a sense of wanting to give something back to the community. She had explained that many volunteers were studying social work and needed to get a certain amount of voluntary hours in and that you got some very good and some ambitious but not so good amongst those people. Bernice was pleased that Faith had come up trumps with a good volunteer, as this case was not straightforward and she felt that Sylvie would be grateful that the family were in good hands with Isobel, especially after the throwaway remark that Faith told Bernice about. Bernice was furious with Josie and Patricia over that; she wanted to say something, but Faith calmed her down and persuaded her not to. Bernice chatted a while with Isobel and Faith and wished them good luck with Mrs Fielding, explaining that she was 'not so bad once you got to know her' and told them how at first she had insisted on pronouncing her name with the incorrect emphasis, and how she'd felt the need to get the upper hand with her. Bernice had phoned and arranged for Faith and Isobel to visit Major and Mrs Fielding the following morning, so saying her goodbyes to them she made her way home to have some lunch and write up the report.

Ralph appeared by Sylvie's desk just as her stomach rumbled loudly. "Well, I don't have to ask whether you are hungry" he laughed. "How about accompanying me to town for a burger? My ulcer is dying for some grease and sugar – that June has had me on a terrible diet!"

"You beast" she said "June has been a saint to put up with you at home for so long, and I'm certainly not encouraging you to eat any rubbish after she's been getting you to eat properly. I don't have time, anyway"

"OK, OK, you win over the food, but NOT the time" he told her, firmly "I want to talk to you about some of the things I've suggested to the chief, so it's a sort of working lunch. Will you accompany me if we go to a healthy sandwich bar and I promise to have something yucky and green with mine?"

"Oh, alright then" Sylvie laughed "You win, so long as you promise to eat your 'yucky' green salad, not just push it around the plate with your fork!"

Chapter 40

Pamela was tired. She tried not to show it as Sandra seemed to be back to her old form having snapped at Rob already and it was only nine thirty. The previous evening had been the first all week that Pamela wasn't doing something or seeing someone, and apart from the Monday evening's fish and chips with Sylvie the other things had been stressful. She didn't just put her feet up and relax, though, as she had begun to feel bad about not having seen Marian for ages so had popped round there before cooking dinner and had been surprised and worried to find Marian tearful.

"Oh, I'm orright, ducks" Marian had tried to reassure her "Don't you worry about me. I've 'ad a bit of bad news about a friend, and it's upset me a bit. Silly me. Now, you sit down; I'll make us a cuppa and you tell me all about yer 'oliday and 'ow things is with yer dad and Carla an' all that"

She really didn't want to sit down for a cup of tea, she wanted to cook dinner and get Carla sitting down to do her homework, so she suggested to Marian that she do just that and come back over to Marian's for a cuppa after she and Carla had eaten. "Dinner won't take long" she'd told her "It's all ready to cook, so I'll be back in about an hour or so if that's OK with you?"

"Ooh, yeah, that'd be good, we can 'ave a real proper natter" Marian had told her.

"Yes, we will, and we won't talk about me and my problems and holiday all evening; we will talk about you, and if you feel you would like to we will talk about your friend with the bad news" Pamela had said to her as she was leaving.

"I'm talking to you, are you half asleep?" Sandra said rudely to Pamela.

"No, just concentrating" said Pamela quickly "I'm sorry, can I help?" she asked

"Hm, I asked whether you'd remembered to pay the electricity for the car park street lamp" She said abruptly.

"I think so, have you looked on the system?" Pamela asked her.

"No. I don't see the point of having a dog and barking myself" Sandra said rudely. At this, several heads appeared above their PC's, and Maureen gave Pamela an encouraging but cautious smile behind Sandra's back.

Pamela gritted her teeth and fixed a smile at the same time. "Let me have a look for you" she said, as pleasantly as she could. She was mentally crossing her fingers, as it was one of the things she had asked Joan and Maureen to sort out for her while she was away in Brittany. There had always been a bit of a mystery over this auxiliary electricity bill and it was, in fact, Pamela who had managed to ascertain what it was for. All she had asked of Maureen was that she got John Meredith to sign it off so Joan could put it on the system ready for the payment run. It was obvious to them all that Sandra was in a bad mood and wanted to fix on something that the team had not done. The system was slow to display the query screen, but when it did it showed that the payment had been made.

"Oh, that's alright then" Sandra said "I'll throw away this final reminder" Pamela was annoyed that Sandra hadn't just given her the reminder in the first place and wondered whether Sandra had any more. She said

"Oh, I could have dealt with that, do you have any more reminders that I should look up? After all, that is what I was taken on for, to save your having to worry about the purchase ledger".

Sandra grunted. She knew that she was outmanoeuvred so she went back to her desk and collected a small pile of post and handed it to Pamela. Pamela thanked her and began to go through the queries and went back into reverie about the previous evening as she did so.

Marian had surprised Pamela on several counts. When Pamela said she'd only tell Marian all about their holiday if she promised to tell her a little about herself she shyly agreed – so Pamela looked at the clock and said "Right then – half an hour about our holiday, which will include how I had to tell Carla about her granddad" Marian's eyes widened at this "and then we'll talk about you and about the bad news you've had from your friend." Pamela wanted to cheer Marian up, so she made sure she included the amusing things that had happened, like Carla and her having a fit of giggles in the middle of the night because of the 'windy snoring' man sleeping next to

Carla. She made light of Carla's belief that she, Pamela, was the one in trouble and just explained that this was why she'd felt the need to tell Carla a version of what had really happened – then she realised that she hadn't told Marian that she did now know what it was her father was accused of, so she relented about her half hour rule and told the full story. "So long as you do tell me about your friend" Pamela said when Marian had admonished her for leaving out half the story.

Pamela popped home to see how Carla was getting on with her homework when Marian laughingly called 'half time' and said she'd make another cup of tea before telling her about why she had been upset before. Carla had finished her homework and had got ready for bed and was watching the television. "I'll just finish watching this, then I'll go to bed" she told her mum "I didn't think you'd escape from Marian's easily" she said.

Marian set down the two cups of tea. "Is Carla orright, duck?" she asked.

"Yes, she's finished her homework and will go to bed once the television program she's watching has finished. I wanted to make sure she was OK as she was doing maths homework, and she has had a bit of a run in with the maths teacher" Pamela felt her cheeks redden as she thought about 'call me Matt' and his leather motorbike gear and she wondered briefly what had come over her. Marian noticed and assuming Pamela was worrying about it she asked what sort of bother Carla was in. So Pamela just said it was probably all sorted now and that she'd been to the school to see the teacher concerned.

"Never mind all that" Pamela had told Marian "We've spoken enough about my family, if you feel up to it tell me why you were upset when I called round earlier"

Pamela finished checking the queries that Sandra had given her and she decided it was close enough to lunch time not to try to continue what she had been doing when Sandra had interrupted. She found herself wondering once more what was making Sandra behave the way she was, and also wondering about her management skills and how she got away with her behaviour. She knew jolly well that she had made it a part of Pamela's job to check the reminder letters – why had she taken it upon herself to start to check them today?

Once again Pamela had had neither the time nor the energy to make herself a sandwich but she begrudged the couple of pounds it would cost to buy one at the local shop, so despite still feeling tired, she wanted to blow the cobwebs away and put some distance between herself and Sandra so decided to walk a little further, to the nearest supermarket. She found herself thinking, inexplicably, as she did the previous evening at Marian's about 'call me Matt' as she now thought of him, and, beginning to enjoy the feeling of being slimmer and possibly also attractive, she decided just to buy some fresh fruit for her lunch.

Walking briskly to the supermarket and back in order to try to shake off thoughts of Matt, Pamela went back to thinking about her evening with

Marian. It truly had been an evening of revelation. Pamela had never considered herself to be a judgemental person, but as the many facets of Marian's life unfolded she found herself realising that she had, indeed, previously been judgemental in some aspects towards people. "Don't you worry ducks" Marian had said to her "Tis natural, tis the way we're all brought up – you've said enough about your Mum for me to see that she's affected you more than you realise. I learned all about 'nature' and 'nurture' and though not everyone agrees I believe nurture has more to do with how we see the world around us."

Pamela chuckled to herself as she hitched up her shoulder bag, checked her watch and slowed her pace a little on the way back to work. Fancy Marian having studied with the Open University! They had, of course, then chatted on long into the night once Pamela had popped quickly back home to check that Carla was asleep. What had started as Marian simply explaining why she had been in tears earlier in the evening had extended into a potted history of Marian's life, an explanation on the workings of Alcoholics Anonymous and the revelation that Marian had a degree from the Open University – or OU as Marian called it. There had initially been a misunderstanding when Pamela had thought that Marian was saying that she, herself, was what some attendees of Alcoholics Anonymous called a recovering alcoholic, but she was talking about her OU friend, Gillian, who she had been told by a mutual friend had 'picked up a drink'. Knowing how important it was to Gillian not to have done so was what had upset Marian earlier that evening. "I knows yer can't live other people's lives for 'em, ducks, but Gillian has a young family and has been trying so hard I've been sort of willin 'er to succeed" Marian had told Pamela.

Marian had explained how she had been involved with OUSA, the Open University Students Association, and how she had become involved in counselling those having difficulty with distance learning or with having to be away from home to go to a summer school. Gillian had come to Marian for advice one summer when Marian was acting as an OUSA representative at the Summer School she was attending at Brighton University as she had heard that heavy drinking was often a part of OU Summer School culture and she wanted at least one person to know she was a recovering alcoholic.

"It's a funny thing" Marian had said to Pamela "But I introduced myself as 'Spike' when we first met; as that's what they calls me in OUSA. 'Course, I've finished me studies now, so strictly speakin I can't be in OUSA no more, but I still goes out wiv 'em all sometimes. An, like you, I ain't normally friendly wiv me neighbours, no more an you are, but there was someat about you I liked from the start." This had made Pamela laugh

"What, and my being so awfully rude to you that very first time you called to help me?"

"Yes" Marian had replied to Pamela's question "Specially so, I spose, 'cos you seemed so natural, even if you was rude!" She paused and sipped her glass of wine. They had progressed from drinking tea to Marian's uncorking a bottle of wine she'd been saving for a 'special occasion' as she put it. She'd said "Sno use waiting for me sons and their wives to come and drink it cos it ain't posh enough for them, being all I can afford to buy. They brings their own on the odd occasions they comes to see their old mum! If we gonna have a real heart to heart we may as well drink to the poor sods like Gillian who can't enjoy the odd glass." And thinking this strange philosophy through Pamela had raised her glass and said

"Cheers" Marian grinned and said

"Cheers" and then she couldn't resist asking Pamela how surprised she was that her 'common' neighbour with what she called her 'Regional Accent' but she had said it with a smile and a very posh accent had 'two posh sons and a university degree'?

This was when Pamela went back to being reasonably serious and had said to Marian that what with what she'd been through during the last year or so, with the split from Michael followed by what her father had been up to and being parted from Carla she didn't think that anything else could surprise her – but that Marian's revelations had both surprised her and pleased her immensely. She was not quite so pleased with Marian's retort of "Oh, so does that mean I'm good enough for you now, then?" but Marian apologised almost immediately and went on to explain about how she saw the 'Nature and Nurture' debate and explained that she believed that everyone has their prejudices, but that some are more prejudiced than others. "Have you read 'Animal Farm?" She asked Pamela. "Yes" Pamela told her –

you mean where 'All Animals are equal, but some Animals are more equal than others? We studied it at school. Wasn't it about politics rather than prejudices? But I am not as educated as you – I only went to college after school, not university!"

Marian had gone on to agree that, fundamentally, Pamela was right about George Orwell's book, but that it had a bearing on what Marian was saying.

"But I will save it fer another day to natter on about all that and to tell yer about me studies" Marian told Pamela "Or else you'll be here all night and you'll never get up for work tomorrow" and it was more or less at that point that Pamela went home laughingly saying to Marian that as it was past midnight it was already technically 'tomorrow' and she hugged her strange neighbour and thanked her for the confidences about her own life and for all the support she'd given her since she'd moved in.

As Pamela walked towards her desk she noticed that Sandra had her head down and was staring intently at something on her desk. Pamela glanced across at Maureen and Joan; both of them looked at her quickly and Maureen nodded towards Sandra and gave a warning look and shook her head slowly at the same time. Pamela assumed that they were letting her know that something had happened and Sandra was best left alone for a while. "Well, that suits me" thought Pamela as she was struggling with letting Sandra get away with being nasty, though she didn't mind so much when Sandra was just nasty to her, but she didn't like to see Lauren upset on the occasions that she was on the receiving end of Sandra's bullying.

Pamela had plenty of work to do, so she settled down and got stuck in while she ate one of the apples she had bought. The walk had done her good. She was still tired, but she knew she had nothing planned until Sunday afternoon when she would go to the cinema with Sylvie. She would organise the washing and housework tomorrow, Saturday, have an early night tonight and give herself Sunday off. She smiled at the thought. Rob saw her smile and was pleased. He also didn't mind when Sandra had a go at him, but he also didn't like it when she was nasty to others; he was relieved to see that Pamela was not upset; he had guessed that she had gone for a walk in her lunch break to get away from the office. Pamela felt someone was looking at her and looked up and saw that Sandra was approaching Rob's desk with some paperwork so she quickly looked down again and got on with what she was doing. She glanced at the time and decided that if she concentrated she could get through everything on her desk before the end of the afternoon and have a clear start with just the incoming post to deal with on Monday.

Chapter 41

Faith pulled up outside Major Fielding's house, leaving room for Isobel to park behind her. As they had decided it would be easier to come in separate vehicles and meet there, Faith had agreed with Isobel that it may be better initially to park outside. Isobel always set great store by creating a good impression when first befriending a new client; she didn't want to antagonise the Major and his wife by just driving in, even though they were expected. Faith was planning to introduce herself and Isobel, and once she'd checked that Mrs Fielding was in as well as the Major and that Isobel felt comfortable in their company, she was intending to go back to the probation office and leave Isobel to get to know them and let them know what, as a Probation Volunteer, she could do to help.

As they crunched along the gravel drive, Isobel looked in admiration at the chrysanthemums growing in the flower bed in front of the house. They were past their best and they hadn't been deadheaded recently and there were weeds at the edges of the drive, as well as between the planting, but the chrysanthemums had been cleverly arranged with tall ones towards the back and short ones at the front, and there was a clump of bronze coloured ones in between. It gave an air of faded gentility, as though someone had run out of either energy, or money to pay a gardener. Isobel loved gardening, but since she'd moved into her little flat she'd not been able to indulge her passion. She did have several nice window boxes; and some herbs growing on her kitchen windowsill but she was looking forward to being able to talk about the chrysanthemums; it would give her a start with the befriending process as she could tell that the planting had been done with love, she didn't believe it possible to have such a lovely planting if it was done clinically by a landscape gardener. She felt sure that the 'chrysanthemum person' lived in this big house.

As soon as Faith pressed the door bell it was opened by a man. "Major Fielding?" Faith asked

"Er, yes" he answered. "But we don't buy anything on our doorstep and we're not interested in religion" he said rather sharply. Before either Faith or Isobel could say anything, the Major was joined at the door by a lady who asked "Who is it dear?" and on seeing Faith and Isobel she started to reiterate what the Major had said. Before she could finish, Faith interrupted and introduced both herself and Isobel. Mrs Fielding invited them in, but she was hesitant and didn't seem very welcoming; she said "Oh you'd better come in then" but she said it almost grudgingly and she was giving Faith strange sideways glances as she led them through to the sitting room.

Both Faith and Isobel were well used to not being the most welcome of callers, but they were expected and were therefore rather puzzled by the coolness shown them. Bernice had said that Major Fielding had agreed to meet a volunteer but that Mrs Fielding had not been so sure, so Faith assumed that this was why Mrs Fielding was looking at her rather strangely. Major Fielding took the lead and offered tea or coffee; Taking her cue, Mrs Fielding then tried to hide her confusion by saying "Oh, yes, I'll put the kettle on, what would you prefer?"

Faith and Isobel looked at each other, and both said at once "Oh we don't mind, whatever is going" Major Fielding, mindful of the fact that it was Daphne who may need support from the volunteer said that he would make tea for everyone while she had a little chatter with them, as he put it.

Daphne Fielding was furious. She had had little or nothing to do with anyone black, but she knew she didn't like black people, and she certainly didn't want any help from this one. Faith and Isobel were still standing; Daphne didn't really want to invite them to sit down, but her good manners overcame her bad ones and she indicated the sofa and said "Oh, please sit down and I'll go and help with the tea"

As soon as Daphne was in the kitchen she hissed to Donald through clenched teeth "They didn't say she was black!" Donald was slightly perplexed.

"Well, I don't think they are allowed to mention it these days" he said to her placatingly, as he put cups and saucers on the tray. "You get us out some nice biscuits, old thing, and we'll soon sort this out" he said as he took the tea things to the sitting room where Faith and Isobel sat waiting. Donald was concerned again about Daphne's health; her hospital appointment was for the following Tuesday, and Donald had not asked Bernice how long it would be between the submission of her pre-sentence report and his court appearance.

There were, of course, other ways for Daphne to get to the hospital for her appointment, but that would mean asking someone or taking a taxi, as public transport links were not good from Crowford. He hadn't suggested this to Daphne, however, as a taxi fare would be expensive, and to ask anyone other than Pamela would mean explaining why he couldn't take Daphne, and he knew Pamela would find it difficult to get time off just after her week's holiday.

Of course, Donald mused as he set the tea tray down on the low table, it was unlikely that his court appearance would be as soon as Tuesday, but he was eager to get it over with and have all 'this business' behind them. He had so far managed to stop Daphne from inviting all their friends for the 'little soiree' as Daphne had suggested; which she had wanted to do when he had confessed all the previous weekend. The initial energy she had summoned at that time had now waned, and she had had several bad nights again with the return of the indigestion and bilious attacks, so it had not been difficult to dissuade her.

Daphne brought in a plate of biscuits and set it down next to the tray of tea things. "Now, I'm afraid I didn't catch your names" she said, looking at Isobel "Would you mind introducing yourself and your companion again, dear?" Isobel hesitated. She was beginning to get a bad feeling about this. She had known Faith a long time, and knew how hard Faith had worked to become a fully qualified Probation Officer. Faith had no hang ups about people being prejudiced towards her because of her colour; she was a confident woman and proud of her achievements. In fact, she had just attended the annual conference for the Association of Black Probation Officers, but she had only done so to please the new Probation Chief, not because she felt the need to belong to such an association. Faith had given a talk to the probation volunteers on what she'd learned at the conference only a couple of evenings ago, and Isobel had been both surprised and appalled at some of the things that Faith had learnt at the conference about the ratio of black people to white going through the criminal justice system, as well as those being treated for mental health problems.

Faith took the situation in hand. "I am Mrs Faith Williamson" she said "I am a Probation Officer working with my colleague Mrs Bernice Liddel, whom you met last week, and this is Mrs Isobel McFarlane, a very valued Probation Volunteer, who I have brought here to introduce to you, and who will be happy to work with you both"

Faith was well aware that Mrs Fielding had assumed that she, Faith was the volunteer, while Isobel was the officer. Having now made the introductions she smiled, sat forward and accepted her cup of tea, declining the offer of sugar and fighting the mischievous inclination to add something about West Indians having to take care that they don't turn into 'the big fat mamma's' of the Tom and Jerry cartoons. Instead she suppressed her smile, making a mental note to mention it to her husband later and give him a good laugh and sat back to enable Isobel to start a conversation and to get to know the Fieldings a little. Faith was confident that Isobel would be able to do so despite the rather rocky start; Isobel was a very down to earth person, and Faith knew that Isobel would have realised that certainly Mrs Fielding was racially prejudiced and it was very possible that they both were, she just rather hoped that it would not put Isobel off from her job of befriending them, but she soon put that thought away, as she knew that Isobel's good nature would overcome her discomfort on Faith's behalf. She smiled encouragingly at Isobel, and as Faith had hoped she would, Isobel embarked upon her usual talk of what she, as a volunteer, could do, what she was and was not permitted to do, and about the confidentiality agreement that all volunteers working on behalf of probation had to sign.

When Isobel began to ask about the chrysanthemums she had noticed planted against the house, Faith took this as her cue that Isobel was happy to continue alone; that she felt comfortable with the Fieldings despite the fact that Major Fielding had pleaded guilty to a crime of a sexual nature. Faith and Isobel had worked together on many occasions, both before and after Faith became qualified, so Faith knew that as soon as Isobel started to embark on a subject unconnected to the crime it was Faith's cue to leave her to it. She rose from her chair and placed her cup on the tea tray on the low table. "Isobel is mad about gardening" she said as she turned to look at the Major and Mrs Fielding "Before she gets started I will take my leave of you, if that is

OK, as I have to go back to the office and have a lot to get through before my weekend can begin"

Major Fielding got up to show Faith out. "Thank you so much for coming" he said to her as he opened the front door "As you can no doubt see, Mrs Williamson, my wife is not at all well, and I am grateful to you for your bringing Mrs McFarlane to help us out at this time"

"You are most welcome" Faith said as she put out her hand. The Major looked nonplussed for a moment; then he remembered his manners and took Faith's hand. He was surprised at Faith's firm handshake and her direct look as she looked him straight in the eye. Remembering why he was in this predicament in the first place, he thanked her again as she walked confidently away up the long curving drive towards her car.

As the Major walked back to the sitting room to rejoin Isobel and Daphne, he decided that the best thing to do was to try to fill in the gaps in his knowledge with regard to the coming court proceedings; Isobel had said in her initial explanation of the remit of a probation volunteer that one of the things she was able to do was accompany a client to court. He glanced at his watch; it was four thirty, he didn't know how long Isobel would stay but he decided to ask her whether she knew how long it would be from the submission of Bernice's report until his court appearance. As he got back to the sitting room Daphne was telling Isobel about his enthusiasm for growing chrysanthemums. He joined in the conversation for a while and then changed the subject back to Isobel's reason for being there and began, tentatively, to ask questions about the impending court appearance.

Isobel asked the Major whether he had ever attended a Crown Court before, initially he was puzzled as he expected her to know all about his case, so Isobel explained that as a volunteer she would have been given a very rough outline of the case, but no details at all. Donald glanced across at Daphne and could see that she was struggling to keep her eyes open. He found that he felt comfortable with Isobel; she was a mature lady of medium height and build. Neatly dressed with nicely cut short grey hair, Isobel was quietly spoken with a slight soft Scottish accent.

Isobel explained that she did not need to know the details of the case; she said "I've been asked to come and work with you both. How often I come to see you, if at all, is entirely up to you. If you decide that it will help to speak about the case at all then please feel free to do so, but I assure you it isn't necessary. If you decide that there is nothing I can do to help you then I shall not be at all offended, please just make use of me if you can." Donald knew that Daphne didn't like to talk of medical matters to anyone, but he risked her displeasure by saying

"I expect that you can see that my wife is a little unwell. She has a follow up hospital appointment on Tuesday morning and I have been very worried indeed that my court appearance may come at the same time". Isobel reassured him that it wasn't possible to arrange the court date that quickly and she explained how it would work. It was not a complicated matter for the court to sort out; she explained how some cases got delayed when someone important couldn't attend, such as one of the main expert witnesses and in such an instance the court officials would look for a simple case of sentencing where someone had pleaded guilty to fit in so as not to waste court time by having a free 'slot' as Isobel explained it.

"So, basically, they may fit your sentencing in when there is a cancellation, but you should get at least a week's notice"

"Thank you" the Major said. "So, I will be able to take my wife on Tuesday, when she is due to get the results of tests she had a while ago" Daphne was concerned that he may elucidate so quickly said

"That's good then, as I am sure you can see, Crowford is quite remote, and we do not have regular enough public transport for that sort of thing."

"Do you not drive, Mrs Fielding?" asked Isobel.

"No, indeed not" answered Daphne "There has never been any need" This last was said rather emphatically, as if to dismiss the subject, but Isobel wasn't easily discouraged:

"That's good then, Tuesday's appointment is sorted. However, should your husband get a community sentence rather than a suspended one he will be obliged to attend at certain times, so if you find that you require follow up appointments at all I can be available to drive you should the need arise"

Isobel was still interested in those chrysanthemums, and she felt that Mrs Fielding may be in more need of her help than she was willing to admit, although, of course, no one at that time could have envisioned just how much, so rather than simply asking whether she should call back to see them another day or just wait to see when the sentencing would take place, Isobel asked to be shown the chrysanthemum greenhouse before she left. The Major was happy to show her, and Daphne was relieved when they left the room as she was not feeling at all well, and she settled back in her chair without even taking the tea tray back to the kitchen and dozed off into an uneasy nap.

Isobel had worked with many sex offenders in her time as a probation volunteer, and didn't feel at all uncomfortable in the Major's company. They walked companionably down the garden towards the greenhouse that housed his chrysanthemums. "Of course, it's very late in the year for them, and these days we no longer heat the greenhouse, but I can show you my stock plants and what I plan to grow next spring" Isobel guessed that it was for financial reasons that the greenhouse was no longer heated and she noticed the same signs of neglect along the length of the back garden as at the front.

"You know, I really love gardening" she told him "As Mrs Fielding is unwell, and you are obviously preoccupied by your impending court appearance as well as your insurance business, I could come and do some weeding and general garden tidying for you, a couple of times a week, if you would like me to"

"Oh, I don't know, is that within your remit as a volunteer?" he asked her

"Oh I can do what I like, within reason" she told him "Maybe it would make Mrs Fielding feel a little better if I were to weed the drive and tidy the front of the house. We're into November now, so there won't be many new weeds popping up unless the weather is unseasonably mild, and I could trim that clematis I saw the other side of the door"

"You really do love gardening, don't you?" said the Major. "That would be very good, indeed. Let's see, it's Friday today, and Daphne's appointment is on Tuesday. What about your coming over Wednesday morning, weather permitting, and I can work with you. I have one of my regular insurance appointments Wednesday afternoon, so the morning is better for me"

"You are on" Isobel said to him. She had brought her small shoulder bag out with her so she didn't need to go back in the house. The Major saw her out to the front of the house "Please, feel free to park on the drive on Wednesday" he said to her "There is no need to park out on the road"

"Thank you, I will" she said "Please say goodbye to Mrs Fielding for me, and I wish you both good luck with Tuesday's appointment. See you next Wednesday, then" They went to shake hands, and both realised that their hands were dirty from handling the flower pots. They laughed, said "Never mind" at the same time and parted amicably.

Major Donald went back into the house to see where Daphne was. He wasn't sure what she had planned to cook for supper, but he wanted to help, as he could see she wasn't well. She wasn't in the kitchen and he couldn't see the tray of tea things, so he went into the sitting room. There he found her, asleep in the chair, snoring slightly. She didn't look unattractive as she had the last time he'd seen her asleep in her bed with her makeup all smeared, but he knew that she felt unwell as her standards were slipping slightly as each day wore on. She would normally have leapt straight up when a guest left; washed and put away the tea things and straightened the scatter cushions and antimacassars and anything else that was slightly out of place in the sitting room.

He left her there to catch up on some sleep. For the first time in weeks, he felt almost optimistic. He hoped that the specialist would be able to diagnose and begin to treat Daphne's condition on Tuesday, and he decided he would throw himself into the gardening with Isobel on the Wednesday, that would definitely cheer old Daphers up, he thought, to have the front of the house looking nice as winter approached.

Chapter 42

Pamela had slept well and was ready for her Saturday morning tidy up. She didn't think of it as housework so much, not as she used to when she was running the big house she and Michael had bought soon after their marriage. Despite its having been a new house, it was never an easy place to keep as Michael liked it; this house was cosy and homely, and so long as she and Carla didn't make too much mess it was easy to keep clean and tidy.

Carla was still sleeping, so Pamela took the washbasket from the bathroom, and checking that Carla had put the things she wanted for her stay at her friend's house, and to watch Emily ice-skating in, she took it downstairs to the kitchen. She put the kettle on, loaded the washing machine and stood looking out at the little back garden. It was looking a bit untidy so she looked out at the clouds and decided to start with a quick tidy up outside so the garden would be nicely spruced up ready for the winter. She wondered how her parents were managing without Peggy. Peggy had never helped in the garden, but by assisting with the indoor tasks, it gave her mother time and energy to spend in her garden. She knew her father wasn't keen on gardening, unless it was connected to growing his chrysanthemums, and she wondered now how her mum would get on at the hospital on Tuesday. She decided that she would phone them later, once she'd achieved the things she had set out to do today. Her evening with Sylvie, the previous Monday, had helped her feel a little easier about her father's impending court appearance and she couldn't help wondering how her mother was coping. In fact, Sylvie had assumed correctly that Mrs Fielding's worst fear was that people would find out, and she had told Pamela that the national press were unlikely to be interested in her father's case, unless, she explained, there was some public outrage on the go at the time with regard to that particular sort of sex crime, then the media would dig up anything they considered relevant. She then made Pamela laugh by mimicking Leticia Fotherington reading a local paper and asking her husband "What is a jumble sale, darling – is it something poor people do?" Pamela wasn't so sure that the Fotherington's didn't read the local papers, but she decided that as it was something over which she had no control, she wasn't going to worry about it.

After spending about an hour in the garden Pamela was putting the next wash load in; having decided it was worth putting the first load out on the line to dry, as it was cloudy but windy, Carla came down the stairs. "Morning Mum" she said "Wow, you've been busy" as she glanced out of the window as she poured herself a glass of orange. "Will that blue top be ready for me to take to Rachel's later?" she asked

"Well, it depends on what time you want to go!" Pamela said to her laughing "If you want to go in the next five minutes it won't be" Carla looked down at herself and took in the rumpled pyjamas

"Mmm, I don't think I'll be ready in five minutes, anyway, I have my homework to do first. I seem to remember that being one of your conditions; I could only go if it was all done first"

"Yes, quite right too" said Pamela, suddenly wondering whether she had any maths homework and not liking to ask in case Carla thought she was becoming obsessed.

"What time are you going shopping?" Carla asked. Pamela told her she hadn't really thought yet, as she'd not intended to spend time sweeping the garden path and tidying the fallen leaves from the lawn and borders.

"I need to change our sheets and vac through" she told her "But it doesn't matter when I do it" Carla said she'd asked because she wanted to watch some cartoons on the TV before doing her homework, then she thought maybe she could get showered and dressed after that and cadge a lift to Rachel's as her mum went out to shop. "Oh, OK, that's a good idea" Pamela told her "That way I can get all the chores done before we go, but there's one condition"

"Oh, what's that" Carla asked warily

"I want a hug!" demanded her mum, grabbing her daughter to her and ruffling her already sleep ruffled hair. Carla laughed and hugged her mum back and kissed her"

"What was all that about?" she asked, but her mum was already half way up the stairs on her way to clean their bedrooms so she didn't answer. She had heard the question, but she could hardly tell her growing daughter that it was because she thought it so sweet that she wanted to watch cartoons in her pyjamas and yet was concerned that her grown up looking top she'd been given by her cousin, Fee would be ready for her to wear with her friends that evening. She'd mentally blamed Michael a few months ago for the changes in Carla, but now she mused that it was all a part of her growing up.

Pamela found that it was she, herself, who had needed to accept that her marriage was over, and during the last few months, as she settled into her new home and coped with all the things that had happened following her father's arrest she had found some peace concerning her feelings for Michael. She even didn't mind now that Michael and Monique were going to watch Emily's dress rehearsal the following morning. She had minded at first, when on asking Carla whether she'd phoned her dad about not going to stay for the weekend Carla had told her that he didn't mind at all, but asked whether he and Monique could go and watch the ice skating and that she had answered "Oh, cool, yes we'll see you there". Pamela had at first suspected that Carla was eager to show Monique off as the cool slim new partner of her father rather than her frumpy mum, but then chided herself for being hard on herself, after all, she had lost weight now and felt attractive.

'Oh no' Pamela found herself thinking, 'Not again, what is the matter with me' as she fought once again to remove images of Carla's maths teacher from her brain. She stripped the sheets from the beds, vacuumed the two bedrooms and the bathroom and landing and polished everything in sight with far greater vigour than was necessary. Pamela left the bedding to air, cleaned the loo, washbasin and bath, washed the bathroom floor and carried the vacuum cleaner downstairs so she could clean there once Carla went upstairs to shower and change.

Carla was still slumped on the sofa watching a cartoon "What sort of time were you thinking of my taking you to Rachel's?" Pamela asked her.

"Oh, I don't know, Mum" she replied "Why, are you keen to get rid of me?" Pamela laughed

"No, love, in fact after all we've been through in the last couple of weeks I'd prefer it if you were staying home here with me, but I won't stand in the way of your having a good time with your friends. It's just that I could do with some shopping now, rather than later as we're almost out of milk – I haven't shopped since Tuesday evening and we need loads of things – there's not even much for lunch. I thought maybe I'd pop out now as you haven't started your homework yet – what do you think?"

"OK, whatever's best for you, Mum" she said, her eyes not leaving the action on the screen.

Pamela nipped back up to her bedroom to change. Mentioning shopping on the Tuesday brought Matt back to her mind; she couldn't help surveying the old fashioned decor in the bedroom and thinking 'goodness, I couldn't bring anyone in here' and then being totally shocked with herself for even thinking it. However, her body had other ideas, and she began to imagine bringing Matt in here and taking off their clothes and.....she pulled herself together and forced herself to think of something else. She decided to shop at the bigger supermarket so she could treat herself to a new shower curtain. She pulled on clean clothes and skipped down the stairs calling out "Cheerio for now, see you later" to Carla she let herself out of the door.

Pamela headed first for the household section to choose a new shower curtain. Luckily her bathroom had a white suite, it was not a modern design, but it was clean and plain and could have been worse; Marian's was avocado green, and Pamela wouldn't have liked that. When Pamela had first moved in, the bathroom was painted a pale mauve, but she had covered that with a couple of coats of white the week she moved there as, although it was clean, Pamela wasn't at all fond of mauve and none of the towels or mats she'd brought with her had looked good in there. Carla's room had had very fussy pink patterned wallpaper and they had stripped that and replaced it with a pale blue and white striped paper with which Carla's bedding looked nice, and Pamela had also bought her some new bedding and a lampshade to match. The one room she'd changed nothing at all in was her own, as she had thought of it as totally unimportant.

Pamela found the shower curtains. They ranged quite a lot in price; from just £4.99 for an amusing one with cartoon frogs or fish on a clear plastic background, to £25 for a more ornate deluxe one. She decided to wander along the aisle and think about it and found herself among the bedding. These last few days were the first that she'd ever thought about the decor in her own room. The wallpaper was old fashioned but a fairly neutral colour but it was the curtains, she decided, that let the room down. Mr Benson had left the upstairs curtains and the bathroom blind for her as they were of no use to him and Pamela had soon changed Carla's but left her own and the blind as it was navy blue and looked much better against the white paint than it had the mauve. Pamela's bedroom window wasn't very big, she didn't know the exact size but she spotted a duvet set which had matching curtains and it wasn't very expensive. A shiver of excitement ran down her spine.

Pamela knew she shouldn't really, as she wanted to pay Michael some of the money back that he had given her for the trip to Brittany, but she put a pretty cream duvet cover and a matching set of curtains in her trolley. When she had bought curtains for Carla's room the smallest size had fitted; Pamela's window seemed to be about the same size, so she took a gamble and chose the smallest as they were also the cheapest. She shrugged; she could always bring them back if they were too small. She would measure the window before removing the curtains from the packaging. She went back to the shower curtains and quickly popped a cheap frog design one in her trolley and moved on to the grocery section and, checking with her shopping list from time to time, she soon filled the trolley with the things she and Carla would need for the following week. She had planned to have steak and a couple of glasses of wine for her dinner, as Carla wasn't keen on steak and would be at her friend's, but as Pamela had been extravagant with the bedding she chose an individual cottage pie instead. She would still have a glass of wine with it as she had brought back a couple of very reasonably priced bottles from France and she picked up some fresh broccoli to go with it. Carla and her friends were planning to have a snack lunch at the ice rink the following day and Pamela was going to have a salad with Sylvie before the matinee film they were going to see.

Pamela was pleased to find that Carla was busy with her homework when she got back with the shopping. Carla was lying on her stomach on the sitting room floor drawing a complicated looking diagram in her science book with her legs waving in the air. "Goodness, I don't know how you can do that" laughed Pamela as she pushed the door open.

"Easy, Mum" she replied "I've done the circles with a compass...."

"Not the diagram itself" said Pamela "I mean doing such a neat diagram from such a contorted body position!" Carla laughed and asked her mum whether she needed help getting more shopping bags from the car. She admitted that she could do with straightening her body out a bit and said she only had a couple more things to do for her homework. "No, you're still in your pyjamas, I'll get the stuff in, maybe you could help put it away once you've finished there?"

"OK, will do, but these 'jamas don't look much different from a tracksuit, you know Mum" she said as she went back to finish her science homework.

"Oh wow, Mum, these are great, at last you've treated yourself to some nice things for your bedroom" Carla said as she emptied one of the carrier bags for Pamela "and I DO like the shower curtain" she said, laughing at the cartoon frogs. "Well, you can take those things upstairs for me, if you will, please, when you go up to get ready. I'm going to have a crusty roll and some cheese and a coffee, would you like something?" "No thanks, I was going to have some cereals but you were right about the lack of milk. I searched in the freezer and found some currant buns at the back and toasted and buttered them – I hope that was OK?"

"Of course, I wondered what I could smell – I'd forgotten they were there." Pamela said to her.

While Carla was upstairs showering, changing and packing her stuff to take to Rachel's, Pamela quickly ate her late lunch and then dusted and vacuumed round, brought in the dry washing and put the second load out on the line. She doubted whether the second load would dry, but she thought it worth a try. She would iron it all later once she'd dropped Carla at Rachel's, then she would not have any housework type jobs left to do apart from putting up the new shower curtain and putting on her new bedding and fitting her new curtains if they were the right size. She had put Carla's clean duvet set in her room, as she knew Carla would put her own on before she went to Rachel's. Pamela was looking forward to making her bedroom look better; she decided to look at it from an outsider's perspective and change things round a little to make it look attractive rather than just functional.

Carla called down and asked whether her top was dry "Yes, it's fine, but not dry enough to wear. Are you planning to wear it tonight?" Pamela answered

"Yes, we are going to Rachel's cousin Tim's for the evening, he's got some friends coming round to his games room" Pamela smiled, Tim's family had a big house with a huge room with a snooker table in it.

"Well, come down and get your top and hang it on a hanger in the airing cupboard until we go, it should be OK later then" she told her.

It was 6 o'clock by the time Pamela got home after dropping Carla at Rachel's. Rachel's mum, Sarah had asked her in for a coffee, and she had accepted as she'd never really got to know Rachel's family as the girls hadn't been friends for very long. The first thing Pamela did when she got home was to pop out the back to see whether the washing was dry; it wasn't very, but it was drier than when she had put it out. She didn't have an outside light, so she had left the kitchen window blind open to she could just about see what she was doing. She brought the things in and put them on her clothes horse in the kitchen to dry off a bit more before she ironed them. She also got the ironing board out from under the stairs as she didn't like ironing, but by setting it up ready she wouldn't be tempted just to leave it until the morning.

Pamela then went upstairs to tackle her bedroom. It was already clean and she'd taken down the old curtains and checked that the new ones would fit earlier, before she took Carla to Rachel's. First Pamela put the new bedclothes on and stood back and admired them. It wasn't a big room and there was only one way the bed would fit. She spent the next half hour rearranging the small items of furniture until she made the room feel more spacious. She then unpacked the new curtains but saw that they would hang better if she ironed out the creases where they had been packed. She went downstairs and switched the iron on and while it warmed up she folded the washing that didn't need ironing and put it in the airing cupboard. While upstairs she popped her head into her bedroom to admire the new duvet cover.

Back downstairs Pamela checked her cottage pie to see whether it was microwavable or not and to see how long it needed to be cooked for. She decided to oven cook it as she wasn't short of time, and she turned on the oven and prepared the broccoli. She spent the next half hour ironing Carla's school shirts and the new curtains and the other few bits that needed doing then she turned off the iron and went upstairs to put the things away and hang the curtains.

Standing back to view her bedroom from the doorway Pamela was delighted with the result. She'd put a couple of ornaments in the back of the built in wardrobe and all she had on show now apart from the book she was reading and a few make up items on her dressing table was an aromatherapy candle. It was very attractive; she was surprised that the new curtains had made such a transformation. She hoped it would look as nice in daylight and looked forward to seeing it the next morning.

Pamela went back downstairs and put the cottage pie in the oven, put the iron, ironing board and clothes horse away and put the broccoli on to boil. She got out one of the bottles of wine she'd brought back from Brittany and pulled the cork and went in search of a wine glass. She chuckled to herself, she was being very self indulgent today! Before she could pour herself a glass, the phone rang. She wondered whether Carla had forgotten something and was glad she'd not taken a sip of the wine as she didn't drink and drive. However, when she answered it was a man's voice the other end "Er, hello, I do hope you don't mind my calling you?" Pamela's heart missed a beat, the voice was familiar in a way, but she wasn't sure; it sounded like Matt Gregory – surely she hadn't conjured him up by thinking of him earlier?

"Er, no, is that Mr Gregory?" she asked rather nervously

"Yes, it is, but for heaven's sake call me Matt!" he said

"How did you know my number?" she asked "and er, what can I do for you, is there trouble at school, is it Carla?"

"No, no trouble at all, but I got your phone number from Carla's school record which is very naughty of me as this doesn't concern Carla" he told her "um, then what does it concern?" asked Pamela haltingly, her heart beating nineteen to the dozen making her feel breathless for some strange reason.

"Well, I wondered whether I could see you" he said "but I don't want to embarrass Carla or her friends" Pamela thought quickly. She did find him very attractive and he had complimented her on her appearance but they had only met the once. Without thinking it through she found herself saying to him

"Would you like to come round for coffee in the morning?" and he said

"Oh, yes that would be very nice. It won't embarrass Carla, seeing me will it?" and Pamela replied

"Oh no, Carla will be out with her friends. Come round at about ten thirty and I will make coffee" By this point in the conversation both of them knew they weren't discussing coffee. Matt said

"See you tomorrow then" and Pamela put the phone down thinking 'Oh my, what on earth has got into me?' She found she was shaking so she poured herself a glass of wine and set the table for her meal.

Pamela thoroughly enjoyed her cottage pie and veg and spent the next hour or two relaxing in front of the TV, feeling alternately elated and petrified at the thought of Matt paying her a visit in the morning. She had never slept with anyone other than Michael, and that hadn't happened for a long time. She suddenly realised that her legs were hairy again. She had not bothered with them for a while so decided to run herself a bath and 'sort herself out'. She pampered herself totally, using some aromatherapy oils she'd been saving – for what she didn't know but decided that this was the occasion.

Pamela didn't expect to sleep a wink, but after first her busy week, then all the housework she'd done today and the glass of wine and warm bath she slept all night.

Chapter 43

Sylvie was thoroughly enjoying her weekend. It was so nice to be doing something different. She loved her parents but was really looking forward to going out to lunch with Pamela and choosing a matinee afterwards. It would have, in fact, been possible for her to visit her parents later that evening as Pamela needed to pick Carla up from Rachel's at about six, but she chose not to tell her parents that, as she felt a complete break would do them all good. The previous evening she'd had dinner at Ralph and June's. June is a very good cook and she had prepared a lovely meal and afterwards over coffee they had had a good talk about how Ralph was going to find working part time for a while and how he was going to manage the stress so as not to become ill again. They had also discussed Major Donald's upcoming sentencing and wondered how that would go. Ralph had known that Faith was going to go to the Major's with Isobel and Sylvie filled Ralph in with how that went; Faith had come back to the office full of what a racist snob Daphne was, but she had a way of telling it that didn't sound like criticism, rather she felt sorry for Daphne for being so narrow minded. She also mentioned that it was obvious that Daphne was not at all well, not that that excused the racism and snobbery, but just that it was something else to feel sorry for Daphne about as well as the fact that her husband had admitted to a sexual offence. Poor woman, Faith had said more than once.

"Yes," Ralph had agreed "Faith is one very good officer; I just hope that the powers that be don't take advantage of her and cause her to 'burn out' before she should. She already organises the volunteer meetings out of working hours, and, I expect that you know she has recently attended a four day conference and that being less than a week, as usual her work wasn't covered by anyone else" Ralph was 'revving up' as June called it for a real moan.

"That's enough" she told him "Faith is young and enthusiastic and for now, although I've not met her, it sounds as though she can look after herself"

"Yes, quite right, she can" Sylvie said to them both. "Is there any more of that excellent rhubarb crumble?" she had asked.

She chuckled as she thought about her second helping of rhubarb crumble. She was still full this morning and didn't want any breakfast. Pamela had very kindly offered to pick Sylvie up she'd said "At least that way one of us can have a drink" and Sylvie was very grateful as she felt like having a glass or two of wine with lunch while they had a good gossip and decided which film to go and see. Still thinking about the second helping of dessert, Sylvie looked at the clock and decided there wasn't time for her to go for a swim. She looked out of the window and saw that although it was overcast it was neither frosty nor raining, so she decided to don her jogging bottoms and go out for a quick run and have a shower and get ready to go out as soon as she got back. That would stop her feeling lethargic and would give her an appetite for lunch.

*

Pamela wondered what felt different as she woke up and then she remembered that she had new bedclothes. She was suddenly wide awake as she remembered why. Had all those crazy lustful thoughts about Matt actually conjured him up and caused him to phone her? As she slid out of bed and made her way to the bathroom she felt mortified at the thought of how easily she had invited him round. She wondered what the time was. After spending a penny and washing her hands she went back to look at the watch on the bedside table. Eight thirty. Not bad, she thought; she was amazed she had slept so well and for so long. Two hours before Matt was due to arrive. She could still smell the aromatherapy oil she had bathed in the previous evening. She brushed her teeth and had a quick wash before choosing an attractive set of undies which she'd kept for years but hadn't fitted her for quite a long time. Deciding to dress casually in leggings and a sweatshirt she began to wonder whether she was imagining that Matt found her attractive. Perhaps he really was lonely and wanted to come round for coffee? She brushed her hair and put on a little foundation and blusher but no lipstick. She would change before going to pick Sylvie up at twelve thirty; she would not need to wear anything really smart to go to lunch and see a matinee, but she didn't want to go in her leggings.

Before going downstairs Pamela looked in her wardrobe and chose the black trousers and a pink tee shirt she'd bought in Brittany and decided to wear them with her warm grey fleece. She realised that she was doing anything and everything to stop herself thinking about what would happen when Matt arrived; she was attempting to convince herself that he was just coming for coffee and that they would politely sit and chat at the kitchen table for an hour or so before she made her excuses to go and get changed to pick Sylvie up. She glanced round the bedroom checking that it was still looking nice after her cleaning and rearranging everything the evening before and went down to the kitchen.

She was too keyed up to eat anything so she had a glass of orange while she searched for the packets of coffee and the filter jug she had brought back with her from Brittany the previous week. She didn't often bother to make herself proper coffee; it was something that she and Michael always used to do at a weekend, she did, in fact prefer filter coffee to instant but she had let Michael keep the coffee percolator as she hadn't wanted to be reminded of the things that had been their routine. She looked at the kitchen clock. Nine fifteen. What on earth was she going to do for another hour and a quarter? She glanced out of the kitchen window and saw that the black sack she'd put the fallen leaves in that she'd swept up the previous morning had blown over, or been knocked over by a nosy neighbourhood cat and some of the leaves had fallen back out.

Pamela decide not to be good as she'd intended and save the sack of leaves to take to the municipal tip, she would stuff it in the wheelie bin instead as Marian had advised her. Mr Benson from whom she had bought the house had been at pains to explain that garden waste was not to be put in the wheelie bin with the other rubbish, but should be taken to the tip. When Pamela had mentioned this to Marian she'd laughed and told her "S'orright for those with the time and money to go swannin' off to the tip with their garden rubbish, but I asks yer what do we pay our rates for, eh? You tuck it all in yer wheelie bin, gel, a good long way down like I do and never you mind what nice old Mr Benson told yer!"

So that's exactly what Pamela did and just as she was doing so Marian came out of her back door and Pamela told her what she was doing. "Hah, good fer you, gel" Marian said "Fancy a cuppa?" Pamela didn't want to tell Marian that she had Matt coming round for coffee, so she thanked Marian and said that she wanted to finish her ironing before she went out for lunch with Sylvie. "OK, me duck, no problem, have a great afternoon with yer friend"

As Pamela went back indoors she saw that only fifteen minutes had gone by. She wondered why she had felt the need to lie to Marian. It would have helped the time go by had she gone round to Marian's but she knew it was because she didn't want to say that she had Carla's maths teacher coming round. She tried to busy herself with something but couldn't get started with anything. She really could have done with reorganising her kitchen cupboards but didn't want to start a job that would mean the worktops being covered with stuff when Matt arrived. She rinsed out her orange juice glass and went into the sitting room. Carla had left her homework books on the sofa so Pamela took them upstairs to Carla's room. She caught sight of a copy of Gerald Durrell's 'My Family and Other Animals' on Carla's shelf and took it down to thumb through. She had studied it at school and hadn't read it since. She remembered Carla saying that her cousin, Paul, had lent it to her. She sat on Carla's bed and smiled as reading through the first chapter took her back to the first time she'd read it. It had been compulsory reading in class and most of her friends hadn't liked it, but she had been so taken with the antics of the Durrell family that she'd read the whole book long before the class had finished studying it. She was still engrossed in it when the doorbell rang. She jumped, but then she replaced the book on the shelf where she had taken it from and went downstairs slowly and opened the door.

It was, of course, Matt Gregory. He was taking off his motorbike helmet and once she could see his face she could see he was smiling shyly. Pamela wondered briefly why she hadn't heard his motorbike but she smiled back and invited him in. She led the way to the kitchen and clicked the kettle on. She was pleased that she'd stopped worrying and become engrossed in the book. Now that Matt had arrived it seemed quite natural for him to be here, although her heart was beating much faster than it normally did; all the fears of earlier flitted unbidden through her mind again. She hadn't undressed in front of any man other than Michael before. She felt herself blush slightly; perhaps the poor chap was just here for coffee?

Pamela stood with her back to Matt while she filled the coffee filter. She suddenly felt him close behind her. He placed his hands gently on her hips and said softly "Shall we have the coffee a little later?" She liked the feel of his touch. She turned to face him. They kissed and she led him silently up the stairs to her room. She had put her prettiest undies on under her old leggings and sweatshirt and now she couldn't wait to take it all off! She was vaguely aware that what she was feeling was lust as there had been little communication between them and she knew she didn't love him. She felt totally reckless, not unlike the way she'd felt the first time she ever plucked up the courage to go down the water chute at the Oasis swimming pool in Swindon.

To think she had worried that she'd misread the situation and then thought that if she hadn't she would be shy of both her own and his body; and here she was, in her bedroom within five minutes of his arriving and she was as busy removing his clothes as he was hers! Once they were both naked Matt pushed her gently onto the bed, on top of the duvet.

An hour and a half later Matt spoke for the first time as they lay exhausted next to one another. "Amazing what you can learn from a book" Pamela laughed; not her usual light laugh but a deep sensuous laugh

"Quite so" she answered not wanting to think about her past love life at all. It had been so staid compared to this. As she lay comfortably beside Matt, her body tingled from head to foot.

"I am glad you said you're not doing anything today" Matt said to her. "I don't think that is what I said" she told him "I am picking my friend up at 12.30 to go out for lunch and then to the cinema" Matt got up lazily and went to his heap of clothes and extracted his watch from it.

"You're OK, it's just turned 12; maybe we'd better have the coffee another time?"

"Sylvie can wait ten minutes, she won't mind. I'll nip down and boil the kettle again; it won't take a minute and you can pour our coffee while I change to go out." Pamela slipped her leggings and sweatshirt on without any underwear and went down to boil the kettle and put two mugs out. She clicked off the kettle just before it boiled and poured the water onto the coffee in the filter. She heard the loo flush and Matt came out of the bathroom as she got to the top of the stairs. "The coffee is brewing" she told him as he went downstairs and she went into her bedroom and collected her undies and the stuff she was going out in. She went into the bathroom and had a very quick wash and got dressed. Nipping back to her bedroom she put on a little foundation and some lip gloss and then ran downstairs to drink her coffee.

Matt was sitting at the kitchen table with one mug of coffee in front of him and the other still on the worktop. "I left yours up there as I didn't know whether you wanted milk or sugar" he said "Thanks. I have it just as it is. What about you – would you like either or both?" she asked him "No, thanks, like you I like it black and I don't take sugar." They sat and sipped their hot coffee in comfortable silence until Matt said "Well, I'd better let you get off to pick your friend up" "Yes, OK" This was the only uncomfortable moment that Pamela felt. She didn't know what the etiquette was for letting your lover out of the front door. She didn't even know whether he was her lover, as such or whether this was just a one off. She certainly wasn't going to ask him. She didn't know whether they would kiss. She led Matt through to the door and as she moved to pass him to open the door he caught hold of her and said "My, but you are a sensual woman" and kissed her on the cheek. He then picked up his leathers and helmet and moments later he was gone.

Pamela looked at her watch. Twelve twenty. She wouldn't be late so wouldn't feel she had to say anything about her morning visitor. She rinsed the coffee mugs, grabbed her bag and car keys and smiled to herself as she closed the door behind her. She pulled up outside Sylvie's exactly on time, but knowing that Sylvie wasn't the most punctual of people she parked and locked the car and walked up Sylvie's path and rang the doorbell. It opened straight away and Sylvie stepped back to let Pamela in. "Nearly ready – I went out for a jog and then needed a shower" Sylvie told her. Pamela grinned. She hadn't been jogging, but her knees were wobbly from the orgasms and she probably should have had a shower but had only had time for a quick wash. "What's funny?" Sylvie asked "Heavens; look at you" she said, looking at Pamela properly for the first time "Whatever have you been up to? You are glowing – have you been buying new make-up?" Pamela had never been one to discuss things sexual and she had absolutely no idea where this thing with Matt would lead, if anywhere, so she wasn't going to tell Sylvie.

"No, no new makeup" she told her "Just a healthy glow from all that walking in Brittany but I do have new clothes" and she took off her grey fleece and gave Sylvie a twirl to show off her new black trousers and pink tee shirt.

"Wow, you look really great" Sylvie told her. "Maybe I need some healthy fresh Breton air. Are you sure that's all it is? There is something very sort of sparkly about you."

"No just the usual old me. Now come on, or we'll not have time for a nice lunch and I am ravenous!"

"OK, OK, I'm coming" Sylvie said. She gave up trying to find out what her friend had been up to, but she knew her well enough to know that it was more than fresh air and exercise that had put that glow in her cheeks. However, she respected her friend's privacy and knew there was no point pushing her.

They managed to get a table at an Italian restaurant near the cinema and Sylvie raised her eyebrows but said nothing when Pamela ordered a large glass of Chablis to go with her penne pesto and green salad. Sylvie had the spaghetti bolognaise and a large glass of Chianti and Sylvie looked quizzically at her friend when they raised their glasses to one another but Pamela still gave nothing away except to say "Yes, I know I never drink and drive, but I have plenty of time before I have to drive again and I will have digested it by then. Sylvie agreed and said that the pasta would help but she was secretly amused as she suspected her friend was kicking over the traces in more ways than just taking a large glass of wine with her lunch.

Not having even checked to see what was showing at the cinema they laughed when they saw the choice they had for an afternoon showing; a horror film that they'd heard about but definitely didn't like the sound of, a Batman film, a couple of cartoons and Lethal Weapon 3. Well, they didn't fancy Batman or the cartoons, so they plumped for Lethal Weapon 3, laughing about the fact that neither of them had seen Lethal Weapon 1 or 2 but Pamela was very pleased that they did as Sylvie was soon completely absorbed in it as she liked Mel Gibson and Pamela could let herself daydream a little while still following the rather weak plot of the film. Weak plot it may have been, but it was very funny in places and they both enjoyed it.

The film finished at 5.30 and as Pamela had arranged to collect Carla at 6 they strolled back to the car chuckling about some of the funnier scenes in the film. Sylvie suggested that they pick Carla up first and then all have a bite to eat at her house. Pamela thought that an excellent idea as Carla had done all her homework and would not be in a hurry to go home. She also was curious about how Michael and Monique had got on watching the ice skating and thought that Carla was more likely to be forthcoming if she asked light heartedly in front of Sylvie rather than asking her when they got home alone.

Pamela's emotions were very mixed. She still felt nice and relaxed following her morning with Matt, but a few times during the film her mind had wandered and she had begun to wonder whether she would see Matt again and if she did how Carla would feel; she had absolutely no intention of telling Carla that he had been round for coffee. Now as the effects of her unaccustomed lunchtime drink had worn off she could feel the slight threat of a headache; she felt that a cup of tea and a sandwich at Sylvie's and a good natter with Carla about her evening at her friend's cousin's would be just what she required. She needed to come back down to earth. She didn't know whether she'd hear from Matt again, indeed, she didn't know whether she wanted to hear from him again. She had no way of contacting him, apart from via the school and this made her feel faintly uncomfortable. She didn't feel used; she was well aware that any 'using' had been two sided but Matt had virtually purloined her phone number from Carla's school records and she didn't have a home number for him, in fact she didn't even know where he lived.

Pamela pulled up outside Rachel's house but as she still looked rather dreamy Sylvie offered to get out and knock on the door to see whether Carla was ready. She was, and they were laughing as they got back into Pamela's car. Sylvie had told Carla that Pamela was 'away with the fairies' as she put it and Carla said it was probably all the emotion from the previous two weeks, what with the week in Brittany and the week back when she didn't have an evening to herself. "I didn't think of that" Sylvie had replied "I thought maybe you and your mum would like to have tea at my place now before going home, then you can tell us all about your weekend and we'll tell you about Lethal Weapon 3" This was why they were laughing

"You got my mum to see a Lethal Weapon movie?" she'd asked Sylvie incredulously

"Yes, but I told you she's sort of' monged out'; I think she'd have agreed to anything, to be honest, even Batman, but I didn't fancy that myself"

"And what are you two laughing at?" Pamela asked them as they climbed in the car

"Just the thought of you two watching a Lethal Weapon movie"

"It was fun, even though I've never seen Lethal Weapon 1 or 2. I suppose I'd assumed it was all violence; I'd not realised it would be so funny" she told her "Are you happy about having tea at Sylvie's?" she asked

"Oh, yes," Carla said. I'll tell you about Emily's skating and all that and you two can tell me about the movie.

Chapter 44

Donald was disappointed not to have heard from Pamela prior to Daphne's appointment today. He had hoped she would call over the weekend but he assumed she was reluctant to call because of the trouble he was in. In fact, what with the call from Matt and his subsequent visit she had forgotten, even though she had intended to. Donald didn't want to call her, as he was unsure what sort of reception he would get, so he decided to wait and see how Daphne got on and then persuade her to call Pamela and tell her.

Daphne had been quite poorly again and Donald had asked her whether she would like him to actually come in with her to see the specialist. Daphne declined as she had always been extremely embarrassed about anything to do with health; her own as well as anyone else's so she had said "No, thanks, just drive me there and wait outside, if you will. I can take it if it should be bad news and I will tell you anything you need to know on the way home."

Donald was not pleased that Daphne was unwell, but that coupled with the fact that he had kept her topped up with her gin and tonics had prevented her from saying any more about inviting their friends round for the little soiree that she had begun to plan the day Donald told her about his involvement with Maisie and the subsequent events. He could tell that

Daphne had lost weight, and he was concerned that she may have something serious. Like a lot of people of his generation he was afraid of the word cancer, he thought of it with dread and was very concerned that it may be what Daphne was suffering from. He hadn't discussed it with her, though, as they never had been in the habit of discussing such things and he would leave it to Daphne to tell him what the consultant said. He was pleased that Daphne didn't want him to go in with her, but he had made the offer genuinely meaning to accompany her should she wish.

Daphne had another reason for not wanting Donald with her in the consultant's room. Her GP had asked her about her alcohol consumption on many an occasion, and especially more recently when she had last seen him to be referred to a consultant for her symptoms to be investigated. She didn't hold with what she considered 'this nonsense' about drinking less than a certain number of units of alcohol in a week, so she had consistently denied drinking more than about two pub measures of gin a week and one glass of wine. Daphne knew that she drank a great deal more than that, but she also knew that she wasn't an alcoholic. After all, she reasoned to herself, alcoholics were nasty down and out people, not respectable people like herself.

The appointment was scheduled for two thirty in the afternoon. Donald and Daphne had decided to have a light lunch and leave in plenty of time as parking at the hospital was known to be difficult and Daphne didn't want to be late. Daphne also wondered why Pamela hadn't phoned, but she didn't mention it to Donald. Pamela had shown a lot of concern about this impending visit to the consultant; Daphne knew not to call him a 'specialist' as her GP had been consistently referring to Mr Mears as a 'highly thought of consultant' and had urged Daphne to be honest if she were drinking more than she had previously claimed. She was very lucky, she had been told, to be seeing Mr Mears himself, as he usually conducted his appointments from his office and allowed one of his junior team members to be the first to see a new patient. Daphne suspected that her doctor had said this in order to encourage her to tell Mr Mears more about herself; her lifestyle and drinking habits in particular but, in fact it just made her more stubborn.

As Daphne laid the table for lunch she hunched her shoulders as she always did when thinking to herself about something serious. Donald noticed and just said "Are you OK, old girl?" She smiled, not minding the affectionate tone in which he called her 'old girl'.

"Yes, thanks, I'll just be glad when all this hospital nonsense is over and I have proper medicine for all this indigestion and tiredness, then life can go on as normal again, well, as normal as possible, what with the court case and all that. Why is that volunteer woman coming to help in the garden tomorrow, anyway?" Daphne asked him.

"I believe she offered simply because she loves gardening, and from a small remark she made I believe she used to have a garden and now lives in some sort of flat." He told her.

"Oh, a flat, how awful" Daphne said and Donald didn't know whether she meant because Isobel no longer had a garden, or whether Daphne meant it in a belittling way. Donald decided not to ask, as he did rather struggle with Daphne's prejudices and snobbishness, but didn't want to upset her today.

It was just as well that Daphne and Donald had set out early, as the car park was worryingly full when they arrived at the hospital. "You go on in and get yourself sorted" Donald said to her as he pulled up by a path that led to the main entrance "and I'll park the car once I can get a space and I'll go and wait for you in the small coffee area"

Daphne didn't like Mr Mears. She supposed she'd set her mind against him when she was told that she was lucky to be seeing him so had tried to like him but he was young and he was Australian and perhaps because of that she felt that he was far too familiar in his dealings with her. She didn't feel that he had treated her with the respect that she deserved. In fact he had been downright rude about her drinking. Cirrhosis of the liver indeed! She was furious, especially as he had all but accused her of lying. He had told her that one of the blood tests had been to determine how much alcohol she had in her blood at that time, and that on the particular day the test was done she would have been over the drink drive limit had she been a driver. He explained that cirrhosis was almost always caused by the consumption of too much alcohol and told her in no uncertain terms that he knew she drank too much and that it was no point trying to pull the wool over his eyes. He also said that unless she stopped drinking altogether immediately she would be dead within five years. Well, she didn't believe a word of it. She had been concerned that perhaps she had some sort of cancer, and if that was not the cause of her illness she was hoping for some strong medicine to treat the debilitating indigestion from which she suffered.

Donald was waiting in the WRVS coffee shop. He had bought himself a newspaper and had just turned to the crossword page when Daphne appeared looking rather determined. "Ah, there you are. Cup of coffee, or would you rather go straight home?" Donald asked her "Home please. I have a prescription to collect first, then home" Daphne didn't tell him that she'd almost forced the prescription from Mr Mears. He had told her she ought to go to her GP for indigestion medicine, he said in no uncertain terms that he doubted that she planned to change her diet and her drinking; he'd said that that in itself would make changes that would improve her digestion. He had offered to refer her to a dietician and suggested she seek the help of a local alcohol counselling service but she had been furious, telling him that she had no such need, that she ate healthily and didn't drink much.

Donald knew not to ask Daphne how she had got on. She hated anything to do with hospitals and would tell him what she wanted to in her own time when she was ready. He thought she looked drained, even though she looked determined. He hoped it wasn't bad news, but was unable to tell from

Daphne's set face. He asked whether she would prefer to be taken straight home to rest and offered to go back out to collect the prescription himself. Daphne had been thinking about the possibility of cutting down on her drinking and the idea worried her; she believed her evening gin and tonics were doing her good, so she said "No, that's kind of you, but we could do with a few groceries, so we could kill two birds with one stone if we stop off at the supermarket, if that's OK with you. We could get a few extra things in for our little soiree; then we will be prepared for it once my medicine starts to work and I feel better."

"OK, then old girl" Donald said, taking the turning for the supermarket he knew Daphne was referring to "We could have a cup of tea first, put a bit of colour in your cheeks before we shop". Daphne smiled. Donald really could be quite thoughtful. What she really wanted was to get a couple of extra bottles of gin in just in case Donald got wind of the fact that the doctors wanted her to cut down, then she could 'squirrel away' a couple more bottles' in case of emergencies'. Donald, of course was not at all keen on this 'soiree' idea of Daphne's, and he didn't know she wanted extra gin supplies in for a different reason altogether, but he decided to go along with her wishes as she was still avoiding the subject of Donald's impending court case, apart, of course, from the odd mention of her little 'soiree' and he didn't want to upset the applecart.

By the time they arrived home Daphne had a little more colour once they had shared a pot of tea for two and had ambled round the supermarket. Even so, Donald made her go and sit down and give her new medication a chance to work while he put away the shopping. He found himself hoping that his court appearance would be sooner rather than later, as this way of life was quite pleasant; he couldn't believe that he had been stupid enough to jeopardise it by returning to see Maisie and risk getting caught out, although, of course, he had had no idea that he was breaking the law, he just thought he may have got caught out doing something that Daphne would consider shameful. Donald knew that his court appearance was likely to come up at short notice. Just so long as his defence barrister was available along with someone to appear on behalf of probation should there be any query with the pre-sentence report (he had also been told that apparently it wasn't even necessary for it to be the author of that report) and the social worker who had brought his actions to the attention of the police then the sentencing could go ahead.

Donald was very pleased that Isobel was to come the following day to help in the garden. He was not normally interested in the garden but even he could see that the front of the house was looking rather seedy, it was, he realised, normally Daphne who had kept it tidy in the past, usually while Peggy was working indoors. Daphne was a great one for appearances, but she was happy in her guise of 'country gentlewoman' taming her garden while the 'help' worked on the unmentionable domestic duties indoors. Once Donald had put the shopping away he turned his attention to how he and Isobel would tackle the garden. He looked in on Daphne in the sitting room and she seemed to be dozing, so he crept back out of the room and slipped out into the garden.

In fact Daphne was not asleep. She had been waiting to see what Donald would do as she wanted to take one of the bottles of gin and put it in a cupboard in her bedroom. As soon as he had gone she opened her eyes and went to the drinks cabinet. She rearranged the bottles so that Donald wouldn't notice one was missing and, having heard the back door open and close she slipped upstairs with the gin. Opening her bedroom door Daphne put the bottle on her dressing table while she peered out of the window to see whether she could see Donald. There was no sign of him so she opened her wardrobe door and took out a couple of plastic boxes containing various selections of hats and summer shoes and felt behind them. There was the satisfying feel of the bottles she had stashed away there a couple of months before also in case of emergency. This she had been in the habit of doing since the awkward business in Cyprus all those years ago – of course, she'd been unable to conceal the bottles when they had to pack to come back home to England, but she'd just put them back in with the other bottles before they moved back as she'd organised the packing anyway. She put this latest bottle in beside the others and replaced the boxes. Straightening up, she closed the wardrobe door and looked at herself in the mirror. She had always been on the stout side but had lost some weight recently. She had dressed carefully for her hospital appointment, but decided now to change into something older to wear at home. She always chose the same type of clothes (apart from a few outfits she used over and over until they wore out for cocktail parties and Christmas soirees) as she knew what suited her. Her preferred mode of dress was a tweed skirt and lambs wool sweater; light weight and light colours for summer and heavier weight and darker colours for winter. She changed from a new version of just that to an older skirt and jumper. The skirt was a little loose on the waistband and the sweater hung a little looser than it had when she bought it but she checked in the mirror and after adjusting the scarf she wore round her neck she was satisfied with the result. She refreshed her makeup, hung up the clothes she had just taken off and made her way back downstairs. Donald was still outside. She put the kettle on and made her way out to find him and let him know she was making tea.

Chapter 45

As Pamela set about sorting the morning's post that Sandra had flung on her desk earlier she wondered, once again, what made Sandra so nasty. Pamela was normally extremely punctual. She hated to be late for anything and it was only because she had argued with Carla this morning that she had been late today. It was the first time she had ever been late since she started the job, so she was shocked at Sandra's reaction as Sandra rarely spoke to anyone else if they were late. Infuriated to be singled out like this Pamela had raised her voice back at Sandra and was ready to be quite rude when she felt a restraining hand on her arm and Rob stood beside her with a mug of coffee in his hand. He said "Oh, sorry, Pamela, I nearly bumped into you. Clumsy of me. Here is a coffee for you, I've made one for everyone" At this Pamela had to thank him and just fired a look at Sandra and sat down to get on with her work.

Pamela felt drained. She hadn't heard from Matt at all. Carla had been behaving rather oddly. On Sunday evening when she and Sylvie had picked her up from her friend's house after the initial laughter at the thought of her mum watching a Lethal weapon film she had been rather quiet and had sat very close to Pamela and been very affectionate and this morning after an innocent question about her maths homework Carla had given a very strange answer and shouted at Pamela telling her to leave her alone and stop nagging! This was most odd, as it had been a genuine question about the homework and had, in fact, been a difficult one as Pamela was trying hard not to think about Matt Gregory at all and so had had to make herself ask the question. She assumed it was all a matter of Carla's age and hormones making her snappy, as when Sylvie asked whether Michael and Monique had enjoyed watching the Ice-Skating on Sunday morning she had been quite non committal, but this morning, after her outburst she had asked whether she could go and stay with Michael the following weekend. "Of course you can, love" Pamela had said, after telling her off for shouting and asking her not to be rude but not wanting to argue any more with Carla and upset her further, although she'd been puzzled by her changeable behaviour.

Pamela sighed as she thought also about the phone conversation with her mother the previous evening. Feeling guilty that she'd not phoned at the weekend she'd phoned to ask her mother how she had got on at the hospital and almost got her head bitten off. "No problem, dear, apart from a rude young doctor who thinks he knows it all" her mother had boomed at her "nothing to worry about. Do you want to speak to your father?" well, poor Pamela didn't know whether or not she did want to speak to him but before she had a chance to answer she found herself speaking to him and he had assumed that she had asked Daphne for him so they had an awkward conversation for a few moments and then both had said goodbye.

Pamela wondered now whether all really was well with her mother. Now she thought about it she really hadn't wanted to speak to her father, and she thought he knew that. They had both awkwardly said to each other that they were pleased that nothing was seriously wrong with her mother, but neither had sounded convinced, and she realised that she hadn't thought to ask her father whether or not he had accompanied her mother to see the consultant. The more she thought about it the more unlikely she considered it to be; her mother was very private about such things, she must have gone in to see the consultant alone.

*

Pamela wasn't the only one having a bad day. Carla was trying to concentrate on her French lesson but her mind kept wandering back to break time when Emily and Rachel had been really unpleasant. She was pleased that they were not in her French class as it gave her a chance to think, but, unfortunately not a chance to concentrate on the lesson.

She had enjoyed her stay at Rachel's on the previous Saturday evening when they had gone over to Rachel's cousin's house and had begun to think that she had imagined a new closeness between Emily and Rachel that was excluding her. However, once the ice skating rehearsal was over on the Sunday morning and Emily came back to Rachel's with them for lunch it became apparent that Carla had not been imagining things. Carla had always felt closer to Rachel than to Emily and had often confided things to Rachel which she would not have said to Emily. Rachel had been the same; feeling comfortable to discuss certain personal things with Carla that she would have been embarrassed to mention to Emily.

Carla now deeply regretted having told Rachel that she had heard her dad and Monique making love when she had been staying with them. In the past a confidence like this would have gone no further and Carla would have just felt better for having been able to tell someone, but Rachel had obviously told Emily, because when Carla told Rachel that Michael and Monique were coming to watch Emily, Rachel had seemed wary about it and Carla had hardly noticed at the time apart from briefly wondering why, but it had become clear when she was saying goodbye to her dad and Monique as she caught sight of Emily making rude thrusting gestures with her hips towards them as Rachel was trying to stop her. This had made her feel uncomfortable but she was not unduly upset, not until break time today when the two of them had begun to taunt her about it until she told them angrily to stop and they called her childish. Emily had taken it further "So, who is your mum shagging then?" she'd asked, nastily. "No one, she isn't seeing anyone" Carla had replied tearfully. Rachel was no help when Carla turned to her as she was laughing with Emily and went on to say "Well, watch out for the old letch Gregory, you know your mum came to see him and he'd shag anything either half or twice his age!" This was something that Emily had started on about the previous day, and it was why Carla had yelled at her mum this morning when she'd asked about the homework. She felt sorry now, as she knew it wasn't her mum's fault. She knew that her dad had left her for Monique. She knew also though that her mum wasn't in such a relationship and she was sure that she didn't want to be. They were happy, the two of them, Carla wasn't sure why she had said she wanted to go to her dad's; she supposed it was just to get at her mum.

This shift in her friendship with Rachel and Emily had been the reason that she had cuddled up close to her mum on Sylvie's sofa. She had felt excluded by Rachel and Emily's newfound closeness in a way that she didn't believe that she and Rachel had ever made Emily feel. Emily didn't used to be one for confidences which is why the threesome had always worked as a friendship in the past. Carla hadn't told her mum any of this, she felt badly enough as it was that she felt left out; voicing it would have made it more real, somehow. The two had not been kind about her mum going to see Matt Gregory either, even before the taunts about his fancying her mum. She felt bad as she remembered teasing her mum about him when they were in Brittany, she didn't want to encourage such thoughts in her mum. She was a bit worried now about having suggested her mum go out with Sylvie, but listening to them both as they told her about their lunch and the film they saw she felt secure in the knowledge that this was just two old friends enjoying an afternoon out, rather than two single ladies on the pull. She had snuggled in to her mum at this thought, and her mum had drawn her closer as she was laughing about something Sylvie was reminding her about in the film.

Carla decided she'd make it up with her mum as soon as she got in, she would say that she would like to get back into the pattern of going to her dad's maybe every other weekend; she had been wondering how the strange little boy, Ben, from next door was getting on, though she mused that he probably wouldn't be out in his garden in this cold weather. Going to her dad's would give her a reason not to be available every weekend to see Emily and Rachel; a rather miserable weekend with her dad and Monique would be better than a miserable one with Emily and Rachel. She could pretend when she got back to school after such a weekend that she had had a wonderful time, even if she hadn't.

*

Pamela managed to get through the rest of the day without another run in with Sandra. She was just logging her computer off when her phone rang. She was loath to answer it as it was probably a supplier who would want the balance of their account and it would mean Pamela logging back in. She looked up and saw Sandra smirking at her so she quickly answered it and was shocked to find it was Matt. Surprised, pleased and puzzled all at the same time Pamela glanced across to Sandra's desk but Sandra had lost interest once Pamela answered her phone and spoiled her chance of having something else to complain about. However, Pamela didn't want Sandra to know it was a personal call; Pamela answered Matt's questions in a professional sounding manner. This amused Matt greatly, as he was asking such questions as 'when will you be free again' and Pamela was answering with "We'll have to arrange a meeting then if you are not currently satisfied with the state of your account" Pamela was enjoying the conversation, but she knew she hadn't given Matt her office telephone number, in fact she didn't remember telling him where she worked. In order to keep up the pretence of it's being a supplier on the phone she hinted that she didn't have a number to call Matt back on by saying

"OK, let me have your direct line and I will call you back when I have checked your latest statement to your account" Matt didn't give her a number to call on though, he just said "Don't worry, I'll give you a day or two to see when you can be free for more 'coffee' this he said very thickly and Pamela was very glad that everyone else in the office were intent on getting their coats on and saying goodbye to one another, as she was trying to suppress a smile and could feel herself wishing that she and Matt could have 'coffee' right then and there! She lowered her voice and said

"OK, then, I'll check which weekend Carla is going to her dad's and I'll await your call" and she put the phone down and went to get her own coat on.

Pamela drove home feeling as though a warm glow was surrounding her, despite the fact that the weather was turning really cold. She parked her little car and let herself in. Carla came running down the stairs saying "Oh Mum, I'm sorry I was horrible this morning" and she gave Pamela a big hug. Pamela hugged her back and laughed saying

"Let me get in the door, its cold outside" but she was thrilled, as two problems seemed to have resolved themselves without her doing anything. She would leave the puzzle of what was bugging Sandra until she had another run in with her – for now Pamela was happy to have heard from Matt and to have Carla back to her usual loving self. Pamela went into the kitchen and put the kettle on. Carla followed her in and got herself a glass of cola.

"I'm sorry I was awful" Carla said "In fact all was well with handing in my homework. I think I would like to go to Dad's this weekend, though, if you don't mind. I'd like to go back to seeing him every other weekend. What do you think"? she asked her mum.

"Sounds good to me" Pamela answered.

Chapter 46

Donald was first downstairs as usual but before he put on the kettle he slipped out of the back door and went round the front to admire his and Isobel's handiwork. Isobel is a remarkable woman, Donald had decided; she told him little about herself but from what she did tell him he deduced that she had had a difficult life but rather than complaining she just got on with it and was very eager to help others. Gardening was her passion, and for reasons she didn't elaborate on she now lived in a small flat without so much as a window box. She had managed to make the fact that even her kitchen window faced north so she struggled to keep a few herb pots going sound funny. Donald smiled as he thought about how Isobel had made him laugh and encouraged him to keep going while they cleared leaves, hoed the last of the weeds whilst taking care not to disturb the bulbs that would flower in spring and generally made the front of the house look smart again. Daphne had been thrilled and had made them cups of tea which they drank in the utility room rather than taking off their mucky shoes. Daphne had been shocked at this to start with, but Isobel had a way with her soft Scottish accent of making everything seem amusing, and to make Daphne feel included by referring to her each time she was worried about the bulbs or perennial plants, so Daphne soon relaxed and let them drink their tea where they wanted to.

Donald had explained to Isobel that Daphne was 'under the specialist for a stomach complaint' and, of course, Isobel was aware there was a problem with Daphne's health as Faith had told her and this was one of the reasons she had offered to help Donald with the garden. Daphne wanted to be on hand, though, while Donald and Isobel were gardening, so she donned her older clothes and cleaned the hallway and polished the brass letter box and knocker on the front door. All in all a very good morning, thought Donald as he went back indoors to put the kettle on for their early morning tea. Daphne had also been very taken with Isobel and had offered her lunch which she had declined saying that she had a dental appointment in the afternoon and had to get home to change. She was so interested in the garden that Donald had given her the full tour of the back, all the way down to the river and he had also shown her his chrysanthemum greenhouse. She was fascinated and had offered to come and help again and Donald had taken her up on this saying he'd consult with Daphne and see what needed doing most. Donald realised that Daphne hadn't been paying her usual attention to the garden, but he wasn't very observant, neither did he really know what should be done in which season, so before Isobel left they went in to consult Daphne again.

Daphne had been pleased and after asking whether she was sure that Isobel didn't mind and accepting Isobel's explanation that she'd once had a big garden which she missed she told Isobel that her 'help' had upped and left and that she and Donald had all the housework to do now and that she'd had neither the time nor the energy to cut back the clematises or prune the wisteria. Daphne was impressed with Isobel's knowledge, and to Donald's delight and amusement a discussion ensued about the best time to prune deciduous ceonothus and forsythia and the various different clematis, and eventually it was agreed that Isobel would return on Friday morning, weather permitting and tackle the clematis Montana.

It was about twelve thirty when Isobel finally left and Donald had asked Daphne how she was feeling; whether the new medication she'd started taking the previous day was helping. Daphne was feeling a little better. Despite the fact that she'd had several gins the previous evening she hadn't had a bilious attack during the night and this had strengthened her feeling that Mr Mears didn't know what he was talking about. She was being very careful to eat only things she knew to be easily digestible, and to take the new medication exactly according to the instructions on the prescriptions. She still had no intention of cutting down on her alcohol intake, let alone cutting it out altogether as Mr Mears had told her she must.

Daphne had told Donald that she was, indeed, feeling a little better, so Donald suggested she sit down while he cooked them both an omelette and that he would drive them both somewhere nice after lunch. Daphne took him up on the offer. He had never learned to cook anything else, but he made better omelettes than she did and would offer to do so occasionally. He prepared the eggs and asked Daphne what she would like with hers as he searched in the fridge for bacon, cheese and mushrooms to put in his. She asked for a plain one so he'd said 'Sit down then, old girl, and I'll make yours first. Where would you like to go this afternoon?"

It was a cold but bright day, and they had decided to follow the river as far as Marlow, and then maybe on to Boulter's Lock, a place they had spent a lot of time when they were young.

That had not been such a good idea, Donald reflected now as he took Daphne her tea. Marlow had been pleasant enough in the weak November sunshine, but Boulter's Lock had seemed to them both seedy and depressing. To his surprise Daphne was awake. She was looking quite pale, as she had no make-up on, but she was just tying her belt on her dressing gown as he tapped on her door and she said "Oh, come in dear, thank you" as Donald placed her cup of tea on the coaster on the bed side table. Unusually for him, Donald had had a couple of stiff whiskies the previous evening, as the change in Boulter's Lock had affected him far more than it did Daphne. She had just laughed it off and said 'Everything changes; let's go back to Marlow and have a nice cup of tea by the river, unless you'd rather go back home for one?" and Donald had answered that yes, he'd rather go home. Neither of them felt like taking a walk along the river as they had in their younger days, when this stretch of the river used to be extremely popular during the summer, and equally pleasant out of season; Daphne because she'd tired herself cleaning the hallway that morning and Donald because he'd felt very oddly unnerved by the changes in the area.

Donald went back downstairs to make some toast. Daphne had been quite comforting the previous evening when she saw that Donald was still a little down. Of course, she didn't know that he tended only to drink tonic water when he poured her gin and tonics, but she'd said kindly "Why don't you have a nice whisky, dear?" when he went to the cabinet to pour their drinks. He had felt quite touched by her concern, but that had somehow made him feel more sad, but he couldn't think why.

He had felt brighter when he awoke this morning and going out to look at the improvements made by Isobel and himself out the front the previous day had helped. As the toast popped up he heard Daphne coming down the stairs; she'd said she would be down soon so Donald put another couple of slices of bread in to toast. He hadn't heard the post arrive, so was surprised to see Daphne with a couple of envelopes in her hand. "More tea, old girl?" he asked as he put the toast, butter and marmalade on the table.

"Yes please" she answered and put one of the envelopes next to Donald's plate. She sat down and busied herself with her toast as she opened her post. Donald put their cups of tea on the table and sat down to open his letter.

Daphne had already opened hers.

"Oh look, dear, Letitia has sent us an invitation. It is for a Christmas drink. She has included a little note explaining why it is so early – it has to be the first Saturday in December because her brother is returning to New Zealand the following week. Goodness, I did wonder, I thought when I read the invitation that the old girl was off her rocker" she laughed. Donald, however, wasn't listening. He was looking intently at his own letter. Daphne looked up to see why Donald hadn't replied. "What have you got there, that you are studying so intently?" she asked him. He looked up

"It's my court date" he told her

"Court date, what court date?" she asked. Donald felt very uncomfortable. Surely Daphne hadn't forgotten? But then he realised that her forgetting was just what he had been working on, and, of course, she wasn't well and had had her hospital appointment in the meantime. So he just said almost dismissively

"You know, old girl, the sentencing for the bit of trouble I was in a while ago"

"Oh, that, of course, I'd forgotten about that. When is it? Donald told her that it was to be on Thursday 2nd December. Daphne replied

"Oh, that's good then, it will soon be all over and we can go to Letitia's on the following Saturday, the 4th. As I said, I thought the poor old girl had gone off her rocker, sending out Christmas invitations this early, she knows our set don't start entertaining until Christmas week, but it's because that brother of hers goes back to New Zealand before Christmas and she would like him there when she entertains again"

*

Isobel had been dreaming about her garden. She awoke feeling refreshed and happy and for a moment or two she wondered where she was. She thought the window was in the wrong place in her bedroom until she woke up properly and realised she was alone in her tiny flat. She hadn't dreamt about her old home for several months now and as she remembered what she was doing the previous day; gardening with Major Fielding, she assumed it was the gardening that had reminded her of her former home. She got up, put on her dressing gown and went to the tiny bathroom and then to the kitchenette to prepare some breakfast.

Normally Isobel would shower and dress immediately; she wasn't one for lingering in bed or wandering about in her night clothes. However, her dream had unsettled her, and she felt once more the loss of her beloved husband, Alasdair. He had died in a car accident, and although the mortgage on their property had been covered by insurance, Isobel knew she wouldn't be able to manage the large house and garden either physically or financially, so she had bravely sold up soon after the funeral and bought this little flat. It gave her independence and it was within easy reach of London where her only daughter lived as a single mother with Isobel's grandson, Iain.

Isobel forced herself to think of Iain and banish sad thoughts of missing Alasdair. Her daughter had not wanted her to sell her home after Alasdair's untimely death, but neither had she wanted to give up her own independence in London and move back home with her mother. This had been Isobel's suggestion as Iain was a tiny baby and Laura was struggling to cope initially as she had just split up with her boyfriend, Iain's father. She smiled as she thought of Iain now. His father, Shumba, was a musician and he had not been ready for fatherhood when Laura fell pregnant. Shumba was now supportive and he and Laura had become friends again and Isobel mused that Laura had made the right choice to bring Iain up in a multicultural environment where his father had easy access to him and he to his father and his family and friends.

Scrambling herself some eggs Isobel thought about how to spend her day. She would phone the probation office to see whether she could get hold of either Faith or Bernice, as they would want to know how she had got on at the Major's on her first solo visit. Isobel enjoyed her volunteer work with probation; she had not worked outside the home for many years as she had kept the books and organised the workload for Alasdair who was a self employed builder. Not wanting to have to find a job was one of her reasons for buying such a small flat, she had bought it outright so only had bills to pay and no mortgage. She had enough savings (she hoped) to keep her going with a fairly frugal lifestyle until she could draw her pension in five years time. Her flat had two bedrooms, so there was somewhere for Laura and Iain to sleep on the odd occasions that they came to stay. Isobel had allowed in her budget for frequent trips to London to see them when she had worked out her finances after losing Alasdair.

Despite Daphne's apparent racism and snobbery, and Donald's slight air of ineffectuality, Isobel had quite taken to them both and sensed a vulnerability not far below the surface. She hoped his court date would soon come up so that they could both get on with life. She wondered whether either Daphne or their daughter would accompany him to court. She would be expected to go, of course, as his volunteer; she couldn't remember the name of his daughter but would ask when she went to help in the garden again on Friday and ask whether Daphne wanted go to court. She didn't think that Daphne drove, so she would offer to take her if she wanted to go. She was just contemplating all this when her phone rang. "Oh it's you" she told Bernice "I was going to ring later to let you know how I got on yesterday"

Bernice explained that Donald's court date was set and after a quick chat about how Isobel got on the previous day and Isobel offering to phone Donald, Bernice said "No, just go to see them tomorrow whatever the weather, then you can offer when you see them face to face, and perhaps you could ask whether they think Pamela, the daughter, will want to go, if it seems appropriate to ask.

Chapter 47

Carla had been avoiding Emily and Rachel as much as their school timetable allowed. Rachel had noticed and had sought her out a couple of times and apologised for 'Emily's little jokes' but Carla knew that it must have been Rachel who had told Emily things she had told her in confidence, so she accepted the apology gracefully but still kept a wary distance from them both.

It was Friday and most people were sharing plans for the weekend. Carla had spoken to Michael and he said that he and Monique would be delighted to have Carla to stay for the weekend and he said he had a 'new toy' to show off to her but wouldn't say what it was. Carla was pleased. She didn't want to feel she was in their way as she was really avoiding being included in Emily and Rachel's weekend plans by going to stay with them. However, every other weekend had been the original arrangement for her to spend with her dad when he and her mum split up, and she was happy to go back to this.

Carla had been intentionally vague when Rachel had asked her that morning what she was doing at the weekend, because Emily was standing by her trying to look contrite but Carla wasn't fooled. She had really enjoyed herself the previous weekend at Rachel's cousin's house; things had only gone horribly wrong the following morning when they had all gone to watch Emily's skating practice and they had ganged up and teased her about her dad and Monique's noisy sex sessions. She wished once again that she had never mentioned it to Rachel, but she shrugged and thought to herself what is done is done but she wasn't going to mention going to stay there this weekend in front of both of them. She was hoping to catch Rachel alone later in the day so she could tell her without giving Emily the chance to be nasty again.

*

Isobel had been pleased to see that the weather was fine as she had opened her little kitchen blind. It was cold, but there didn't seem to be a frost so she would be able to prune some of Daphne's climbers. Despite the fact that Bernice had asked her to go to Donald and Daphne's whatever the weather, Isobel felt more comfortable having a reason to go. She had not, in fact, had a dental appointment the previous Wednesday; she had made that up as an excuse not to stay for lunch with her new clients. This was partly her volunteer training and partly common sense; as a trained and experienced volunteer, Isobel knew the dangers of becoming too friendly too soon, this could lead to two things; either the client(s) could become too dependent on her, or they could tire of her company. In either case she would be less effective as a volunteer and she did not want that to happen. She had not gone in to volunteering to give herself a social life; it had been with the intention of doing something helpful that could give her a sense of satisfaction.

As she pulled into the sweeping driveway she admired the tidy flower beds that she and the Major had worked on the previous Wednesday. She always called him 'Major' when addressing him as she considered it important to treat him with respect, as she did all her clients, no matter what they had done. She checked her watch. It was exactly ten o'clock; the agreed time for her to arrive. The front door opened as she approached it and Daphne invited her in. She had a little more colour than she had two days previously and she was dressed in her old clothes. "Good morning" she said to Isobel "Would you like a cup of tea before we start work?" she surprised Isobel by saying.

Isobel thought quickly. She didn't really want a cup of tea, but she had thought that she was going to be working with the Major this morning. She had assumed that Daphne wasn't well enough to do gardening. She had never had the chance yet to speak to Daphne alone, so she said "That would be lovely, Mrs Fielding, thank you" Daphne, as usual, made proper tea in a pot and served it in the living room, so it was a while before she came in with it after showing Isobel in there and declining her offer of help. There was still no sign of Donald, and when Daphne brought in the tea she only had two cups on the tray.

"Ooh, lovely, thank you. Is the Major not here, Mrs Fielding?" Isobel asked.

"No, dear, just you and me for gardening" she replied. "He has had to go out to see an insurance client" Well, that was all the information Daphne was willing to give. Playing things close to her chest was something she had learnt from a very early age. If she didn't want to tell someone something then she didn't, and she made it very difficult for anyone to question her. Isobel, however, was trained to try to open up closed subjects and to persuade people to talk when necessary. She decided not to put those skills to work just now, though; she would work in the garden with Daphne and see whether Daphne would respond to questions about Donald. Isobel didn't know whether Daphne was aware of the impending court date, but she did know that Daphne knew about the offence and she was keen to know how Daphne actually felt about it. Isobel had worked with sex offenders before, but they had been different; the last one had been a young man who was not in a relationship and he lived alone. One of the many reasons that Isobel had been assigned to befriend the Fieldings was that in sex offence cases couples often split up, and it was thought that with their respective ages it would be hard for them to settle apart, and depending on Donald's sentencing it would be the responsibility of the probation office to ensure that Donald attended whatever was set for him to do, and also that he kept to the court order to keep away from the area surrounding the street where May Bridges lived.

Daphne cleared away the tea things and said "Right, then, let's set to it!" and she led the way to the shed where the gardening tools were kept and they spent a companionable morning with Daphne actually making the pruning cuts and Isobel doing the heavy work clearing away the cuttings. Isobel managed to bring the subject of their conversation round to the major a couple of times, first by praising his chrysanthemums and again, later by asking whether anyone had been injured in the accident for which his clients were claiming on their insurance. Daphne, however, was still reluctant to talk about her husband, she agreed he was good at growing chrysanthemums but said she knew nothing of his insurance business. Mindful that Daphne had been ill and not wanting her to overdo it, Isobel suggested they take a break. They stood back and admired what they had done and Daphne said "You are quite right, my dear, we have done well. Let's go in and prepare a little lunch; my husband should be home soon, once he has conducted his business."

Once indoors, Isobel decided to tackle the issue more directly. She had decided to accept Daphne's invitation to stay to lunch in order to have more time alone with her. After removing their gardening shoes and washing their hands, Daphne accepted Isobel's offer of help in the kitchen and after being shown where to find things Isobel laid the table for the three of them. Daphne had asked "I do hope you don't mind eating in the kitchen, as we are in our working clothes?" and it was just the opening Isobel had been looking for

"No, of course not, it makes sense to do so" she went on to say "You do know why I am helping, don't you Mrs Fielding?" Daphne tried to ignore Isobel but Isobel persisted "When I came here with Faith, my Probation Volunteer Liaison Officer, we spoke about the offence to which your husband pleaded guilty. As I understand it his court date has been set. Has he spoken to you about it?"

"Oh, that, yes. The letter came yesterday. In the same post we received a Christmas invitation from my very good friend Letitia Fotherington. She is local. Do you know the Fotheringtons?" Isobel shook her head but didn't reply as she wanted Daphne to carry on talking. "Well, it is a very early Christmas function, I thought old Letitia was losing her grip, our set never entertain for Christmas until Christmas week itself – it's just not done. However, when I read the accompanying letter I realised that it is because her brother, the surgeon, is returning to New Zealand the following week and she wants to entertain while he is still there." Daphne smiled triumphantly as though this explanation was all that was required. Isobel persisted.

"So, you say that Major Fielding heard about his court date in the same post?"

"Oh, that, yes. That was what I was saying. His date is Thursday December 2nd and Letitia's Christmas cocktail's are to be held the following Saturday. Do you see?" Isobel didn't so she shook her head "Well, the thing for my husband will be settled and so we can go to Letitia's and not mention a thing."

Isobel was a little confused still, as she had no idea that Daphne had been planning to invite her friends and play down the 'incident' in case something got into the newspapers, but she wanted to know whether Daphne meant to go to court. "Oh, I see" she said, though she didn't really "So are you planning to accompany Major Fielding to court? What about your daughter, do you think she will want to attend?"

"Good Lord, no dear, on both counts. Our daughter, Pamela, has been inconvenienced quite enough by the whole business already, what with her estranged husband absconding with my Granddaughter, and I certainly don't want to be involved. He got himself into this and he can get himself back out of it" Daphne said determinedly.

Before Isobel could reply they both heard a car pull round on the gravel. "Here he is now, dear, now let's get this lunch on the table." Daphne said. Isobel had learnt what she needed to know, so she helped to put salad, ham, cheese and butter on the table just as Donald entered the kitchen with a fresh crusty loaf of bread. "Oh, here we all are, very good, very good" he said, jovially, as he set the bread down on the breadboard and reached for the bread knife. Now, how did we get on this morning, not overdone it at all, have we?" he smiled at Daphne.

"No, dear, we have done very well but Isobel very kindly did the heavy work while I clipped and chopped" she told him.

"Well, there's some colour in your cheeks" he told her "but don't overdo it." Seeing the three places set for lunch he thanked Isobel for her help and said "Sorry I couldn't be here this morning, I had to visit a client who had had a slight car accident. I see you are staying to lunch, are you able to help a little more this afternoon? If so, I will work with you and we should encourage Daphne to take a nap"

Isobel thought this a great idea, as she could discuss the impending court appearance with him and at the same time offer to drive him there. She was reassured that Daphne wasn't planning to throw him out, she may be almost ignoring the whole thing, but she had said they were both to attend her friend's Christmas function the Saturday after his court appearance, so she obviously still intended to stand by him, even though she wouldn't go to court. She decided to get Donald to fill in the gaps in her understanding of what Daphne had said earlier, about her friend's party and, more importantly about her daughter's estranged husband and their granddaughter.

*

Pamela hadn't heard from Matt. She had a weekend to herself, as Carla was going to Michael's, and she was just wondering how she could, perhaps, get hold of Matt when Sandra approached her desk with some papers. At that point Pamela's phone rang but Sandra looked pointedly at Maureen so Maureen took Pamela's call for her so Sandra could talk to her. Sandra had been quiet all day so far, and Pamela wondered whether the paperwork she was bringing meant some sort of trouble, especially as she had indicated to Maureen that she wanted her to answer Pamela's phone. However, Pamela needn't have worried, Sandra had been in John Metcalf's office to get something signed and he had given Sandra the paperwork to give to Pamela. Pamela knew what it was; she had requested the latest statement and a lot of copy invoices from Randalls, one of their biggest suppliers and her contact had said his boss was coming in for a meeting with John, so he said he'd send them to her via his boss, as there were a lot of them. Sandra felt it necessary to explain in great detail what checking the statement entailed, completely missing the point that Pamela had obviously checked the previous one otherwise she wouldn't have requested copy invoices. She resisted the temptation to tell her so and just thanked her.

Sandra looked pointedly at Maureen "Well, do you have a message for Pamela, then?" she asked "Uh, no, not really" Maureen answered "What do you mean "Not really" Sandra asked "Either you do or you don't"

"Oh, it's OK; he said he would call back" Maureen answered a little uncomfortably. Pamela felt awkward and wondered whether it had been Matt.

"So was this a business call, or was it, perhaps, a personal call that you took for Pamela?" Sandra asked pointedly. Then she went into a lecture about how personal phone calls were rather like stealing from the company as it was a twofold thing; whilst taking such a call one was either not working at all or working more slowly, and a call in may hold up an important business call while a call out would cost the company money as well as loss of staff time.

Everyone was looking up from their desks now but no one spoke. Suddenly Maureen stood up and said "Sandra, I have no idea whether the chap asking for Pamela was a business or a private call. As she has such a good but professional rapport with all our suppliers it could have been either. I don't know about the others, but I, personally, resent being treated like a child with regard to lateness, telephone calls and the like. You have wasted far more time making us all stop and listen to your lecture than Pamela may have done on a two minute call to make an arrangement for her weekend, that is, assuming it may have been a private call in the first place!"

Sandra was visibly shocked. She stood, stunned, for a moment and the office collectively held its breath waiting to see what she would say. However, she surprised them all by bursting into tears and running from the office. Everyone let out their breath and Joan got up and went to Sandra's desk and picked up her handbag and car keys. Maureen mumbled an apology and said she hadn't been able to take any more. Joan smiled and said "don't worry; poor Sandra had been rather unbearable of late, I wouldn't be surprised if she wants to go home. Hand me her coat, if you will, and I'll go and find her and suggest I tell John she has gone home poorly."

Pamela glanced at her watch. It was almost three o'clock. She looked at the work on her desk and was just trying to decide whether to finish what she had started or whether to leave that until Monday and work on the Randalls account, or whether to leave the Randalls statement until Monday and finish what she'd been doing, when her phone rang. It was Matt. Pamela looked round guiltily but there was no sign of Sandra so she asked him: "Did you phone about twenty minutes ago?" and he said

"Yes, I asked for you but was told you were busy. It was lady I spoke to and she offered to take a message, but knowing what we wanted to arrange I didn't like to say!" Pamela laughed at this but she said

"Look, we've had a bit of trouble here this afternoon, I'll explain when I see you, but I don't want to be on the phone for long. I'll be alone from tomorrow late morning until Sunday mid afternoon, so take your pick"

"OK, that sounds great, how about if I come to your house tomorrow afternoon, about two-ish?" "Excellent, see you then, sorry, I'll have to go now"

"No problem" Matt replied "See you tomorrow".

Only about three minutes had passed but it seemed like much longer to Pamela. She was pleased to see that no one was taking any notice of her phone call; all eyes were on the office door to see whether Sandra would come back with Joan or whether Joan would come back alone, and if she did they were wondering whether she would say anything about Sandra. Pamela felt hot. She knew she wouldn't be able to concentrate on work for a while; Matt's call had really unsettled her. She had intended to ask him for a contact phone number but in the circumstances hadn't wanted to prolong the call. She felt both excited and uncomfortable when she thought about what she had just arranged. To hide her confusion she went to put the kettle on but found that Rob had had the same idea. "Great minds think alike" he laughed as he gathered up everyone's mugs. "Tell you what, I'll wash up the mugs and you ask what everyone would like; they were so busy trying to see out to the car park that they didn't even notice my taking their mugs!" he said to her.

"Well, unless Sandra and Joan come back in there aren't many to ask" Pamela said, feeling herself calm down with Rob's easy going manner. "Lauren only drinks cola and that leaves Maureen, who always has black coffee and Wendy has gone to the dentist now. That leaves you and me so I'll wash up the mugs and you pop back round the corner and see whether Joan is back"

Rob grinned at her "Coward" he muttered quietly as he went back to the office from the little kitchenette area. Joan was, in fact, just coming back in as Rob went to look, so he said "The kettle is on; what would you like?"

"Oh, tea please, that would be lovely" she said to him gratefully.

*

Isobel and Donald cleared away the lunch things and insisted Daphne went to take a nap while they washed up. Daphne was quite happy to do so as she was now tired but she was pleased with what had been achieved that morning and she had issued instructions as to what she would like Donald and Isobel to do next. They started by building up a bonfire with the cuttings from the climbers and added the leaves that they had gathered from the front garden before setting light to it. Next they started work on the long flower bed that led all the way down to the river; the flower bed that had been created when the strip of land had been sold off some years before. Donald admitted to Isobel that he had never realised how hard Daphne worked in the garden; Peggy, their help had come three mornings a week to do the heavy housework and the laundry, and Daphne had had a routine then that Donald admitted to having barely noticed at the time; she would tidy and dust and polish and put freshly cut flowers in the rooms on a Friday, but the rest of the time she was in the garden. He had always fondly referred to it as Daphne's 'pottering', but now that she hadn't 'pottered' for several weeks, Donald realised just how much she had been doing to keep the garden reasonable.

Isobel probed gently to get answers to the questions she had but it was easy enough; Donald seemed at ease with her and was happy to talk. She started by asking him to confirm that Peggy was the mother of the girl with whom he had got involved and subsequently in trouble due to her having learning difficulties. She asked how long Daphne had been unwell and what the consultants opinion was with regard to her illness. This was something, of course, that Donald didn't really know so Isobel asked whether Daphne had gone to see him alone. Donald had said that, yes, indeed, she had. He explained that they had never discussed health and such-like, and this gave Isobel an opportunity to ask a few delicate questions before saying that she had worked with sex offenders before, but that he didn't fit the usual profile.

Donald stopped raking as she said this and straightened up. "Well, my dear, that's very nice of you to say so. I know I shouldn't have done what I did, and I especially shouldn't have gone back to her house, but no one apart from that barrister I was interviewed by after I pleaded guilty has asked why I went back. I really wanted to know whether they wanted me to dispose of or bury their little dog.

"OK, fair enough" Isobel said to him "But could you not have asked the girl's mother that when she came to work?"

"Yes, of course I could, but she doesn't do Fridays, Peggy popped in on a Friday to tell us what had happened. I was not there; I had been to visit an insurance client and then went on to the Golf Club, where I was treasurer until they asked me to leave because of all this. I went to Peggy and Maisie's house that afternoon when Daphne told me what had happened, then I went again the following day, Saturday to offer my help"

"But you did find Maisie alone again, didn't you?" Isobel confirmed. "Yes, I did, and I'm afraid I couldn't help myself this time when she made it obvious that the same thing was to take place as it had the previous afternoon"

Isobel straightened up too and stopped putting leaves in the wheelbarrow. "I am not here to judge" she told him "Did the barrister give you any indication of what sentence he thought the judge may give?" she asked.

"No, he didn't. He didn't say much to me at all apart from ask questions. In fact, he rather put my back up and there was something he asked which I didn't answer. I really didn't feel comfortable with him. Now I am wondering whether I was right not to do so or whether it may come out anyway."

Isobel looked at Donald. He looked troubled. "Do you want to talk about it?" she asked, kindly.

Donald looked at her. "Do you know, I believe I do" he told her feeling quite surprised with himself as he said that to her. Isobel carried on weeding the border so Donald didn't feel pressurised to talk and Donald explained to Isobel what took place a long time ago in Cyprus, and told her that when the barrister asked whether there was anything that might get brought up from his past that could affect the sentencing, he just said no, there was nothing he could think of. He then said to Isobel "I will use all my little nest-egg, of which Daphne knows nothing, if I am to hire the barrister. I am seriously thinking of contacting him and saying he is not required. What do you think?" he asked her.

Isobel was worried. The probation service was responsible for a client while they were under sentence. Their job was not to become involved between the prosecution and the defence. So she said "Do you know, I feel this is something we should discuss with Bernice. If the prosecution have looked into the end of your army career then a defence may be necessary. I am only a volunteer. Bernice will know what to do for the best".

"OK, can I leave that to you please to ask her? I didn't feel at all comfortable with that barrister. I have paid him for the initial visit and am seriously thinking of saving the rest of my little nest egg and cancelling his appearing for me." Isobel agreed that she would contact Bernice then call him and let him know what she said. They continued gardening companionably for another hour and then went in for a cup of tea. Daphne had awoken from her nap and served them tea in the utility room as they requested, as they wanted to do a little more in the garden afterwards.

Donald was now in a very reflective mood and Isobel wondered whether he would mention anything about Cyprus or the court case to Daphne. However, when Daphne came with the tea Donald changed completely again and thanked her and told her that he had never realised how hard she had worked in the garden before she was ill; he didn't mention Peggy's having left and Daphne now needing to do her own housework. Isobel began to wonder whether they always lived in an unreal world; a little world of their own.

Back out in the garden Isobel told Donald that she had asked Daphne whether she planned to accompany him to court. He wasn't at all surprised by her reply, and said to Isobel "She is quite right, of course, I shall be fine on my own" Isobel asked him whether he would tell his daughter when it was and whether he would like her to attend. "Oh, Lord, no. I don't want to have to discuss it with her at all. The whole thing was so shameful, really, when I think of it in terms of how she would feel. I did once try to explain to her what had happened and the look on her face was so horrified that I just couldn't bear for her to hear the details."

"OK" said Isobel "But I don't like the idea of your going alone. Would you like me to collect you from here on the day and drive you there?" she asked him.

"Oh" he said "That is very kind indeed. Yes, perhaps I would like that, yes, you are very kind."

Chapter 48

Pamela had started the washing machine early. She had tidied the house the evening before and now all she had left to do was vacuum and dust round. Carla was going to her dad's, so she would do Carla's room later or Sunday morning. There would be no point putting the washing on the line as it was cold and foggy. She would do the couple of wash loads and put the baskets of wet washing in the airing cupboard. She didn't want to have wet washing on the radiators when Matt arrived. It was really very foggy. She wondered whether he would ride his motorbike. Perhaps he wouldn't come today? She put that thought away hurriedly. She was even more eager to see him than she had been the first time. She knew she wouldn't invite him to bed this time, but at least now she knew that she hadn't imagined that that was what he wanted. She sighed as she thought of his hands on her body.

"Goodness, Mum, that was a big sigh" Carla said, startling Pamela out of her reverie. "Do you have an awful lot to do? Should I stay and help? I could call Dad and tell him to pick me up this afternoon if you'd prefer" she said to her mum. Knowing she still had no way of contacting Matt, and not wanting Carla to know that she was seeing him just yet she said

"Oh I was just wondering how to dry the washing, as it's so foggy. It's not worth putting out on the line. What time are you being picked up?"

"About half past ten. I have an hour or so. I tell you what, I'll get changed and sort my stuff out and then I'll hang some of the washing over the radiators for you" Pamela smiled to herself. She heard enough parents complain that their children did nothing at all to help at home and here was Carla being too helpful, in the circumstances.

"You get ready, love, and I'll put this first load in the airing cupboard then we'll see about the next one. Are you going to have some breakfast?" Pamela always insisted Carla eat breakfast on schooldays, but she let her make her own mind up on weekends, especially if she slept in late.

"Yes, please, I'll have some toast" she surprised her mum by saying. "Dad has something he's described as a 'new toy' he wants to show off to me, so I don't know what the plans are for the weekend."

Pamela put a couple of slices of bread in the toaster and went upstairs with the laundry basket. She hung as much of the washing as she could on hangers on the inside of the airing cupboard and draped the rest over the copper pipes. As she was doing this she let herself imagine Matt's hands on her body again, and found herself thinking about how dexterously he had produced and then put on the condom he had brought with him. She thought again how irresponsible it was of her not to have even thought about some sort of protection. She had been on the pill for years when she was married but at her last appointment at the clinic some months ago she had been advised to take a break from the pill, and as she'd not been sexually active for a long time, she had not bothered to consider the options suggested to her. Pamela couldn't believe that she hadn't felt at all shy with Matt. She hadn't even had a chance to get to know him. Apart from knowing that he was a teacher and he rode a motorbike and knowing how he liked his coffee, she knew nothing about him at all. She wondered what had attracted him to her.

"Mum, is this toast for me?" Carla called up the stairs. Pamela started guiltily

"Yes, love" she answered and went downstairs to spend a little time with Carla by having a coffee while Carla ate her toast.

"So what are you going to do today?" Carla asked her mum. Pamela was stumped for a moment but Carla didn't notice. She asked instead "Is it tomorrow we are going to dinner at Sylvie's Mum and Dad's?" That was easier to answer:

"No, love, that's a week tomorrow, Sylvie's birthday" she replied.

"OK, I'll get Dad to drop me back about 6pm tomorrow, then, shall I?"

"Yes, that will be good" Pamela told her "I'll do us a roast and then we can do something with the leftovers on Monday" she said

"Oh, good, could we have chicken, please?" she asked her mum. Pamela said a non committal "we'll see" and Carla finished her toast and went upstairs to get ready to go to her dad's. Pamela had tidied the house the previous evening and was organised with the washing and cleaning; but she'd not thought ahead about shopping. She had no idea how much time she would spend with Matt. They'd not had the opportunity to discuss that on the phone, and Pamela would have been far too shy to ask. It was one thing having an amazing tumble on her bed with him after not being sure she'd read the signs right, and she'd not been at all shy actually doing it but apart from flirting on the phone she certainly didn't want to talk about what they'd done or what they might do in bed, so even if she'd been able to talk for longer she wouldn't have asked what he wanted to do in case he told her! She was hoping they'd go out for a drink or something this weekend. She had thoroughly enjoyed the sex with him but wanted to get to know him a little more.

*

Carla kissed her mum goodbye and turned and waved to her as she put her holdall in the back of Michael's car and climbed in the front seat next to him. He waved a polite salute to Pamela and she put her hand up to him in return. Carla turned to her dad and said "So what's the big secret then? What is your new toy?" Michael just grinned and waved his hand as he pulled away from the kerb and drove the couple of miles to his house. "What?" Carla asked.

"There" and Michael pointed to a black plastic thing on the ledge in front of the gearbox.

"What is it? Oh, is it a phone?" Carla asked, excitedly.

"Yes. I've only had it a few days and it's been very useful for my business already"

"Wow" said Carla "I'm impressed. Some people say they don't work very well, though. Is this one good?"

"Yes" Michael answered. "It's digital, you see, not analogue. We looked into it, and this is a Motorola 5200...."

"Whoa, stop! Enough technical details" Carla complained, laughing. Just show me how it works; that's all I'm interested in"

"OK, when we stop again I'll show you" he told her.

"Can't you use it while you are driving?" she asked "Not a lot of point having one if you can't"

"Oh yes, you can use them while driving, it's just that I'm not used to it yet, so I have to look at it to see what I'm doing. I can program some phone numbers into it, but I haven't yet. Maybe you can help me when we get home?" Carla noticed her dad was already calling the house he was sharing with Monique 'home', even though it could only be rented for six months maximum. She was very pleased that her mum had bought a house that was to be their home for the foreseeable future. She now no longer walked along the ring road to catch the bus further along by the bigger houses; she was no longer embarrassed to say she lived in a small terraced house. She couldn't remember really why it was that she had felt that way at first. Only when that funny neighbour of theirs challenged her about it and explained the dangers did she really think it through. Marian had been waiting in their house the evening she'd avoided going to her Grandma's in Crowford and she had gently persuaded her that it was too dangerous. She was still surprised that she had told Marian why she was doing it; Marian was so easy to talk to, and she had promised faithfully not to tell her mum about it so long as she agreed not to do it anymore. Since then Carla had often popped round to Marian's for a chat whilst waiting for her mum to come in from work.

Michael parked the car on the drive outside the garage. Carla wondered whether Monique was at work or whether her car was in the garage. She was hoping to get some time on her own with her dad but rather than ask, she waited until they got in the house. She quite liked Monique, but she did enjoy time alone with her dad. As they entered the house it was evident that Monique wasn't there, but she wasn't at work; Michael explained that she was out shopping. For the next half hour or so Carla sat and chatted and read out phone numbers to him from his Filofax as he programmed them into his phone.

"Hi" Monique shouted as she came in the door with a bag of shopping. Carla and Michael went out to help her unload the car and Michael laughed and asked whether she'd bought enough to feed an army. "No, but I need to sort out the bags. Some of it is for Rosemary, next door. She is pregnant and suffering from morning sickness, and it is little Ben's birthday tomorrow so I offered to get some shopping for her as her husband is working today. They took all the bags into the kitchen and Monique sorted out what she had bought for her neighbour. Carla offered to take the bags round and Monique said she'd make some coffee.

Carla hadn't been in the house next door and she had never spoken to Ben's mum, Rosemary. She shifted all three carrier bags into one hand and rang the doorbell. A very pale looking lady came to the door and Carla introduced herself. "Ah, the fence lady!" Rosemary exclaimed. Ben came running to the door and stopped and looked at Carla. He said

"Hello Carla Maffoos" very politely. Rosemary said to him

"Carla has brought the shopping for your birthday" but he screamed

"No" at the top of his voice and ran away.

"Oh dear" said Carla, "Is he OK?" Rosemary led the way to the kitchen and sat down on a stool. She looked exhausted.

"Oh, I don't know" she told Carla. "He has these moods when I can't do anything with him. I've heard of the 'terrible twos' but somehow this seems more severe. When he is like this I can't comfort him. His dad gets terribly frustrated. He will be three tomorrow and I am supposed to be organising a party but I feel so wretched." Carla felt very sorry for Rosemary. She didn't know anything about young children or pregnancy, but she offered to help Rosemary.

"I'll just pop next door and tell my dad I'll be here helping you for a while, if you like?" she said. "That is very kind of you" she told Carla. I'm supposed to be making him a cake. Bernard, my husband, will be very cross if I haven't done it by the time he comes home this evening, but when I think about mixing the butter and eggs it makes me feel very sick again."

"Well, I've never made a birthday cake before, but there's a first time for everything" Carla said, brightly "Let me have the recipe and show me where everything is, and maybe you can do something else that needs doing while I do the cake."

Carla left Rosemary sitting on the stool and let herself out. She hoped that her dad wouldn't mind, after all, it was she who had said she wanted to come for the weekend. "No, you go and help" he said to her, "she seems to have a lot to put up with, poor lady."

"Yes" added Monique "When Ben has one of his tantrums we often hear Bernard shouting as well, usually shouting at both Rosemary and little Benjamin. I don't know why. She certainly doesn't have it easy."

As it turned out, Carla stayed until evening, until just before Bernard was due home. She had thoroughly enjoyed herself. Once the sponge cake had cooled while they had some lunch she had covered it in chocolate buttercream icing and had made it look like a clock with chocolate buttons, with the time set to three o'clock, as Ben was to be three, and she had put the 'Happy Birthday' sign written in gold that Rosemary had produced from a kitchen drawer and written 'Ben' in broken up chocolate buttons underneath the sign. Rosemary was very pleased with it. Carla had quickly realised that it wouldn't do to let on to Bernard that it wasn't Rosemary who had made the cake, but she wasn't sure about saying that to Rosemary. It did sound, however, from the odd things that Rosemary had let slip through the afternoon as they worked companionably together that Bernard had no time for weaknesses of any sort in his family. "What is his job?" Carla had asked whilst applying chocolate buttons and Rosemary had said that he worked at the hospital, but she didn't say what job he did there.

Rosemary had made fish fingers and oven chips for Ben's lunch, and a ham sandwich each for the two of them and they had sat and eaten companionably at the kitchen table and Ben had eaten his lunch quietly and not been at all naughty. Ben didn't seem to want to talk; he was very serious for one so young. He always called her 'Carla Maffoos', rather than just Carla, but she didn't mind. Rosemary explained that he didn't like anything to do with change. He didn't even like his name shortened; he preferred to be called Benjamin. New shoes were the worst, Rosemary explained. He would scream and scream until he became used to them; then when he grew out of those it would all start over again. Carla wondered about what one of her school friends had told her about autism, but she didn't like to approach the subject in case Rosemary was offended. Instead she asked whether he went to playgroup, and what the other mum's thought.

Rosemary started to look pale again, and Carla wished she'd not asked. Changing the subject so that

Rosemary didn't have to answer Carla asked whether she should put the kettle on so she could make her a cup of tea. "Oh, yes, please, that would be lovely" she said "I don't know why I am feeling so grotty all the time with this pregnancy; I wasn't like it with Ben. Somehow I can always manage a cup of tea if someone else makes it, but not if I make it myself."

Just before four thirty Carla was saying goodbye and Rosemary was thanking her. "Oh, I've enjoyed myself" Carla told her "I just wish the cake wasn't quite so amateurish, I'm sure it would have looked better had you been able to make it"

"I doubt it" Rosemary said, laughing. It has a certain 'rustic look' Bernard will think it was me who made it"

"Well, better let him think that, then, I don't want him to be cross because I've been round here wasting your time" she said, tactfully. Rosemary thought what a kind understanding girl she was, as she closed the door and went to see what Benjamin was doing.

Back with Monique and Michael Carla agreed with them that Bernard seemed to give Rosemary a hard time. However, they soon forgot about their neighbour and her problems because Michael wanted to talk to Carla about Christmas. "It's less than seven weeks away now" he'd said "and it would be good if we plan what we are going to do, as George has invited us to their place, Monique's parents have invited us to France and I want to see you at Christmas"

"Goodness" said Carla "sounds like a busy time. I won't leave Mum on her own"

"No, of course not" replied her dad "But I thought we'd start discussing it as soon as possible" "Has your Mum said anything about visiting her parents?" he asked. Carla had not spoken to her dad at all about Granddad Fielding's trouble, and he had not mentioned it as Pamela had made it quite clear that although Carla knew about it all now she didn't want the subject discussed. This, however, using Christmas, thought Michael, was a legitimate area for discussion.

"Oh, I don't know. Mum and I haven't talked about that. Mum has complained about how much Christmas stuff is in the shops already, and she asked whether I want to eat Turkey on Christmas day, so I guess she's intending it to be just the two of us. Mum has phoned Grandma to see how she got on at the hospital, but she's not been to see them since we got back from Brittany. Carla didn't hold it against her dad that he had made out her granddad was ill rather than telling her the truth. Despite the fact that she had misunderstood at the time and had for a while had the horrific belief that it was her mum that was in trouble, now she knew all was well with her mum the business with her granddad seemed quite distant to her. Just so long as the girls at school never found out she was not interested. Carla was pleased that her mum was seeing more of her friend, Sylvie, again, her mum she could discuss it with her if necessary, but Carla herself had quite enough troubles of her own with her friends teasing her; she did not want to think of her grandfather in a sexual context, any more than she did her parents, especially as what he had done was apparently against the law.

*

As Pamela dropped Matt off at the corner of his road she smiled at him as he bent forward to give her a kiss. When he had arrived without his motorbike leathers she had assumed it was because of the bad weather, but he soon explained that there was something wrong with his bike and he would need the afternoon to fix it. He had travelled by bus to come and see her, so she had offered to drive him home after his visit. She felt faintly let down, though, as she had hoped to get to know him much better and, perhaps, go out for a drink or a meal together. He had tried not to show it but had obviously been very disappointed when she explained shyly that she had her period so sex wasn't on the agenda. Pamela made fresh coffee and they chatted about the school and Pamela's office but Matt carefully deflected any of Pamela's attempts to ask him about his own background and also made it clear that he wasn't free for the whole weekend as he had to fix his motorbike before Monday.

Marian had watched as Pamela and Matt walked up her path to her car. She was not being intentionally nosy, but she had planned to return a book that Carla had leant her and she knew Carla needed it back before Monday, but she had just been about to leave her house when she saw Matt walk up Pamela's path and knock quietly on the door. She had wondered why he hadn't rung the doorbell, then she wondered whether he was the same chap she had seen the previous week; he had the same build, but the previous week he had been wearing motorbike leathers and had quietly pushed his bike next to Pamela's car and looked furtively round as he walked up her path. 'So, that's it,' she thought mischievously to herself, 'Pamela's got a boyfriend! Well, good for her' and, of course, she decided not to disturb them. She assumed that Carla was out, so she would look out for her return and give her the book when she saw her.

Chapter 49

Isobel phoned the probation office early Monday morning to try to get hold of either Bernice or Faith. Neither was available. She did not want to ask for Sylvie as the phone had been answered by Josie, and Isobel knew the delicate situation regarding Sylvie's friendship with Pamela and that Josie was one of the officers who disapproved strongly that Sylvie even knew the details of Major Donald's case. All Isobel felt she could do was to leave a message for Bernice to call her with some urgency. She knew she should really go through Faith, as Volunteer Liaison, but she knew from experience that using the proper channels slowed messages down and she wanted advice on this one urgently.

Josie had said that Bernice was not expected in the office until the afternoon. Isobel had shopping to do and bills to pay, so she decided to go to town straight after leaving the message for Bernice to call her, so that she would be back home to take Bernice's call. She had told Major Fielding that he could leave the matter with her, but she didn't really feel the confidence she had implied to him. She knew that his defence was not a matter for probation, but she hoped that Bernice would understand and would know what, if anything, to do with the information with which the Major had entrusted her, with regard to his leaving the army and returning from Cyprus.

Marian smiled to herself. She was having a good morning. Her health wasn't good and she sometimes found it tempting not to get out of bed on a Monday morning these days. She still marvelled at the fact that she was officially retired. She had been signed off sick for the two years prior to her 60th birthday; she had sustained injuries in a car accident and had been unable to work, but had to be continually reassessed each time the government brought in new rules about sickness benefit. This had used to irritate her immensely; she was no sponger; she had sustained whiplash injuries which meant she could no longer work on a keyboard for any length of time. She had loved her job, despite the fact that while studying with the Open University she had had dreams of, perhaps, working at something that used her brain a little. For the twenty years before the accident Marian had worked in the parts section of a large garage. She was one of only two women who worked there, the other being Rose, the receptionist. Marian was still in touch with Rose but didn't see much of her. She supposed that Rose had always been a little jealous of her relationship with the mechanics; where Rose used to get told off for booking in too few or too many jobs – it had seemed to her she could never get it right and was blamed whether they were too busy and when there was too little work. Marian, known by all the mechanics as Spike, because she had unruly hair, which instead of trying to tame she coloured red, was their pet; they would always say "Never mind using the computer system; if we have a part here Spike will know and she will know where it is".

Marian had been quite lonely once she'd recovered enough from the accident to live a fairly normal life, but not recovered enough to go back to work. Money was short but that was nothing new to her and didn't worry her. She didn't make friends easily but had found good friends in both Pamela and Carla, next door. She smiled again as she thought about her conversation with them both the previous evening. She had seen Michael's car pull up to drop Carla off and had hurried round with the book Carla had lent to her, knowing she needed it for school the following day.

Carla had been full of information regarding mobile phones; how they were the communication of the future and how reliable her dad's new phone seemed to be compared to ones owned by some of her peers' parents. Pamela, on the other hand, had been reticent when Carla had asked her how she'd spent her weekend, and Marian had smiled secretly to herself as she remembered seeing Pamela and the young man walking to Pamela's car. Pamela had offered Marian a cup of tea, but seeing that they were about to eat roast chicken she declined, pleased that Pamela had offered.

*

Donald was startled to find Daphne already up and dressed when he took her up her morning tea. Not only was she up and dressed, but she had put almost the entire contents of her wardrobe on her bed. "What on earth are you up to, old thing?" he asked as he set her tea down on the coaster on Daphne's bedside table. "I'm looking out something suitable to wear to Leticia's on the 4th" she told him. It won't be quite Christmas time, so I am looking for something appropriate and need to check whether it needs any attention before it can be worn. Oh, thank you for the tea" Donald felt he had been dismissed so went back downstairs and left Daphne to her organising. He thought she had lost some weight recently; not surprising considering how unwell she had been before she started taking her prescription. Donald wondered whether she would need a new outfit. He decided to offer to take her shopping for one later. Money was quite tight, but if he decided not to spend his money on this barrister he would be able to treat old Daphers now and then. He considered that life was pretty good just now. He would be glad when the court case was over and he could put all the silliness behind him. He decided to be strong in the future and never to get embroiled in anything like it ever again.

*

As Sandra went into her Monday morning managers' meeting Pamela went to the little kitchen area to make everyone tea or coffee. It was the last full week before month end and they were all very busy, including Rob who was ploughing away preparing a new interface which would allow the payroll journal to be uploaded into the system. This annoyed Sandra, as did any progress or change to the system, but it would mean that Maureen would no longer need to process the time consuming journal onto the system line by line. Pamela carried the tray of drinks to the office and quietly put a drink down on each desk. As she did so she thought to herself 'I must shop for a birthday present for Sylvie for Sunday'. She had not enjoyed her weekend and she was cross with herself. She knew she was not in a relationship with Matt but nevertheless had been disappointed that not only did he not stay long at her house on Saturday but neither was he open to her suggestion that they meet for a drink or something once he had fixed his motorbike. He had said that he didn't want to let her down by not turning up in case he had a bigger problem than he first thought with the bike, but she did, in fact, feel let down by his not making an arrangement for their next meeting and also for not giving her a number on which to contact him. This she blamed herself for, however, as she had not liked to press him for it and so she assumed he had meant to give her his phone number but had just forgotten. Pamela should have really gone to town over the weekend to buy a birthday present for Sylvie, but after her short visit from Matt she felt demoralised and couldn't be bothered to do anything and had spent the rest of the weekend doing very little.

As Pamela put Rob's coffee down on his desk he said to her "Good heavens, you are deep in thought – a penny for them?" Pamela grinned and told him her thoughts were not worth a penny. "If you are worried about your work load and getting everything on the system, I can help, if you like" Rob offered. Maureen looked up at this

"You just get on with that magic computer program of yours. If I no longer have to key in the payroll journal I will be able to help Pamela with her work – the payroll journal usually takes me half a day to key in, but if I make a mistake it can take another half a day to find it and put it right until it balances – and you tell me that I will never have to do that again once you have written the interface – you get on with it" she said to him with a laugh. Rob looked at Pamela who smiled and nodded in agreement.

"OK, outnumbered by the women again" he said, good-naturedly.

"Not all of them" said Maureen darkly referring to the fact that Sandra didn't want any of the journals automated.

*

Josie had a dental appointment Monday afternoon. It was she who had taken Isobel's message. Despite the fact that Isobel had asked first to speak to Bernice, and had said it was urgent that Bernice call her back, Josie decided to leave a message for Faith instead. Josie didn't agree with volunteers by-passing the system and as Faith has the role of volunteer liaison, it was into Faith's already crowded in tray that Josie popped the piece of paper with the message to call Isobel. She didn't mark it as urgent, as she didn't like the idea of being told to do so by a volunteer, especially one who wouldn't tell her the details of the case in question when she had grudgingly enquired whether she, herself, could assist Isobel with whatever it was.

Isobel had known that Josie was not particularly keen on the probation service using volunteers. She was concerned about having left the message with Josie. On getting home from town she checked her answer-phone, but no one from probation had called her back. Isobel didn't want to make a nuisance of herself or, indeed, risk getting Josie on the phone again so after putting away her shopping and filing away the receipts for the bills she had paid, she settled down with her lunch and to wait for Bernice's call.

*

Sylvie had had a good morning. The previous week there had been a meeting with Eddy Mitchell, the Chief Probation Officer. Ralph had attended the meeting in order to talk to all the probation officers about the dangers of stress in the workplace. One of his suggestions had been that the Chief think seriously about allowing people to work from home when they had several reports to write. Most of the probation officers had a home computer and those computers had compatible word processing packages so Ralph pointed out that it was much easier to get a report written at home than in the office where there was always noise and disturbance and phone calls to be answered. He suggested that a rota be organised to allow for working from home, and to everyone's surprise even agreed that it would be necessary for everyone, including himself, to fill in the 'who is where' board and to leave a contact phone number when working from home.

Sylvie had been lucky enough to have been on the rota for the first Monday morning to work from home and had completed two of her outstanding reports. Not having wanted any breakfast as she had eaten an enormous meal at her parents' house the previous evening, she had eaten a quick sandwich before driving into the office. She wondered whether her father had had a word with her mother about not nagging her about her love life, as she had really enjoyed the evening with her parents. She had told them about the good time she had with Pamela the previous Sunday; their lunch and trip to the cinema and she had also told them that Pamela had said she would love to come to dinner with them all the following Sunday, Sylvie's birthday.

Sylvie's mum, Doris, had always said that she could never get into the swing of preparing for Christmas until after Sylvie's birthday, and as that was on November 28th Doris claimed that she then just got on with it and never panicked about Christmas the way some people did.

As Sylvie parked her car and walked up the stairs to the office she wondered briefly what Pamela would do at Christmas this year, the first year on her own with Carla. She wondered whether Carla would spend part of the time with Michael. She knew without having to ask that Pamela would be very welcome to have Christmas dinner with her parents; they had both been thrilled when Sylvie had told them Pamela was coming for her birthday. She had been such a big part of their lives while the girls were growing up and although both Sylvie's parents often asked after her they hadn't seen Pamela for many years.

As Sylvie hung up her coat she asked "Any important messages?" there were a couple of head shakes in answer so she sat down and began to go through her in-tray. Bernice came in soon after Sylvie, having spent the morning at the Magistrates court. Bernice asked the same question, receiving the same negative reaction as Sylvie. Noticing Sylvie, Bernice asked her

"Hey, it's your birthday soon, isn't it? When are we having cakes?" Sylvie grinned

"Yes, you are right, my birthday is on Sunday. I'll bring in cakes on Monday" she replied. One or two of the other officers looked up briefly and said

"Oh good" and one said

"Oh no, what about the calories?" and they all chuckled before getting back to their work.

Chapter 50

Pamela was keeping her head down. Sandra was in one of her worst sarcastic moods. Being the last day of the month they were preparing to close for month end. Rob had successfully downloaded the payroll journal thus removing the need for Maureen to spend the whole morning keying the figures in manually. Freed from the need to do this she had first offered help to Joan with the sales invoices then to Pamela. Neither needed her help so when Maureen offered to help Lauren with the filing; Lauren was very pleased to accept. It was at this point that Sandra, who had been quietly smouldering and making sarcastic remarks all morning, finally exploded. "May I remind you all that I am the Office Manager here and if there is to be any reallocation of tasks it is to me that you will all refer". She snapped loudly.

At this John Meredith appeared and looked round at everyone and asked pleasantly how the arrangements for month end close were going. Pamela realised that Rob must have had a quiet word with John. This wasn't the first time he had appeared as though by coincidence when an argument was about to break out in the office. Pamela had always had a lot of respect for him and now she realised that he knew there was a problem with Sandra's behaviour and that this was his way of dealing with it.

Pamela wondered why John didn't deal with Sandra in a more direct manner, but as Rob explained to John that the payroll journal interface was a success, and as this meant a lot less work for the staff, Sandra was just looking to see who could help who elsewhere, Pamela understood that John knew exactly what he was doing with regard to the running of the office. She looked back down at her desk and carried on inputting the rest of the invoices which she had received back in the internal mail authorised for payment. She had chased up each department with large value outstanding invoices as this would save her time the following day as she would not have to accrue for the large values after month end close. This would not only save her a lot of work but would also be more accurate than the guess work that accruing usually entailed.

Sylvie had told Pamela on the way to Sylvie's parents the previous Sunday that Donald's court date for sentencing was to be the following Thursday, December the 2nd. Sylvie had asked tentatively whether Pamela would like to attend court. Pamela had declined, saying that she had heard no more from her father on the subject, and, more importantly she had heard no more from Michael and that was the most important thing for Pamela; that Carla would remain unaffected by the whole thing, apart from what had already taken place.

*

Carla was, in fact, at that very moment extremely pleased that she had never confided in her friends what had really happened when she had been away for a week supposedly because her grandfather was ill. The previous week or two had been reasonably pleasant with Carla not feeling pushed away or not included by her friends. She was aware that some of this was down to her having remained a little aloof after the last bout of teasing, and having first spent a weekend at her father's, then saying she was 'busy' this last weekend with her mum's friend, Sylvie's birthday. This had at first caused the two girls to be curious about what Carla found interesting at her dad's; particularly his new portable phone and the time she had spent next door to her dad's at Ben's house preparing the birthday cake.

However, today was different. For some reason the taunting had started again. She tried not to mind, but she had been friends with Emily and Rachel since primary school. She didn't have any other close friends and up until now they had always been close, particularly Carla and Rachel. It hurt that now Rachel was spending more time with Emily and aping some of her ways and siding with her when she tormented Carla.

Carla walked along with her head down. She was on her way to her next lesson and almost bumped into Matt Gregory. "My, you are looking serious" he said to her "Are you OK?" he had made her jump

"Oh, yes, yes thank you, I am fine" she answered before hurrying on her way to her next class. Emily and Rachel had noticed.

"Ha, so you're after him too now are you" quipped Emily

"Yes, not enough that your mum fancies him" added Rachel. Carla tried her best to ignore them both, but she was feeling very unhappy as she entered the classroom and got her books out of her bag and sat down.

*

Donald had not heard from Isobel, so he had made up his own mind with regard to using the barrister and he had telephoned and cancelled the appointment with him explaining that he would conduct his own defence as he was sentenced. Daphne had been pleased when Donald had offered to take her shopping for a new outfit to wear to Leticia's early Christmas evening. "Oh, but are you sure we should spend money on clothes just now?" she had asked him when he offered.

"Yes, old thing, I do" he had replied "You've been unwell and seem to have lost some weight. You are getting the colour back in your cheeks now so let's cheer you up even more with a new outfit. We could go into Reading if you like, to Lewis' and see whether they have something you like".

Daphne had accepted and they had gone to the department store the previous Friday and she had, indeed, found an outfit she liked, and when she told Donald the price he had not hesitated and had bought it for her. Daphne had been really chatty on the way home, almost like her old self. Donald had told her she looked stunning in the new clothes and that the others at Leticia's would think she looked marvellous.

"I don't know about that" Daphne had laughed " but it is very kind of you and leaves my usual Christmas outfit free for me to wear when we have our own Christmas soiree"

*

In fact Isobel had been having troubles of her own. Having not heard from Bernice by 4pm the previous Monday afternoon she had just decided to leave it until the following day and try phoning the probation office again when the phone rang. Surprised and at first pleased to hear her daughter's voice the pleasure quickly turned to alarm. "Mum, don't speak, just listen" Laura had said to her "The bairn is in hospital with suspected meningitis. Can you come?" Isobel went instantly cold with fear and after asking which hospital he was in she agreed to get there as soon as she could. Quickly throwing the things she thought she might need into her large handbag Isobel threw caution to the wind and phoned for a taxi to take her to the station. She caught the first fast train that came along that was going to Paddington and once on it she studied the underground map in the back of her diary to determine the easiest way to get to the hospital.

Isobel did well. An hour and a half after receiving Laura's call she met her in the children's ward where Iain had been admitted. He looked terrible; he was listless and uncomplaining as the nurse hooked up a drip and explained that it was just a rehydration fluid to counteract the effects of his high temperature. They must await the results of his tests before they could treat him with any medication. Isobel hugged Laura to try to give them both strength. "Have you called Shumba?" she asked.

"No, I haven't had the time. That's why I need you here. I haven't even called work to tell them what is happening. Iain was just a little bit poorly in the night and this has all happened so quickly since then. Isobel was happy to have something practical to do.

"Well, it's a little late to call your office; I'll do that in the morning. Let me have the numbers of the places Shumba is likely to be and I will track him down" Isobel said to Laura.

"Thanks Mum, I knew I'd feel better once you arrived" said Laura as she stroked Iain's little hand.

Isobel didn't, in fact, manage to get hold of Shumba. She left messages for him everywhere she phoned; explaining that his little boy was ill in hospital and Laura wanted him there as soon as possible. Once she had done her best to locate Shumba, Isobel rejoined Laura at Iain's cot-side. Isobel and Laura tried to buoy each other with encouraging words, but they gave this up after a while and took it in turns to talk softly to Iain to reassure him and sooth him. He was conscious but listless, occasionally sucking his thumb, his dark curly hair plastered to his head just looking at them with big dark puzzled eyes. Isobel was faintly surprised and amused that Laura had referred to him as 'the bairn' when she had called. Laura had never lived in Scotland, and, unlike Isobel, she didn't sound at all Scottish. Isobel supposed that at times of stress one resorted to what was familiar, and Isobel herself often referred to her grandson as 'the bairn'.

The nurse came at regular intervals to check on Iain but she had no news as yet with regard to his condition. It was late evening and neither Isobel nor Laura had eaten anything. They weren't hungry. Another parent had very kindly brought them each a cup of tea earlier; it was out of a machine and didn't taste very nice but they had both drunk it automatically as it was put in front of them. As Isobel thought of it now she couldn't remember them thanking the person who brought the teas. The door to the little side room opened and a large imposing looking black man with huge dreadlocks came in. "Oh, Shumba" cried Laura, softly; "thank goodness" Isobel slipped softly out of the door. She was quite fond of Iain's father, despite his early lack of support towards Laura and the fact that he was pursuing his dream of a career in music and had no money to give Laura.

Isobel went in search of a sandwich machine as she had no idea how long they would all be there with Iain. One thing was sure; none of them would move until Iain's condition was diagnosed and he began responding to treatment.

It was five days later when an extremely exhausted Isobel got back home to her flat. She thanked the taxi driver and let herself in. She wondered what sort of image she projected; her usually neat hair was in need of a wash and she was wearing a pair of her daughter's leggings and a large woolly jumper under her coat and had her own clothes that she had worn for far too long in a carrier bag. She didn't care. Most importantly Iain had been discharged from hospital and was on the mend. Never had Isobel ever felt as afraid as she did while Iain was so ill. Shaking off any negative feelings Isobel took off the clothes she'd borrowed from Laura and had a shower. After her shower she put on her dressing gown and looked in the fridge. The milk, mercifully, hadn't gone off so she made herself a cup of tea. She was not hungry as once Iain was discharged from hospital they had gone to the other extreme and eaten very well; Shumba's friends and family bringing and sending over many delicious Jamaican delicacies. After checking for phone messages and briefly sifting through her post for anything interesting or urgent, Isobel slipped into bed despite the fact it was only early evening and slept without waking for the next fourteen hours.

Isobel had spent the weekend quietly, just phoning Laura a couple of times to check on young Iain's progress. Satisfied that he was on the mend Isobel turned her thoughts to what the following week had in store for her. There had been no message from Bernice, so Isobel assumed that, not getting hold of her, she would have contacted Major Fielding herself, guessing that it would be in connection with his case that Isobel had needed to speak with her urgently.

Isobel phoned Major Donald on the Tuesday morning, two days before his sentencing in order to apologise for not being in touch before and to ask him what time he would like to be picked up.

*

"Who was that dear" asked Daphne, as Donald put the phone down.

"It was Isobel" he answered.

"Who?" asked Daphne

"You know, Isobel; the lady who has been helping with the garden.

"Oh, that's nice dear, is she coming to do some more gardening?" Daphne asked.

"Not just yet" Donald answered her "She was just calling about picking me up on Thursday" he told Daphne

"Picking you up?" she asked "Why, where are you going?" Daphne had forgotten again about Donald's forthcoming court appearance for sentencing. He didn't really want to remind her as life had been quite pleasant over the last couple of weeks.

"Oh, that little business to do with the court. Isobel has very kindly offered to drive me there on Thursday. Don't know why. Could easily drive meself, but it's kind of her. I can discuss what we are to do next to help you with the garden, if you like, old thing?" Donald said, in order to deflect Daphne's thoughts from the court visit.

"Oh, yes, that will be nice. Do you think she will come in first, for a cup of tea before you go?" Daphne asked.

"No, she has arranged to come here at 9.30 sharp. Seems her grandson has been ill and each day she likes to call and see how he is progressing. So she will do that and come straight to get me. We can come in when we return, if you would like" He said to her.

Chapter 51

Isobel drove over to Crowford feeling quite cheerful. She had phoned Laura before leaving her flat and Laura had confirmed that Iain was on the mend. Isobel had now caught up on all her lost sleep and had dressed carefully to accompany the Major to court. As Isobel's car crunched on the gravel drive the door opened and the Major stepped out closing the door behind him. "This is very kind of you" he told Isobel as he climbed into the small car.

"Not at all" Isobel told him, smiling "How is Mrs Fielding today?" she asked him.

Donald told her that Daphne had been quite well now since her appointment with the specialist but was still becoming tired easily. "In fact, she was still in bed when I took up her morning tea just now, but I know she would like you to come in with me when we return" he told Isobel.

"That will be nice" Isobel said to him. She put the car in gear and pulled away. Once out on the main road she began to ask him about his decision with regard to using the barrister, and what Bernice had thought. Donald was puzzled. He had assumed that as he had heard from neither Isobel nor Bernice that they didn't think his worries re his army career were important so had cancelled his meeting with his barrister. Isobel realised that for some reason or other Bernice had not received her message. It was too late to worry about that now, so she said something reassuring to Donald and concentrated on negotiating the morning traffic. Isobel had attended Crown Court before as a volunteer for Probation and knew where to find the Probation Liaison officer. She explained to Donald that the best thing would be for him to go on into court as his letter had told him where to report to, so she would drop him near the court while she went off to find a parking space.

Isobel had needed to go quite a way to find somewhere to park. By the time she got to the court and found the probation liaison officer the Major had already been called. Isobel was shown into the court and was very pleased, indeed, to see that Sylvie was in attendance. She knew that the officer who wrote the report would not necessarily be required to attend, but she knew that Sylvie, with her family connections would not be there in an official capacity. This was highlighted by the fact that Sylvie sat in the public gallery rather than in the seats reserved for probation officers. She had said she would attend if time and circumstances permitted. Isobel hoped to be able to have a word with her as soon as there was a break.

The preliminaries began. The prosecution read out the indictments against Donald. Isobel was surprised to learn that initially there had also been accusations of both rape and buggery. The prosecuting officer then explained that these had been dropped and that Major Donald Fielding had pleaded guilty to two charges of indecent assault. The officer went on to say that there was another matter recorded against the Major in 1967, but the judge interrupted to say that this was not going to be taken into account as even though it was a sexual matter it was such a long time ago that the court felt that it was not relevant to what was taking place now. Surprised at this, Sylvie turned to look across at Isobel. Isobel returned her look and Sylvie thought that Isobel looked almost relieved. She wondered what it was about, and decided to try to speak to Isobel as soon as the judge called for a break.

The preliminaries continued. The prosecution applied for costs of £935. The Pre sentence report was introduced as were three letters and a psychiatric report. The judge asked whether Major Fielding was being represented and was told that he was not; that he was representing himself.

The morning wore on as the prosecution laid out the facts of the case and the judge asked many questions. The judge had received the Pre sentence report in plenty of time, but he had not had a chance to read the psychiatric report submitted by the victim's social worker. Citing this as a reason to break early for lunch, the judge called a halt at eleven thirty and asked that the court reassemble at two o'clock prompt. The court rose, the judge left and Sylvie and Isobel turned to one another. Seeing they both had the same idea; that they wanted to speak to each other Sylvie signalled to Isobel to leave by the nearest door but to wait for her outside.

They both began to speak at once. So as they both stopped Sylvie said "Looks like we have plenty to discuss. Let's go get a coffee and a bite to eat away from here where we can talk" Saying no more she lead the way. Isobel followed, relieved that she had someone to talk to about the case. Isobel looked surprised as Sylvie led her into a pub and headed straight to a corner seat. "It's a bit smoky in here, I'm afraid. Do you mind? It's just that I know this place, they do nice coffee, unless, of course, you'd like a drink?" Isobel shook her head, conveying both that she didn't mind the smokiness and she didn't want a drink. Sylvie carried on "We can speak freely here as we will see who else comes in. The court restaurant is quite good, as are the two tea shops nearby, but here we can get a good sandwich and coffee and talk without continually looking over our shoulders" Once she could get a word in edgeways, Isobel spoke.

"Yes, it's fine by me. Goodness, but I am pleased you are here. I think there may have been a breakdown in communication, as I'd tried to get hold of Bernice; then I had to go away for a few days.

"Bernice has the 'flu" Sylvie told Isobel, she's been off since the middle of last week. She's not the only one off with it so we've been stretched more than usual. Ralph is representing Probation today, in case the judge has questions regarding Bernice's report. I really shouldn't have come but I have plenty of flexi time so booked some time off as soon as I knew the date. This has had a terrible effect on my friend Pamela, did you know that her ex-husband took her daughter away for a week and wasn't going to let her live at home with Pamela again because of what her father has apparently done?"

"Yes, I do know that, Mrs Fielding told me. The thing is, do you know about Cyprus 1967?"

"No" said Sylvie "I was shocked when it was mentioned. I take it you do know?" she asked.

"Yes, Major Fielding told me the whole story, I was very worried as he'd told no one else, and he had begun to wonder whether the prosecution would dig it up and have it used against him, but he didn't have any faith in the barrister so left it to me to tell someone. Oh, I have failed miserably in that as I left a message for Bernice to call me urgently, then my grandson was rushed into hospital and I dropped everything and went straight to London to be with him and support my daughter"

"Well, don't worry" Sylvie told her "You heard the judge. He said he will not take it into consideration. You can't blame yourself. How is your grandson now?"

"Oh, he is on the mend now, thank you, but he was very seriously ill" she told her.

"What is this judge like? I don't think I've heard much about him"

Sylvie looked thoughtful for a moment before saying "To be honest he is a bit of an unknown quantity. He doesn't usually cover our circuit. Ralph knows of him and said that from what he'd heard he has been known to hand out harsher sentences than some, he's not known as one of the softer judges"

"Oh, then it's just as well that he is not taking what happened in Cyprus into account" Isobel said. Sylvie agreed and suggested that they order their coffee and sandwiches and then Isobel could tell her about Cyprus, if she wanted to.

"Yes, yes, I do" Isobel told her. "Major Fielding decided to get it off his chest and definitely wanted me to tell the probation office. I know you are a friend of the family, but I have to tell someone and I know we can't make a difference now, especially as he decided not to use the barrister"

"Yes, that was a surprise to us, his not using the barrister" Sylvie said to her, then she asked Isobel what she would like to eat. She told her they did a very good 'hot chip butty' which she described as 'naughty but nice' so Isobel said she'd like one as well. Sylvie went up to the bar to order, and Isobel sat contemplating where to start with the Major's story.

Walking back to the court Sylvie was silent and thoughtful. Isobel walked companionably by her side but didn't speak. She had told Sylvie what Major Donald had told her about events in Cyprus and, for Isobel's sake, Sylvie was glad that the judge had said the court would not take it into consideration when sentencing the Major for the offences to which he has pleaded guilty. Sylvie had told Isobel not to feel guilty that she hadn't got the message though to Bernice; she had told her emphatically that it had been the job of the duty solicitor and then of Donald's barrister to advise him re such a matter. It was not the job of probation, so she told Isobel to stop worrying on that account.

Isobel and Sylvie were back in the public gallery by ten minutes to two. Isobel had been shocked by the size of the chip sandwich served at the pub; she had been unable to eat all of hers although it was delicious and she had watched in amusement as Sylvie ate every last crumb of hers. They sat down, next to one another, and waited for the court to settle down and the judge to arrive.

In her time as a Probation Volunteer Isobel had accompanied quite a few clients and their families to Magistrates Court. She had attended County Court several times with one client as she battled to gain custody of her children. She had attended Crown Court on a few occasions as part of her volunteer training but this, however, was the first time Isobel had attended Crown Court with a client. She watched and listened avidly as the afternoon's procedure went on. She had become quite fond of the Major and his wife during the short time in which she had befriended them; looking at him now Isobel could see that he looked strained.

Major Fielding had not yet been called to speak for himself and Sylvie had told Isobel during their lunch break that the judge may not ask him to speak. Sylvie thought it a mistake that the Major had not asked anyone to speak for him as a character witness; he had not even asked anyone to write a letter on his behalf. Isobel believed that she understood why this was; apart from committing the offences in the first place the Major's only thoughts had been to protect his family from adverse publicity.

The judge had a couple of queries regarding the pre sentence report and called for a representative from Probation to clarify the matters. Sylvie and Isobel watched as Ralph went into the witness box and took the oath. He explained that he was not the officer who had written the report but that he was in a position to answer questions. Sylvie had told Isobel over lunch that this was normal procedure as it was not possible for every officer to be available to speak for their own report at every court hearing. She also said that it was sensible for her not to speak with Ralph at any time during the day, but she needn't have said so because Isobel was aware that Sylvie was attending the court as a friend of the family and not as a probation officer. The judge had marked a couple of paragraphs in the report and it was to these that he now referred. Such reports are meant only to contain facts; probation officers are not allowed to include opinions that they have formed about the client during their interviews, but a probation officer can convey sympathy toward a client in many ways, should they feel any empathy toward the client, without breaching the set guidelines.

The judge obviously felt that this report had elements in it of such a sympathetic manner. The two things he queried were the number of times Bernice had stressed the Major's age, and the remorse that the Major felt with regard to how any publicity regarding his offences would affect his wife and family. Before answering Ralph looked at the Major who was standing as if to attention and though very smartly dressed was looking strained and showing his age. Ralph answered "I am sure that Mrs Liddel was eager to convey to the court that Major Fielding shows remorse for his offences and that he is concerned about any shame and disgrace that is felt by his wife due to his actions and Mrs Liddel is also keen to remind the court of the Major's age" The judge thanked him and he stood down.

There was a slight stir in the courtroom and the judge took a message from the clerk of the court. He cleared his throat "Ah, yes. I see Dr Brown is required in another court shortly; so we will call him now" Dr Brown, being the psychiatrist responsible for writing the report regarding the victim's impairments. Isobel was surprised to hear Dr Brown describe May Bridges as 'a defective with severe impairment', as Isobel was more used to the socially accepted terms for those with learning difficulties.

Isobel was surprised to see that it was still not yet three o'clock when the judge said "This is rather more difficult than I imagined. I will go out to deliberate. You will all remain where you are while I do so" and at that he left the court. A lot of talking broke out but immediately the Usher called for silence. The judge's chambers were, in fact, close behind the court and silence was required. A very short time later the door opened again, the Usher called

"All rise" and the judge came back into the court.

The judge waited for the court to be seated and become quiet. He then began to speak "Major Fielding, this is a very serious offence. Plainly you knew the victim was impaired and with you being a lot older you took advantage. The pre sentence report makes it clear that this young lady was associated with your family for the whole of her life and that here was a breach of trust; a breach of confidence. I have taken into account your guilty plea and I have taken into account your age. Your age is a double edged sword. Some would think a lenient sentence would be in order due to your advanced age, on the other hand you are old enough to know better. The pre sentence report indicates that you show remorse with regard to the effect on your family, but it does not, however, indicate that you show remorse with regard to the offence against the victim. I therefore sentence you to twelve months imprisonment concurrent for both offences." The judge then thanked the court and turned and left. Isobel was speechless. Sylvie remained rooted to the spot; she had been waiting for the judge to add 'suspended' and add a length of time for the suspension.

Sylvie sat still looking shocked. Isobel looked at her and asked "So he is actually going down? He's actually going to prison now?"

"Yes, yes he is" answered Sylvie "Goodness, we must get our skates on. It will probably be in the evening papers. What is the time?" Isobel realised Sylvie was thinking aloud but she said

"It's three o'clock. What do you want me to do?" Sylvie was busy thinking. "Let's go and find Ralph. He will, hopefully, be allowed to see Major Donald and he can reassure him that we will talk to his family. I will seek out Pamela before she gets home as she may not want her daughter, Carla, to know. Will you go and explain to Mrs Fielding?" They walked down towards the front of the court where they had last seen Ralph. As they walked Isobel answered

"Yes, of course I will. Should I go straight away?" Sylvie thought for a moment then she spotted Ralph. As soon as they reached him he said

"Bloody hell; that was a surprise! I was quite sure it would be a community service or a suspended sentence."

"Didn't we all" answered Sylvie.

"Do you have a plan?" asked Ralph.

"Yes" said Sylvie. "Will you go and see the Major now?" she asked Ralph "If so, we will wait to see whether he has messages for both his wife and daughter; then I will go to see the daughter and Isobel will go and tell his wife"

Ralph agreed readily to this. He didn't know the Major but he knew that his daughter was a childhood friend of Sylvie's. Isobel looked at Sylvie. They hadn't agreed where to meet and Isobel could see the court was preparing for the next case. Sylvie was deep in thought but she could feel Isobel looking at her "Come on" she said to Isobel "We'll wait for Ralph outside. He will know where to find us"

They didn't have long to wait. Ralph approached them looking thoughtful. "Poor old beggar" he said when he reached them "Just keeps saying it's all a big mistake and that when they realise it they will release him. I asked whether he had messages for his wife and daughter and he just repeated it. They are going to put him in the hospital wing first off until they find him a place under rule 43" Ralph looked at Isobel as he said this and she nodded to let him see she understood "Will you be able to explain to Mrs Fielding?" he asked her.

"Yes" she told him "It was all part of our volunteer training. I understand about the categorisation of prisoners and I know most of the slang terms for sex offenders as I have a few I have been writing to since becoming a volunteer. Should I go now to Mrs Fielding?" Ralph and Sylvie looked at one another. Sylvie replied;

"Yes, please. I want to get hold of Pamela, Major Fielding's daughter, my friend, before she leaves work. Will you be OK? Ralph will let Bernice know about his sentence as soon as she is back at work and she will arrange to visit him as soon as possible."

"Yes, I'll be fine. I am not looking forward to telling Mrs Fielding, but I will do it. I am so glad you were here" she said to Sylvie "Should I tell Mrs Fielding that you are telling her daughter?" she asked. Before she could reply Ralph said

"Sorry to interrupt but I am off now" Looking at Sylvie he said "You know where I am if you want me" and then he said goodbye to both Isobel and Sylvie as he left the court building.

Sylvie then answered Isobel's question; "Yes, please do tell Mrs Fielding that I was in court and that I am now going to see Pamela. It is quite likely that his sentence will make the newspapers. It is always best for the family to be forewarned".

Chapter 52

Sylvie found a telephone box and called Pamela at work. Pamela had sounded pleased to hear her when she answered the phone. Sylvie quickly cut in to say that she had something important to tell her and asked if there was somewhere near to her place of work that they could meet. Pamela had said "No, not really, it's a trading estate with the odd pub, but no coffee shop" and had suggested Sylvie come to her house. Of course, Sylvie didn't want to do that but didn't want to explain why over the phone so she said "Tell you what, meet me in the foyer of the Hotel on the ring road roundabout, they do a nice coffee and I can tell you what this is all about" She rang off after agreeing a time and Pamela grumbling good naturedly that it was all a bit mysterious but that she would be there.

Pamela had said that she couldn't leave work until five o'clock and that she would be at the hotel at about twenty past depending on the traffic. Sylvie was relieved. She had rung off abruptly on purpose so that Pamela had no time either to ask questions or decide that meeting with her wasn't such a good idea after all.

*

Isobel pulled into the drive and parked just past the front door. She had thought Daphne would hear the car and come to the front door. She didn't. Isobel rang the door bell. When she appeared Isobel said "Hello Mrs Fielding" but Daphne interrupted and asked

"Doesn't he have his key?" and before Isobel could answer she looked around and asked "Well, where is he?" Isobel didn't answer

"May I come in?" she asked instead. "Oh, of course, where are my manners?" said Daphne as she showed Isobel in. "I have something to tell you. Not good news I am afraid. Would you like to sit down?" before Isobel could continue Daphne said

"No, I would not like to sit down. If there is something to tell me then please do so" Isobel stepped towards Daphne and put a hand on her arm. Daphne looked concerned but pulled her arm away. Isobel said to her "There is no easy way to say this. Major Fielding has been sentenced to twelve months imprisonment"

Mrs Daphne Fielding's mouth dropped open. She put her hand up to her mouth. She almost whispered the word "Prison? But where is he now?" she seemed in a daze. Isobel said gently

"That is where he is now. He was sentenced and taken straight down to the cells. He has been sentenced to twelve months, but he will serve six and be released on licence and be monitored by the probation service" Still Daphne didn't speak. They were still standing in the hallway. Slowly Daphne walked to the kitchen where she lowered herself into a hard backed chair at the table. She looked at Isobel

"Prison?" she asked again. "Which one, where? How will he manage? What about his things?" She was very pale. Isobel was worried

"Shall I put the kettle on?" she asked. Daphne didn't answer so Isobel put it on anyway. This was not the first time that Isobel had been asked to inform a family member that a loved one had been imprisoned, but it was the first time she had to do it with someone of the Major and Daphne's ages and the first time she had done so with someone of their apparent social standing.

Isobel made tea. Daphne still sat impassive at her kitchen table. Isobel put a cup of tea in front of her. She looked up "Oh, thank you dear" she said, rather absently. The she asked again "What about his things?"

Isobel asked "What things?" Daphne said

"Well, toothbrush, things like that?" Isobel sat down with her tea

"They will provide everything he needs to start with. There are rules about what prisoners can have. He will be given a basic kit that includes a cheap toothbrush and disposable safety razor."

Daphne still looked vague "A prisoner, Donald? There must be some mistake. Have you spoken to him?" Isobel answered her

"No, I haven't spoken to him but one of the probation officers has; Ralph Stone. He went down to see him in the cells to ask him whether he had a message for yourself or your daughter" Daphne cut in

"Oh my God, what about Pamela?" Isobel told her that Sylvie had gone to talk to her. Daphne looked deflated again. She seemed so shocked that she couldn't concentrate on any one thing for long. Isobel drank her tea. Daphne seemed to have forgotten hers. Isobel spoke again.

"I will have to go home soon. Are you going to be OK?" she asked. Daphne didn't answer. Instead she said

"I don't drive, you know" Isobel assumed that Daphne was worried about how to get to see her husband.

"It's early days for a visit yet" she said to her. Daphne was puzzled

"A visit?" she asked.

"To see your husband" Isobel answered. Daphne was vague again

"But the car, what about the car?" she asked. Isobel became firm.

"I am sure you can sort out a friend, or perhaps your daughter to start the car from time to time so it runs for your husband when he is home again. Now, I must go home now, will you be alright? Is there a friend or neighbour I can call for you?" Daphne looked horrified

"Friend? Neighbour? Whatever for?" she asked. Isobel explained to Daphne that she had had a shock and that perhaps she shouldn't be on her own. Daphne bristled at that and at last seemed to be aware of her surroundings. She sipped her tea and told Isobel that she would be fine. Isobel promised to call again the following day. She said she would give Daphne all the details she would need then. Daphne showed Isobel out and went into the living room. She poured herself a large gin, saying to herself 'A snifter's what you need old girl. Best thing for shock. Mother always said so' as she did.

*

Sylvie pulled into the hotel car park moments after Pamela and they got out of their cars. Pamela noted Sylvie's grim expression and followed her into the hotel. Sylvie didn't speak until she had ordered a tray of coffee and biscuits and then she ushered Pamela into a corner where there were two armchairs and said "Sit down". Pamela trusted her friend so she did as she was told and then asked

"Come on, what is this all about?" A waitress appeared with the coffee and biscuits which she placed on the low table between them. Sylvie pushed the table away from them and turned to Pamela and took both her hands in hers.

"Your Dad has been sentenced to twelve months imprisonment" she told her.

Pamela looked at Sylvie and withdrew her hands slowly "Holy shit!" she said. Sylvie almost wanted to laugh. She had never heard her friend say anything like that before. Sylvie poured them each a coffee and explained how the court case had gone and what the sentence meant in terms of how long he would actually serve. Pamela told Sylvie that she had tried to figure out what it was Sylvie wanted to tell her and that she now understood why she wouldn't say over the phone. She thanked her.

"No problem" said Sylvie. "We need to decide what, if anything, to tell Carla. It will quite likely be in the newspapers; possibly this evenings local. Michael will soon know and we need to be prepared for his reaction"

"What about my Mum" asked Pamela "Does she know?" so Sylvie explained that Isobel, a volunteer with the probation service had accompanied her father to the court and had gone to tell her mother.

"Where is he? Do we know how he is? Surely no one was expecting him to get a custodial sentence? Why? Is he a danger to the public?" Pamela now couldn't stop asking questions. Sylvie answered as best she could. Indeed, no one had expected there to be a custodial sentence. Bernice had written a fairly sympathetic report and the judge had agreed not to take his army offence into consideration. Sylvie started "What is it?" asked Pamela.

"There is something else you need to know. Something that came out in court but that the judge told the prosecution that he wouldn't take into account. It explains why your parents came back from Cyprus when they did, if the prosecution got hold of the information then the newspapers will be able to. Do you want me to tell you?"

"I'll need to let Carla know I will be late home" Pamela said "Yes, I suppose I'd better know what it is you know. Have you always known?" she asked her friend

"God, no, I only found out today" Sylvie assured Pamela. "Your dad had confided the whole thing in Isobel, the volunteer, bizarrely while they were gardening together" Pamela vaguely remembered her mother saying that the nice Scottish probation volunteer had been helping in the garden "Will Carla be home yet?" Pamela looked at her watch

"Oh, yes, she'll have been in a while, unless she's next door chatting to Marian. Those two have become quite pally" Sylvie suggested that she phone Carla and think of a reason to tell her she'd be late so that Sylvie could tell her what she could expect to be reported in the newspapers. Pamela asked Sylvie whether she'd mind her telling Carla that Sylvie had a problem with a neighbour and needed a chat. Sylvie said that was a good idea and that after she'd told Pamela what she needed to that they could both go to Pamela's with a takeaway for all three of them, and that would give them a chance to check the evening newspapers.

Pamela sat back down. She'd phoned Carla and explained she would be home later with Sylvie and a takeaway. Carla asked if Pamela were OK, she must have detected a wobble in her voice but Pamela laughed it off and said she was concerned about Sylvie and once they'd had a good chat they would be back with the promised takeaway. Carla, in turn, asked whether they could have Chinese and when Pamela said yes Carla promised to do her homework so that they could sit together and enjoy their dinner.

In the meantime Sylvie had ordered more coffee. Once the coffee arrived Sylvie began to explain what Pamela's dad had told Isobel.

Sylvie began by saying "What you need to remember is that this, of course, is your Dad's version of events, I am not explaining it sympathetically, just, as best as I can, word for word as he explained it to Isobel. I'm afraid you may be shocked, as I was; used as I am to such things it is a skeleton in your Dad's cupboard, and if he had not been brought to court it could have remained firmly in the cupboard. However, I feel it better that you hear your Dad's version before a newspaper decides to print their version, if they ever do."

"I understand all that" Pamela cut in "Please, just tell me"

"OK, well as children we never really wondered why you and your parents came to England and lived at Crowford with your grandparents. I know it was explained why you then stayed on there, rather than finding a place of your own. That was because your grandfather died and your grandmother wanted you all to stay to help her manage the large property." Pamela knew all this, but knew better than to stop Sylvie as this was the preamble to the explanation as to why her father left the Army and then had to try to find suitable work. "As you know, your father's Army career had taken him to several postings abroad, the last being Cyprus, where he was a Major. Your mother had been hoping that he would be promoted to Lieutenant Colonel and posted somewhere in the Far East, possibly Hong Kong.

Your father was not as ambitious as your mother was for him, but he was happy in the Army and was happy to progress both for that reason and to please your mother. It looked as though a promotion was likely until an unfortunate event took place with a young man" Pamela looked startled at this, but still she didn't speak, she just listened. "This young man was very well connected; his uncle being a Major General and his father a Brigadier. The young man was a Second Lieutenant and was in trouble for having overspent on his bar bill. He had been unable to pay at the end of the month and this could not be allowed to continue, so he was sent to your father to be reprimanded, as your father was a member of the management committee of the officer's mess. This chap was blond and a real charmer and before your father had a chance to speak to him instead of standing to attention he walked round to your father's side of the desk and pulled up a chair beside your father. Naturally, this would have been exceptionally eccentric behaviour in a subordinate in the Army, so your father waited a moment to see what he would do next. Well, this is the tricky bit;" Sylvie paused and took a sip of her coffee and looked at Pamela "He put his hand on your father's leg and began to rub. Your father got an erection immediately; so the young man unbuttoned your father's trousers and after a bit of fumbling in his underclothes he took his penis in his hand" at this Pamela did interrupt

"But why didn't he stop him? Why did he allow the young man to walk round his desk in the first place? She asked

Sylvie continued "You have to remember I only know what Isobel told me. She didn't ask your father any questions, she just allowed him to speak; to get it off his chest. "Anyway, where was I? Oh yes; your father was sitting there with the young man his side of the desk and it was quite obvious that something was going on when the door opened and in came your father's superior officer. There was an enquiry, of course, but despite your father being the higher rank the young man was so well connected it was your father's career that came to an end. He resigned but was allowed to keep the title 'Major'. Well, that's all I know, but better you hear it from me than read it in the papers, or to have to explain it to Michael if he gets to hear of it." Sylvie looked at Pamela. Pamela was shaking. "Are you OK?" Sylvie asked her.

Pamela answered hesitantly "Er, yes I think I am OK" she said, slowly "It answers so many questions; questions I'd never asked and had never intended to ask, but which had been in my head for many years. We had quite a big house in Episkopi, and I do remember a kerfuffle when I got home from school one evening and Mummy was moving into a bedroom of her own. I know they have slept in separate rooms since we came to England, but, until that moment I'd forgotten that their sleeping apart began in Cyprus. I suppose I wasn't that interested in the reason at the time.

"Yes" answered Sylvie "and then you were concerned with the move and settling into a country of which you had only vague memories and settling into the new school"

"Yes, and thank goodness you were new to the school too" Pamela said "Oh you've always been such a good friend to me" and she leant over and squeezed Sylvie's hand.

"Well, it goes both ways" Sylvie said "I may have only moved a couple of counties but I wasn't used to moving as you were, what with the different Army bases. You were a comfort to me too. And still are – we'd better get our story straight for Carla – what's supposed to be my problem?" She asked

"Goodness knows" Pamela said to her "Carla won't expect chapter and verse. Let's go now and order a Chinese and see what evening papers are available" They went out to the car park. Before she got in her car Pamela turned to Sylvie and said

"Oh Lord, what about my mother? I know she's a funny old thing but I can begin to see where some of it has come from. What should I do? Should I phone her?" Sylvie thought for a moment and then said

"Let's think about that while we are waiting for our food. If you do decide to call her I can sit in the sitting room with Carla and we can make out you are ringing my 'lost love' or neighbour or whatever."

Pamela agreed and so they both drove off and pulled in to the little parade of shops not far from Pamela's where the Chinese takeaway was situated. They placed their order and then went into the newsagents. Pamela was almost afraid to look, so Sylvie picked up an Evening Post and a Gazette. She said to Pamela as they went back to the Chinese to await their order "I don't suppose there will be anything in the Gazette; I think they plan it days before it comes out. Come on, let's check the court pages of the Post" There was, indeed, a small article about the Major's sentence, but apart from naming him and the charges against him to which it said he'd pleaded guilty, there was no more information. Sylvie looked thoughtful "Does anyone at Carla's school know your maiden name?" she asked

"Not as far as I know" Pamela replied "If you remember it was because Michael saw the original article about Daddy's court case that he took Carla away for the week, but no one at the school questioned what we said about her grandfather having been taken ill."

"That's a relief, then" Sylvie told her. "You would be surprised how many secrets are kept even about pupil's parent's serving prison sentences, or going into mental health care institutions, without their school friends ever finding out. Apart from what goes in the press, confidentiality is a wonderful thing. The media will only pick up on a story if the subject is currently important in the political sphere; only if it is a season with very little new news will they bother with something as old as the Cyprus story. They may become more interested in the fact that he has been imprisoned for taking part in, what seems to be, a consensual sexual act. It is, as you know, only because of the girl's mental age that she is protected in this way. Some journalist may dig around and make a story out of it, we will remain vigilant; I know where to look for such articles" As Sylvie said that, the friendly lady behind the counter called out their number. She'd had to call it twice, and she teased them saying that they were too busy gossiping so they couldn't be hungry. Sylvie took the local papers and one of the bags of food and took them to her car. "See you at your place" she called out to Pamela as she got into her car.

Carla opened the door for them. "Great, I'm starving" she said as she helped them in with the bags of food. Are there prawn crackers?" she asked "Oh, Sylvie, are you OK?" she then remembered to ask. Sylvie was very tired now, after the emotional strain of telling Pamela what she had discovered, so it was not difficult for her to sigh and sound tired as she said "Yes, thanks, I'll be OK". Carla had laid the table so all Pamela had to do was put the containers in the middle and say

"Help yourselves"

Both Sylvie and Carla tucked in but Pamela just picked at hers. "Glad to see you're not hungry, Mum, I'll eat your share" Carla said to her cheekily.

"Oh, I've not had the best of days at work, you carry on and eat as much as you like" her mum said to her. Sylvie looked up

"Are you going to make that phone call for me?" she asked Pamela. Pamela looked thoughtful and then said

"Yes, OK, if you think it will help matters" "What do you think?" asked Sylvie

"I think you are right" Pamela said to her

"OK" said Sylvie to Carla "Can I come and watch TV with you while your mum tries to get through to my dotty neighbour for me?" Carla was most amused

"Of course, come with me and we'll leave Mum to it".

It took quite a while for her mother to answer and then it took Pamela a while to make her understand who was calling. She wondered whether her mother had been drinking. "Mummy, it's me, Pamela. I wondered if you were OK after today's awful news"

"News, dear, I haven't seen the news today" she said.

"No, Mummy, the news that Daddy is in prison. I understand that the probation volunteer called Isobel came to tell you?"

"Oh that business, dear; just some misunderstanding. Daddy bought me a new outfit because we are going to Leticia's on Saturday. A little soiree, sort of a Christmas one but it's only just December..."

"Mummy, I don't want to know about Leticia's soiree, I want to know whether you are alright; how are you going to manage?" Pamela didn't get any further sense out of her mother, but she decided that she obviously wasn't extremely upset as she had thought she would be, so she rang off and went back downstairs. Carla was engrossed in the TV so Sylvie and Pamela went to chat in the kitchen. Pamela explained that her mother had not made much sense and that she thought perhaps she had had a drink but that she didn't sound upset.

"Don't worry, for now, then" Sylvie said to her. "She's probably in shock. Isobel will look after her; that's what our volunteers are for. Goodness, but I am glad Isobel is involved she is a very pleasant no nonsense sort of woman." She hesitated then said "I need to get off home now and sort out some stuff for tomorrow. Will you be OK?"

"Oh, yes, thank you for everything. I will be fine. It's Thursday today, I'll call Mummy again tomorrow evening and if I don't get any sense out of her I will drive over to see her on Saturday morning. Carla is due to go to Michaels's this coming weekend so I'll be able to talk freely to Mummy."

Chapter 53

Pamela couldn't think what on earth had possessed her to agree to seeing Matt today. She had felt dreadful at work yesterday as she'd not slept a wink after Sylvie's news the previous evening. She had got up early, dressed nicely and applied a lot of makeup as she hadn't wanted Carla to ask why she was distressed. Pamela wasn't totally convinced about not telling Carla that her grandfather had gone to prison, but she was following Sylvie's advice for the time being. Sylvie had explained that her father would only serve half his sentence i.e. six months and had suggested that perhaps Carla need never know.

Pamela had phoned her mother again on Friday and she hadn't sounded too bad; she was not quite so vague as she had been the previous evening and she had said that Isobel had offered to take her shopping on a regular basis. Pamela was relieved about that as her mother had never learned to drive and that was one practical consideration taken care of. What was worrying her, however, was how her mother was going to cope in general; how she felt about the whole thing and whether she would, in fact, have her father back once he had served his prison sentence.

Right now, though, Pamela was trying to get her head round the fact that Matt was due to arrive in an hour's time. Michael had just picked Carla up as arranged and Pamela was doing the usual Saturday morning juggle of washing machine, vacuum cleaner and clean duvet covers. She had not intended to see Matt. She hadn't known when he phoned whether she'd need to go and see her mother. She was feeling so rotten when he phoned that she just agreed that it was, indeed, Carla's weekend to see her dad and that yes, it would be OK for him to come to see her. He had heard the flatness in her voice but assumed that it was because Pamela didn't want anyone at work to know she was making a social arrangement and so he had just said brightly "Great, I'll see you tomorrow, then"

Pamela had cleaned and tidied her bedroom and put clean bedclothes on her bed. Despite the fact that she was still upset about the news that Sylvie had imparted she had felt a small frisson of excitement as she had looked back at the clean tidy room before pulling the door to.

*

Carla settled herself into the front seat next to her dad. She asked him if there were any plans for the weekend. "Not really" he told her "Except that Monique is working tomorrow, so we can do something just the two of us if you like" Carla was thrilled. She quite liked Monique but it would be really good to just be with Dad for most of a day. Carla had to be back with her mum by about six pm, and she knew Monique's shift would be the early one as it would be Sunday "What do you fancy doing?" Michael asked her. Carla racked her brain

"I don't know, but I'll think of something" she told him with a grin. He said he'd try to think of something too and they spent the rest of the short journey in companionable silence.

*

Matt wandered round the supermarket deep in thought. He didn't want a permanent relationship with anyone, but he quite liked Pamela and she was a good shag. He didn't want to invite her round to his flat, as, to him, that signified a commitment and he wasn't into all that at all. Neither did he really want to start taking Pamela out, as that would cost him money and, in his book, that also signified commitment. Interestingly, in his opinion, shagging did not signify a commitment. Matt did realise, however, that he would have to do something 'nice' to hold Pamela's attention and therefore keep him in her good books. This is why he was in a supermarket. He wanted to buy something easy to cook for two, a bottle of wine and some flowers and or chocolates and with these offerings he was hoping he would be invited to stay the night. As he understood it; Carla spent every other weekend with her father. He had inveigled himself into relationships several times with the single mothers of his pupils, the more successful usually being with recently the separated. It was an arrangement that suited him. He usually found such women to have a low self esteem and to be grateful for the sort of relationship he was offering. Of course, they didn't tend to know just how little was actually on offer, and when they found out he usually moved on; just as he now had to Pamela. In such cases, he found it much easier if the previous person had neither a phone number nor an address for him as he then had no hassle. Of course, they could always trace him through the school, but none of his previous lady friends had wanted to do so, much to his relief.

*

Pamela sighed as she arranged the damp washing to dry in the airing cupboard. She thought it a nuisance that Matt was coming to see her today, even though she liked him and enjoyed his company, as well, of course, as the wonderful sex they had. She perked up a bit at this thought; she had considered it would be better to be alone with her thoughts; there was no one she could confide in about her dad, unless she decided to tell Marian. She had now changed from worrying about how her mum would cope; she had never felt close to her mum, and she didn't really feel that way now. She had actually begun to wonder how her dad was feeling; Sylvie had said she would be able to visit, but she had dismissed that thought as soon as Sylvie had said it. However, Sylvie was used to this sort of reaction from the families of those first sentenced to a custodial sentence; especially when such a sentence has been rather unexpected. Sylvie had explained all this to Pamela and told her that when it all had had a chance to sink it she would feel differently and although her dad would only be inside for six months, she had plenty of time to arrange a visit; in most cases visits were not permitted immediately, anyway. Sylvie had told her that her dad would be housed initially in the hospital wing of the prison; he was a sex offender, and as such would be classed as a 'vulnerable prisoner' liable to attack from other inmates, so he would remain in the hospital wing until a suitable place could be found for him under Prison Rule 43. Sylvie had told Pamela that she could phone her at any time if she had any questions or if she were particularly worried about anything to do with her dad's sentence. Pamela hadn't been able to take in everything that Sylvie had told her. It was only two evenings ago and Pamela had had a busy day at work the previous day after a sleepless night. She knew there was absolutely nothing she could do this weekend and she really didn't want to go to see her mother; she had been relieved when she had sounded reasonably OK on the phone the previous evening.

The doorbell rang cutting across Pamela's thoughts. She had momentarily forgotten about Matt. She went to let him in and was surprised to see he was carrying shopping bags. He kissed her as he walked into the hallway and through to the kitchen. "I've bought us lunch and dinner" he told her as he unpacked the bags. "I hope you like steak and red wine" and as she nodded that she did he handed her a box of chocolates and said "and these are for you" He set to putting things away in the fridge as Pamela made coffee. "I've also brought fresh rolls and some nice cheeses for lunch, as we're going to need our strength later" he told her leaving her in no doubt about what they would need their energy for. She actually found herself laughing and relaxing; well, she thought to herself, she'd been wondering how to get through the weekend; sounds like he's planning to spend the night, and she found that she rather liked the idea.

*

Carla was out in the garden. She had said hello to Monique and then she had spotted Ben, the strange little boy next door, out in his garden with his little duffle coat on with his hood up, so she had gone outside to talk to him through the hole in the fence.

While she was out there her dad's portable phone rang. Michael and Monique looked at each other; it was the main contact number on the advertising literature that Monique had designed for Michael's new business; providing gymnasium equipment, but it was Saturday, not a day when many people enquire about new business. Michael answered the call. Monique watched and listened with interest as Michael grabbed a pen and notepad and was scribbling notes as he asked and answered questions. He finished off by saying "I'm sure it will be fine, despite the short notice. Let me speak to my colleagues and I will call you back within the hour". He was smiling broadly as he disconnected the call. "Well" he said to Monique "It will rather mess things up for the weekend with Carla, but that was a hotel. They are intending to install a gym and have just seen our leaflet and would like me to give a presentation tomorrow"

"Tomorrow?" asked Monique, surprised

"Yes, apparently they have a couple of other companies to see, but they liked the look of our stuff and as they are independent and refurbishing they wondered whether we'd be up for it at short notice".

"Well, it would be a marvellous opportunity, so why not?" she asked him

"Well, what about Carla? I know she will understand, but I've just told her that she and I can do something nice tomorrow as you are working, now it looks like we are both going to be working and that's hardly fair – I will have to take her back to Pamela's"

Monique looked thoughtful. "You are right, that is hardly fair. I know she would have loved to have you to herself, it's only natural, and I'd be a poor substitute, but do you think she would like to come with me? I could sign her in as a guest and she could use the facilities. She's not old enough, unfortunately, to use the health suite; sixteen is the lower limit for that, but she could swim and I could wangle a squash or badminton court if we're not too busy and have a couple of games with her. What do you think? Then maybe we could meet up for a late lunch."

"You are a star!" Michael told her. I'll give her a shout and see what she thinks. If she doesn't want to do that she can either stay here on her own for a few hours or go back to her mum's this evening."

Carla did like the idea. She was a little disappointed not to be having time alone with her dad, but she knew that his new business was important to him, and she was pleased for him to have this opportunity. Also, she liked the idea of going to Monique's exclusive club. The girls at school were still giving Carla a hard time, and she liked the thought that she could go in on Monday and tell them she'd been playing squash and swimming at the club, especially as Monique had loads of 'cool' sports outfits and had offered to let Carla try things on to see if any of it would fit her. Monique was quite petite, so Carla was looking forward to borrowing some nice things of hers. Carla's feet were actually bigger than Monique's though, so she would need her own trainers, which she had not brought with her. "Never mind" Monique had told her "We have to go quite near your mum's to get to the club from here; I'll drop you there on the way early tomorrow and you can pop in and pick them up"

"Ok, it's a deal" said Carla, as they went upstairs so she could to try on some tracksuits and shorts and tops. Michael smiled and said

"and I suppose if this is a success I'll be buying you some nice sports clothes?"

Chapter 54

Matt was very pleased. In fact he couldn't believe his luck. Although Pamela had seemed slightly distracted at times she had been as willing as she had the last time they'd been to bed and the afternoon and evening had gone very well, indeed. Pamela had produced one of the bottles of wine she had brought back from Brittany and between that and the wine he had brought with him they had become quite relaxed and enjoyed a companionable evening, first eating and chatting and then, later on, watching television. Matt was comfortable. Good food, good company and plenty of shagging. He smiled as Pamela sighed contentedly in her sleep and he slid further down the duvet and went back to sleep. He had thought he'd heard footsteps, but decided it was his imagination and went back to sleep.

*

Monique was rather puzzled at first. Then she became concerned and, after twenty minutes she became angry and drove away. Still feeling rather like the 'other woman' in her relationship with Michael she had parked around the corner from Pamela's in order to let Carla nip out and get her trainers. Carla had said she would only be a couple of minutes as she knew that Monique's shift started at seven o'clock and although it was still only six thirty there was at least a twenty minute journey to the sports club and Monique needed to sign Carla in as a guest, and to persuade one of her colleagues to cover for her while she had a game of squash with Carla.

*

Carla eventually stopped running. She was unsure where she was. She had not wanted to disturb her mum at six thirty on a Sunday morning so she had let herself in very quietly. She had smiled as she crept up the stairs and heard her mum snoring gently. Tentatively she opened her mum's bedroom door torn between not wanting to disturb her and wanting to give her a kiss before grabbing her trainers and getting back out to Monique. Carla had felt faintly disloyal to her mum trying on Monique's sports gear to borrow and for that reason she was in her own jeans and jacket as she hadn't wanted her mum to see her in Monique's stuff, should she happen to be awake.

She sat down on a low wall in front of someone's house. She felt really miserable. All her worst nightmares had come true. Not only was her mum sleeping with someone, but that someone was Matt Gregory, her maths teacher; the person that her friends had said her mum fancied! What did they know? Was she, Carla, the only person in the world who didn't know her mum was seeing Matt Gregory? Carla shuddered. She felt sick. She wasn't used to getting up at six o'clock in the morning any day of the week, let alone a Sunday. She wondered where she was. After the realisation dawned that there were two figures in her mother's bed she had pulled the door to quietly feeling absolutely disgusted. The only thing that would have embarrassed her more would have been those two sleeping figures knowing that she was there.

She began to feel cold. She stood up and tried to get her bearings. She was in a housing estate, but not one she recognised. She tried to think rationally. She felt numb; both mentally and with the cold. She didn't feel like crying. She wanted to feel safe and warm. She didn't want to see her dad or Monique; briefly she wondered how long Monique had waited and she felt a little guilty. Never mind; she didn't want to be with anyone who had anything to do with sex. She wondered why it had to smell so nasty. She'd not realised what it was when the bedroom door had been left open at her dad's; she'd assumed it was something of Monique's she wasn't keen on. However, when she smelled the same smell coming from her mum's room she realised with disgust just what it was.

She was walking now. She reached a junction at the end of the road she had run into. She could see the ring road from here but as it was Sunday and it was so early there was no traffic. Suddenly she thought where she could go. She would go to Eastbourne and stay with Grandmom and Grandpop. She took a deep breath. She would work out how to get there. There was no sex nonsense there. Goodness, she thought, even her other grandfather was in trouble for having sex. Was there no end to it? Yes, she thought, Eastbourne, surely that can't be too difficult?

Carla put her hand in her jacket pocket. Her purse was still there; luckily it hadn't fallen out when she had run away from the house. She checked her money. Her dad had given her five pounds in pound coins so she could get things from the vending machine and she had a five pound note of her own. She decided to walk to the station; it would probably take her at least half an hour or more but she didn't suppose there would be many trains on a Sunday; and probably not this early, either.

In fact it took her an hour and a half of steady walking to reach the station, but that included a few wrong turnings and stopping at a paper shop where she bought a flapjack and a bottle of orange. She ate half the flapjack and drank a little of the orange intending to finish both on the train. Her feet were sore when she reached the station as she was wearing her little flat heeled black patent leather shoes without any socks. Her socks were in the sports bag in Monique's car.

A bored looking ticket salesman said "yes" as she approached his window.

"Er, Eastbourne, please?" she asked, tentatively.

"Via where?" he asked

"Oh, er, I don't know. I've only gone by car before. What are the choices, please?"

"None, on a Sunday" he laughed rather unpleasantly, but when he saw her looking upset he said

"No choice, I meant, not no trains. It's via Clapham Junction today. The next train to Clapham will leave here at eleven thirty and there will be quite a few connections from Clapham to Eastbourne. That'll be twelve pounds fifty, please" Carla was shocked then she realised he had quoted the adult fare.

"Oh, a child's fare, please" she said to him. "Any ID?" he asked. "Er, no" she told him "I'm thirteen. I didn't expect to be catching a train today. I didn't know I'd need identification, I'm sorry."

"Well I'm sorry too" said the ticket salesman. This time he sounded as though he was sorry. "You look older. No ID, no child's fare. It's more than my job's worth, sorry"

"OK" Carla said to him. "I don't have enough for an adult fare" she muttered and feeling rather defeated she left the station.

Carla contemplated her options. She didn't seem to have many. The more she thought about it the more she wanted to go to Eastbourne. She wondered how far the motorway was from the station. So far all distances had seemed further than she thought. She was determined, however, so she set off towards the ring road roundabout that led to the motorway slip road.

*

Daphne awoke eventually. She knew no one would disturb her as it was Sunday, and she had phoned Leticia the previous day to say that they would be unable to attend her soiree as the Major had bronchitis. She had then, instead of having any supper, proceeded to try to get extremely drunk. It hadn't really worked. Daphne's system was quite accustomed to alcohol and she hadn't found the oblivion that she sought. Instead, she kept thinking of Donald's various kindnesses; pleasant things he did for her, or they did together on a daily basis. Isobel had told her, gently, that the event leading up to their leaving Cyprus had been mentioned in court but that the judge had dismissed it saying that it wouldn't be taken into account as it was such a long time ago. Daphne, however, believed that despite what the judge said he had, indeed taken it into account; after all, she thought now, it showed just the same weakness as Donald had shown by allowing the girl to do what she did to him. Daphne firmly believed Donald's side of the story about both incidents; whatever else he was and whatever else had taken place during their marriage Donald had always been a truthful man. She wondered now how he was managing; two nights now in that dreadful place. Isobel had explained he would be on a hospital wing for now, but what did that mean? He still didn't have his freedom; freedom to perform the morning rituals that everyone, even those claiming not to be creatures of habit, undertook.

With shaking hands Daphne made herself tea. Without thinking she had taken down the mug that Peggy had always used for herself and poured the hot water over the teabag as she'd seen Peggy do many times. She found a strange comfort in prodding the teabag and lifting it out with the spoon and then adding milk to the mug. Never normally coming downstairs until dressed, Daphne was in her nightdress and dressing gown. She felt dreadful.

Despite not being able to find oblivion in her gin the night before she had drunk enough to sleep a dream filled sleep for most of the night. She hadn't eaten the previous day at all; in fact, she couldn't remember when she had last eaten, apart from some bread and butter after Isobel had left on the Thursday. She opened the fridge. There was nothing there that tempted her, in fact there was very little milk left; she would have to start drinking coffee instead of tea. She drank her coffee black and with sugar, but as Donald didn't drink coffee she rarely did so. However, drinking coffee would do until Isobel came to take her shopping. She couldn't quite remember when it was that Isobel said she'd do that, but she thought she said she'd call the following day, Monday.

*

It was a mild morning so Sylvie had jogged and swum. She was far more stressed than usual as this time a part of her work had impinged on her private life. The exercise had helped calm her but hadn't changed the fact that her closest friend's father was in prison. She was wondering how she would get through the evening at her parents' house without saying anything. So used was she to never speaking about her job she didn't, at first, consider telling them about Major Donald, but, the more she thought about it the more she realised that she could, in fact, tell them. It wasn't her case; it stood a chance it would be in the papers; it was something in the public domain anyway that she hadn't simply learned about through her work so there was, actually, no reason for her not to tell them. They would be shocked, of course, as they knew Major and Mrs Fielding from when the girls were friends as children. They'd not kept in touch as the girls grew into adulthood, though, as the two families had nothing in common other than their girls' friendship. Sylvie began to feel better. Even if her Mum just spent most of the time bustling around in the kitchen as was her wont Sylvie would be able to talk her feelings through with her father in a detached, intellectual manner. She began to look forward to it. Probably the first evening with her parents she'd looked forward to apart from her birthday meal recently which Pamela had shared with them.

*

Carla was surprised and disappointed just how difficult it was to hitch a ride with a lorry. All the big ones just drove straight past her without even a second glance. She was cold. It had been alright while she was walking, but in light clothes and no socks she was now feeling the cold. At least her sore feet were getting a rest while she stood trying to get a lift. She wasn't really sure which way to stand and which thumb she should put out towards the traffic but just as she was contemplating this a flatbed truck pulled up and a friendly sounding voice called out to her.

She climbed up into the cab. The driver introduced himself as Harry and asked where she was headed. "I'm Carla" she told him "and I am going to Eastbourne"

"Well," Harry said to her "Eastbourne eh" and he scratched his head "I'm headed for Kingston upon Thames, I don't usually work on a Sunday but we've got a big contract on and we're only a small company." He paused as he changed lane to let a car join the carriageway from the next slip road. "You've picked an odd route to get to Eastbourne; you'll need to get to the M25 then down to the coast from there. I'm staying with the M3, so maybe I'd better drop you at Fleet Services and you can get a ride with someone there who is going more in your direction."

*

Pamela smiled as she saw Matt out. He kissed her gently as he left. His motorbike was parked around the corner and she smiled as she thought how considerate this was of him. She shivered slightly; it was not really cold but it was colder out than in so she pulled the front door to and turned the heating thermostat up a little. Matt hadn't wanted any breakfast but Pamela was ravenous. She grinned to herself; she supposed it was all the sex making her feel so hungry. What a lovely relationship this was turning into. Soon she would be able to tell Carla and she and Matt could see one another openly and maybe do things together, the three of them. She didn't know where the relationship would go; Matt was a few years younger than her and would, surely, one day want a young lover; one who he would want to marry and have children with. Pamela suddenly thought that she, herself, was only thirty six; still of child bearing age but then she immediately dismissed the idea telling herself not to be so silly; Matt was bound to want someone younger on a permanent basis. She didn't think she loved him anyway, this was just a fun relationship that suited them both for the moment but there was no reason why they couldn't soon tell people and enjoy an open relationship instead of a furtive one.

Pamela looked at the clock as she poured muesli into a bowl and added milk. Eleven thirty. She chuckled to herself, well, she thought, I wanted my mind taken off my present troubles and it certainly has been. She briefly wondered whether she should phone her mother but dismissed the idea. She had sounded as though she was coping last time she'd spoken to her and that nice Probation Volunteer, Isobel, was keeping an eye on her and would take her shopping. Pamela realised that there was an awful lot that she had never known about her parents and she thought that their marriage must have been be very strong to have survived the Cyprus ordeal; she did, actually, believe her father's account of what happened with the young man and thought what a difficult thing it would have been to argue his case against that of the young, well connected homosexual. She was well aware that at that time homosexuality had only ceased to be a crime a few years before and was most certainly not acceptable in the armed forces. She didn't think that her father leaned that way, but she could understand the fascination that he may have felt towards the young man. She didn't, however, feel the same way about his involvement with the daughter of their home help; especially as he had, evidently, gone back for more with Maisie. This did disgust her. She could understand why the law protected those with learning difficulties. She knew that her father had insisted that Maisie had initiated proceedings, but she knew equally that someone or something had taught Maisie to be sexually precocious and that, according to Bernice, she could have been that way since a very early age. Pamela believed that her father wasn't the sort to 'groom' a youngster in the way that Bernice had explained many sexual predators do, but she did understand that he had become a person who had encouraged Maisie's behaviour. She shuddered now and pushed away her muesli. She no longer felt hungry. She drank her coffee and wrenched her thoughts away from her father's sexual behaviour.

Pamela wandered round the house looking for something to do. She tidied her rumpled bedclothes smiling as she did so. She reorganised the washing that was drying in the airing cupboard and set up the ironing board so she could iron the dry things. Whilst waiting for the iron to warm up Pamela went to find her TV mag to see what films were showing in the afternoon. Realising she didn't have this week's mag as she hadn't shopped for the weekend she switched off the iron and wrote a quick shopping list before putting on her coat and setting off to the supermarket.

*

Daphne realised that she should eat. She was feeling shaky and hadn't taken her medication She looked at the clock and was surprised to see that it was mid day. Finding herself still in her nightclothes she went upstairs to get dressed and while there she got another of her secret supplies of gin out from the bottom of her wardrobe.

Downstairs again, now fully dressed she looked in the fridge and saw some bacon. That's it, she thought, I'll have a bacon sandwich then I can take some of those pills that stop me feeling so ill. Several hours later with her sandwich only partly eaten, Daphne fell asleep in front of the television. The gin bottle was empty.

*

Carla thanked Harry as she climbed down from his cab in the lorry park. He has apologised that he doesn't have time to help her find someone to take her along the M25 but he has been very kind and helpful and told her which M25 junction she needs to leave at to find her way onwards to Eastbourne. He also explained that there were strict rules now for lorry drivers working for large companies with regard to taking hitch hikers, so he recommended that she wait in the lorry park and ask drivers who look as though they drive independent vehicles, like himself. With a wave of his hand and another shout of "be careful, look after yourself" he pulled back out of the lorry park and back onto the M3.

Carla felt very alone now. It had been warm in the cab and it was chilly in the lorry park. She didn't want to spend any money as she realised she'd probably need to catch a bus or something for the final part of the journey that would actually take her to her Grandmom and Grandpop's Eastbourne address. However, she decided to go into the service area where it was warmer and, rather than spending any money on a warm drink and a sandwich she would eat the rest of her flapjack and drink the rest of her orange juice. Standing in the lorry park was making her feel nervous; she wasn't really sure how to recognise independent lorries; she thought maybe it would be better to just ask kindly looking people who came into the service area; after all, she thought to herself, it doesn't have to be a lorry, maybe a nice family could accommodate her in their car just so long as they were going to travel along the M25; everyone this side of the services was, after all, travelling in the same direction, there must be an equal amount of people joining the M25 as staying with the M3.

*

Monique wasn't enjoying her Sunday shift. Since meeting Michael she begrudged having to occasionally work at weekends, but today had been going to be different as she wasn't going to be able to spend time alone with Michael anyway, as Carla was to be with him. This she didn't mind; although she liked Carla she realised Carla needed time alone with her Dad. No, the reason that she wasn't enjoying her work today was because she was still cross and faintly worried about the fact that Carla had stayed indoors with her mother. If Michael had been there he would have gone to knock on the door to see what had become of her, but she, Monique, couldn't do that as she was Pamela's husband's 'other woman' and she still felt a little guilty at being the catalyst that had signified the end of their marriage. Monique knew deep down that Michael loved her in a way that he had never felt about Pamela, but she did sometimes wonder whether Pamela and Michael would have just continued to jog along together in rather passionless but pleasant marriage for the rest of their lives had she and Michael never met. She looked at the clock; almost two o'clock; no wonder she was feeling low, she hadn't eaten all day. She checked that her colleague was watching the swimmers and indicated that she was slipping away for a bite to eat. She got herself a coffee and a cheese roll and went back to join her colleague. She sighed and looked again at the clock "Not much longer" he said to her as she tucked into her late lunch "I know Sundays are hard, especially when you have someone nice to go home to" he said to her. She smiled in agreement. She hadn't told anyone about what had taken place with Carla; it was all a bit too complicated to explain and no doubt her colleagues would have just dismissed it as typical teenage behaviour. She tried to convince herself that it was, indeed, just that and decided to think about something else. She wondered how Michael was getting on with the presentation at the hotel. She would finish her shift at three and she and Michael would actually have some extra time alone together with Carla having gone home to her mother; Michael usually had to drop her back there at about six, so without the need for that they could have a nice long evening together.

*

Carla looked in the mirror at herself. She had been standing just inside the entrance to the service area and she had only had a chance to ask a couple of people whether they were heading for the M25 when a couple had walked past her and she heard the wife say disgustedly "I didn't think they tolerated beggars in these places" She had taken a moment or two to realise that they were talking about her, so she went into the ladies to hide until they had gone. As she looked herself up and down in the mirror she could see why they had thought that. Her jeans were marked with mud where they had rubbed against the dirty cab of Harry's flatbed lorry. Her shoes were scuffed where she had walked so far prior to getting her lift. Her bomber jacket, of which she was so proud now looked rather tatty to her as opposed to grown up. Her hair was a mess and her face was ruddy from the cold and the exertion of the walking. Now she could see why Harry had suggested she try to get a lift in the lorry park. Worried that a security guard may have been called by the couple assuming she was a beggar, Carla looked carefully around as she emerged from the ladies. She made her way out to the lorry park and began to wait for a suitable looking small lorry so she could ask the driver where he was headed. Carla didn't notice a scruffy young chap who was watching her as he had been since following her from the service area.

Carla approached a friendly looking man as he jumped down from his cab "Excuse me" she said politely "Would you be going to join the M25? I am trying to get to Eastbourne" he looked doubtful for a moment then said "I'm just popping in for a bite to eat, then am going to Gatwick" she looked disappointed as Harry hadn't mentioned Gatwick, but the driver carried on "If I drop you near junction ten on the M23 you can make your way to Eastbourne via East Grinstead" Carla brightened up. This made sense, as although her geography was scratchy to say the least Harry had mentioned East Grinstead and also she could remember going through there with her dad that last time she'd gone with him when he 'spirited' her away from her mum. In fact he had stopped there to use a pay-phone, this was why she remembered the name of the place.

"Oh, thank you, that's very kind; could I wait in the lorry?"

"No, sorry, kid, my insurance company wouldn't like that. I'll only be about twenty minutes; I'll see you back here then"

*

Clive was very pleased. He rarely had the chance to get a nice looking girl to himself in such easy circumstances. He would wait in his car, an old white Fiesta and he would follow the lorry until it dropped the girl off. He could barely believe his luck and could feel an erection beginning as he thought about how he would pull over and innocently ask her if she needed a lift.

*

Richard wasn't sure whether he was looking forward to his evening out or not. It was a long time since he had been to a theatre and this was only a pantomime they were going to rather than a play. However, the enthusiasm of the other members of the Open University Students Association (OUSA) to which he belonged was beginning to rub off on him. They were going to a theatre in Brighton as someone they had met at summer school was taking part and he had implored them to come and see him perform. It was Richard's friend, Sally, who had persuaded him to come and when he had pointed out the difficulties he would face she had found a solution to them all. In the face of all that it would have been churlish to refuse. "You know I can't manage the loo on my own, don't you" he had said to her when they were planning the trip. So far he had only gone out for drinks with them when one of them was willing to load him and his wheelchair into their car at the local OUSA meeting place and had managed not to need the loo.

"Ah, I did wonder about that, I hope you're not cross with me, but I did ask Keith, in case that were the situation, whether he would help you. He was, of course, very eager to oblige...." Richard had raised his rather bushy eyebrows at this, something his failing muscles still allowed him to do and Sally, used to

Richard's sense of humour, had doubled up in spasms of laughter at that.

"No, silly, he's not THAT eager; you know Keith as well as I do, he is as hetero as you and I, I just wanted to be sure I'd dotted all the i's and crossed all the t's before telling you we wanted you to come with us" she explained once she had stopped laughing long enough to do so.

*

Pamela flopped down on the sofa. She was feeling pleasantly tired but the house was clean and tidy, there was a chicken roasting slowly in the oven, the ironing was all done and she had made hers and Carla's packed lunch for the following day. My goodness, she thought to herself; sex must be good for efficiency! When she'd got home with her shopping she had checked the TV mag and found that there was an old black and white film on that she had seen many years ago as a child. She settled down to watch it and do the crossword puzzle in the TV magazine and looked forward to a nice evening with Carla when Michael dropped her back home.

*

Carla was back by the lorry twenty minutes later. "OK, hop in" the driver told her. She had spent the time in the service area and, in order to allay any suspicion that she was some sort of beggar, she had done her best to comb through her hair with her fingers and brushed the mud from her jeans and then gone into the shop for a browse around. "So" the driver said to her "I have to go to Gatwick. I don't want to leave you at the side of a road as it will be getting dark by the time we get that far. How about I drop you somewhere in Crawley?" She looked dubious "Geographically challenged, are you?" he asked and laughing he passed her his map. "Take a good look" he told her "You'll see that there is more than one way of getting to Eastbourne" he looked at her more closely than he had before "You're very young, aren't you?" he said. She didn't answer "Why Eastbourne" he then asked. She didn't think there was any danger in telling him so she just said

"Oh, I'm off to see my grandparents." And in case he thought that odd she added "They are expecting me, but they think I'm coming by train" when she didn't elaborate he didn't ask any more questions. He wasn't very interested anyway; he didn't like working Sundays and it was nice to have some company on the way, but he was rather concerned that she seemed so young; this was why he wanted to drop her somewhere where there were plenty of people. She didn't seem very streetwise and he didn't think she was really used to looking after herself. He thought that she seemed a nice girl, worth adding a few miles and minutes to his journey. He was making good time anyway, as the plane he was picking up from wasn't due to land until six pm and it was still only three thirty.

An hour or so later the driver pulled up by a garage. He was right, it was dark but it was well lit all around the garage area. "If I were you I'd phone your grandparents, love" he said to her "maybe they could come here and pick you up?" She nodded assent and thanked him for the lift. She felt very alone as he pulled away and looked dubiously towards the bright lights of the garage forecourt. As she hesitated, a rusty white Fiesta pulled up alongside her.

"You look lost" a voice said to her "I'm going to Eastbourne" he lied "Can I drop you anywhere on the way?" Carla couldn't believe her luck

"Goodness, what a coincidence" she said to him "That's where I am heading"

"Well, jump in, then" he said to her and he pulled away.

*

Michael was already home when Monique pulled in. "Where is Carla?" was Michael's first question, so Monique explained what had happened and how she had not wanted to knock on Pamela's door. Michael fully understood this and agreed that, out of character as it was for her to be quite so rude, when she had got indoors she had decided to stay at home instead of going to the gym with Monique. Having cleared that up Monique went on to ask Michael how his presentation had gone at the hotel. He was thrilled; it had gone extremely well. It wasn't just the one hotel, he told her excitedly, but a small chain. A small chain of hotels independent of any large organisation, and as Michael was in the same position with his new company they were inclined to give him the business. They were taking on and renovating five old hotels to begin with; and each of these hotels was to have its own gym. Provided Michael could come up with the desired equipment at a reasonable price the job would be his.

"But that's fantastic" Monique enthused, "how about eating out this evening to celebrate?" "Good idea, but as we are alone, albeit unexpectedly I have other ideas just now about how I want to celebrate" and he pushed a laughing Monique up the stairs to their bedroom.

*

Sally was driving her Micra. Richard was in the front with her; three others were squeezed into the back seat and the rest were following with Keith in Keith's Escort. The 'comfort' stops as they had called them when planning the trip had been carefully worked out beforehand, mainly in case the two cars became separated. Sally thought she had seen Keith pull in to the Little Chef but it turned out to be another Escort the same colour. She parked up and they waited for Keith and his group to arrive.

*

Pamela was getting worried and a little cross. Michael usually dropped Carla off at around six, and he had not said anything about being any later. OK, it was only twenty past six, but the chicken was cooked and Pamela didn't want it to dry out. When there was still no sign of Carla at a quarter to seven Pamela phoned Michael.

*

Monique had just come out of the shower and was deciding what to wear. Michael had said he was starving as he hadn't eaten all day and had suggested they go a fish restaurant that he knew Monique loved. "Come on, lazy bones" she said to him as he was still reclining on the bed "Go and have your shower, I thought you said you were hungry" but just as he started to move the phone rang. It was Pamela

"What do you men, where is she?" Michael asked "She came home to you at some unearthly hour this morning" Pamela cut him off

"What on earth are you talking about" she demanded "I haven't seen her since you picked her up yesterday. What on earth do you mean about her being here with me?" Monique's blood ran cold. It was obvious from Michael's end of the conversation that Carla was missing. She loved Michael and was very fond of Carla. Michael put the phone down and looked at Monique. His face was ashen. He asked her to explain again exactly what had happened when she dropped Carla off to collect her trainers. He said to her

"I am sure there is some explanation. I must go over there, you do understand, don't you?"

"Of course I do" Monique said to him, tearfully

"Oh come here" Michael said, hugging her close. "Whatever happens you are not to blame. Please stay here in case Carla comes here or tries to contact me here, is that OK with you?"

"Of course it is" Monique told him tearfully. "You just go and do whatever it takes to find her safely"

Chapter 55

Mrs Arnold put the phone down. She returned to the dining room where Sylvie and her dad were happily tucking into their roast dinner. They looked up as Mrs Arnold just stood there rather than sitting back down to her dinner. "That was Pamela on the phone, dear" she said addressing her daughter. "Carla is missing and has been since early this morning but through some mix up no one realised. Pamela is very distraught. She needs you there, love" Sylvie stopped eating immediately and got up to collect her coat and handbag

"God, that's awful. I'm so sorry about the lovely dinner Mum, but I must go"

"Of course you must" said both her father and mother at the same time.

*

In the short time it took Michael to arrive at Pamela's Marian was with Pamela. Pamela had quickly gone next door to ask whether she's seen Carla, but being afraid that Carla may try to contact her she was almost incoherent. Marian had just grabbed her key and said "Go on home, ducks, I'm coming" and had followed her, sat her down and made her explain what had happened. Of course, Pamela didn't know what had happened; she assumed that Carla had found out somehow that her grandfather was in prison and this is what had prompted her to take off. Marian asked Pamela, just as Michael was pulling up outside whether she planned to tell Michael that the Major was in Prison and she said "Well, I'll have to now; it must have some bearing on why Carla has run away. My friend Sylvie is on her way over, she may have some ideas"

Michael parked up and Marian let him in and introduced herself. Marian hadn't had a chance to ask Pamela about the motorcyclist that she was obviously seeing, but she didn't want to ask in front of her ex-husband. She couldn't help but feel that, if Carla knew about it, this new relationship of her mother's may have more to do with Carla's disappearance than what had happened to her grandfather. However, there was no opportunity to mention it because just as Michael and Pamela reached agreement on what to tell the Police when they called to report Carla missing Sylvie turned up.

*

This wasn't turning out as Clive's fantasy had promised. He had had great hopes as he wanted Carla to be very relaxed and comfortable with him until he was ready to enjoy her fear. Fear was what turned him on. The last couple of girls he'd used had been tarts and the last one, the worst; he was sure was mocking him and faking fear while he wanked over her. No, this would not do. He had tried to make Carla feel relaxed, he had introduced himself as Billy, although it wasn't his real name and tried to chat to her remembering to call her by her name in order to reassure her. She didn't seem to feel reassured though, as he was not worried about driving towards Eastbourne once she was in his car and she had queried the fact that they hadn't turned towards East Grinstead. That's all I need, he thought to himself, a silly tart who knows her way around. But he thought again, of course, she wasn't a tart, not like the others; this one should be able to show real fear and he would reach full satisfaction rather than coming too quickly and feeling disappointment, like last time.

"Don't worry, there is more than one way to Eastbourne from here, if you know the back roads as I do" he had said to her, but she turned towards him, fear showing in her eyes. It was real fear and he felt himself harden. No, not yet, he told himself desperately. He glanced across at her. She looked very young; younger than she had seemed when he was following her at Fleet services. Never mind, he said to himself, she's the best I've picked up there so far and he tried to take his mind of her fear lest he should come too soon and become angry instead of relieved

*

Sally got out of the car to look out for Keith and the others. She wondered whether Richard needed the loo but didn't want to ask him in front of the girls. She needn't have worried, within a few minutes Keith pulled in, and spotting her waving, he pulled in and parked next to her. "Good grief; has that Micra of yours got wings?" he asked her, laughing. Sally just shrugged and prepared to help Richard out of the car and into his wheelchair. None of them offered to help as they knew that she and Richard had this process down to a fine art, and they would only get in the way if they tried to help. Richard was lagging behind a little as he preferred to manipulate the wheelchair himself, but he was now more used to the electric one he used at home, this was his folding chair that he only used on car journeys. His muscles were constantly becoming weaker, though, as the ataxia worsened. He knew that he may need his strength later on so he called out

"Oh, go on then, give us a push" and one of the girls willingly turned back to help him into the restaurant.

*

Marian made tea for Michael, Pamela and Sylvie as they waited for a policeman to arrive and take a statement. They didn't really want any but Marian felt it was the thing to do. When the two uniformed officers arrived, one a middle aged chap and one a young lady; Marian handed them cups of tea too. It all seemed so surreal that Pamela felt she wanted to giggle, she could imagine Marian making tea if the world was threatened. Realising it was just hysteria Pamela pulled herself together and concentrated on what Michael was telling the police officers. She suddenly realised that Marian was staring at her, and making almost imperceptible nods towards the kitchen. "Would you excuse me, just a minute?" Pamela asked everyone in the room and she went out to the kitchen followed closely by Marian.

"What?" she asked quickly.

"Your young man, the one with the motorbike. I'm not being nosy, ducks, but I know he stayed last night. Are you going to tell them?" Hastily grabbing the biscuit tin so it looked as though this was the purpose for the trip to the kitchen Pamela went back to the sitting room with Marian. Pamela hadn't even thought of this but she did begin to wonder. Perhaps this had nothing to do with what had happened to her father after all? Michael was still explaining exactly where Monique had dropped Carla and at approximately what time. The male officer seemed to be the more senior; he was the one asking the questions at this time.

"So" he said to Pamela, declining Marian's offer of a biscuit with a wave of his hand and a smile "You were asleep and heard nothing. Were you alone?" Marian looked at her.

"No, no I wasn't" she said to him, blushing slightly. Michael almost jerked upright in surprise and Sylvie's eyes widened like saucers. "I have been seeing a friend called Matt" she said, strongly and almost defiantly, but with a slight wobble in her voice, as she looked at Michael "He spent the night here with me" The young female police officer smiled reassuringly at her; her attitude seemed to say 'and why not' and made Pamela feel slightly more at ease after having to announce to all present that she was sleeping with someone.

"And where is this Matt now? Does he have a surname? We will need to speak to him" this was the male officer speaking again. Pamela realised yet again that she had no contact phone number for Matt. "His surname is Gregory. He left here late morning, I'm not sure of the time" she told the officer "I will get you his number later" and she left it at that. After all, she couldn't think that Matt had anything to do with Carla's disappearance and she could always give them the school's phone number.

The police sergeant went out to the car to radio Carla's details as a missing juvenile. The constable stayed in the house and took over the questioning. "Is there anything else; anything at all that any of you think may be relevant?" she asked them. Initially no one spoke. Then, tentatively, with a shy glance towards Pamela, Marian explained that when Pamela and Carla had first moved in that she'd seen Carla walking along the ring road early on a couple of mornings, and, when she'd challenged Carla, Carla had explained that she didn't want some of the rather bullying girls at school to know where she had moved to. These particular girls were not as well brought up as Carla, and Carla felt that they would taunt her for having moved from what they called a 'snobby area' to 'the pits' so she caught the bus from a stop that looked as though she'd moved into an upmarket new development. Pamela was amazed; she had never known this, but now she remembered that this was the reason that Marian had come to her door that very first time.

"Looks like this is news to you" said the lady constable, kindly

"Yes" Pamela confirmed "Is there anything else I should know?" she asked Marian.

"Don't feel badly, ducks" she said to Pamela "Carla felt you 'ad quite enough to worry about so once I'd challenged her on that we became friends. She promised me she'd not do it no more, once I pointed out the dangers, and I told 'er she could always come and talk to old Spike (that's me nickname)" she explained to the constable "If she 'ad any troubles" They looked at her expectantly to see if there was any more. "So, yes, lately she told me she'd fallen out a bit with her two closest friends....Oh, god, Pamela, if only I'd made her tell you...."

"Now don't upset yourself, Mrs Rodgers, I am sure Carla was very lucky to have someone like you to confide in. So please, let's just all work together to find her safe and sound" This was the WPC again.

At this point the sergeant came back in and made arrangements to take a photo of Carla back to the station with him, and explained that Constable Madeleine Harvey would liaise with the family and let them know of any developments. Michael said he wanted to go out and look for Carla and explained that he had a portable telephone; the sergeant said that it was up to him if he could think of places to look for her, and he took Michael's number, as did Sylvie and Pamela.

*

"Are we stopping for coffee, or just sneaking in to use the facilities?" Keith asked as they went into the restaurant

"Well, speaking for myself" said Richard, with a grin, "I'm a bit conspicuous for 'sneaking'!" The others chuckled

"We don't need to be in Brighton until seven, we have plenty of time to stop for a coffee if everyone agrees?" they all did, and Richard quietly told Keith that in that case he'd use the facilities on the way out, if Keith didn't mind. Twenty minutes later Sally's passengers were strapped back in her back seat and Sally and Keith's passengers were waiting for Keith and Richard to return from the gents.

Keith was pushing Richard's wheelchair when Richard suddenly said to him "Stop, what on earth is that?" Keith stopped and they both listened. Someone was sobbing. The reason Richard had heard it first was because that someone was nearer his level than Keith's. The sound was coming from the road side of the bushes that bordered the car park. Richard put his finger to his mouth and indicated to Keith that he should leave him there and fetch some of the others to walk round the other side. As Keith walked away Richard said "Don't worry, we're coming to help you. Please don't be afraid" The sobbing stopped briefly and a voice said

"Who's there?" very timidly.

"My name is Richard" he said "and I have some very nice friends with me and they are coming to help you. Curiosity got the better of the person in the bushes and the shaky voice asked

"Why..." she meant to ask 'why not you, then?' but couldn't get the words out. However, before he could answer Sally was the other side coaxing the person to come out.

"Oh you poor girl" Sally said and tried to hug her

"Don't" she cried, starting to sob again "I am dirty, he, he..."

"Come on, love" Sally said to her reassuringly "Whatever has happened is not your fault. You are not dirty as far as I am concerned. Let's look at you and decide what to do. Do you need an ambulance?" Reluctantly Carla crawled out from under the bushes and explained that she had accepted a lift with someone as she was trying to get to Eastbourne. Sally took in the torn jacket and the scratches on Carla's face. "I think we need to call the Police, what is your name, love?" she asked.

"Oh no, I can't go home" Carla said and started sobbing again.

"Well," Sally said "You need help. Let's get you into the restaurant, no, don't worry; they are not very busy, I am sure that they will give us a table in a corner where we can sit and decide what to do. I really do think we should call the police, though, if you say a man did nasty things to you." Sally had realised that Carla was very young and didn't want to use the words 'rape' or 'sexual assault'. Carla agreed reluctantly to go inside the restaurant.

"I'd seen the lights from where I fell from the car; I jumped out while it was still moving, and I headed in this direction. Then I didn't want to go in, not, not like this, you know..." Sally told her that she understood, but she would accompany her into the restaurant. Carla then caught sight of Richard in his wheelchair and understood why it was that he spoke to her from the car park side while the others climbed over the flower beds to reach her.

In fact, Sally's confidence was misplaced as the manager of the restaurant was very reluctant to let Carla in. "She doesn't look badly injured to me, but you want me to call the police? Police cars are bad for business..." However, the manager wasn't prepared to argue with Keith. Normally a very mild mannered, quiet man, he was outraged by the manager's attitude and exploded into a diatribe of

"How would you like it if this were your daughter? Or are you not man enough to have daughters? This is a nice girl, you can tell..."

"OK, OK, sorry" he eventually said and led them to a corner table away from the few diners that he had in.

Carla had watched this exchange; she didn't know how she felt about things at home. She knew that the manager was calling the police on her behalf; and after all she'd been through in this last hour or so she began to feel she wanted the comforting presence of her parents.

Sally had looked briefly at Carla's injuries and, deciding they looked superficial had told the restaurant manager to call only the police; they would know whether they wanted Carla taken to hospital. Carla had a nasty graze, which was bleeding, on her wrist where she had hit the ground, but she began to explain that the car had not been moving fast when she had managed to wrestle the door open and jump out. Sally did not want to distress the girl by asking her about the actual assault; she knew that the police had proper ways of extracting the information delicately and in such a manner that they had a chance to identify the perpetrator so she wanted neither to upset Carla unnecessarily nor to cloud the police investigation that was bound to follow. Keith had gone back out to tell the others what was happening so they could work out whether they were going to make it to the pantomime. Not wanting to crowd Carla they had initially all waited outside, Keith only going to the rescue when he heard that the manager was not intending to let them in.

Sally was also wondering whether they were still going to get to the pantomime. She glanced at her watch and was surprised to discover that only about ten minutes had passed since they had first left the restaurant after their coffee. Sorry though she felt for this girl she knew that their friend would be upset if they didn't turn up as they had told him they were coming. By now the manager had brought a bowl of warm water and some industrial paper towel; now more helpful and apologising that he didn't have anything softer with which to wash Carla's wrist. As Sally ministered to Carla's injuries Richard was now talking to her. Carla had by now thanked him for having heard her and sent his friends to help and asked where they were heading for. When Richard mentioned OUSA she said "I know what that is" and explained that her next door neighbour, Marian had once belonged when she was studying. Richard looked in amazement "Well, it is a small world, that sounds like Spike!" Carla agreed that Spike was indeed Marian's nickname and said that she had become very fond of her since they'd moved in next door.

*

When the police left there was an uncomfortable silence. Marian broke it by saying "Well, ducks, I don't think as I can do nuffink sittin 'ere wiv you, so I'll get meself back off 'ome unless there's anything I can do?" Pamela, Michael and Sylvie looked at one another and Sylvie said

"I tell you what, you go home but if we think of anything you can do for us or if there is any news at all one of us will come and get you" Pamela was grateful to Sylvie; all she wanted was to know that Carla was safe, and she didn't think that three of them sitting in the house would do any good. She was pleased that Michael wanted to drive round and look for her; they'd already phoned all her friends' houses to ask whether anyone had seen her, but after Marian's revelation about her not getting on so well just now with those friends that had, indeed, been the waste of time they thought it might be.

Sylvie saw Marian out and Pamela and Michael talked about any likely places that Carla might have gone. Michael had asked no questions about Matt; he realised that he had no right to do so, but he was concerned about his being a teacher at Carla's school. He hadn't met him as in the days when Pamela and

Michael used to go together to parents' evenings she had had a different maths teacher. The police sergeant had obviously had the same concern, as, much to Pamela's embarrassment, he had asked her several times whether she slept heavily and whether she would have known whether Matt had left her bed for any length of time. She had answered honestly; saying that she might not have noticed should he have gone to the bathroom, but she felt she would have known had he left the bedroom long enough to spirit Carla away before coming back to bed. The sergeant didn't say so but this was one of his main concerns. He would run a check against Matt Gregory just as soon as he returned to the station, to see whether there was any information against him.

*

Carla was beginning to get a little more colour in her cheeks. Almost without her realising it; Richard was gently coaxing the reason from her that she had initially said that she couldn't go home. His voice was becoming more gravelly as he spoke as his throat muscles were also affected by his ataxia. She seemed comfortable with him, though, and Sally assumed that was because he knew her friend and neighbour with the strange nickname. Sally just sat quietly not wanting to interrupt. She knew it wouldn't be long before the police arrived and Richard was trying to ascertain whether there was anyone at home who had, or had wanted to hurt Carla. He had ascertained that her parents were separated and that her dad lived with a lady called Monique. She had said she quite liked Monique and felt a little guilty that she had run off and left her round the corner from her mum's without saying anything. It was when Richard asked whether her mum had a boyfriend that the tears started again. So, thought both Richard and Sally; this was it. "Has he tried to hurt you?" Richard asked very gently. Sally was alarmed, as she knew that the police should be asking such questions rather than strangers.

"Oh, no" she told them through sobs. I didn't even know mum was seeing him until I saw them in bed together this morning.

"Do you know him, then?" asked Sally, joining in the conversation for the first time.

"Ye, ye , yes" Carla sobbed. "He is my maths teacher" At this Sally had to stifle a giggle. Luckily it sounded both to Richard and Carla as a sharp intake of breath. Sally had two teenage boys and had been bringing them up alone for a couple of years. She knew all about the embarrassments that teenagers felt towards their parents; especially a single parent who may want to start a relationship. She had a very good relationship with her sons, but they were very forthright, especially her eldest and she could imagine him just coming out with

"Hey, mother, what's this about your shagging our maths teacher?" and again she almost wanted to stifle a giggle.

Luckily, at this point, a Sussex Police patrol car had arrived and the restaurant manager was pointing the two officers in their direction. While Sally was busy composing herself after her flight of fancy about a conversation with her eldest son Richard had persuaded Carla to allow him to telephone Marian.

*

Marian didn't know what to do with herself. She was very worried, indeed, about Carla but didn't feel she could do anything next door. She had drunk a surfeit of tea and nibbled a couple of biscuits she didn't really want so she had no appetite for the meal she had been preparing when Pamela had called round in her distress. She was just surveying the bits of the meal she had been preparing and deciding what to throw out and what could be kept when her phone rang.

She answered it and wondered for a moment as the voice sounded quite rough and raspy. "Spike?" said the strange voice "Is that you?" She could barely understand the caller. "Spike, it's me, Richard, Richard from the OU" he managed to say.

"Richard!" she said to him with pleasure "How the devil are you, long time no......" but he cut her short.

"Listen, I probably shouldn't be making this call, I slipped off with an excuse just as the police arrived" Marian wanted to tease him and ask what he'd been up to, but there was a seriousness to his voice despite his obvious trouble speaking. "We have found a girl called Carla.." Marian's hand flew to her mouth and she gasped

"Oh my god; is she OK?"

"Yes, yes, she is OK from the point of view that she is not badly injured. However, she has had a close brush with a nasty sounding young man who has attempted to assault her and she had to escape by jumping out of his car as it was moving" He had to stop to take a breath. "Something happened at home this morning to make her run away. She was trying to get to Eastbourne, to her paternal grandparents, where she feels comfortable." Marian had to be patient as Richard had to breathe again for a while before he could continue speaking. "But she has allowed me to phone you, as when I mention we are on an OUSA outing she said she knew what OUSA was and mentioned you" again he paused for breath. "She realises now, especially after what she has been through, that both her parents will be very worried, but she doesn't know how she feels about coming home and, of course, the police will need a statement, and, possibly samples from her" Marian shuddered and wondered just what this nasty young man had managed to do to her before she jumped from his car. "Is her mother at home; could you go and tell her that Carla is safe?"

"Of course I will, but where on earth are you? You haven't said" Richard explained they were at a roadside restaurant not far from Crawley. Marian asked which police force was attending and he told her Sussex. Marian then told him "I'll go and explain to Pamela, could you please tell the police there that a Constable Madeleine Harvey from Hampshire police is acting as family liaison with regard to Carla being a missing juvenile?"

"Yes, of course I will, that's a very good idea" Richard told her and after saying their goodbyes and promising to keep in touch he rang off. As he made his way back to Sally, Carla and the police officers, he thought about Marian; or Spike as she liked to be known in OU circles. She had answered the phone with an enquiring 'ello?' and he knew she liked to use her local accent with most people but once she realised who he was she had spoken as she usually did with her OU friends.

*

Pamela jumped as she heard a knock at the door. She looked fearful and hopeful at the same time but seemed rooted to the spot. "I'll go" Sylvie told her. At the same time the phone rang and Pamela had to answer at as Sylvie had gone to the front door. Sylvie came through with Marian and was trying to tell Pamela that Carla was found but there was a police officer on the phone telling Pamela the same thing.

Chapter 56

It had been a long night. Carla was now tucked up in bed and Michael and Pamela were drinking coffee in Pamela's kitchen. There was a closeness between Michael and Pamela that they hadn't felt since Michael had first told Pamela about Monique. It seemed to go further than simple relief that their daughter was safe. They could both feel it but found it hard to define. Michael had admired Pamela's independence but had previously found it difficult to say anything as each time he'd tried Pamela had told him not so be so condescending. Now, however, they were talking as fairly close friends might. Michael was being supportive about Pamela's relationship with Matt but he didn't know that Pamela had never been to Matt's home nor had she ever actually been out with him and she had no contact number for him. Luckily, the number she'd given the police the previous evening, the phone number for the school, had not been put to the test.

Pamela was beginning to acknowledge, to herself, that Michael had really found love with Monique; he had changed in many ways and Pamela put this down to a new found understanding about what made people tick and could only think that he had found this through Monique. This actually made her quite cross, because if only Michael could have been more like this during their marriage perhaps things would have turned out differently. She wasn't, however, about to spoil the ambiance of the morning by voicing these thoughts. Pamela realised that she had simply been flattered by Matt's attention but that he was really a slippery character and she had no intention of ever seeing him again. This would be easy, as both she and Michael agreed that Carla would be far better off at a school closer to her new home here at Pamela's and there were three schools that could be considered.

Both Michael and Pamela were exhausted as they had been up all night. They were just discussing how to move forward with regard to contacting the schools; Carla had not expressed a preference when they'd suggested a move but had been very relieved when they told her she was to have a week at home with Pamela before going back to school and that she didn't have to go back to her old school. Pamela had phoned in sick but hadn't specified what was wrong. She would sort that out once she had a chance to think straight. She had gone to find a phone book to look up the school numbers when her phone rang.

"Hello" she said tiredly into the receiver. "Are you Mrs Pamela Matthews?" a voice asked and when she confirmed that she was he went on to say "Then I am sorry to tell you that your mother, Mrs Daphne Fielding has been taken ill and is in hospital in Reading". Pamela listened to the rest of what he had to say and put the phone down and turned to look at Michael.

"Whatever is up?" he asked her

"You'll never believe this" she said to him "That was a police officer. My mum has been rushed into hospital and they want me to go and see her"

"Well, of course, you must go. I'll stay here with Carla, but goodness me, you poor thing; I didn't think anything else could go wrong! Do you think you will be OK to drive?"

"I'll be OK, thanks. I'll call you from the hospital when I know what is what"

"OK, would you like me to call the schools?" he asked her

"Oh, yes please, then we shall at least have something constructive to tell Carla later" she replied.

*

Michael listened in the hallway for a while for any sign that the phone call had woken Carla, but when a few minutes after Pamela had quietly closed the front door behind her all was still quiet upstairs, Michael went back into the kitchen. He ran a tired hand over his stubbly chin. He didn't want any more coffee but he did feel hungry. It was strange for Michael being in this house that was familiar and unfamiliar at the same time. There was furniture and there were ornaments and pictures from the home they had shared as a family; unlike the house which he shared with Monique which they had taken as a short term furnished let. Quietly Michael looked round for something to eat and finding some bread he put a couple of slices in the toaster and checking the cupboards he found some peanut butter. As he did so he got out his portable phone to call Monique. They had not had a chance to speak since he had let her know that Carla was safe. He knew that she blamed herself for parking round the corner and not then having been able to see Carla run out of her mother's front door. However, his battery was flat and he didn't have the unit with him with which to charge the thing. He wasn't sure about using Pamela's house phone; it was one thing helping himself to her bread and peanut butter but quite another to use her phone to call Monique.

As he thought about Monique he smiled. He knew she wasn't working this morning but had an afternoon and evening shift. He decided that he was being over sensitive and that a quick call would be acceptable and he knew that she would be pleased to hear from him. She answered the phone quickly so he guessed she had been waiting to hear from him. He explained that Pamela's mum had been taken ill and that he had a lot more to tell her about that side of the family but that it would have to wait until he got home. He told her that he would wait there until Pamela was back and Carla was awake so they could make arrangements to visit some schools now that they had all decided that Carla should change her school.

Eating his toast Michael settled in to await Pamela's return. He considered himself very lucky, indeed. He had fallen in love with Monique in a way he had never previously understood was possible. He and Pamela had had a good relationship and marriage and he knew that until his parents had met Monique and seen them together that they, and especially his father, had never been able to understand why he had thrown away a good marriage; but once they'd seen the changes in their son they accepted that he loved Monique and she him in that special way that not everyone finds. Michael's mum had seen the changes in her son and warmed to Monique immediately she met her. She had never understood how she had managed to produce a son with such rigid views on life and was pleased that he had mellowed since being with Monique.

Michael had initially struggled with the idea that Pamela had found someone with whom to have a relationship and then he realised he was going back to what Monique called his 'silly old stuck in the mud' ways. She said this with her attractive French accent and it amused and pleased him when she did so. Monique had shown Michael a very different way of looking at the world, rather than the fixed 'black and white' 'right and wrong' he had thought was right before he met her. He realised now why Sylvie had come to dislike him so much and had stopped coming to dinner with them; he had spiked her up on purpose in front of his friends in order to be able to air his views with regard to offenders and sex offenders in particular. He cringed now as he also remembered condemning those who looked outside their marriage for what he would refer to as 'cheap thrills'; oh how judgemental he had been!

*

Driving to the hospital Pamela didn't know what to think. The police officer had been kind. He had explained that Isobel, a friend, he had called her; but

Pamela remembered that she was the probation volunteer who had been supporting her parents, had called them when she couldn't get an answer from Daphne and they had broken in, found her unconscious and had her taken straight to hospital. Pamela tried to empty her mind. She was exhausted and thinking made her feel worse. Rather than dwell on what had happened and how bad her mother might be, Pamela cleared her mind and concentrated on driving. It was almost ten o'clock but the Reading traffic was as bad as ever and Pamela knew that parking at the hospital would be a challenge.

Eventually having found a space and bought a two hour ticket Pamela made her way to A & E where she assumed she would find her mother. However, when she asked at reception she was surprised to find that her mother had already been admitted to a ward. Wearily Pamela made her way to the floor to which she had been directed and found a nurses station where she asked where she might find her mother. A lady approached and asked whether she was Pamela. When Pamela said yes, she was Isobel introduced herself. "I'm sorry I had to call the police to break in, I didn't know how to contact you..." Pamela cut her short

"Thank goodness you did, but how is she, what happened?" "Oh, you poor lamb, haven't they told you anything? Your mum has come round now but they won't tell me anything as I'm not family" The busy nurses, seeing that Isobel and Pamela had found one another carried on with their tasks so Isobel took Pamela to see Daphne.

Daphne was looking very pale and small in her hospital bed. Seeing Pamela she immediately said "Oh, sweetie, I'm so sorry to have been such a nuisance. I forgot to eat; I think it was all the shock, you know. I think the doctor wants to see you, but he is talking a load of rubbish. I just forgot to eat, that's all. I really want to go home" Pamela was puzzled, as she still didn't know exactly what had happened. She bent to kiss her mum.

"Don't worry; I am sure we will soon get you out of here" As she said that a young doctor approached and asked whether she was Mrs Fielding's daughter and asked her to come to his office for a few moments.

"Please, take a seat" the young doctor said to Pamela after introducing himself. She hadn't caught his name, it sounded quite unpronounceable to her ears but he said he worked with Mr Mears, the consultant with whom her mother had had an appointment recently. "I won't beat about the bush, Mrs Matthews" he said to her "Your mother was found in an alcoholic coma. She has an alcohol problem, which she won't acknowledge and she is suffering from cirrhoses of the liver. She has been told this; she has been told that unless she stops drinking her health won't improve. This is not unusual in those with an alcohol addiction. All we can do unless she accepts that she needs help is to bring her in and dry her out when she collapses in this manner. I am sorry if all this is a shock to you, but neither Mr Mears nor I believe in beating about the bush"

And so it was with all this ringing in her ears and an Al Anon leaflet in her hands that she made her way back to her car. She told no one, not even her mother, about what had happened the previous day to Carla and no one had queried why she wasn't at work; why she was at home when the policeman called her. Isobel had very kindly offered to stay with Daphne and drive her home once she was fit enough to leave the hospital.

Isobel had thought Pamela very distant and almost uncaring. She supposed it must be to do with her father's offence and subsequent sentence, unless she had always had such a relationship with her parents. She wouldn't be surprised. What had surprised her, though, was that she hadn't objected when Isobel offered to take her mother home. Isobel had expected that Pamela would want to do that herself. Oh well, she shrugged her shoulders as she thought about the mess they had found in Daphne's house. There was a strong smell of vomit and Isobel suspected that there was more to clear up than the pool that poor Daphne was found lying in. Well, she thought, she had offered to help and help she would. She hadn't been told what Daphne was suffering from; Pamela had thanked her profusely for being willing to take her mother home, but all she had said about what the doctor had said was "There seems to be a conflict between what the doctor thinks and what my mum says. She has had neither a heart attack nor a stroke, thank goodness, and she will be allowed home later today".

Pamela drove back slowly to allow herself time to think. She was feeling rather sick and light headed as she had been awake now for over twenty eight hours and hadn't eaten properly in any of that time. She wound down the window despite the cold in order to help her to stay awake. She was very relieved that the obviously capable Isobel was looking after her mum. She could explain to both her mum and to Isobel why she was in such a rush to get back home later in the week. Carla was her main focus now and she wasn't going to let anything at all get in the way. Pamela was hovering between being pleased with the way Michael had accepted the news that her father was in prison and angry with him for being so tolerant now after the way he always used to behave. He had even blamed himself for having taken Carla to Eastbourne without telling Pamela when he first discovered that Major Donald was in trouble. They had all acknowledged that once they realised that Carla had been trying to get to Eastbourne to see Michael's parents that they, especially Michael, should have thought that she might have headed that way.

Pamela looked so white and shaky when she entered her house that Michael led her straight to a chair and sat her down. "Great" she said to Michael "My father's in prison and now they tell me my mother's an alcoholic. God, I feel sick" Poor Michael didn't know what to say. Pamela had explained about her father's prison sentence during the long night while they were at the police station waiting while the police surgeon saw Carla with the family liaison officer. Michael knew that Pamela hadn't eaten; he hadn't either until he had made himself the toast while Pamela was at the hospital. Much though she wouldn't feel like it he thought food and sleep would be the best things for Pamela just now. He had looked in the fridge earlier, in case Carla woke up and knew there were eggs and milk. As he had made himself some toast with peanut butter on earlier he was feeling better than he knew Pamela was.

"I know you won't feel like eating, but I'm going to make you some scrambled egg and a cup of tea" Michael said to Pamela. Pamela didn't argue. She didn't know what she felt like.

Half an hour later she fell asleep in the chair she was still sitting in and where she had eaten the eggs. Michael tucked a fleece jacket round her that he found in the hall cupboard. He didn't want to go upstairs and risk disturbing Carla. Michael had had at least an hour's doze himself after eating his toast and before busying himself phoning the three schools within easy travelling distance and making appointments for the three of them to attend. All he had said to the administrators with whom he spoke was that Carla was experiencing difficulties and that he and his estranged wife would like her to change to a different school. All three had been equally helpful and had been happy to arrange appointments for later in the week. Two of them had said, also, that they had a place should they want Carla to start the following Monday.

Pamela had been asleep about two hours or so when Carla came sleepily down the stairs. As she came into the sitting room Michael put his finger to his lips and pointed to Pamela, but Pamela had heard Carla come in and woke up feeling a lot better. Carla was happy to see that her dad was still here, as he had promised he would be, but she was still obviously very shaken by her recent experiences. However, she went off to the kitchen and came back into the sitting room with a large bowl of cereals smothered in milk and sugar and sat next to Michael on the sofa.

Carla had spent a lot of time during the night with the police constable she now called Maddy. Constable Madeleine Harvey was a trained family liaison officer and in that capacity she had taken Pamela to collect Carla and had called Michael on his portable telephone so he could meet them at the police station. It was Maddy who accompanied Carla the whole time as she was seen by the police surgeon and her statement was taken and then the samples taken from her clothing by a scenes-of-crime officer. Carla had been upset at that point as she didn't want to wear the temporary clothing on offer and she said she never wanted to see the clothes she had been wearing again as they were disgusting. She had found herself able to talk to Maddy about why she had run away and explained that to then have ended up with that horrible young man trying to molest her was revolting to say the least. She was well versed in the facts of life, far more so than her mum had thought, but when he ejaculated over her she had been horrified. Understanding all this Maddy went out to speak to Pamela and Michael to see whether they could arrange to bring some clean clothing of Carla's own to the station for her to change into. Knowing that Carla would be quite some time yet before she could come home, having agreed to do all she could to get this man caught, Pamela went home herself to get clothes for Carla as she knew what she would feel most comfortable in.

Carla looked a little brighter once she had eaten her cereals. She was realistic enough to understand that her parents were not getting back together, but they had promised her before she went to sleep in the early hours that together they would sort out a new school for her and they would always communicate properly with regard to where she was and who she wanted to be with, and, most importantly, there would be no more secrets. She had explained as best she could in the car on the way home why she had run away. She had talked to Maddy about how she found the smell of sex extremely disgusting, but she had told Maddy she couldn't bring herself to actually say this to her mum and dad as it was far too embarrassing. Maddy had helped her to find a way to explain to her parents how she felt and why she had run away without embarrassing herself and so using some of her own feelings and some of Maddy's words she told them both how she felt. In turn Pamela told her that her grandfather had been sentenced to a short spell in prison and that they had initially thought that Carla had found out and that was the reason that she had run away.

Now Pamela and Michael had the job of telling Carla that on top of everything else her grandmother had been admitted to hospital. They had not had the opportunity to discuss how much to tell her, so Michael simply put his arm around Carla and said "Your mum has something else to tell you, your grandma is not very well" and Carla looked askance at Pamela.

"Yes, I've had to go to Reading this morning. It seems the shock of my dad's prison sentence has just got to my mum and she collapsed and was taken to hospital" It all seemed a bit remote to Carla but she did ask how she was and how long she would have to stay in hospital and who would look after her. Never having been very fond of her maternal grandmother she then surprised both Michael and Pamela by saying that she thought they should go to see her as soon as they could. Michael said that he would leave that to Pamela and Carla to decide between them, and that he would soon need to go home. Carla looked worried again and asked about school. Michael told her about the appointments that he had booked while Pamela went to Reading and reassured her that the three of them would go together to the schools. Pamela and Michael sorted out the logistics of meeting up at the schools and Michael left to go home.

Despite the fact that Carla had not been actually raped Maddy had explained to Pamela that Carla would feel many of the same reactions that rape victims experienced. She advised her to contact Victim Support if Carla felt the need. So far the only outward sign that Carla showed was wanting the clothes she had been wearing to be burnt and wanting a bath before she went to bed when she got home in the early hours. Pamela thought that this was totally natural and to be expected. She had read through the leaflet with Michael and they had agreed to wait and see whether Carla herself felt she needed help or counselling. For now Carla was content to cuddle up with her mum on the sofa in her pyjamas and a warm cosy sweatshirt. Once again she said to her mum "Oh Mum, I'm so sorry. I can't believe I was so stupid" and once again Pamela hugged her daughter to her and said

"It's all over now, you are safe. By the way, I didn't want to say it in front of your Dad but I definitely won't be seeing Matt Gregory again." Carla pulled away and looked at her mum. Pamela smiled "One day I hope to meet someone nice, someone who I will be proud to be with and who will be proud to be with me. I realise now that you and your friends were quite right about your Mr Gregory but I was lonely and flattered by his attention." Carla shuddered so Pamela changed the subject "What do you want to do now?" she asked her

"I don't know" she said "How about absolutely nothing, just as we are now?" she suggested snuggling back against Pamela. They had been cuddled up for quite a while and had hardly noticed that it had become dark. Suddenly the door bell rang and made them both jump. Pamela went to the door. It was Sylvie

"Goodness" she said "I didn't think there was anyone in" as Pamela ushered her in at the same time thanking her for having stayed with them the previous evening. "No problem" she said "But I wanted to see how things were and I remembered we'd decided to chuck the chicken you'd roasted away as it had been congealing on the work top for hours – would anyone like a takeaway?" Pamela drew the curtains and put the light on. Carla was pleased to see Sylvie

"Hiya" she said to her "Has Mum told you about Grandma?" Sylvie looked at Pamela

"As if we didn't all have enough to worry about, my Mum was rushed into hospital this morning. Isobel had arranged to go and see her and not getting any response she called the police. They broke in and found her collapsed and called an ambulance." She put an arm round Carla. "She's now been sent home. Isobel is caring for her for now and we will go to see her tomorrow. It would seem that she had quite a few drinks but forgot to eat. The young doctor gave me this" she said indicating the Al Anon leaflet "but Mum denied any such problem so we shall have to see. Carla, Michael and I have appointments at three different schools and Carla is our priority..."

"But, Mum, I really do think we should go and check on Grandma as soon as we can. We don't have any schools to see until Wednesday. Just think what Grandma has been through; let's go and see her tomorrow" Carla was becoming enthusiastic now "We should talk to that lady from probation, too, Isobel, is it? Maybe we could arrange to take Grandma to visit Granddad..."

"We'll see, all in good time" Pamela said enigmatically "Did you mention a takeaway? I think I could eat a horse!" she said. Sylvie and Carla laughed

"I don't know of anywhere local that does horsemeat, I think we'd need to go back to Brittany for that!" Carla said.

"So, what's it to be then?" asked Sylvie "Chinese, please" Carla said so Pamela went to the kitchen to get a menu.

"Let's choose and phone through, then you won't have to wait so long" Pamela suggested.

"Can I stay like this?" Carla asked indicating her pyjamas and sweatshirt. "Of course you can, so long as you are warm enough" Pamela said feeling extremely relieved. Carla was not as yet displaying any of the signs Maddy had warned her to look out for. She was also touched that Carla was concerned about her grandmother after all she had been through.

"I tell you what, I don't want to phone Grandma just now in case she is sleeping, but that nice lady, Isobel gave me her number so I will call her and ask how things are and I can thank her for taking Mum home. She must have thought me terrible that I didn't stay to take her myself." Pamela phoned through their Chinese order and told Sylvie it would be ready in half an hour.

Pamela went to phone Isobel and Sylvie sat down with Carla. "So, is everything OK with you?" Sylvie asked her

"Yes, thanks, I'm fine" Carla told her "I know that what I did was very stupid, but I was upset. When I realised I was stuck in that horrible man's car I thought I'd never see Mum or Dad again. They've both been wonderful about it and the police are pleased that I gave such a good description; they said they've been trying to catch this man for a few months. They called him a 'little toerag'. I've never heard that expression before." She was quite animated telling Sylvie all this and Pamela grinned at Sylvie

"Quite something, this daughter of mine, isn't she?" she said.

"She's not the only one" Sylvie said "Fancy your having a fella to stay and not telling anyone, not even your best friend!"

"Yes, well, doesn't that tell you something?" she said to both Sylvie and Carla "I shan't tell Michael just yet, but you can, if you want" she said to Carla "I won't be seeing Matt again. I realise it was a mistake. I've told Carla I shall meet someone nice one day and then she'll just have to learn to put up with it!" and she hugged Carla once more and Carla said

"Oh, Mum, really" then she asked "What did Isobel say about Grandma?"

"Oh, Grandma is quite tough, I think she's had to be" she said glancing at Sylvie. This new promise of no secrets didn't have to include details of things from the distant past, only recent events that could affect the family. "Remember last time we had takeaway – was it really only last Thursday?" she said almost to herself "Well, the reason Sylvie and I met was so she could tell me about your Granddad's prison sentence; it wasn't a problem with Sylvie's neighbour..." "No" interjected Sylvie "I have lovely neighbours!"

Sylvie looked at her watch and said it was time she went to get the food. She asked whether Pamela wanted anything from the shop next door to the Chinese and Pamela suggested "Something naughty, either chocolate or ice cream or both and plenty of cola!" and so, laughing, Sylvie went to collect their order. Pamela and Carla flopped back on to the sofa, both of them exhausted physically and emotionally.

"I love you, Mum" Carla said cuddling up close.

Sylvie let herself in with the key Pamela had given her the evening before. She put the takeaway and 'naughty' things in the kitchen and went into the sitting room. Pamela and Carla were cuddled up on the sofa fast asleep. Sylvie went upstairs and took the duvet off Carla's bed and wrapped it round them. She went back to the kitchen and put the ice cream in the freezer and the chocolate in the fridge. She left Carla and Pamela's takeaways next to the microwave and, smiling, she slipped quietly away leaving mother and daughter entwined on the sofa.

Printed in Great Britain
by Amazon.co.uk, Ltd.,
Marston Gate.